JUST A FRIENDLY KISS

"All right," Libby said. "No one's ever accused me of welshing on a bet. You win." She closed her eyes, coiled her hands tightly, and puckered her lips.

Chase moistened his lips with the tip of his tongue. Deliberately, he lowered his gaze to her mouth.

She kept her hands curled against his chest, as if she could keep him from doing to her heart what he was doing to her body. Oh, why had she agreed to this foolish bet?

Cupping her face with his hand, Chase dipped his head down toward hers. Like the whisper of breeze that surrounded them, his lips brushed hers—once, twice—before claiming them fully. A deep feeling of pleasure curled through her. A sound, a moan, came from deep in his chest as he pressed her closer still. Like a skein of wool too tightly spun, Libby felt herself unraveling as his kiss deepened. Somewhere, in the dim recesses of her mind, while her body turned to molten liquid, she knew this wasn't the friendly kiss they'd agreed on.

BARBARA ANKRUM
CHASE THE FIRE

ZEBRA BOOKS
KENSINGTON PUBLISHING CORP.

Barbara Ankrum's first Heartfire romance, *Passion's Prize*, is the winner of the *Romantic Times* "Best Western Romance by a New Author."

For Barbara Joel, whose encouragement and friendship keep me on the right path. And for my family—David, Challee and Brian—whose unfaltering love, and occasional housework, allow me to dream these dreams.

To the memory of Kristi Coll Coppin, thanks for the light.

ZEBRA BOOKS

are published by

Kensington Publishing Corp.
850 Third Avenue
New York, NY 10022

First printing: July, 1991

Printed in the United States of America

10 9 8 7 6 5 4 3 2

Character is that which reveals
moral purpose, exposing the class
of things a man chooses or avoids.
—Aristotle

Prologue

Battle of the Wilderness
Virginia—May 6, 1864

"For God's sake, man—shoot me!" the grimy-faced Reb screamed, his voice ragged with pain. Clutching the jagged tear in his gut with one hand, he grasped the sleeve of the officer in Federal blue lying beside him and pulled himself closer. A bullet hole in the Reb's upper arm leaked in a spreading crimson stain that merged with the one on his belly. "Don't leave me here to die this way," he begged.

Artillery shells roared around them, pocking the earth from every angle. It was impossible to tell from which side the shells came. It didn't seem to matter anymore.

In the dim light, Major Chasen Turner Whitlaw could see the other man's mouth move, but his screams were swallowed up by the deafening roar of the battle which was being played out a hundred rods beyond them—toward Federal lines.

Chase dropped his head wearily against his forearm, the taste of the rusty, crimsoned earth bitter on his lips. A fiery pain branded his right thigh like a white-hot poker. He tried to ignore it. He back-handed the moisture trickling down the side of his face. Sweat or blood? he wondered with vague disinterest. He felt it pool in the hollow of his ear and cut a warm swath down the grime on his neck toward his chest.

How long had he been unconscious before he'd roused to the man's moans and the sounds of battle? Moments? Hours? The ground quaked like violent thunder. The air, acrid with spent gunpowder and smoke from burning trees, seared his lungs and darkened the sky. Razor thin shafts of sunlight shot through the tree branches above him, through the windblown smoke, dappling the ground with shadow.

The dead and dying lay all around him in the tangle of brush. The shallow, body-strewn creek nearby was garnet red in color. A final gift to Southern soil, he reflected perversely. Were they all destined to die in this blood bath they were calling a battle? The hell of it was, he admitted silently, until a few moments ago, he hadn't thought he cared anymore.

Beside him, the Reb coughed and groaned. Chase's fingers curled around the smooth walnut stock of the Army Colt still in his hand. One bullet to put this gut-shot soldier out of his misery. Like he would a horse or dog in pain.

But this was a man.

His enemy, yes. But a man just the same. Killing him in the heat of battle and setting a loaded gun against his temple were two different things.

Closing his eyes to shut out the other man's cries and the searing pain that shot up his own torn and bloody leg, Chase ground his cheek against the earth.

Remembering.

They'd been sighting down the barrels of their

6

respective guns at each other, he and the Reb, preparing to blast one another to hell when a howitzer shell had done it for them. He remembered his Colt kicking in his hand and the exact moment when his body had been flung into the air—as if his mortal essence were a thing apart—weightless, spinning in an agonizingly slow arc back down toward the earth.

In those long ticks of a moment before the ground came up to meet him—before the murderous, crashing pain in his thigh and head hit him like a shore-breaking wave, snuffing out light and breath and all conscious thought—it occurred to him that he wasn't ready to die. In spite of the despicable things he'd been forced to do in the name of the Union, in spite of a soul sickness that clawed at his mind and heart, what he wanted at that moment, and with every fiber of his being, was to live.

He'd felt the life force buck within him like the exploding barrel of a .44. Then the light had splintered into utter darkness and had eventually filtered back again.

He clung to it now as he fought back the waves of nausea and pain that threatened to defeat him. Lying side by side in the unclaimed ditch, he and the Reb had crossed some invisible barrier that once separated them. No longer on opposite sides, they were now simply two men straddling the ever-shifting boundary between life and death.

The Reb pulled his knees up to his chest with a groan, his pleading hand still tangled in Chase's sleeve. "Help me. . . ."

God, how long had it been, Chase wondered, since he'd considered the humanity he'd put aside for this damned war? Now, as he looked at the man whose uniform made him an enemy, compassion warred with conscience, mercy with duty.

7

A sick feeling rose in his throat as Chase pulled the hammer of his walnut-stocked Army Colt back to half-cock and spun the cylinder to check it.

It was empty. Bereft of pity. He had known it would be. His last bullet was lodged in the man's shoulder, a good six inches from where he'd been aiming before the explosion.

His hand went to his hip where his cavalry saber should have been. It, too, was gone. Through the haze of smoke, he spotted it along with his ammunition belt lying in a twisted heap twenty feet away, where it had been ripped clear from him in the explosion.

Chase swore and his eyes closed as he silently counted the number of men he'd watched die like this Reb. Hundreds of them. Such deaths were mercilessly slow. Agonizing. Life had become expendable during this bloody war—death a commodity to be tallied in faceless numbers. The up-close stench of it muted the colors of a man's loyalties and made them suddenly . . . irrelevant.

Chase untied the knotted neckerchief at his throat and pressed it against the soldier's bloody belly. "My gun's empty, Reb."

The Reb groaned and pushed the cloth back. His teeth chattered uncontrollably and his whole body was gripped by a tremor. "N-no . . ." he said, squeezing his eyes shut against the agony. His breath whistled past clenched teeth and his Adam's apple bobbed in his throat. "I'm gut-shot . . . let it be, Yank. I'm a dead man, only I'm still breathin'."

Chase watched him reach for the simple silver chain around his neck, give it a tug, and break it free. Emotion bunched on the soldier's features as his bloody dirt-encrusted hand squeezed around the square-shaped locket that dangled from the chain. He pressed it to his chest.

"M-my wife." The man slurred the words. "I tol' her . . . God forgive me . . . I tol' 'er I'd be . . . comin' home."

Another widow, Chase thought darkly. How many others had this war made? Hell, how many had he personally made? He was suddenly grateful he had no ties. No woman to mourn him when he went under. No wife to make his dying all the harder.

The man pressed the locket into Chase's hand. "Git it to her, bluebelly. I wouldn't ask ya . . . but I got me no one else. T-tell her . . . I loved her." He squeezed his eyes shut tight. "I'm such a . . . bastard. I always . . . meant to say it . . . more."

Chase rubbed the back of his sleeve across his face, wiping the blood from his eyes. "You got a name, Reb?"

"Honeycutt . . . Lee Honeycutt, p-private with . . . the Georgia 4th. It's . . . it's all there, inside the locket. Everything you need to find her. She's—"

The rest of his words were lost to the explosion that rocked the ground and peppered them with sharp clods of dirt and stones. Chase threw his arms over his head and flattened himself on the earth, closer to the Reb. The sharp movement cost him, the pain shooting up his leg nearly causing him to pass out. He lay still for a long minute, regaining control.

When he dared to move, he looked up to see Honeycutt, who had made no move to protect himself, now bled from a dozen tiny lacerations on his face and hands. For a moment, Chase hoped the explosion had finished the man. Only the trembling movement of fingers above his wound betrayed the awful truth.

9

"Christ!" Chase swore under his breath, brushing shards of dirt and rock from the other man's face. "Oh, Christ . . ."

Honeycutt gasped, his breath rattling in his throat. "I gotta . . . Oh, Gawd, help me git up. I can't . . . I can't breathe . . ."

Chase slipped his arm beneath Honeycutt's shoulder, and he lifted the other man until the private's head rested against his chest. That was as far as his own fast-draining strength would take them. He felt Honeycutt's hand tighten around his wrist.

"My . . . my wife . . ."

"I'll get the locket to her, Honeycutt. If they don't kill me, too, I swear I will." A tremor quaked through the other man, and then Chase felt the Reb slowly relax against him.

He coughed and squeezed his eyes shut against the fire in his leg. The staccato barrage of gunfire and artillery drowned out the screams and shouts of the panicked, desperate soldiers nearby. Smoke drifted over them, redolent with the scent of death. How long he and Honeycutt lay unmoving before he heard someone shouting his name, Chase didn't know.

"Major! Major Whitlaw!"

Chase tried to turn to the voice, but his body responded with sluggish indifference. He blinked at the vaguely familiar face of the stocky soldier in blue looming above him in the haze.

"Major! Thank God you're alive. We gotta get the hell outta here," the soldier shouted. "They're pushin' us back, sir. You hurt bad? Gimme your hand, Major, I'll help you up."

Chase looked back down at the Reb, and his arm tightened around him. "Wait—"

The sergeant ignored him and shoved the body of

10

the Reb from his arms. Chase bit back a scream as the sergeant threaded an arm beneath his and hauled him to his feet. Fighting back the gulf of darkness that threatened, he steadied himself against the other man.

"That bastard's dead, Major Whitlaw," the sergeant shouted above the din of cannonade and gunfire. "He was a Butternut, sir. Nothing but a goddamn Reb."

"Yer wrong, Sergeant," Chase slurred, as the soldier dragged him toward Federal lines. Tightening his fingers around the silver locket, he slipped it inside the rough wool pocket of his uniform. "He wuz . . . a man. Just a man."

Chapter One

Leaden clouds, heavy with the promise of a drenching rain, scudded along the snow-capped granite peaks of the Sangre de Cristo Mountains and gathered wraithlike in their craggy hollows. Overhead, vultures lingered, wings tipped to the fickle air currents, awaiting their share of the spoils.

Libby rammed a brass-tipped paper cartridge into the breech of her Smith Carbine rifle, slapped the gun shut, and cocked the hammer back. She fit the walnut stock against the curve of her shoulder and aimed it at the ruff of sand-colored fur darting between the rocks some thirty feet distant. The gun's recoil jammed her shoulder backward as she squeezed off the shot. A puff of dirt erupted beneath the coyote's feet, evidence of her unfortunate aim. The creature was just moving too darned fast to hit.

"Damn!" she muttered under her breath, rubbing her tender shoulder.

"Damn!" echoed the eight-year-old towheaded boy beside her, his eyes trained on the retreating animal.

13

Chagrined, Libby couldn't help the smile that crept to the corners of her mouth at the perfect inflection he gave the word. Mercy! The word had slipped past her own lips smooth as butter. What was getting into her anyway, swearing like one of the men?

"Tad . . ."

The boy shrugged. "We're down to our last two cartridges," he supplied in self-defense.

"I know." She let out a long sigh and ran a hand over her son's hair. More and more, he was the image of his father; the same fine silvery blond hair, the same willful brown eyes and stubbornly set jaw. He was growing up too fast. Too fast for a boy without a man to keep him on the straight path.

Releasing the catch on the top of the barrel, Libby broke the rifle open at the hinge and ejected the spent cartridge. She reached into her pocket and slipped a fresh one into the breech, then snapped the rifle shut. Resting the stock against the sandy soil beside her, she reached down to stroke the velvety muzzle of the newborn foal whose head lay on her son's lap. The filly's breath was warm and moist against her fingers. She was one of Diablo's foals. Libby could tell by the fine shape of her head and her distinctive ebony color.

Hours ago, she had considered and dismissed the most practical solution to their problem: putting the abandoned foal down and leaving her to the pack of scavengers in the distance. Her fingers found the silken fur behind the foal's ears. Sometimes practicality had nothing to do with the right and wrong of things.

Lee would have argued that point with her—called her an emotional female. She admitted there was undoubtedly some truth in that. He'd always con-

14

sidered emotions something of a liability, a character defect women were saddled with—like the monthly curse.

Shrugging off her thoughts of him, Libby tipped her face up to the darkening sky. "Rain's coming. Fast."

"I'm *going*, Mama."

"No." Libby clamped a hand on her son's arm.

"What else are we gonna do?" Tad argued, sitting back on his heels. "Sit here all night until they come for us?"

Libby had been asking herself the same question for the past hour. After picking off three of the scavengers, she'd thought the gun would eventually scare the coyotes away. She'd been wrong. Apparently, they'd decided her aim didn't warrant an all-out retreat. They were waiting her and Tad out, holding them in siege; slinking around just beyond the rocks, taunting them.

"It's not safe," she argued. "What if they chase you? What if you fall off your horse?"

Tad screwed up his mouth and looked at her with all the indignation an eight-year-old could muster. "Ma, when was the last time you saw me fall off a horse?"

He had her there. "I-I just don't want anything to happen to you. . . ."

"Okay, then," he replied with a logic annoying in a boy his age. "You go. *I'll* stay here with the foal."

"No!"

"Well, then? She's too heavy to haul up onto—"

"I know, I know." She let out an exasperated sigh and tossed her flaxen-colored braid back over her shoulder. They'd already tried to lift the filly atop Libby's horse, but had found it impossible between the two of them without risking injuring her. "Can you get the team hitched up to the buckboard by yourself?"

"Early taught me," Tad replied eagerly, hope sparking anew in his eyes.

Libby prayed she wouldn't regret this. "All right then. Bring Straw back with you if he isn't three sheets to the wind by now. First help me collect some rocks. When my ammunition runs out, I'm going to need something to hold them off 'til you get back. I'm afraid a fire'll be a waste of time with the weather that's coming."

She and Tad collected two armloads of rocks, in the process pitching a few at the overly brave scavengers. They set them in a pile on the ground beside the foal. Libby laid a soothing hand on her spooked dun-colored mare, whose brown eyes rolled backward with fright at the sound of the coyote's yipping. She tied the horse's reins to a branch of the scrubby mesquite tree behind her and pulled her India-rubber poncho from behind her saddle. Gently, she slid it over the foal to keep her dry. The black filly nickered softly and raised her head up off the ground for a moment, too weak to protest more.

"There, little one. You'll be all right," Libby soothed, stroking her behind the ears. "We'll take care of you."

She turned to Tad. "Be careful, darlin'," she whispered, and pressed a kiss on his forehead. "You hear?"

Tad squirmed under her mothering, anxious to prove himself worthy of her trust. "Don't worry," he assured her, climbing up into the saddle of his white-tailed sorrel. "I'll get back as soon as I can."

She swallowed her fears and smiled back at him from behind her fingertips as he kicked the horse and tore off across the darkening landscape.

The rain started a few minutes later. Fat droplets plopped against the weathered brim of her hat and slapped against the poncho covering the foal with the sounds of popping corn. The pungent smell of damp sage and creosote bushes filled the air.

Libby tucked her long mane of golden hair up under her hat, pulled her trouser-covered knees up to her chest, and tightened the worn, wool coat around her, cursing the timing of the storm. Why did it have to come on a Saturday night when all the hands had headed into town for their regular weekend blow-out? Only Straw remained back at the ranch. No hope of him hearing the gunshots, she thought miserably. Straw was only a thimble shy of being deaf as a doorknob.

In the dusky darkness, the coyotes set up a mournful yipping that sent a shiver straight through her. The sound no longer came only from in front of her. It seemed to surround her now. She gathered the gun to her, tightening her finger on the trigger. "Come on, you flea-bitten hunks o' mange," she growled low. "Just try and sneak up on me. I'll give you a taste of gunpowder even if I can't blow your heads off."

Her only answer was the sound of the rain pounding against her back and shoulders as she crouched low against the deluge. Tiny rivulets of water streamed past her, cutting paths in the gritty soil. Thunder rumbled across the mountains, and a flash of lightning split the sky in two. The rugged landscape flashed bright as day for several seconds, then faded back to murky lavender.

The cold rain stung her face, and she blinked it back while a bone-rattling shiver raced down the length of her. Slipping down further inside her over-sized coat, Libby kept her eyes trained on the rocks

17

straight ahead. The coyotes, she noted, had taken shelter under them while she sat out in the middle of this gully-washer, getting soaked to the skin. All for a little filly who would not, in all likelihood, survive the night.

Libby frowned and wiped her eyes with the back of her soggy sleeve, her mood disintegrating with the weather. "Damn you, Lee!" She cursed him out loud to the angry evening sky. The valley brightened briefly with a flash of lightning.

Tipping her face defiantly up to the needle-sharp rain, she shouted (at the top of her lungs now, having gathered courage from her solitude), "Damn you for leaving me alone out here." Her voice ricocheted around the rock-enclosed valley, coming back to her like the drawn-out echo of thunder. She sniffed and pressed her mouth against her wool sleeve. "Damn you for leaving Tad without a father," she mumbled. "And me . . . without a friend."

Chase Whitlaw tugged the collar of his leather-caped, oilcloth duster up around his ears, pulled his hat down low over his eyes, and squinted at the black specks circling low over the valley a mile distant.

Turkey vultures.

Damnable creatures, he thought with a sickening shiver. What are they after this time? He'd caught enough sign of game in this valley to account for dozens of possibilities: deer, bear, rabbit, even a few human tracks. None of which, he decided, were his concern. He put the scavengers out of his mind.

His own destination weighed heavily upon him. Glancing at the thunderheads gathering in the distance, he wished he'd taken El's advice back in Santa Fe and waited until morning to head out to the

18

Honeycutt place. God knew, he'd waited two years. Twelve more hours couldn't have hurt.

But somehow, he couldn't bring himself to put it off. He wanted it done. Over with. Maybe then he could—

The sound of a gunshot echoed up the canyon walls, causing him to jerk in the reins of his horse and duck down instinctively. *Bloody hell!*

The odor of sweaty horseflesh mingled pungently with the familiar scent of his own fear. He took a deep breath and trained his eyes on the high copses of rock rimming the canyon ahead. This country could play tricks on a man's ears, he knew.

Straightening slowly, he stared in the direction of the vultures again. Could have been thunder, he thought reasonably, looking at the gunmetal gray sky. He drew his Henry rifle from its scabbard beneath his right knee in spite of his doubts, and nudged his mount in the direction of the sound.

The rain started with a whimper and gathered fury as the heavens opened up in a torrent. Thunder pounded heavily across the valley, and the downpour cut Chase's visibility by more than half. Suddenly, from behind the solid sheet of rain, a horse shot past him. Its diminutive rider he could only assume was a young boy. Though only fifty feet separated them, Chase knew the boy hadn't seen him.

"Hey!" Chase called over the din of the rain. But the boy rode on, hellbent for shelter, no doubt. For a moment, he thought about chasing him. Was the boy the shooter? he wondered.

He didn't have to wait long for the answer.

The high whine of a carbine split the air again, easily distinguishable from the surrounding thunder. *Damn.*

Chase touched his horse with the tips of his spurs,

and the beast took off at a run, splashing across the muddy ground. Within minutes, he spotted a huddled figure beside a poncho-draped heap as a flash of light jagged across the sky. It only took him a few more seconds to realize the bedraggled unfortunate was holding off a pack of hungry-looking coyotes with only a rapidly shrinking pile of rocks and the upended stock of a carbine. Shouldering his Henry, Chase took aim at the nearest animal and fired.

The crack of a gunshot startled Libby so that she fell backside-first into the mud with an undignified splat. The barrel of her gun was now buried nose-deep in the mire. The coyote that only moments ago had been sneaking up on her had been lifted off the ground by the forceful thud of a bullet and tossed a few feet away, to land dead as a tree stump.

Libby turned to seek out the source of the shot. Like some kind of avenging demon, a hulking shape on horseback was galloping toward her. The man's gleaming duster flew at his sides like wings, while his rifle belched another round of fire. A second coyote slammed into the ground muzzle-first and twitched in death throes.

"Oh, my!" she cried, scuttling backward toward the foal. The man cocked his rifle again and picked off another retreating animal. The rest scattered, like windblown tumbleweeds, in every direction. He fired two more shots at their heels in quick succession, then turned his horse back toward her and came on at a lope.

The stranger pulled his horse up short and dismounted, slogging through the mud to Libby's side. Her eyes widened, taking in the size of him, and she scooted back farther. Fear crept up her spine, setting the hairs on the back of her neck to bristling. He could be anyone, out in a storm like this, she thought with a jolt of panic. Outlaw, cattle rustler . . . Fear overcame her sense of gratitude, and she raised her mud-clogged rifle and pointed it in his direction.

"That's close enough, mister."

The man stopped short, blinking back his surprise. His lips parted when he saw the barrel of the gun pointed at him, and he took a wary step back.

Chase could have sworn it was a woman's voice that came from that lump of rain-sodden clothing in front of him, but he thought his mind was playing tricks on him again. What in hell would a woman be doing out in the middle of nowhere, holding off a pack of coyotes?

Alone.

He narrowed his eyes. Rain dripped off the brim of his hat in a steady stream, and his fingers tightened around the stock of his Henry. "That's pretty unfriendly of you to point that thing at me, considering I just saved your neck," he said at last.

"Maybe," the distinctively feminine voice allowed.

I'll be damned. He couldn't get a good look at her face, not with her hat pulled down that way. But the voice peaked his interest. It was throaty, with a hint of a soft Southern drawl. He took a step forward, his eyes on her gun. "You a woman?"

He watched the mud-clogged tip of the gun waver slightly. It took her a moment to answer, as if she were considering the possibility of an outright lie.

"That's none of your business. I thank you for your help, but I'll be fine now," she declared with cool dismissal. Another streak of lightning tore at the sky close-by.

A harsh bark of laughter escaped him as he tipped his face up to the driving rain. *"Fine?* Yeah, that's perfectly damned obvious."

21

Before she could react, he crossed the distance between them and yanked the rifle from her hands, wrenching a surprised gasp from her throat.

"Didn't anyone ever tell you not to point a gun at a man unless you intend to shoot him!" he snapped.

Shock and anger warred inside her, and Libby strangled a scream of frustration as she leaped to her feet. "Give that back to me!"

"You can't shoot a man without any bullets, lady," he parried, holding the gun out of her reach. "That's a damn dangerous bluff out here in the middle of nowhere."

"What makes you so sure I was bluffing?" she demanded, jamming her hands down on her hips. She bit down hard on the inside of her lip to keep it from quivering.

"Right . . ." he said, ejecting the gun's spent cartridge onto the wet ground. "And I suppose you were trying to cold-cock those coyotes with the butt end of this thing for the hell of it." His gaze took in the smudge of mud that traversed her face from cheek to chin. He couldn't see much more of her than that under the brim of her battered old hat.

Libby's scowl traveled from the damning evidence at the man's feet back up to him. His speech branded him a Yankee, probably a stray from the war. She'd seen enough men like him drift through the territory in the past year to recognize one on sight. Most of them were harmless, but he looked far from that. She lifted her chin with false courage. "So maybe I was bluffing. I wasn't going to shoot you. I just wanted to . . . to warn you off."

That scoffing laugh echoed again. "Lady," he said, with a disparaging shake of his head, "if I was the kind of man who needed warning off, that stunt would have been too little, too late."

22

His words rang ominously true. "And how do I know you're *not?*" she asked.

"Not what?"

"Not . . . that kind of man."

He snapped her gun shut with a crack. "You don't," he replied. "That's my point."

Libby swallowed hard and forced herself to breathe. "Well, what did you expect me to do, riding up to me that way in the dark?"

"I'd *expect*," he replied, gritting his teeth together, "that a woman with a lick of sense wouldn't have gotten herself into a dangerous situation like this in the first place." His beard-darkened jaw was grimly set.

Rain pelted Libby's back and gathered in a small pool on the brim of her hat. She shot him a disgusted look. "You don't know what you're talking about. How could you? You're . . . you're a man."

"Ah, you noticed that right off, did you?" He didn't smile. He merely shifted the rifles in his hands and cocked a knee insolently.

Libby's face flushed a bright pink. "That's not what I meant."

The stranger ignored her, turning to the small, moving lump beneath the rubber slicker. "You got somebody hurt under there?" he asked.

"Not somebody. Something." Libby saw one dark eyebrow go up.

"I beg your pardon?"

"It's . . . it's a horse," she told him as a shiver of cold raced down her back.

He cast a suspicious look at the smallish mound. "Did you say a horse?" The brim of his hat concealed a frown, but she heard disbelief in his voice.

"I did." She threw her shoulders back defensively. "A small horse. A foal, actually."

23

His head came up with a snap. "Good God, woman! Are you telling me that you're sitting out here in the middle of a driving rainstorm, working on a good case of pneumonia, trying to save the life of some . . . some foal who's probably half-dead anyway?"

"Yes." The challenge in her voice was clear. "That's exactly what I was doing."

He let out a snort of disbelieving laughter. "Either you're a fool, lady, or you're just plain crazy."

She let out a snort of her own. "Maybe I am. But that's my business, not yours, isn't it?"

"Yeah? Well, you just made it my business," he countered. He ignored her indignant expression, stooped down, and lifted the edge of the poncho to get a good look at the foal. Balanced on the balls of his feet, he let out a disgusted sigh.

"Listen, Mr. . . . whoever you are—"

"Whitlaw. Chase Whitlaw. And I suppose this is your rain gear protecting her instead of being on your back," he accused, breaking off her thought.

She raised her chin a defiant notch. "I don't know where you're from, mister, but around here life is too dear to part with so easily and foals are too precious to squander."

He didn't look up at her—didn't even move—but she saw his broad shoulders bunch with tension. She shifted her stance when he didn't respond. "Besides, I . . . can't afford to lose her."

"How old is she?" he asked finally, with his back still to her.

Libby wiped the rain from her face and stared down at the moisture gathering on the back of the stranger's muscular neck. It beaded and ran in small rivulets toward the collar of his coat. "A few hours, maybe not even that."

24

"Where's the mare?"

Libby glanced off into the darkness and muttered. "Well, if I knew that, she and I wouldn't be sitting here in the rain would we?" Libby folded her wet arms across her chest and shivered. "She's probably dead."

Chase stood up and let out a long breath. Without another word, he stripped off his long oilcloth coat and handed it to her. "Put it on."

She glared at him. "I will not. It's . . . it's yours."

"Damn it lady, don't argue with me," he snapped. "We're both getting wetter by the minute and I'm not in the mood to sit here and trade insults with you." He shoved the garment into her hands and, in the fading light, caught the angry flash of her silvery eyes. Before he allowed himself to dwell on their fascinating color, he turned and whistled for his horse.

Libby was stunned to see the big-boned gray come trotting up like an obedient dog. It was the darndest thing she ever saw. After slipping his rifle back into its scabbard, and thrusting hers back into her hands, he scooped the foal up—covering and all—into his arms.

"Wh-what are you doing?"

"What does it look like? You've got a spread some-where nearby, I assume?"

Tight-lipped, she tipped her head affirmatively as she pulled on the too-long duster.

"Get your horse and let's go."

She'd never met anyone so infuriating in her entire life. He was bossing her around like he had the right! She wanted to scream, stomp her feet or slap that smug expression off his face. But she didn't do any of those things. The truth was—and it pained her greatly to admit it—she needed his help if she was

25

going to save the foal. She and Tad had failed in that. Miserably.

Libby slogged back to her horse, which was partially hidden by the leafed-out screw-bean mesquite, and gathered up the reins. From behind her mare, she watched the stranger stand perfectly still with his burden for a moment in the driving rain. Confoundingly, he crooned softly to the frightened foal to quiet her before lifting her up with him onto his horse. Then, he settled her, with surprising gentleness, across his knees. He made the awkward movement seem effortless.

Groaning inwardly, Libby remembered how she and Tad had struggled together to get the foal up on her mare's back. But the squirming, ninety-pound creature was too much for the two of them. She swept the long tails of the stranger's coat out of her way as she swung up into her saddle.

Whitlaw's horse shied a bit at the unfamiliar scent of the foal on its back, but the man soothed his mount with a gentle hand. "Lead on, lady."

Libby pulled back on the reins of her horse and sent the stranger a hard look. "Look, just so we're clear on this, Mr. Whitlaw, Lady is my mare's name, not mine." An irritating grin softened the part of his face she could see beneath the brim of his water-stained hat.

"My apologies, ma'am," he drawled mockingly, insincerely touching long, gloved fingers to that brim. "But I don't recall hearing your given name."

"My *given* name is Elizabeth, Mr. Whitlaw," she replied with a slightly superior air. "But you may call me Mrs. Honeycutt."

Without another word, she kicked her horse into a lope and faded behind the curtain of sheeting rain.

Chapter Two

Chase felt as if the bottom had dropped out of his stomach. Dumbstruck, he swallowed hard, tightening his grip around the squirming foal.

Honeycutt! Bloody hell!

He realized he'd just broken out in a sweat—in spite of the cold rain. With a touch of his knees, he nudged the gray forward, inordinately glad for the distance the woman had put between them.

He tried to reconcile the dirty, bad-tempered urchin he'd just met with the silvered image of the woman he'd carried with him for the last two years. It didn't seem possible these were the same woman. He'd expected . . .

Hell, he didn't know what he'd expected, he admitted with a frown. A ridiculous sense of disappointment filled him, and he swallowed it back. He had no right to feel disappointment or anything else, not about her, he reminded himself.

He was here for one reason and one reason only.

In one hour, maybe two at the outside, he'd have his business done and be gone. He shrugged his rain-soaked shoulders with new conviction.

Right.

The rain fell harder, if that was possible. The storm seemed to be hovering over the valley, snagged there between the mountains like deadwood in a stream. Chase felt the cold drive right through his body, and he reached down to rub his achy thigh. Cold weather always made it worse.

Night had enveloped what little landscape had been visible through the torrents, making the going not only tricky, but treacherous. Ahead, he saw the Honeycutt woman waiting for him—steady, sitting straight astride her saddle, uncowed by the storm. She was shouting something at him.

"What?" he called as he drew closer.

"We'll take the road!" she yelled, motioning to him with a wave of her hand. "Footing's better, even though it's a little farther that way."

He caught up to her and a flash of light illuminated her face. Moisture beaded her full lips and the part of her cheeks visible beneath the brim of her battered hat. His gaze fell to the smudge of mud that ran across the hollow of her cheek and down her chin. A wet strand of hair was plastered against her face, but she didn't seem to notice it. He had the craziest impulse to reach over and brush it back, but thinking better of it, he dug his fingers deeper into the rubber slicker covering the foal.

"She all right?" Libby asked.

"Snug as a bug," he replied with an involuntary shiver. "How much farther is it?"

"Only about a mile or so." She sniffed and rubbed her nose with the back of her hand. "Tad lit out to fetch the wagon just before the storm started. I don't want to miss him cutting cross-country."

"Who's Tad?"

Her head tilted sideways for a split second, as if she were studying him. "He's my son." Yanking on the reins, she touched the heels of her boots to the mare's side and took the lead again.

Son? Chase's memory supplied the image of the boy streaking past him through the rain. Honeycutt hadn't mentioned a boy. Could he be their son? She looked too damned young to have a boy that age. Chase clamped his mouth shut on any more questions and struck out after her.

He had to admit that she rode a horse as well as any woman he'd ever seen. Then again, he'd never seen a woman ride astride the way she did. He supposed there were a lot of things about this particular woman that were . . . unique, if his first meeting with her was any indication. As irritated as he was with her for getting herself into this mess, he was nonetheless intrigued.

Soon, the lights from her place wavered in the distance like a full moon over the water, beckoning them with the promise of relief from the dank, miserable weather.

The hollow swell of thunder rumbled closeby as Chase followed the woman down the mud-rutted wagon path toward the house; he couldn't bring himself to call it a road. It was a far cry from the paved streets of Baltimore, he reflected without so much as a twinge of regret. The rustic feel of the land held a strange appeal for him in spite of its stark nature. Maybe it was that very starkness that attracted him.

A man could find solitude in a country like this. Maybe even . . . peace.

A hundred yards or so from the house, a flash of lightning revealed a small picketed grave plot with three white markers. Chase supposed one of them belonged—in name at least—to her late husband. One freshly turned mound caught his eye and, as the plot disappeared behind them, he wondered who she'd buried lately.

The house was a small, natural-colored adobe that

29

blended in perfectly with its surroundings. Round wood beams poked out the sides just under the eaves of the flat, grass-covered roof, and rainwater gushed from several broken drainage spouts to form a small lake beneath the wooden-barred front windows before which two scrawny rose bushes struggled to survive.

The door hung slightly askew on its leather hinges, and slender triangles of light streaked out from the inside. The inky night prevented Chase from seeing much more, but he suspected the rest of the house was as badly in need of repair as the front.

The dwelling was flanked on the right by a wooden barn, from which the soft glow of lantern light spilled. Another adobe building, slightly larger than the first, he guessed was a bunkhouse. A corral lined the area between the two structures, and a remuda of horses stood nose-to-rump beneath the shelter of two cottonwood trees. Anger seeped through him again as he realized the kind of life she must have. Why the hell hadn't she sold out and moved in with family somewhere?

Libby breathed a sigh of relief as she spotted Tad through the open barn doors, still inside hitching up the team. She called out to him, but the pounding rain swallowed up the sound of her voice. Behind her, she saw Whitlaw drawing near with the foal, and she dismounted, hitching Lady, for the moment, to the rail beside the house.

"Take her inside," she told him, pointing toward the adobe house. "It's warmer in there, and she'll be too weak to try to nurse from old Ruby anyway." Grabbing hold of his reins, she tied them to the hitching post and waited for him to comply.

He stared at her for a moment and shook his head, wondering if he'd heard her right. "In the *house?*"

What woman in her right mind would bring a horse into her house? None of the women he'd ever known.

She stared back at him, her impatience thinly veiled. "If it's not too much trouble."

"No trouble at all, if you're sure that's what you want."

"It is," she answered, arms akimbo.

Chase slid the foal up off his thighs and scooted back, resting the bulk of her against the saddle tree, partially supporting her with one hand. He didn't trust his right leg to take the full weight of both him and the foal, not the way it felt. He swung free of the saddle, but even without all the extra weight, pain shot up his thigh as his right foot hit the ground. He grimaced and stumbled slightly, muttering a breathy curse through gritted teeth.

Libby heard the sound and ducked under the neck of his horse, coming up beside him. "Did you hurt yourself, Mr. Whitlaw?"

He scowled down at her. "No!" he returned with a growl. He gathered the foal back into his arms.

She didn't believe him. Not for a minute. The pain she'd seen in his eyes was real. But she wasn't about to argue the point with a man who had given her a look that would back down a grizzly bear.

With a critical eye, she followed behind him up the stream-rutted pathway to the low-beamed covered portico. His collarless blue cotton shirt and dark wool vest were plastered to his broad shoulders and arms. Her eyes were drawn downward to his tight-hipped torso and long, muscular legs. It was the right leg he favored, she decided, appraising him as she would one of her geldings. The limp might not even have been noticeable, except to one with an eye trained to spot such things. The fact that he worked

31

so hard to conceal it told her something about the man.

"Are you going to get the door or should I just kick it open?"

His voice broke into her thoughts, and she realized, with a rush of heat, that she'd been staring unabashedly at his backside.

"Land sakes, no!" she cried, lifting the flimsy wooden latch. "This door's only hanging by a thread anyway." She swung it open for him and stepped out of his way. She watched the finesse with which he fit both himself and the foal through the narrow opening. Not an easy task. Alone, the man seemed to dwarf everything else in the small room.

"Over here," she told him, directing him to a corner. "By the fireplace." Libby shoved a fresh log and a handful of tinder onto the banked fire to build it up. The dry wood caught immediately sending a blast of warmth into the chill air.

Libby watched the foal struggle in Whitlaw's arms. Her spindly legs flew out in all directions at once, causing him to grunt in pain. With a soothing voice and a gentle hand on her neck, he quieted the frightened creature again, then obligingly delivered his load onto the floor near the warmth of the mesquite-scented blaze in the fireplace. The hard-packed earthen floor was covered with a crisply woven wool *jerga,* whose black- and white-checkered pattern lent warmth to the plain, sparsely furnished room. Several chests and a cupboard lined the walls; a polished wood rocker sat near the fire beside a worn, burgundy horsehair sofa.

Libby brushed her hands against her pants, shoved her hat down tighter on her head and headed for the door.

"Where are you going?" he asked, straightening to his full height.

She turned back to look at him. Lord, he was tall. He was six-three if he was an inch. She shivered again, but wasn't sure if it was from the chill or . . . him. "I'm going to put the horses up. They shouldn't be—"

"No," he said, brushing past her. "I'll take care of them. You get yourself dry."

Ignoring him, she tried to slip past him. "I'll do it—uhnh!" With a grunt of surprise, she ran smack into the solid, wet wall of his chest as he stepped in front of her, blocking her path. "Oh!" she cried, splaying two hands across the sodden muscled expanse. She tried to push away from him, but his large hands bracketed her shoulders, holding her there. Beneath her fingertips she felt the steady thud of his heart against his ribs. The sensation triggered a hammering in her own chest.

"Let me go!" she demanded, glaring up into his shadowed face.

She felt the pressure of his fingers against her upper arms, where his steadying hands lingered for a moment, thumbs roving back and forth against the cold, wet fabric. Then, as abruptly as they had collided, he set her away from him. "You're cold. Stay here," he ordered. "I'll go."

"But—"

"You said you had a brood mare out there?" he asked.

"Yes, but—"

"What does she look like?"

"I can do it—"

"I'm sure you can. Tell me."

Libby sighed. "She's a sorrel, in the third stall from the front. Her name is Ruby."

He turned toward the door. "I'll get some milk for the foal and be back soon."

"Mr. Whitlaw!"

He stopped again and angled a look over his con-siderable shoulder at her. "Yeah?"

"My son's out there. In the barn, I mean."

He turned around fully now, a frown playing at the corners of his mouth. He blinked at her, unsure of her meaning. "Does that worry you? Him being with me?"

She swallowed hard and shrugged. "Yes . . . no . . . I mean . . . he doesn't know who you are, that's all." The lie tripped so easily off her tongue. She knew nothing about him. He *could* be an outlaw for all she knew. Her fear returned in a rush. Tad was all she had. All that was important to her. She didn't take chances where he was concerned. "I should tell him I'm back." She stubbornly placed balled fists on her hips and glared at him.

Slowly, deliberately, Whitlaw reached up and lifted his low-crowned hat from his head. He raked his fingers through his dark, wet hair, leaving four furrows behind, and then looked up at her.

Libby's lips fell open as she got her first good look at his face. The eyes that regarded her from under a sweep of dark lashes were the clear, green color of newly sprouted piñon needles—and were too beautiful for a man's face, she thought absurdly. Yet, they were hard eyes, dangerous—filled with the kind of trouble one could only hope to avoid in a lifetime.

Like the rest of him, his features were unsparingly lean and taut. His face could have been sculpted by an artist's hand, but for the imperfections that made his handsomeness rugged. His nose looked as if it had been broken once and veered slightly off center. The blue smudges under his eyes betrayed a fatigue that went beyond a single night's lost sleep, and fine lines curved around his full mouth and eyes. She somehow doubted they'd been born of laughter. A pity, she thought, for his mouth looked as if it was made for smiles.

A thin, crescent-shaped scar traced a path from his cheekbone to his hairline. The sinister quality it added didn't detract from his face in any way, but rather added to its mystique.

It had taken her all of ten seconds to peruse the visage he'd offered up for inspection—for she had no doubt that was exactly what he'd done—and to decide, grudgingly, he meant them no harm. It had only taken another two or three to realize the inherent danger in prolonging her stare.

Libby looked away and flushed guiltily. "I . . . I'm . . ." she faltered.

"I'll give your son a hand unharnessing the wagon, Mrs. Honeycutt," he interrupted, settling the hat back on his head like an old friend, "after I introduce myself." His smile softened the hard edges of his mouth.

She could only nod curtly and watch him head back out into the rain-swept night. Libby closed the door and leaned up against the jamb. She closed her eyes and listened to the rhythmic thudding of her heart.

Mercy, she thought, pressing her fingertips to her lips. Who is that man?

Chase gathered up the reins of the two horses standing with heads down against the steady drumming of the rain, and started for the barn. Shaken, he took his time, allowing his throbbing leg the comfort of a limp and the heartbeat hammering in his ears a chance to slow.

Hell, he thought. This was a bad idea, coming here like this. Seeing her. He'd had nearly two years to prepare himself for this. Two years to convince himself that both of them could get through this painlessly. Two years of careful planning out the window because of the goddamned weather.

"Don't go, Chase. Send the damn locket out by the mails," his stepbrother Elliot had warned him back in Baltimore as Chase had packed. "Write her a letter if you have to, but stay the hell away from her. She's the widow of a Reb, for God's sake, man. You go looking for forgiveness and you're likely to find a bullet for your trouble."

"It's not forgiveness I'm looking for," he'd countered, turning away from the man he'd practically grown up with.

Grabbing Chase's shoulders in frustration, El had shouted, "What then? What can you possibly hope to accomplish by—"

"I don't know!" he'd cried, jerking away. "I . . . I just know I have to go. Finish it."

"Nothing good will come of it, Chase."

Now Elliot's words echoed in his ears. He'd had no answer for them then, nor did he tonight. He had nothing to offer her, no words of comfort or solace. Those soft feelings—the ones a man shared with a woman—had died in him, had long ago been interred with the bloody memories of the war.

So why was he here?

His rain-slick fingers closed around the locket he kept in his pocket. His reasons had less to do with the war than with the picture he had carried with him all this time. He couldn't explain to El that her face, a tiny photograph in a locket, had seen him through

36

the worst of the pain when he lay near death in that godforsaken Army hospital in Washington. It was *her* picture the woman nursing him had pressed into his hand, thinking it a picture of his wife. How could he ever explain that he owed Elizabeth Honeycutt a debt for that? How could he explain it without sounding as if he'd lost his mind?

The boy was fumbling with the belly-strap of the lead horse when Chase walked through the double doors of the barn and led the two horses inside. Tad's head came up with a thwack of surprise against the belly of the mare he was working on, bringing an irritated snort from the animal. At the horse's feet stood a black and white mutt of a dog. Its ears pricked up sharply at Chase's approach, and a low growl rumbled in its throat.

Rubbing the back of his head, Tad straightened and stared at Chase from under the gelding's neck.

"Tad, isn't it?" Chase asked, stopping a few feet away. He was instantly struck by the boy's uncanny resemblance to the Reb who still haunted his dreams. A chill shot through him.

"That's Ma's horse. Who are you, and what are you doin' with it?" the boy demanded, his eyes wide and scared.

"Name's Chase Whitlaw. Your ma's in the house. I ran into her out in the storm and helped her bring the foal back."

"You did?"

"Um-hmm." Chase casually rubbed his mount's muzzle. "We sent those coyotes scattering for greener pastures, too."

Tad moved out from behind the horse and stood before Chase. The dog moved with him as if the pair were attached at the kneecap. Amused, Chase watched the boy's huge blue eyes scan him as if he

37

were a climbing tree and Tad were looking for the best branch to get a footing on.

Finally Tad stuck out his hand. "Pleased to meet-cha."

Chase grinned and took the small hand in his. "Likewise." It gave him an odd feeling to close his fingers over a hand so small, yet so strong.

"This here is Patch, my dog," the boy said, indicating the mutt who'd taken a decidedly less defensive stand beside Tad since the boy had welcomed Chase.

Chase reached down and let the dog sniff his fingers, then scratched him behind the ears. "Nice dog."

Tad nodded, shoved his hands in his back pockets, and shrugged at the half-hitched team. "I almost got 'em hooked up. Guess we won't be needin' 'em now."

Chase walked over and inspected the harnesses. "Appears you did a fine job of it, too." He slapped a palm across the roan's rump and glanced at the boy. Pride lit Tad's eyes at Chase's compliment. "I imagine you're a big help to your ma around here."

"Yeah . . . well . . . she don't—doesn't—let me help unless there's nobody else," Tad said, attacking the buckle he'd just fastened. "She's always afraid I'll get hurt or something."

"Mothers tend to be that way," Chase agreed solemnly.

"Was *your* ma like that?"

He frowned thoughtfully, sliding the long leather latigo free from his horse's cinch. "Yup. But it was generally just a matter of learning how far I could push it. My pa usually set her straight."

Tad dropped his head. "My pa's dead."

Chase could have kicked himself back to Santa Fe. He glanced up at the boy. "I'm sorry, Tad."

"He died in the war. The dirty Yanks kilt him."

Chase swallowed hard and looked down at his

38

hands. "A lot of good men died in the war. On both sides."

Tad's eyes widened. "You fight in the war, too?"

Chase fixed his gaze back on the task at hand, wedging his hand under the latigo to loosen it. "Yeah."

"Maybe you knew my pa," Tad said hopefully. "His name was Honeycutt, too."

A sick feeling rose in Chase's throat. It hadn't occurred to Tad that Chase might have fought on the other side. A boy Tad's age couldn't know how complicated the world really was, and Chase couldn't bring himself to tell him. Not yet. "It was a big war, Tad."

Disappointed, Tad shrugged and slid the harness off the mare's back. "I know. I just thought . . ."

"You know," Chase said, sliding the saddle off his horse, "Blue, here, sure has a hankering for a good meal. You think we could scratch up a flake or two of hay for him?"

Tad brightened. "Sure. We got oats, too. He like oats?"

A smile eased the edges off Chase's expression. "Oats are pretty near his favorite thing. Next to carrots."

"Blue. That his name?" Tad headed for the oat barrel. "I used to have a lizard named that . . . pertiest lizard you ever did see. . . ."

Chase felt a ripple of pleasure as he listened to Tad go on about the lizard. It had been a good long time since he'd experienced a child firsthand. Tad had put the memories of his father aside as easily as he had the harnessed team. If only life could remain that uncompromisingly simple.

Plink. Plink.

39

Kerplink.

Libby captured the annoying drip of muddy rainwater in the last of her wooden bowls and stared disconsolately about the room. Rapidly filling containers were scattered everywhere. Chilled, despite her change of clothes, she rubbed her hands briskly up and down the sleeves of her red flannel shirt. The roof leaked like an old, worn-out shoe. Every time it rained it was the same story. She supposed she should be grateful that rainstorms were few and far between here on the high desert.

Lee's father, Malachi, hadn't been one to make repairs even when his health had been good. In the four years since Lee had left for the war, the ranch had gotten more and more run-down. Starting with the roof and ending with its profits, Libby mused glumly.

Her disappointing visit that very day with the banker in Santa Fe, Sam Darnell, had dampened but not squelched her hopes of making a go of the Double Bar H. She still had three months to round up enough horses to fill the Army's order. If she succeeded, she wouldn't need the extension Darnell was so dead set against giving her.

She wasn't a stranger to hard work, she reasoned, giving herself a mental shake. She'd had to work her whole life. Nothing had come easily to her. Not her growing-up years back in Georgia, not her marriage, not even her son, whom she loved more than life itself. But none of that mattered. Lee used to tell her that once she had her mind set on something, she went after it with the grit of a bulldog. And thinking of that now, she guessed it was true. The ones in town who'd started calling her Crazy Libby Honeycutt for trying to hang on to this patch of land all by herself since Malachi's death four months ago didn't know that about her.

Libby leaned against the three-foot-wide strip of green calico that circled the walls of the outer room, protecting her clothes from the white-washed adobe. She peeked through the lace curtain toward the barn. Lantern light spilled from the half-open doors, but there was no sign yet of Tad or the stranger.

Her fingers tightened around the sill for a moment, her watchful stare dissolving into a frown. She'd never seen Chase Whitlaw before he'd come blazing up to her in the rain, but she had the nagging feeling she should know who he was. Still, his wasn't a forgettable face. If she'd seen him before she would remember, Libby told herself reasonably, pushing away from the window.

Still, there was something familiar—no, *intimate*—about the way he'd looked at her. As if he knew something about her she hadn't revealed.

She almost laughed out loud at that crazy notion. Oh Libby, she scolded silently. You've been out in the rain too long. Reading such things into a simple straightforward look. He's a drifter. Nothing more. Nothing less. And downright irritating, to boot. He'll be gone after a hot meal and a dry night in the barn.

She went to the black iron stove and stirred the stew she'd thrown together earlier that day, then checked on the pan of cornbread in the oven. The scent of it filled the small common room and made her stomach growl impatiently with hunger. Though Tad had relished his noon meal at The Exchange Hotel, a real luxury she and her son rarely afforded themselves, Libby's meeting with Darnell had effectively stolen her appetite. Frankly, she hadn't even thought about food until now.

She picked up a fresh towel and knelt beside the little foal. Warmed by the gentle blaze, the foal stared up at her with enormous brown eyes.

41

"Now listen, you"—Libby took the no-nonsense approach, rubbing briskly at the shaggy brown coat—"I darned near got myself eaten trying to keep those coyotes away from you, and I did get soaked to the skin for my trouble. Not to mention having to put up with that . . . that know-it-all Yankee. So if you have any ideas about going the way your mother did, you'd better get them right out of your head. Dying is simply out of the question."

A cool gust of air fanned the flames in the fireplace, and she turned to see Tad burst through the door. "Ma! Chase let me feed his horse. Did you know his horse's name was Blue? Just like my old lizard? Whew, it's really wet out there!"

Libby's glance went from her son to the tall man in the doorway. The stranger hovered near the opening, dripping wet, an uncertain look on his face. His saddlebags were slung over one shoulder. The Henry rifle was suspended in one hand, a bucket of mare's milk in the other.

She stood and wrapped her arms around her wet son. "Well," she replied, "I see you two have gotten acquainted. Tad, settle Patch down out on the portico. He's muddier than a mare in fly season." At that, the dog made a whining yawn and headed back outside. "Come in, Mr. Whitlaw," Libby continued. "No need to stand there in the cold."

It took a second or two before Chase heard what she'd said. He was too busy taking in her transformation from drowned rat to breath-stealing beauty. She'd shed her shapeless, wet clothes and traded them for a man's oversize flannel shirt which she'd tucked in at the waist of a dry pair of Levi's, cinched with a belt. He'd never seen a pair of denims filled out in quite such an appealing way. They hugged her long slender legs and the attractive flare of her hips. The sight sent his heart skittering along his ribs.

Her hair, waist-long, was the golden color of flax. She wore it in a loose, practical braid down the center of her back, out of her way, as if she were completely unaware of its splendor.

Her delicate face had been scrubbed free of the mud. She wasn't beautiful in the classic sense of the word, he decided critically. Her dove gray eyes were a touch too wide-set, and her bow-shaped mouth was too generous to be strictly beautiful. But taken as a whole, she was the kind of woman who conjured up a man's sweetest fantasies and set a lustful heat stirring in his loins.

Right now, he realized with a jolt, she was frowning at him.

"Is it that you're not used to seeing a woman in trousers, Mr. Whitlaw? Or are you always this rude?"

His heartbeat kicked back into rhythm, and a smile twitched at the corners of his mouth. "I beg your pardon?"

"You were staring." Her eyes narrowed at his half-smile. "Have I done something to amuse you?"

"Yes . . . no, and not exactly," he answered obtusely.

"What?" she asked, looking at him now as if he were completely out of his mind.

"Yes, I'm not used to seeing a woman in trousers. No, I'm not always this rude." He grinned again at her fuming expression. "And *amused* isn't exactly accurate."

Libby had absolutely no idea how to respond to him. So she turned to her son, who had watched the whole exchange with a mouth primed for fly-catching. "Tad, don't stand there dripping on the rugs. Hang your coat up on the coat tree." Almost as an afterthought, she reached out and ran the backs of

43

her fingers down his cheek to soften her words. Tad grinned knowingly at his mother, then did as she asked.

Deciding on a plan of action, Libby cleared her throat. "My . . . my husband will be back from town shortly," she lied, "but you're welcome to warm yourself by the fire and have a bite to eat." At Tad's incredulous expression, she shot him a quelling look.

The stranger frowned, first at her and then at Tad. "Your husband?"

She smiled thinly. "Yes."

"I already *tol'* him, Ma," Tad interjected in a low voice, catching on.

Her eyes went toward her son, who sent her a helpless look. "You *what?*"

"I tol' him about the Yanks killin' Pa."

"Oh, Tad! How many times have I—? Oh, for heaven's sake, never mind." Libby flushed bright red and swallowed down the lump stuck in her throat as her eyes flicked up to Whitlaw. He was watching her, with an infuriatingly unreadable expression. She ran the pads of her fingers along one eyebrow. "All right. So I'm a widow," she admitted. "And there's no man coming through that door tonight. But my ranch hands will be back soon."

"You're not afraid of me, are you, Mrs. Honeycutt?" he interrupted, shifting the gun in his hand.

"Afraid?" She gasped silently. Oh, she'd botched the lie, but good. "No, of course not. Just letting you know where I stand, is all."

Chase nodded, arching one dark brow. "That's good. Because you've got nothing to worry about." One corner of his mouth lifted in a parody of a grin. "I'm not particularly dangerous . . . unless I'm provoked."

44

He reminded her at that moment of a sleek, green-eyed mountain lion that prowled the high country near her ranch. She had no doubt Whitlaw's anger, when provoked, could be lethal.

"We milked that old brood mare like she was a milch cow, Ma," Tad announced, breaking the taut silence that stretched between her and the drifter. "Chase said I did a good job with the team. Said I hooked 'em up real good. That old gelding Charlie didn't want to get all rigged up in this weather, but I settled him down." He beamed proudly at Chase. "I told ya I could."

Libby's gaze flicked up at the man, then back to her son. "I'm real proud of you. And I'll have to remember to thank Early for teaching you how to do it. Did you find Straw?"

Tad nodded, then smirked, rolled his eyes, and flung his arms wide dramatically to indicate Straw's state of consciousness. Or more aptly, the lack of it. Libby shook her head and tried to keep a straight face. Tad had a flair for making her laugh even when the situation wasn't the least bit funny. Straw's drinking problem was something she couldn't deal with that night. And certainly not when he was face-down drunk in the bunk house. She'd just have to think about that tomorrow.

Tad hung up his coat, then made a beeline for the foal, and dropped down beside it. "Chase said—"

"Tad, where are your manners?" she scolded, then reined in her irritation at her son's complete acceptance of the man. More calmly, she added, "It's Mr. Whitlaw, not . . . Chase."

Chase shrugged. "It's all right. I don't mind. In fact," he added, looking directly at her, "I prefer it."

Libby felt heat creeping up to her cheeks. She turned back to her son and cleared her throat. "Sweetheart, you go get out of those wet things, before you catch a chill."

"But Ma—"

"No buts." She raised an eyebrow and pointed a finger toward his room. "You can see the foal after you get dry."

Chase watched Tad disappear into his room and then turned his attention back to the boy's mother. Her silvery eyes rose to meet his gaze. Chase ran his tongue over the moisture on his lips and found it suddenly difficult to swallow.

"You've made quite an impression on him." Libby admitted in as steady a voice as she could manage. The truth was, Tad had taken to the stranger like grease to a pot. She made a mental note to teach her son not to be so trusting. Particularly of rootless drifters like Chase Whitlaw.

"He's a good boy. You must be proud of him." Chase watched that reluctant smile steal across her face again.

"I am." She slid her hands into the back pockets of her denims and looked at the tips of her stockinged toes. "I'm sorry I was so short with you in front of him. I'm afraid the weather's gotten the best of my temper."

"You have nothing to apologize for. You were right. I was staring at you. But"—he stooped to prop his gun against the wall beside the door—"you must be used to that."

Libby had never set much store in her looks, though she knew some men found her attractive. Looks didn't run a ranch. They didn't fill an Army contract, and they certainly didn't make the other ranchers take her seriously.

"Most of the men in these parts think I'm crazy," she replied challengingly. "Why, you yourself called me that after knowing me all of two minutes."

46

A fist-sized clump of wet sod fell with a punctuating splat into one of her water-catching bowls. He shook his head. *"My* mistake . . . obviously."

The amusement in his voice ruffled her feathers all over again. She watched his disbelieving gaze take in the dozens of leaks pouring into her house.

"Yes. Well, at any rate, it looks like you're stuck with me until this storm lets up."

Silence stretched between them. Chase listened with a flash of irritation to the steady *drip, drip, drip* of the water leaking into her house. He tipped his hat off, sending a fresh stream of water cascading to the floor. Libby stepped closer and took the hat from him.

Her hands caught his eye. They weren't the soft, unblemished hands of the women he'd known back East. Hers were strong, unpampered hands, rough from work. Inexplicably, the sight of them made anger coil low in the pit of his stomach. This was no place for a woman alone. It was no place for a woman, period. He wondered again why she'd stayed.

A flush of color brightened her cheeks. The same pulse-quickening confusion he felt, seemed to be reflected in her eyes.

"How's the foal?" he asked.

"Warmer, at least," she answered, forcing her attention back to the foal. She placed his hat on the edge of the pine chair to dry. "She must be hungry as a—" Her eyes went suddenly wide. "Oh, my! There you stand, dripping wet. You must be freezing."

Chase glanced down at his clothes. He'd forgotten about the rain and the wet. He felt, as a matter of fact, unusually warm.

"I think I have some clothes you could change into while those things dry," she told him, turning toward a large pine chest in the corner. "They'll be a

47

little short on you. They were my husband's—"

"No!" The word came out more harshly than he'd intended, and she stopped midstep and turned back to him. He ran a rain-slick hand over his mouth and across the rough day-old stubble on his jaw. "I mean, I have extra clothes of my own," he told her, lifting his saddlebags off his shoulder. "I would have changed in the barn, but it wouldn't have done me much good." He hooked a thumb toward the rain still battering the window. "I'd be obliged if you'd just show me where I could . . ."

"Oh. Of course. Well . . ." The edge of her bottom lip disappeared between her teeth.

From what he could see, the house consisted of three rooms: this main room, which served as a combination kitchen and parlor; the bedroom Tad had just closed the door on, and one other room. It stood to reason that one was hers. He could see the dilemma in her eyes. A woman's bedroom is a private place, and he was a stranger. He shifted the saddlebags onto his shoulder again.

Tad came loping out of his room in time to save her from having to make excuses for propriety's sake. The boy's flannel shirt was buttoned wrong, and his feet were bare against the *jerga*.

"Tad," she said, with obvious relief. "Show Mr. Whitlaw your room so he can change; then you can come back and give me a hand with the foal."

Tad happily ushered Chase into his room, dodging the pots on the floor and the steadily dripping leaks.

As the door closed behind Chase, he looked around the small room. It was, like the rest of the house, poor but neat as a pin. A double bed with a trundle underneath took up one side of the room. A small dresser and washstand stood against the wall closest to the

48

door. It wasn't a child's room. The bed was too large. He wondered if it had once been Honeycutt's and Elizabeth's.

Elizabeth. Over the past two years, he'd tried a hundred names on her in his imagination, but none had seemed to fit her as well as that one. He toyed with the sound of it on his tongue, remembering the way she'd said it. Haughty, proud, straightforward, as if she expected to be met on her own terms, not coddled because she was a woman.

Yet, beneath her tough exterior, he knew there lurked a vulnerable woman. He'd seen it in her eyes out there in the rain and again when she'd spoken of her son. It made him want to reassure her, protect her.

Chase let out a bitter laugh. *Protect her from what? You, you crazy bastard? That will be the day when you have something to offer a woman like her.*

Chase peeled off his wet clothing and pulled on dry garments. He gathered up the wet things and was about to open the door when his eyes fell on a wrinkled piece of paper, spread out flat, evidently with infinite care, on Tad's dresser. Moving closer, he recognized it for what it was—a letter from the Confederate States Army.

He went suddenly and sickeningly cold. He'd personally been responsible for sending enough of these letters to paper this room, but seeing it now in Honeycutt's own house sent an eerie feeling down his spine.

Hesitantly, he picked up the letter and read it:

24 JUNE 1864

Confederate States Army
Georgia 4th Infantry
Brigadier General John B. Gordon

Mr. and Mrs. Malachi Honeycutt
Mrs. Leland Draper Honeycutt
Santa Fe, New Mexico Territory

It is with sincerest regret that we inform you of the death of your son and husband, Leland Draper Honeycutt, Private, C.S.A.—4th Georgia Infantry, on the sixth day of May, 1864. His valorous sacrifice on the field in the Battle of the Wilderness in Virginia will be remembered with deep gratitude by the people of the Confederacy and all those who continue to struggle for the Southern cause.

Yours with deep sympathy,
Brigadier General John B. Gordon, C.S.A.
Georgia 4th Infantry

Carefully, Chase replaced the letter on the dresser where Tad kept it the way other boys kept boxes full of shiny rocks and secret treasures. Damn little for a boy to remember his father by, he thought. Damn little for a boy to hold on to.

Chase closed his eyes and took a deep steadying breath, surprised by the long-dormant emotions the boy and his mother stirred in him. He bit those feelings back ruthlessly. He had no illusions anymore about who and what he was. He'd come from nothing, and that's what he was headed back to. Only one thing had brought him here, and he'd put it off too long already. He'd tell Elizabeth about her husband after they got the foal straightened around.

And then she'd show him the door.

Chapter Three

"You can hang your things over those chairs to dry, Mr. Whitlaw."

Chase glanced over at Elizabeth as he ducked on coming through the low, narrow doorway of Tad's room. She was sitting on the floor, holding a cleaned-out liniment bottle filled with milk, trying to coax the filly to take the makeshift burlap nipple into her mouth.

Chase spotted the carved pine chairs Libby had placed near the fireplace. He deposited his clothes on them, pulling one of his wet leather gloves from the pocket of his pants.

"Is that contraption working?" he asked, lowering himself carefully down onto the floor beside the woman. He clenched his jaw against the pain in his leg as he stretched it out straight.

Libby's eyes followed the movement for a fraction of a second, then returned to the foal. "No."

The word had a desperate quality that drew Chase's eyes back up to her face. Seeing her now, with the firelight playing off her cheeks, he thought again that the photograph in the locket hadn't done her justice. He wondered if the Reb who'd died in his arms knew what a lucky man he'd been.

Chase rested a forearm on his bent left leg and dragged his gaze away from her. "I'm not surprised. Burlap doesn't smell a whole lot like horse."

Libby flashed him a look. "If you've got a better idea, I'd like to hear it."

"As a matter of fact, I do. Got a needle?"

Libby narrowed her eyes. "A needle? What in the world for?"

"Do you want her to eat?"

"Well, that's—Of course, I do." She frowned at him, tossing her long braid over her shoulder.

"Then get me the needle."

Tad glanced from his mother to Chase, a stricken look on his face. "She ain't gonna die, is she?"

"No, darlin'." Libby's voice was firm as she rose to get her sewing kit. "She's not gonna die. We simply won't let her." She handed Chase the needle and unavoidably their fingers brushed; his calloused and strong, hers inexplicably trembling.

Libby's eyes roamed over the breadth of his shoulders as he turned to his task. She watched the way his muscles worked beneath the blue chambray shirt that clung to his still-damp skin. Heat surged unexpectedly through her veins, like the flash of a resin-fed fire. She blinked and backed up a step, glad his back was to her so he couldn't see the reaction he sparked in her.

Chase opened up the top of his leather glove and poured the warmed milk down inside it until it was half-full. Then he twisted the top and aimed the needle at the tip of the thumb. He was rewarded with a steady stream of warm milk.

"What do you say, girl? Hungry?" He rubbed the milky glove back and forth across the filly's mouth until she opened up to him and allowed him to slip the engorged thumb into her mouth.

52

Libby watched the process with a frown. Though she was grateful the foal was taking the nourishment, it irked her that this stranger had succeeded where she had failed.

Again.

"It's an old trick," Chase commented, angling a look at her.

Libby let out an exasperated sigh. "You needn't gloat, Mr. Whitlaw."

"Me?" he replied with feigned innocence.

"Yes, you. You've made it perfectly clear you think I'm woefully inept at ranching and"—she made a sweeping gesture at her leaky house—"everything else."

"I never said you were inept. I just pointed out that . . . you're a woman—alone."

"I'm well aware of that, thank you."

Chase dragged a palm across the day's growth on his cheeks. "This land doesn't strike me as particularly forgiving, Mrs. Honeycutt," he said with a frown. "It doesn't allow for mistakes or inexperience. Without a man at your side, it can be downright belligerent."

Libby drew herself up. "Are you saying that I need a man to survive here, Mr. Whitlaw? Because if you are—"

"That's exactly what I'm saying. This country is too wild and unpredictable for a woman on her own. You're a widow. That makes you easy prey for every lawless character within a hundred miles of here."

"Like you, you mean?" she accused, her lips drawn into a straight, angry line.

"Me?" His thumb pointed toward his chest in a gesture of disbelief. "You think *I'm* bad? Lady, you were plain lucky when you met me."

She let out a peal of laughter. "How humble of you

to say so. I have men working for me, Mr. Whitlaw. Experienced men. I'm hardly alone."

"You were tonight."

"I don't know why you feel the need to point all this out to me. I'm perfectly aware of my situation," she told him, getting to her feet and crossing to the stove. "And, I might add, perfectly happy with it." The stew-pot cover clanged against the black iron stove, and she jammed a wooden spoon into the thick mixture. Outside, thunder rumbled long and low.

"I just thought . . . maybe you have friends or family you could go to."

"Naw," Tad interjected, reminding them both that he was between them. "Only Mr. Harper. He asked Mama to marry him."

"*Tad!*" Libby shot the boy a frown.

"Well, he did," Tad argued. "You said so."

Libby looked back at Chase, to find him watching her. His mercurial leaf-green eyes narrowed speculatively, and an unreadable expression flicked through them. But the look was gone as quickly as it came.

"As a matter of fact," Libby told him, "We don't have any other family. And even if we did, we still wouldn't go. This is our land, Mr. Whitlaw. Mine and my son's. It's all we have. It may not be much, but it's ours and no one can make us leave. Not yet, anyway." She turned her back on him again and attacked the stew. "Now, if you're hungry you'd better wash up, because the only danger here tonight, mister, is that you're going to yammer your way out of a helping of my best jack-rabbit stew."

Chase clamped his mouth shut and shook his head. His glance traveled down the golden braid that fell between her shoulder blades. She was the stubbornest woman he'd ever run up against, with more pluck than an entire roomful of hothouse-bred Baltimore debutantes.

And she was right.

Who in the hell did he think he was, coming in and telling her what she should do when he couldn't make heads or tails out of his own life? It *was* none of his business.

So why the hell do I feel like it is?

Chase finished feeding the foal and settled her back down again, before getting up himself. He massaged the stiffness out of his thigh while Libby's back was to him, then he headed for the sink where Tad was already elbow-deep in a bucket of water.

Libby avoided looking at the stranger as he headed for the sink. She busied herself with putting the bowls of stew on the table. Then, retrieving the cloth-covered jug of milk from its cool nook in the thick adobe wall, she poured a glass for Tad.

As she wrapped her hand in a towel and scooped the hot spider of cornbread from the oven, her eyes strayed to the man sharing space with her son at the sink. Whitlaw had rolled his sleeves up to his elbows, past the corded muscles of his forearms, and was sluicing water over his face and across the back of his neck. It was a simple gesture. But, ridiculously, it sent a low, curling flutter to the pit of her stomach. He is handsome, she thought, looking away. Too blasted handsome for his own good.

Or hers.

The sooner he is fed and gone, she decided, the better I'll feel.

Libby looked up to find him watching her. Rooted there, she could only stare as his eyes caught and held hers. He ran a wet palm down the moisture on his face, then shook the wetness from his hands. "Got a towel?"

Libby blinked. "Wha—? Oh, yes." She reached for a clean linen dishtowel on a shelf.

"Thanks."

He took the towel from her, and she heard the rough scrape of his day's growth of whiskers as he slid the cloth across his face. Flustered, she turned and finished setting out the food.

The silence stretched between them as they ate. To her surprise, Whitlaw didn't attack his food the way the other men on her ranch did when she served them a meal. He didn't slurp, belch, or hold his fork as if his food were about to escape as they did, either. As much as his quiet manners pleased her, they struck her as oddly incongruous with the image of him she'd already locked in her mind. And that she found most irritating.

"Mmm-mm, jack rabbit, you say?" Chase said breaking the silence as he savored a bite. "Tastiest I've ever had."

"Have you ever *had* jack-rabbit stew before?" she asked doubtfully.

He grinned around another mouthful. "Nope."

She chuckled. "I suppose I should say thank you for all you've done for us tonight."

Chase reared back in mock surprise and waggled a finger in his ear as if to clean it out. "Was that a kind word I heard?"

Libby pressed her lips together to keep from smiling. "That was gratitude, Mr. Whitlaw. You've no doubt heard of it."

"I just didn't know you had." His smile slid into a grin.

"I give credit where credit is due."

"That's good to know. A little bit of that might have come in handy out in the rain when you had that Smith Carbine pointed at my chest."

She looked at her hands. "That was different."

"It was?"

"Of course."

"How?"

"I didn't know you. You were a stranger."

"Ah . . . that's right." Chase replied, poking at the food in his bowl. "A desperado." With a force as inevitable as the pull of gravity, his gaze collided with hers. "And now?"

"Now?" Her breath quickened and her cheeks became warm under his intense scrutiny. "Now you're in my house, feeding my foal, eating at my table. Still, I don't know who you are."

"Chase Whitlaw—drifter," he replied with a half-grin. "Isn't that what you called me?" Chase jabbed a piece of meat on the tines of his fork and indolently popped it into his mouth.

"Was I wrong?"

His easy smile faded away. "No. Not particularly." Truth was, she'd hit painfully close to the mark. He *was* a drifter. With the temporary exception of Elliot Bradford, Chase had untethered himself from the bonds of his past—a past that couldn't be reconciled with his present, or, for that matter, his future. His past had left him with a dull aching void where purpose should have been.

Libby pulled her gaze back to her own bowl. "I . . . I didn't mean to make it sound like name-calling."

He shrugged. "I'm not partial to labels, regardless of who deals them out."

She was plainly guilty of that and it stung to hear him say so. She'd been the object of just such mud-slinging herself in Santa Fe since she'd made it known she intended to keep the ranch going on her own. "We have that in common, then."

"Do we?" His gaze lingered on her face.

"Yes."

57

"Imagine that." His voice was low and husky and it sent a shiver up Libby's spine. Outside, the rain splattered musically against the soaked ground.

"Blue comes when Chase whistles for him, Ma," Tad put in when the two adults stopped talking.

"Blue?" Distracted, Libby looked blankly at her son.

"His *horse*. You-u-u know."

"Oh, yes. Blue." Libby's eyes flicked back up to Whitlaw and found him still watching her.

"Well, I seen—I saw—him do it," Tad went on. "It was really somethin'. Chase, you think you could teach me to make a horse come that way?"

A muscle jumped in Whitlaw's cheek, and his expression tensed. "Well, I, ah—"

"I'm sure Mr. Whitlaw doesn't have time for that, Tad. After all, he was on his way somewhere when we waylaid him with the foal." She glanced up at Whitlaw. "Were you headed for Jonas Harper's place? It's the only ranch around here for miles besides mine."

He shook his head, then added thoughtfully, "Harper. That your fiancé?"

"*No.*" Libby replied a little too emphatically. She took a deep breath and tried again. "No. We're not engaged, for heaven's sake."

"But he's asked you," Chase persisted.

"Yes, but that doesn't mean . . ." A shutter dropped over Libby's eyes, and she pressed her fingertips against the bridge of her nose. "I don't know why I'm discussing this with you."

"Why not?" *Do you love him?*

"Why *not?*" she sputtered. *Don't look at me that way!* "Good heavens! Because I don't even know you, that's why."

Chase tried to keep his shrug casual. "Just curious why a woman in your situation wouldn't jump at a proposal of marriage."

Libby stiffened her shoulders. "I don't see any wedding band on your finger, Mr. Whitlaw. Should I ask you the same question?"

"Touché," Chase acknowledged with a nod of his head.

Suddenly, a log in the fireplace shifted, letting out two sharp pops that sent Chase's chair scraping against the table leg as his fingers closed around the gun at his hip and he nearly leaped to his feet. Sweat broke out instantly on his forehead and his heart hammered at his ribs before he recognized the sound for what it was. Across the table from him, Elizabeth Honeycutt and her son gawked at Chase as if he were mad.

Christ! he swore silently, rolling his eyes shut. Will it ever stop?

He braced his palms against the smooth wooden table, let his chin drop to his chest, and swallowed hard. "I'm . . . sorry."

"It was only the fire," Libby said, as her gray eyes searched his face.

Silent, Chase raked both hands through his hair and then slumped back down into his chair.

As Libby watched the flush of embarrassment fade from his tanned cheeks, her anger evaporated, leaving behind confusion and a brief stab of pity. "Are you all right, Mr. Whitlaw?"

A barely audible huff of self-deprecating laughter escaped him. "Yeah." He looked up through a fringe of dark lashes at her. "I didn't mean to scare you."

"You didn't," he heard her say, and he could see she meant it. Though Tad regarded him with wide eyes, they were filled with curiosity, not fear. Libby asked none of the questions written so plainly on her face. And he offered no free answers.

It was time for him to leave, time to finish what he'd come here to do.

"Listen," he mumbled, standing. "I . . . I'd better be going."

"You haven't even finished your dinner, and it's still raining out," Libby argued. "You're welcome to sleep in the bunkhouse tonight if you want. There's an extra bed, and it's the least I can do, considering everything you've done for us."

Her kindness caught him off guard. A flash of heat stirred Chase's blood as he looked at her. He was a bastard for wanting to stay, to prolong it, but it was too late to question his own motives for coming here. The locket he'd come to deliver suddenly felt like a lead weight in his pocket.

"Yeah, stay, Chase." Tad's blond head came bobbing up between his mother and Chase. "You can teach me how to whistle in the mornin'."

Chase shook his head. His heart pounded, and his mouth went dry as cotton. Reaching into his pocket, his fingers closed around the locket. "There's something I need to—"

A loud rapping on the door stopped Chase midsentence. He looked questioningly at Libby. "Are you expecting someone?"

"Not this early," she told him. "But if it were someone I didn't know, Patch would have announced him." Libby lifted the latch on the door and swung it open.

The bow-legged cowboy in the doorway doffed his hat immediately and grinned around his droopy, graying mustache. "Evenin' ma'am."

"Why, Early!" Libby exclaimed. "What are you doing back so soon? I didn't expect you until late tonight."

"Well, with this here goose-drownder stirrin' things up, I thought I should get back here and see that everything was all right."

She smiled warmly. "You're a gem, Early. Thank

60

you. Come on in out of the rain. You must be soaked through."

Early ducked to get his tall, lanky frame through the doorway, slapping his wet hat against his coat-covered thigh. He frowned when he spotted Chase near the scarred wooden dining table, and his questioning glance slid back to Libby.

"Early, this is Chase Whitlaw. Mr. Whitlaw, my foreman, Early Parker."

Early wiped his wet palm along his dry pants first, then offered it to Chase.

Chase had learned, over the years, that one could tell a great deal about a man by his handshake. When he offered his hand to Libby's foreman, he wasn't disappointed by what he discovered.

"Howdy," Early said, appraising Chase with a quick, curious once-over. "That your gray gelding I seen in the barn?"

Chase nodded, releasing the other man's hand. "It is."

"Good piece o' horseflesh," Early noted.

Chase guessed the ranch hand to be on the shy side of forty-five, though his sun-weathered face made him appear older. A swath of pale skin above the sweatband line of his hat, indicated that he was seldom without it.

"Mr. Whitlaw helped me to bring in this foal who'd been abandoned out by Piñon Flat," Libby explained, gesturing toward the sleeping animal.

Early's scruffy blond eyebrows went up with surprise. "You was out in that gully-washer on yer own? Hell's bells, ma'am. I told ya it warn't a good idea to be out here on yer own on Saturday nights."

She brushed the dust off the knee of her pants. "If I didn't let the men blow off some steam on Saturday nights I'd have a revolt on my hands. Besides, it wasn't raining when we rode out, Early," she said in

61

her own defense. She didn't, however, miss Whitlaw's self-satisfied look. She took her foreman's coat from him as he stopped to examine the foal curled up on the floor.

After she'd put a steaming cup of coffee in Early's hands, she filled him in about the foal, the missing mare, and the way Chase had shot the coyotes.

"We never found the dam," Libby went on. "I'll send someone up to look for her tomorrow. My guess is she's already dead, leaving her foal the way she did."

Early shook his head. "You was pure lucky to find that foal 'fore them coyote's got her, and luckier still they didn't decide to make a meal outta you. Where was Straw all this time?"

Libby sent him a pointed look, and he held up his hands. "Never mind," he countered. "You don't need to tell me. Straw's a good farrier, but he ain't got no tolerance for liquor." He looked back at Chase. "Obliged to ya fer helpin' out the way ya did, Whitlaw."

Chase shrugged self-consciously. "I was just in the right place at the right time."

"Lucky fer us." Early's friendly smile came as easily as did his territorial drawl. He took a pull off his mug of coffee and grimaced as it burned its way down his throat. "That kind of shootin' kin come in mighty handy around these parts," he speculated. "You as good on a horse as you are with a gun?"

"I can handle myself," Chase replied, wondering where this line of conversation was leading.

Tad's blond head bobbed up beside Early. "He can make a horse come by just whistlin'!"

"Can he, now?" Early replied, ruffling the boy's towheaded mop of hair.

"Where are the others?" Libby asked, steering the

subject away from Chase Whitlaw. "Are they staying in town tonight?"

"Last I saw Bodine and Miguel, they was linin' their flues with forty-rod down at Conchita's, and Bodine was breakin' up the place." He hesitated, rolling his thumb across the top of his tin mug. "Nate and Wilson . . . they ain't comin' back."

It took Libby a few seconds to grasp what Early was telling her. "Not coming back? You mean . . . they *quit* on me?"

"'Fraid so."

"Oh, my God." The loss seemed to tighten like a cord of drying rawhide around Libby's throat.

Early's fist curled tightly around his coffee cup. "I tried to talk 'em out of it, Miz Libby, but they weren't having none of it. Wilson said . . ." He broke off.

"What?" she prodded. "What did he say?"

"Aw, hell. He said him and Nate was tired of the short pay they was gettin' here and tired of takin' orders from a . . . woman. Said you was gettin' a bad-luck reputation around these parts and they didn't want no more part of it."

"I see." Libby's face flushed, as much with anger as mortification. She stared at her hands. "Is that how you feel, too, Early?"

Early's brown eyes widened in his deeply tanned face. "No, ma'am," he answered earnestly. "No, it ain't. Hell, I say you're better off without 'em. No-account lackwits. There ain't no loyalty no more."

"Did they say where they were going? Did they hire on at another spread?" she asked.

The wrangler shook his head. "Can't say. They was being tight-lipped 'bout the whole thing. But I heard rumblin's that Les Bidwell's still hirin' over on the Pecos." He stopped again, gauging her reaction. "Word is they're takin' on men at Three Peaks, too."

Her lips parted in surprise. "Jonas Harper's place? Why would he do that to me? You must be mistaken, Early. Jonas is a friend. He knows how much I need those men to get that order of horses together."

Early looked at the muddy toes of his boots. "Stillwell and Harper got business on their minds first and last, ma'am."

"You're wrong, Early," she told him flatly, refusing to believe that Jonas would go up against her, steal her men right out from under her. No. She wouldn't believe that of him. "As far as Nate and Wilson go, there's nothing for it but to go on."

Early glanced up skeptically through the hank of blond hair that had fallen over his eyes. "If you're still meanin' to meet that army contract deadline, you're gonna need some more men."

"What kind of a contract?" Chase asked.

"Sixty broke geldings by first of August," Early answered. "Army mounts. They ain't got much use for mares."

Chase had a feeling he'd regret asking his next question. "How many have you got already?"

"Twenty-five. Not all of 'em broke, an' not enough men to do the job."

"I've still got you, Early," Libby argued. "Bodine, Miguel and his son; Straw, for what he's worth. And me. That's six."

Early shook his head. "It ain't enough. Straw ain't good for much but shoein' and feedin' stock. Miguel'll do to cross the river with, but Esteban ain't yet a full grow'd man. An' Bodine . . . well, he's got more guts than you could hang on a fence, but he's a jingle-bob shy of bein' all there, if'n you know what I mean."

Chase watched Libby sink despondently into the chair behind her.

"No one will hire on here at the wages I'm offering," she said. "Nate and Wilson only stayed on as long as they did out of respect for Malachi."

"Who's Malachi?" Chase's question bought the attention of both Libby and Early.

"Malachi Honeycutt," the foreman answered. "He was Miz Libby's father-in-law. Died here, oh, four months ago or so. Heart just plumb give out. Never did get over Lee dyin' in the war."

Chase remembered the fresh grave he'd glimpsed when they'd been riding in. The pieces to the puzzle of Libby Honeycutt were starting to fall together in his mind. The hell of it was, the more he discovered about her, the more he felt responsible. She'd told him she wasn't any of his business. But, damn it, he'd seen enough to know she was sinking fast—and without a paddle to hold on to.

Chase fingered the locket, nestled against him as it had been these past two years. Hell and damnation! He should have given it to her hours ago.

"What about you, Whitlaw?" Early asked, barging uncannily into Chase's troubled thoughts. Chase shifted his stance uneasily. Libby's cool gray eyes came up to warily meet his gaze, sending a knot to twisting in his gut.

The foreman's gaze narrowed as he sized Chase up. "We could use a feller like you around here. If'n yer lookin' fer work, you just walked yerself smack into a job."

Chapter Four

The four walls of the small room seemed to close in on Chase. Good God, how had he gotten himself into such a mess? Work for Libby Honeycutt? It was impossible. Out of the question.

Wasn't it?

Hell yes.

Yet, he realized it was exactly what he'd been considering for the past hour. Chase mentally throttled the rampant feelings that had dogged him since he'd gotten here. He had a job to do all right, but it had nothing to do with breaking horses and fixing leaky roofs.

He let out a harsh breath and shook his head, pulling his gaze from Libby. "No." He pushed away from the chair and strode purposefully over to retrieve his hat near the fire.

Early smoothed his thumb and forefinger down the brush of hair above his lip and studied the other man. "No, you ain't lookin' fer work? Or no, you ain't lookin' fer it *here*."

Chase brushed at the still-wet leather brim of his hat, absentmindedly reshaping it with his long, tanned fingers. "You're barking up the wrong tree, Parker." He settled the low-crowned hat on his head

66

and reached for his oilcloth coat. "I can't help you."

"Wasn't me I was thinkin' of." Early's gaze followed the other man's movements. The storm outside clattered hard against the outer walls of the adobe, and a peal of thunder rumbled again close by.

Chase glanced at Libby. "I can't help her either."

Libby rose from her chair, throwing her shoulders straight back. "Well, you needn't talk about me as if I weren't here!" She glared first at Chase, then at her foreman. "Either one of you. I'm perfectly capable of speaking for myself, just as Mr. Whitlaw is. If he says he can't stay on, we'll have to accept that. There's no sense in trying to back the man into a corner, Early."

Early chewed on the edge of his mustache and looked at the tips of his muddy boots. "Maybe backin' somebody else into the corner you've got *yer-self* into, ain't the worst that could happen, Miz Libby. Anyways, I'm thinkin' Mr. Whitlaw here is the kind of man who makes decisions by his own self. Ain't me or nobody else gonna make 'em for him."

Chase didn't reply. He merely shrugged on his leather-caped oilcloth coat.

"My offer to spend the night in the bunkhouse still stands, Mr. Whitlaw," Libby told him. "There can't be any place so important to get to, you'd ought risk being out in this storm again."

Chase hesitated in the doorway. With the boy and Early Parker standing here, this was no time to tell her what he'd come to say. He decided it could wait until morning. "I'm not partial to bunkhouses, Mrs. Honeycutt," he said looking toward the sound of the rain. "But I noticed a loft in your barn. If it wouldn't put you out any, I'd be obliged for the use of it tonight."

Her shoulders seemed to relax a little. "You're more than welcome to it."

"Thanks." He glanced at the foal stretched out asleep near the fire. "You want me to take her with me to the barn? She'll be a lot of trouble tonight. I don't mind looking after her."

"No, thank you, Mr. Whitlaw. That won't be necessary. It's only for a few hours, and I can handle that. In the morning, I'll put her with Ruby."

Chase nodded and touched the brim of his hat. "Well, I'll say good night then. Thank you for the supper, Mrs. Honeycutt. It was a fine meal."

"And thank you for your help tonight, Mr. Whit-law. I'm afraid I wasn't very gracious in accepting it," she admitted, "but I'm not sure we could have saved the foal without you."

Leaf-green eyes met silvery gray across the narrow room and Chase felt a wave of regret sweep through him, wondering how it would have been if they'd met another time, another place. Stubborn and proud. She was both those things and more. So much more. "Good night then."

"Hey, Chase!" Tad's voice stopped him as he was halfway out the door. "You gonna let me feed Blue in the morning?"

Chase gave the boy a tight smile, hefted his saddle-bags onto his shoulder and picked up his Henry rifle. "Sure. I'll be counting on it." He turned and, without looking back, headed out into the black cocoon of rain.

Tad moved to his mother's side, staring with her out the door. "He's gonna leave tomorrow, ain't he, Ma?"

Libby ran her fingers through the boy's white-blond hair. "It's for the best, I think. Men like Chase Whitlaw never stay in one place too long. We'll be just fine, you'll see," she said with more conviction than she felt. Libby glanced at Early, who looked

68

decidedly unconvinced. "You'll see," she repeated, turning away from the door.

The first streaks of dawn that filtered into the barn found Chase staring vacantly—as he'd been doing for the better part of the night—at the rafters of the low-slung roof above him. It wasn't the lack of sleep that bothered him. He'd battled insomnia since the war, and what sleep he got was often punctuated by hellish nightmares and remembrances of things best forgotten. No, his restlessness was different this time. His troubled thoughts were focused on the golden-haired woman he'd walked away from last night.

Absently, his fingers caressed the smooth, silver locket in his hand. Holding it didn't seem to make his decision any clearer, though he'd hoped it would. Instead, it made everything more complex. With a practiced flick of one finger, he popped the locket open. In the pale morning light, he stared at the picture within.

Libby's flaxen hair was pulled back tight, concealing its beauty. Her delicate mouth held a shy, almost sad smile. Why hadn't he noticed that sadness before? He'd seen it last night too, although he was sure she hadn't intended for him to. The daguerreotype couldn't capture her vibrancy, her spirit. It was that inner fire that held him here now, when he should have been long on his way.

Chase broke off a piece of hay and twirled the stem between his teeth with his tongue, pondering his dilemma.

She needs help. Help I could give her.

You didn't come here to get involved.

Who said anything about being involved? All I want to do is help the woman out for a while. I could

*use the job. She could use my experience. Hell, she's
just stubborn enough to dig herself an early grave by
trying to make this place work. If her husband were
still around, she wouldn't be in this damn situation.*

*Yeah, and it was your bullet that helped to kill
him, remember?*

It was war. He was aiming for my heart as well.

*So what? Do you think that will matter to her? Do
you think she'll let you work here once she finds out
that little detail?*

Chase slammed his eyes shut, running into the
same brick wall he'd been hitting all night. She
wouldn't.

Damn right, she wouldn't.

Disgusted, he gathered his gear and climbed down
from the haymow. He brushed the flecks of hay off
his clothes and straightened, contemplating a course
of action. Meeting the flesh and blood Elizabeth
Honeycutt last night had been akin to taking a swift,
unexpected punch to the gut.

Why was he having such a hard time giving her the
damn little trinket? For two years now—during the
last, violent year of the war as he lay in a hospital bed
recuperating, and in the year that followed—the
locket had burned a hole in his pocket and his conscience. It was time he was shed of it. Long past
time. He shoved the locket back into his pocket.

He'd told her he couldn't stay. So why couldn't he
just give it to her and get the hell out?

Heedless of that cautioning inner voice, he veered
toward the narrow tool room, picked up a heavy ax,
and headed to the fallen cottonwood he'd caught
sight of last night. It had splintered several rails of
the corral during the storm.

As the sharp edge of the blade bit into the wood,
Chase savored the feel of the jolt that traveled up his
arm and reverberated through his body. He swung

again and again, working his way up the slender trunk, venting his frustration on that fallen tree. Featherlike white seeds shook loose of the spring blossoms and drifted like snow on the morning air currents. For Chase, the chore blotted out all arguments, pro and con. All that remained was the wood, fragmenting beneath the honed blade.

Libby awoke to the dull thunking sound of an ax biting into wood. The steady rhythm invaded her sleepy mind as if it had been a part of the fitful dream she'd been having only moments ago. She blinked and rubbed her eyes, sitting up straighter in the old cherrywood rocker that sat near the banked fire. She stretched out her denim-clad legs, then reached up to massage the back of her neck. She hadn't bothered to change into nightclothes last night, knowing she'd spend little time sleeping. Her achy stiffness reminded her that she would have been better off curled up on the floor beside the demanding foal than sitting up all night in the rocker.

The animal had awakened her on and off, and Libby had fed it the mare's milk as Chase Whitlaw had instructed.

Whitlaw.

Unbidden, he invaded her thoughts, just as he had all night while she had lain awake: his green eyes, impossibly broad shoulders, and—worst of all—the memory of his long slender fingers touching hers, sending unwanted tingles up her arm. The very air around him seemed charged with blatant masculinity. Libby squeezed her eyes shut, shaking off the thought. *What's wrong with you, Libby Honeycutt, thinking of that stranger in such a . . . a carnal way?*

Heaven knew, it had been a long, long time since she'd even thought of a man in those terms. Why, not

71

even with her husband, Lee, had she—

Libby cut off the thought before it could come to full fruition. There was no sense dredging up what might or might not have been between her and Lee. She had loved him always. Their marriage had been the natural culmination of years of friendship. And while the transition from friend to lover had been awkward for them both, the birth of their son, Tad, had cemented the bond between them as nothing else could have. Yes, she thought, Lee had loved her as well, though he had seldom said so. She had to believe that.

Libby rubbed the bridge of her nose with the tips of her fingers. She'd gotten used to being without Lee. In fact, it was hard for her to picture him before he'd gone off to war—he'd been strong then, healthy, and, she'd thought, invincible.

Very much like the man who'd slept in her barn. The thought came like a gust of cool wind.

She glanced toward the window. Whitlaw was no doubt gone already, and it was for the best. What she didn't need in her life right now was a man who flustered her by simply being in the same room.

Libby stretched out her stiff legs. As she stirred, so did the foal. Blinking large, brown eyes, she stared at Libby and nickered softly. Then, without warning the animal gathered her legs under her and lurched to a wobbly standing position.

"Ah, feeling better, huh, girl?" Libby crooned with a smile. "I'd better get you out of here before you hurt yourself or my house." Wrapping her left arm around the front of the foal's chest, Libby grabbed her tail with her other hand and steered her awkwardly toward the door. She lifted the latch with her elbow and swung the door open, guiding the animal outside. "It's time you got acquainted with Ruby. I think you're going to like each other."

As Libby passed the corner of the house with the foal, she saw him and stopped dead.

"Oh, my," she murmured under her breath. She straightened and released her hold on the foal. The pale morning light washed over Chase Whitlaw's naked back as he bent to the task of cutting up the aspen which had, only yesterday, shaded part of her corral.

"Oh, my," she repeated in a barely audible whisper, gaping at both the man and the destruction. Why was Whitlaw still here, and what was he doing chopping down her tree? Libby swallowed back the questions. She was suddenly inexplicably glad he hadn't left without saying goodbye.

She watched him, transfixed and unnoticed. The powerful muscles in his back and arms bunched as he reared back for another blow. A fined sheen of sweat coated his tanned skin despite the morning chill that still clung to the air.

After a moment, he stopped to toss a log aside, then turned, as if he suddenly sensed she was there. He swiped his forearm across his mouth. His expression told her nothing, though the dark circles beneath his eyes said he hadn't slept much better than she had.

Reaching automatically for his shirt, he shrugged it on. "Morning."

She cleared the frog that had leaped into her throat. "Good morning." His limp, though still there, was less noticeable this morning, Libby decided, watching him saunter toward her. "I'm surprised to see you still here. I . . . I thought you'd be long gone by now."

So did I, Chase thought. The foal, like some wild thing she'd gentled, stood still at her side, watching him, too. Chase's gaze roamed over the wisps of burnished golden hair that haloed her face where it had come loose from her night braid. Her stunning gray eyes met his. Even after an undoubtedly sleepless night, Libby Honeycutt was prettier than a field full of wild lupines. The sight of her sent heat spiraling through him.

"I noticed this tree came down in the storm last night, and thought you could use a hand with it."

"My men would have gotten to it eventually, after they'd nursed their hangovers from last night," she added with a smile. "Thanks. It looks like I owe you another meal."

Chase dismissed the debt with a dip of his dark brows. "You don't owe me a thing," he told her, buttoning his shirt. Glancing up at the thin curl of smoke coming from her chimney, he knew she hadn't even started a proper fire yet. "But I wouldn't turn down a cup of coffee later if you get some brewing."

"That seems like the least I can do," she answered. "There'll be a cup waiting for you."

Chase flashed her a smile. He liked the sound of that. Too much.

Without warning the foal gave its head a shake and made a little hopping buck in Libby's direction.

"Hey!" She laughed as the foal collided with her hip. "Settle down, you!" The foal, spooky as a gawky fawn, looked up at Libby.

Chase stepped forward to corral the foal in his arms. "She's feeling her oats this morning I see. You gonna put her with the mare?"

Libby nodded, a pleased smile on her face. "That's the idea, but she seems to have a mind of her own now that she's gotten a little food in her."

Chase bent down and easily lifted the foal in his arms. "Let's go."

As he sauntered off, carrying the foal, Libby briefly contemplated arguing with him about helping her with it, but decided against it.

The air inside the barn was sharp with the scent of

damp earth, hay, and horses. From her stall, Ruby dropped her neck across the stall door and snorted, picking up the scent of the young horse. The foal responded in kind as Chase set her down.

Chase led the mare out and tied her up by her halter, so she'd be less apt to kick the smaller horse if she were so inclined. Libby guided the foal up toward the mare's head so she could get a good whiff of her.

"You ready to be a mama again, girl?" Chase asked, stroking the mare's muzzle soothingly. "Here's your chance."

Libby's gaze took in Chase's strong, gentle hands calming the mare. She held her breath as the mare bent to sniff the baby, then threw her head up with a snort, causing the wobbly foal to take a surprised step back. Ruby shook her mane and pulled against the ropes that held her.

"Easy, girl," Libby soothed, patting the mare's neck.

"Don't get in the way of her hooves," Chase warned. "If she should take it into her head, she could get pretty ugly about all this."

Libby looked across the mare's back at Chase. "You don't have to worry about Ruby. She'd never hurt me, and I seriously doubt she'd hurt the foal either. Some horses are born mothers, and Ruby is one of them. Why, since her foal died a few days ago, she's been trying to steal one from every mare on the place."

"I hope you're right," Chase answered, eying the pair of horses. For Libby's sake, he did. He'd hate to see her have to put a perfectly healthy foal down for lack of a mother. But he noticed the determined look in Libby's eyes. She is one who doesn't accept defeat easily, he decided. From personal experience, he knew that could be both a blessing and a curse.

Libby watched with growing concern. The baby

75

became more aggressive in her approach, cruising along the mare's flank, making little smacking noises with her mouth, instinctively searching for the nourishment she knew was nearby. Repeatedly, the mare moved just out of the foal's reach, snorting impatiently. Libby may not have known about gloves making nipples, but she knew what to do now. She'd seen Lee and Malachi put orphaned foals with dams before.

She looked up to find Chase watching her, as if he were waiting to see if she knew what to do.

"Get me that bucket," she told him, grabbing hold of one of the lead ropes holding Ruby.

His eyes flicked up to hers assessingly. But without questioning her, he reached for the oak bucket nearby, and handed it to her.

"Hold Ruby for me, up close to her head," she told him. The mare was clearly irritated when Libby stooped beside her and began milking her. She let her know it by stomping her hooves. Managing to stay just out of reach, Libby filled the bucket with an inch or so of milk. "She's got her dam's scent on her," Libby explained as she worked, "and if we don't try to erase that, there's a good chance Ruby won't accept her."

Carefully, Libby poured the still-steaming milk over the foal's neck and back, the two places the mare would instinctively go to sniff at her baby. She smiled up at Chase. "It's an old trick," she told him with a grin and stood back to watch.

Chase returned her smile with an approving one of his own.

Several minutes passed, but finally the mare snorted again and lowered her head to take in the familiar scent.

The foal blinked her doelike eyes and wobbled forward again on stiff, determined legs. This time

Ruby didn't back away as the filly nosed her way along her flank, making its way to the udder. Cooperatively, Ruby widened her stance to allow the foal access, and she latched on triumphantly, as if she'd never gotten her milk from any other source.

"She's taking her!" Tears of relief sprang to Libby's eyes, and she unthinkingly grasped Chase's arm. "Oh, thank God, Chase! She's taking her!"

But Chase wasn't watching the foal anymore. His eyes were on Libby, on her arm touching his, on her eyes glittering with happiness. With her gaze riveted to the two horses, Chase realized Libby was probably unaware she'd called him by his given name or that her touch sent heat steaking up his arm. He felt something tighten down deep inside, and he looked away before it could get hold of him.

At the same moment, Libby realized what she'd done and loosed his arm as if it were a burning log. She flushed pink up the tops of her ears. "Oh, I . . . I'm sorry. I'm afraid sometimes I let my emotions carry me away."

Chase's eyes met hers. "Nothing wrong with that. It's a woman's prerogative, I hear." A small grin tipped the corners of his bow-shaped mouth.

"For any other woman, maybe that's true," she answered.

"Any *other* woman?" he repeated. "What, you're not allowed?"

"No," she answered without hesitation, flicking at the hay on her pantleg. "I can't afford to let emotions get in the way of what I have to do."

He arched a dark brow curiously. "And that is . . . ?"

"Make this ranch succeed. Carve out a place for Tad and me. So we can survive in a man's world."

"Is that what you really want?"

Her eyes darted up to his, meeting his penetrating

stare. "Yes," she replied unequivocally. "It is. Is that so hard to understand?"

"I guess I have to wonder why you've chosen such a tough road for yourself."

She looked away, through the open double doors toward the house. "Most of the choices in my life haven't been my own. Up until now, that is. Of course, I could sell the ranch, pay off the mortgage, and use what's left of the money to head for Denver City. Buy a small house for us. I could take in sewing or maybe washing or run a boardinghouse. But that's not what I want."

"This"—drawing in a deep breath of the fragrant hay and horsey scent, Libby gestured at the barn and the land beyond—"this is what I want . . . for myself . . . for Tad. I want it more than I've ever wanted anything. It's ours, this ranch, this land. I have things to learn, but I'll learn them because I have to. I'm not afraid of it. I'm not afraid of any of it."

She stopped short, suddenly embarrassed at having revealed so much to him. She couldn't explain it to him anyway. Not him or any man.

Whitlaw was watching her, a strange expression on his face, as if gauging her potential. He probably thought she was crazy as a loon, just like all the others. She half expected him to burst out laughing, or at the very least, scoff at her dreams. What he said took her by surprise.

"You're an unusual woman, Mrs. Honeycutt."

She gave a small, uncertain laugh. "Well, now, Mr. Whitlaw, I'm not sure if I've just been complimented or insulted."

He laughed, too, and for a moment, the barriers they'd erected between them vanished. "Complimented," he acknowledged, "but I'm afraid my technique is a bit rusty. I guess I'm out of practice."

"And I'm out of practice in receiving," she

admitted, smiling back at him. Glancing at the mare and foal beside them, she decided to steer the subject toward him. "Tell me, how is it you seem to know so much about horses? You have a wonderful way with them."

"I was raised around them," he answered with a shrug. "My father oversaw a large stable of blooded Thoroughbreds back East. His reputation as both a trainer and a breeder bordered on legend. He'd forgotten more about handling horses than most men ever know." The teasing light disappeared suddenly from Whitlaw's eyes. "I was fifteen when he died. The man my father worked for gave me the chance to take Pa's place."

"And did you?"

He nodded. "For five years or so."

"Yet you left."

Chase shrugged and bent to retrieve the bucket. "It's hard to live up to a legend." He dumped the contents of the bucket on a pile of used straw, closing the subject. "I prefer to be on my own."

Yes, she had already guessed that he was a loner. It also struck her, suddenly, that this was the most he had talked since they'd met in the rain last night. At least about himself. She was intrigued, but afraid to press him anymore.

He walked beside her into the early morning sunshine toward the corral. Chase walked to the water trough, dipped the bucket into it, and swilled the water around inside, cleaning it. The air between them sparkled with unspoken words.

"You needn't feel obliged to finish the tree," she said finally, casting about for some safe subject. "I'll have one of my men finish it today."

He glanced at her, his expression once again closed off from her. "I like to finish what I start."

The door to the bunkhouse crashed open, and

Trammel Bodine stumbled out into the early morning sunshine with a hand clamped against his forehead, moaning like a bog-stuck longhorn. A chill ran through Libby. She didn't like Bodine; not his tactics or his unpredictable disposition. But she had little argument with the job he did for her. In her situation, she had no choice but to keep him on. All the same, Libby was relieved to see that Early followed him out the bunkhouse door.

What Bodine lacked in size, Libby mused, he made up for in pure meanness. She guessed his age at around twenty-two, but his hair-trigger temper and steely fists had already earned him a reputation in both Santa Fe and Taos Pueblo as a man to be reckoned with.

He was compact—the way a badger was compact—and when he was drunk, the two shared the same disposition. She'd heard he could bring down men twice his size in fistfights. Fortunately, Libby reflected as she watched him head for the horse trough, he restricted his drinking bouts and his fighting to Saturday nights. On Sundays she made sure she stayed out of his way.

"Mornin' Miz Libby," Early said. "Whitlaw."

Libby started to reply, but Bodine moaned again.

"Ohh-h-h, my achin' head." He carelessly thrust his hat against Early's stomach and leaned over the trough beside Libby and Chase, splashing water on his face.

"Oh, quit yer bellyachin', Bodine," Early growled at the smaller man. "It's the same thing every Sunday. Ain't nobody forcin' that forty-rod down yer gullet."

Bodine swiped the water from his mouth and grinned boyishly up at Early. A fresh shiner gleamed below his right eye. "No, but it sure as hell is fun while I'm a-doin' it. That damned bluebelly hardly

80

knew what hit him." Bodine cast a cursory glance at Chase, and dismissed him a second later when Chase's expression told him he was decidedly unimpressed.

Bodine splashed his face again and straightened, letting the water slide unchecked down the open front of his shirt to glisten on his tautly muscled chest. Libby averted her eyes, but not before he'd caught her looking. Trammel's grin was wicked, self-assured and aimed directly at her.

"Yeah, well, that greener got in a few licks of his own," Early retorted.

Bodine's fingers went gingerly to the discoloration under his eye. "Lucky punch."

"You didn't have any call to rough up that feller, Trammel," Early said to him. "He was mindin' his own business as far as I could see."

Trammel ran both damp hands through his hair. "He was cozyin' up to a little *señorita* I'd had my eye on all night. That was reason enough for me. 'Sides," he added with a snort of laughter, "I didn't like the color of his eyes."

Early shook his head. "Conchita's gonna kick your butt outta her place fer good if'n you break it up one more time."

Bodine cast a shimmering look at Libby. "No, she ain't. Conchita knows when she's got a *real* man under her sheets. She's right fond of me, that one is."

"Bodine . . ." Early warned.

Bodine slid his spread palm across his wet chest and let his eyes roam insultingly to Libby's breasts. His eyebrows arched in wicked, unspoken invitation. "Anyways, my theory is when one door closes, there's always another one openin'." He cast a crooked-toothed grin at Libby.

In spite of her determination not to let him get to her, Libby flushed to the roots of her hair. She'd heard enough. More than enough. She started to turn on her heel, but Whitlaw caught her arm, stopping her. Surprised, she flashed a look up at him, but his eyes were trained on Bodine.

"Wait a minute, Bodine. I say you owe the lady an apology for that crack," Chase gritted out, his eyes suddenly cold as green jade.

"Oh yeah?" Bodine let out a huff of laughter. "And who the hell are you?"

Chase took a threatening step closer, towering over the younger man. Though his temper flared close to the flashpoint, he kept his voice low and dangerously quiet. "I'm the man who's about to teach you some manners, boy."

Bodine smiled in disbelief at the challenge and began shrugging off his unbuttoned shirt. "Boy? Hear that, Early? This here Yank thinks he can whup me."

"Stop this, both of you!" Libby ordered, glaring at them. "I won't have fighting on my ranch. You know that Bodine." She couldn't decide which man she was more furious with; Bodine for his rude mouth or Chase, for interfering where he was uninvited. To her utter consternation, Chase ignored her, not taking his eyes from Bodine.

Early took hold of Bodine's arm. "Jerusalem! Don't be a horse's hind end, Trammel. Do what he says. That ain't no way to talk around a lady and you know it."

Bodine's uneasy glance flicked from Early to Libby to the formidable stranger scowling at him. His Adam's apple rose and fell in his throat as he considered his options. Clearly, he saw his job about to slip through his fingers. "Aw, hell, I didn't mean nothin' by it." The cocky grin still twisted his mouth. "I was just funnin' ya a mite Miz Libby, that's all."

Libby wasn't amused. Nor was she about to fire the man for an off-color remark. All the men were wont to make them from time to time in her presence. After all, they weren't serving teacakes at some Sunday school picnic. They were ranch hands. Her ranch hands. But if she was going to demand their respect, she knew she had to earn it.

"In the future," she said, "keep your exploits at Conchita's to yourself, Bodine. I'm *not* interested. Do we understand each other?"

Bodine's expression sunk into a scowl. "Yes, *ma'am*."

"Good." The fire in her eyes scorched even Chase as she turned on her heel and spun toward the house, leaving them all behind.

A muscle tightened in Chase's jaw. Incredibly, he realized she was angry with him, too. Women! What the hell had she expected him to do? Stand there and let that sonofabitch treat her that way? Anger churned up inside him as he twisted the cuffs of his shirt, threading the buttons into place.

"Watch yerself," Bodine warned Chase. "She didn't say nothin' about takin' you on in my off time. You try to tear me down again in front of the boss and I'll have a piece of you."

Chase indolently raked his gaze down the length of the shorter man, and he let out a humorless laugh. "You can try." Without waiting for a reply, he started after Libby.

Early shoved Bodine's hat back at the younger man's chest and shook his head. "Nice goin', jackass."

Furious, Bodine whipped around on him, ready for a fight. "Who you callin' jackass?"

"You, you ham-fisted hothead," Early replied, unimpressed. "You looking to make her set you on a quick drift? Yer a good wrangler, but sometimes that

83

mouth of yers needs a spade-bit on it."

"Hell." Trammel let fly a wad of spit. "She's so damn prissy she squeaks, that woman. She needs a little oilin' up."

"Leave her alone. She's got enough troubles without fightin' you, too," Early told him.

Bodine's glare shifted to Chase's retreating form. "And who the hell is that bastard with her anyway?"

"Name's Whitlaw, and he could teach you a thing or two about manners, boy. Didn't yer mama teach you nothin'?"

Bodine spat on the ground and let out a bark of laughter. "Yeah." He sneered. "She taught me everythin' I know."

Early shook his head. "Yer gonna find yerself at the tight end of some man's rope if you ain't careful, Bodine. Someday, you'll find somebody faster than you, or stronger." He glanced at Whitlaw's retreating back. "You ain't gonna be able to smile or fight yer way out of that. Mark my words, boy. You gotta settle that wild streak in ya."

"I don't gotta do nothin' 'cept stop listenin' to your bull, old man." Bodine carefully settled the hat on his head and rubbed his temple. "I'm gonna find Straw and see if he's got him some more of that hangover remedy he cooks up. My head aches somethin' fierce."

"Yeah, well, jingle yer spurs. We got us a lost mare to account for. Get your hungover butt back out here in ten minutes."

Bodine waved him off without looking back. Early watched the younger man saunter away, his stride graced with all the cocky sureness of youth. Early slapped his hat across his thigh. He had a sneaking suspicion more than just Bodine's head would ache if he decided to tangle with a man like Chase Whitlaw.

Chase caught up to Libby before she reached the

door. "Wait a minute," he said, catching her arm. "You mind telling me what the hell is going on here?"

Libby glared at his powerful hand on her arm and then up at him. "Going on? I don't know what you mean."

He freed her wrist. "You're angry."

"Angry?" She turned icy silver eyes on him. "Yes."

"With *me*?"

She took a deep calming breath, seeing the confusion in his eyes. "I'm sure you thought you were trying to help, but you didn't." She started to walk away from him again, but his voice stopped her.

"Correct me if I'm wrong, but I thought we were on the same side back there."

"The same side?" she repeated incredulously. "How could you possibly know what my *side* is? You don't know anything about me or what I'm trying to accomplish here."

A muscle jumped in his square jaw. "It seemed pretty clear-cut to me. Bodine was taking liberties with you, and somebody had to take him down a peg or two. Your foreman, Early, sure as hell wasn't doing it."

"I don't recall *asking* you to jump into it on my behalf, Mr. Whitlaw. Maybe where you come from, things are as black and white as the stripes on a skunk. Out here they're not. You have no idea how difficult it is for a woman in my position to be taken seriously by men like Bodine and Early . . . to earn their respect."

"Respect? Is that what you call what just happened?"

"I can handle Trammel Bodine myself, Mr. Whitlaw." Libby tilted her chin up, demonstrating more conviction than she felt. "In my own way."

Chase took a step closer, so close she could feel the

heat from his body, catch the infuriatingly masculine scent of him. It terrified and yet drew her.

"You know what I think?" His voice was suddenly hard and unforgiving. "I think you don't have any idea how to deal with a bastard like Bodine. I think he's been trampling all over your fancy ideas about how a woman can run a place like this all by herself, hasn't he?"

"No he—" Libby stepped backward and came up hard against the rough adobe wall.

"And you know what else?" Chase went on, holding her with those green, green eyes, pinning her against the wall without the slightest touch. "I think he scares the hell out of you."

Anger buffeted her like a hot desert wind, and she fought for control over it. That he was uncannily, almost eerily perceptive about her feelings toward Bodine, in no way softened the edge to her anger. "How *dare* you come in here, presuming to know what I think and how I feel? You're no different than the other men who have warned me to fold and get out while I still can. I've given up wasting my breath trying to convince them otherwise, and I'm not going to waste it on you either."

"Did you ever consider they may be right?"

"I think you'd better leave."

He stared at her for a long moment. "That's funny," he answered without smiling. "Because I was just thinking I'd better stay."

Chapter Five

Libby's mouth fell open and she blinked up at him in disbelief. *"What?"*

"You offered me a job last night, didn't you?" Chase asked.

Suspicion flared in her eyes. "Which you flatly refused. Are you saying you've suddenly changed your mind?"

"I guess I am."

"Why?"

Because I'm a coward, he thought. Because I don't have the courage to leave you hating me for what I did. But he said, "I don't know."

"I . . ." She narrowed an obstinate look at him. "If you're thinking of staying on my account, it's not necessary. I'm entirely capable of—"

"—taking care of yourself. Right. Even if we both believed that, it wouldn't change the fact that you're short-handed and you've got a string of horses to chase down." He saw her facade crack ever so slightly when he mentioned the ranch. Instinctively, he knew it was her weak spot, her Achilles heel.

"Truth is"—it was a lie. A small lie—"I could use the job. I'm running low on funds. So, is the offer still open or not?"

"I thought you were headed someplace," she argued.

"I was," he answered, shuttering any emotion from his face. "It can wait."

His eyes told her what his expression did not. They were bleak, stark, disillusioned slashes of green. They were the eyes of a man who'd seen too much of life . . . more, she imagined, than a man should be allowed to witness.

Yes, she'd seen it last night, but she'd been too preoccupied to recognize the hurt and pain he struggled to hide. Someone or something had wounded him grievously in the past and she knew it went much deeper than the limp that hitched his walk.

Could it be that he needed her, needed a place to settle for a while as much as she needed him?

"Well?"

Chase's deep voice invaded her thoughts. He was waiting for an answer.

"Yes. The offer is still open, if you want it."

"Good."

"But before you decide to stay on, let's be sure we understand each other, Mr. Whitlaw. I'm the boss, and those who work here, work for me. Nobody tells me what I should and shouldn't be doing, and if that doesn't sit well with you, you might just as well mount up on that big gray of yours and head out."

A muscle flicked in Chase's jaw, but his face remained impassive.

"Pay's too little and the days are too long," she continued. "I can't offer as much as some of the other spreads around. Not nearly as much as Harper pays his men. But he runs longhorns, not horses."

"There's a clean bed in the bunkhouse, three solid meals a day and as much work as you can handle. I don't allow drinking anywhere near my horses, and I insist you keep it confined to your free time. If you don't, I'll fire you. Same goes if I catch you gambling on my time. Does that suit you?"

He arched one dark brow. "Right down to the ground." He wondered briefly how much of her little speech Bodine had heard when she'd hired him. Then again, maybe she'd inherited the little bastard along with the rest of her problems when Honeycutt's father died.

Chase let a long moment tick by while he studied her face. Her eyes were like quicksilver, her golden skin now flushed to a tawny, appealing pink. Her lips, pursed with stubbornness, sent a sudden flood of desire coursing through him.

Silently he cursed his lack of control over his wayward thoughts. He damn well needed a woman to stem the tide of need rising him, but it wasn't this woman. Not by a long shot.

Libby steepled her fingertips together before her. "Well, then—"

"Just two things," Chase amended. "First, if I'm going to work here, I answer to Chase, not Mr. Whitlaw."

"All right."

"And second, I'll sleep in the loft. If," he added, echoing her earlier words with a hint of a smile, "that suits you."

It was infuriating that he made her want to scream and smile at the same time. She fought the answering grin that crept to her lips and thought again how handsome he was when he smiled. "That suits me fine . . . Chase. When can you start?"

He glanced at the half-finished tree. "I guess I already have." He thought of Elliot waiting for him back in Santa Fe. Damn. Why hadn't El listened to him back in Baltimore and stayed where he belonged?

He didn't look forward to the argument he was sure to get from him about staying here. "I have to tie up a few loose ends in Santa Fe. It shouldn't take long." Dragging his gaze back to her, his eyes roamed briefly over the wisps of hair escaping from last night's braid. His fingers itched to touch it. He backed up a step. "You need anything?"

She shook her head in answer. Need? There were a hundred things she needed, but would never get: she needed her husband, Lee, beside her—guiding her, making her strong. She needed time she couldn't have and a loan that the bankers of Santa Fe weren't willing to give to her. Most of all, though, she needed Chase Whitlaw to stop looking at her and making her want things she hadn't wanted in a long, long time. "I . . ."

The sound of Patch's barking brought Libby's head around toward the narrow dirt lane that led to her house. An elegant black fringed surrey pulled by a matched pair of ebony Morgans were heading toward them. "Oh, no," she cried. "What time is it?"

Chase frowned and looked up at the sun cresting the tops of the Sangre de Cristos to the east. "Seven . . . seven-thirty, I'd guess."

Libby's expression sank into panic as she cast a disparaging glance at her appearance and swept a hand over the unruly wisps of hair flying out every which way. "And look at me. . . . With everything that's happened, I completely forgot!"

"Forgot what? Who *is* that?"

"My neighbors. Patch! Come!" she shouted. Obediently the dog raced to Libby with tongue lolling. With one hand on its head, she raised the other to wave at the two who had pulled into the yard. At the carriage's helm sat a solidly built figure of a man, beside him a dark-haired young woman

90

who looked to be close to Elizabeth Honeycutt's age.

"Elizabeth," the man called, reining in the team near the hitching rail. He frowned down at Libby's appearance and didn't try to hide the disappointment in his deep voice. "You're not ready. Don't tell me you've forgotten your promise to join us for services in town this morning."

"Actually, until you drove up, I had," she admitted. "I'm truly sorry, Jonas."

Jonas. Jonas Harper. Chase's gut tightened at the sight of the man who would one day marry Libby Honeycutt. Harper had the solid, barrel-chested body of a younger man, though his graying hair and sun-lined face hinted he was pushing forty. From the expensive cut of his black wool frock coat and fawn-colored trousers to the polished tips of his leather boots, everything about the man spoke of money and power.

Harper's gaze flicked momentarily to Chase before he climbed agilely from the surrey and dropped a kiss on Libby's cheek.

"No matter," he replied in a clipped drawl that Chase knew had its origins not in the West but in the deep South. "If you hurry, we can still make it."

A frown darkened Chase's expression as he watched Libby stiffen under the familiar kiss. Either Mrs. Honeycutt didn't like being kissed with an audience, he thought, or she didn't like being kissed by Jonas Harper. Chase tipped the brim of his hat down lower and folded his arms across his chest. For reasons he chose not to explore, he preferred to believe the second.

Harper's gaze turned unerringly to Chase, and one gray-flecked eyebrow arched up. "And who's this?"

Libby half turned, remembering Chase, who was leaning with one shoulder against the cool adobe house, watching Harper with obvious interest. When she caught his eye, he blanked his face of all expression. "This is Chase Whitlaw, my new wrangler. Mr. Whitlaw, Jonas Harper and his sister, Nora."

Nora greeted Chase with a smile, but, curiously, Jonas Harper looked as if he'd swallowed a fish. Whole.

"New wrangler?" The line that bisected his brows furrowed deeper.

Chase pushed away from the wall, touched the brim of his hat to Nora, and extended a hand to Harper. "I've just hired on."

"Ah-ha." Harper's appraising gaze slowly traveled the length of Chase before he accepted his hand. "I didn't think I remembered seeing you on Libby's place before." His eyebrows flicked expressively.

Harper turned back to Libby. "I wasn't aware that you were looking for new hired hands, Elizabeth. Though I have heard you've had a spate of bad luck lately."

Libby stopped and her expression grew serious. Just how far had the rumors flown? she wondered. "Exactly what have you heard?"

"Jonas." Nora's dark brown eyes flashed an apology to Libby. "Those who listen to rumors are no better than those who start them."

Harper frowned at his younger sister. "You know I'm no rumormonger, Nora. And I doubt Libby will mistake my concern for that. She knows she need only to say yes to my marriage proposal"—he snapped his fingers for emphasis—"and she can be shed of this albatross in a minute."

Beside Libby, Chase shouldered the wall again and folded his arms across his chest, narrowing a glare at Jonas Harper.

"Please, Jonas, we've been over this ground

before, and I hardly think," she added, glancing at Chase, "that this is the time to discuss such things."

Chase watched the color rise in her cheeks, saw the firm line her lips took. He'd told her nearly the same thing only minutes ago, yet hearing Harper belittle her chances sent a ripple of anger through him. He suddenly regretted having added to her already full burden.

"Oh, please, Libby," Nora pleaded, "Say you'll come with us today." Sweeping aside the mud-dappled splatter blanket covering her lap, she hopped down gracefully beside her brother. "I've been so looking forward to your company."

Nora's lilac, shot-silk taffeta gown flowed like a cloud around her and fit her slender body to perfection. Libby had nothing to compare with it.

"Come on," Nora prodded again gently. "I made up a picnic basket for after church. I thought we could take it along the river and make an afternoon of it."

"I'm afraid you'll have to go without me today," Libby answered. "As you can see, I'm nowhere near ready and to tell you the truth, I have too much to do."

"Everybody needs to take a few hours off, now and then, Libby," Harper said, shaking his head. "You're going to wear yourself out if you keep on going the way you have since Malachi's death."

Libby sighed. "Well, I won't be starting today. I have at least one missing mare, a fence to be repaired, and a garden to weed." Rubbing her fingertips across her tired eyes, she added, "I'm sorry I forgot my promise to come today, Jonas, really I am. Can we make it another time?"

"Of course." Harper drew a finger across his jaw. A sure sign of irritation, Libby thought. A chill took hold of her as his malachite-colored eyes traveled the length of her trouser-clad legs and he shook his head again.

"Perhaps next time, I'll see you in a dress befitting a woman as beautiful as you."

If the prickly pear lose their spines, she thought wryly, imagining herself riding through the long spiked underbrush in a fashionable gown.

"We'll see," she answered. "Don't worry about me. I'm fine. Really."

Seeing the exhaustion written on her face, Chase wondered how many times in the past few months Elizabeth Honeycutt had been forced to put up an indefatigable front. Too often, he guessed.

Tad tumbled out of the house, tousled and sleepy eyed. "Hi, Miss Harper." And less enthusiastically, "Hullo, Mr. Harper."

"Tad!" Nora exclaimed. "I was just wondering what had become of you. Have you been practicing on that new slate I brought you?"

"Uh-huh. I mean, yes'm," he amended sheepishly.

"You're working wonders, Nora," Libby assured her. "He's been working hard on his sums."

"Good," Nora replied. "I'll see you on Thursday, then, as usual. The McGuffey Readers are due in any day now. I'll try to bring one when I come."

"Come along, Nora," Harper told her, taking her by the elbow. "Enough talk of this teaching nonsense. I could use a few more pies and a few less McGuffey Readers at my table, I can tell you. A schoolmarm, for God's sake."

Nora smiled patiently at this familiar argument. "'Knowledge is the mother of all virtue. All vice proceeds from ignorance.'" she answered, quoting a proverb. "Soo Ling and Maria keep plenty of pies on your table. There's no shame in teaching. It's perfectly proper. You keep on working, Tad. 'Bye, Libby." She glanced at Chase. "It was good to meet you, Mr. Whitlaw. Heaven knows, Libby needs all the help she can get here."

Chase nodded to her. "Pleasure, ma'am."

"I'll be seeing you soon, I hope, Elizabeth," Harper said, taking Libby's hand again and brushing it with a kiss.

"I'm sure you will."

Harper and Nora climbed into the carriage and waved their goodbyes as Trammel Bodine sauntered past them toward the corral. Saluting with one finger off the brim of his hat, Bodine casually acknowledged both the rancher and his sister as they drove off.

Chase's fists tightened at his sides as he watched Bodine. He disliked Jonas Harper, but his feeling for Trammel Bodine ran deeper than that. Chase couldn't give Libby back the husband she so desperately needed on this place, but he intended to make damn certain Bodine didn't ride roughshod over her anymore.

Chapter Six

From a distance, the silhouette of Santa Fe could hardly be distinguished from the land surrounding it. Many of the sun-baked adobe buildings—wrested from the heavy clay soil they stood on—had already outlived two generations of the cottonwoods that grew along its perimeter.

Chase rode beneath the high wooden archway that marked the town's entrance. He was struck by the sameness of the architecture and the poorness of the town. Squeals of delighted laughter erupted from a group of barefooted Mexican children who ran down the muddy *avenida*. Pursuing a rag-ball with a stick, they dodged in front of Chase's horse as he rode into the plaza. He hauled back on the reins to keep from running them down.

He laid a soothing hand on Blue who stomped his hooves against the muddy, rutted street. By some miracle the children managed not to be trampled by any of the dozens of vehicles or animals that crowded East San Francisco Street. Still, he couldn't help but smile at the children's utter preoccupation with such a simple pleasure as chasing a ball. Chase watched as they disappeared into the whitewashed gazebo that graced the star-shaped center of the square. For a moment, he could almost remember a time when stickball was as serious as life got.

He lifted his hat off his head, swiped at the beads of sweat trickling down into his eyes, then fit the hat back on. His shirt stuck to his back and what he wanted most was a cool drink of water. The late morning sun had made the ride from the ranch seem long, though it had taken little more than two hours. Hot, hungry, and uneasy about what he had to do, he scanned the town square to get his bearings.

At the far end of the plaza was the long, low, adobe Palace of the Governors, a building that seemed to take up an entire block. Surrounding this on the east and west sides of the plaza were dozens of *tiendas*, or stores, run mostly by American merchants. He'd passed Gold's Mercantile and the Gamete Building's City Cabinet Shop. To his left, a freshly painted sign announced Frank MacDonald's Household Furnishings. According to the small print on the sign, MacDonald also served in the capacity of carpenter and undertaker.

Chase steered his horse through a malodorous flock of milling sheep and toward the cool shade of the cottonwoods which lined the irrigation ditch bordering the large plaza at the center of town. He'd heard the locals call the ditch an *acequia*. It meandered through the maze of streets in Santa Fe like an undecided snake. But along with the overhanging trees that sprang from the moisture-laden soil around it, the *acequia* offered a cool oasis where the heated morning breeze skimmed along its surface.

"Frijoles, señor?"

Chase glanced down into the face of the serape-clad vendor who'd spoken. The man smiled up at

97

him, exposing a dubious set of teeth, his ancient face like a worn piece of shoe leather creased with age. Several caged chickens squawked in protest beside him.

Chase didn't need to speak the man's tongue to understand the tantalizing scent rising from his small cookfire. It teased Chase's appetite and set his empty stomach to growling.

"Tortillas?" the man asked, pointing to the flat rounds of cornmeal his wife was rolling atop a square, flat stone. *"Muy deliciosas.* You want, *señor?"*

Regretfully, Chase shook his head. He had business to finish before he could attend to his stomach.

On the southeast corner of the plaza, the sun glinted off the shiny glass windows of the Exchange Hotel. Real windows were a rarity and enough to drive men for miles just to catch a glimpse of them— which attested to the success of the hotel.

Like the crowded streets, the hotel portico was littered with a remarkable variety of men lounging in its shade: skin-clad trappers, well-dressed merchants, traders looking to barter their newly arrived goods to the highest bidder.

The same dove-colored adobe as the rest of Santa Fe, the Exchange stood out from the other buildings because of the Americanized, narrow, white picket railing that topped it's flat roof. Chase tied Blue up outside the hotel, removed his saddlebags and rifle, and headed into the cool darkness of the lobby.

Resolve quickened his step. His booted heels clattered against the earthen tiles that paved the length of the corridor that led to the room he had taken yesterday with Elliot. He rattled the doorknob on the oak-slab door emblazoned with the number fourteen. It was locked.

"El?" Chase called into the door frame. "It's me.

98

Open up." The only response from inside was a long, drawn-out moan which sent needles of fear shooting through Chase.

"Elliot?" Yanking the key from his pocket, he swore and jammed it into the lock. The door swung open and Chase stumbled to a stop at seeing his step-brother.

Elliot was sprawled across the bed, one knee cocked and an arm thrown across his battered face. He raised the arm momentarily to cast a disparaging glare at Chase, then dropped it back down over his eyes. Beside him, his black medical bag sat propped open. Bloody clumps of lint and a bottle of whiskey were on the small side table beside the bed.

"Good God, El," Chase said, moving over to the bed. "Are you all right? What the hell happened to you?"

"I could ask you the same question," Elliot replied sourly.

Relieved to hear him talking, Chase dropped his hat onto the colorfully woven blanket that lay, neatly folded, at the foot of the iron bedstead. He ran his hand through his hair.

"I can't leave you alone for a minute." Chase gave a small disbelieving laugh and sat down on the edge of the bed. "Anything broken?"

"Hell, yes." Elliot's usually neat blond hair spiked out comically in several directions. "My nose undoubtedly, a rib, possibly, not to mention my pride." He fingered his split lip.

"Well, you came out here looking for adventure. Lucky for you there's a doctor nearby," Chase quipped.

"Very funny," Elliot replied humorlessly, glaring at Chase with one sky blue eye. "What I could have used was an extra pair of fists."

"I was . . . delayed."

99

"Apparently. I thought you were coming back after you gave her the locket."

Chase leaned over Elliot, pulling his arm back to get a better look at his face. Beneath his carefully trimmed mustache, his lip was split, and his right eye was swollen and was turning an ugly shade of purple. One side of his nose was packed with lint and blood had spattered down his white shirt, in graphic tribute to what Chase decided must have been a hell of a fight. "Who did this to you?" he asked, avoiding the subject of the locket.

Elliot let out a snort of laughter. "Some little piss-ant cowboy started it, and the rest of the damned *cantina* joined in. Honest to God, Chase, that bastard could throw a punch to beat hell. A little late, I'm afraid, I learned of his somewhat infamous reputation with his fists."

In all the years he'd known him, Chase had never seen Elliot willingly pick a fight with anyone. It went completely against his gentle nature and— philosophically, at least—against the Hippocratic oath he'd taken when he'd become a physician.

"I take it he didn't bother to introduce himself," Chase ventured.

"You mean before or after he yanked the little doe-eyed *señorita* out of my lap?" Elliot flopped his head back down on the pillow and groaned.

"Ah-hah . . ." Realization struck that Trammel Bodine was the particular little piss-ant Elliot was referring to. Chase suddenly wished he had knocked that considerable chip off Bodine's shoulder this morning after all.

Elliot cracked an eye open again, this time a glint of mischief was in it. "Damn. She was a sweet little thing, too. If things had worked out, I wouldn't have missed you at all last night. Speaking of which, where the hell *were* you?"

"I went to the Honeycutt place."

"Tell me something I don't know. You said you'd be back before dark. If you weren't such an ornery cuss, I would have been worried about your hide in that storm. As it was, I had to be satisfied with silently cursing you as that peabrain's fist was making mincemeat out of my face. I don't remember much about the outcome, except that I was the loser and he went off with the girl."

"Trammel Bodine."

"Huh?"

"The peabrain. His name is Trammel Bodine. And he works for Libby."

Elliot shot a disbelieving glance at Chase. "He works—" One eyebrow shot up and he hiked himself up on one elbow. *"Libby? Is that her name?"*

"It's Elizabeth. Elizabeth Honeycutt." Restless, Chase moved to the half-open window overlooking the street and stared through the glass. The sounds drifted up to him as he leaned a shoulder against the solid pine armoire that stood beside him.

"You called her Libby," Elliot amended, easing up to a sitting position. "What the hell went on there last night anyway?"

"Nothing," Chase snapped turning back to the man on the bed. "At least, not what you're thinking."

Elliot's shoulders relaxed a fraction. "Well, anyway it's done. The sooner we can get out of this mud puddle of a town, the better off we'll both be," he said, fingering the sore spot on his ribs.

"I'm not leaving." Chase let the words sink in for a moment as he stared out onto the rutted, muddy streets of Santa Fe. The heavy bells of the San Miguel Church tolled somberly in the distance.

"What?"

"I said—"

"I *heard* what you said. Are you out of your mind?"

101

Elliot got to his feet and steadied himself against the bed.

"Probably."

"Is this about the Honeycutt woman?" At Chase's silence, Elliot shook his head. "My God, Chase, you can't be serious. Did you give her the locket?"

Chase shook his head.

Elliot tightened his fist around the gold-painted ball at the tip of the bedstead. "Ho, boy—"

"Look, I know what you're going to say and believe me, it's nothing I haven't already told myself." Unable to meet Elliot's eyes, Chase stared blindly out the window. "She offered me a job, and I took it. She needs help, and I'm going to help her." As the silence lengthened, Chase glanced back at Elliot. "I warned you not to come with me."

Elliot's mouth opened, then shut in frustration. "This isn't about me, you crazy bastard. It's about you. You're getting into something here you have no business getting involved in. Look, I know you feel responsible for this woman, just from being in the same bloody *war* with her husband. . . ." Elliot broke off in frustration, raking his hands through his hair. "If it's money . . . all you have to do is ask my father—"

Chase shot him a murderous, silencing look. "It's not about money, and if it were, she wouldn't take it. Neither would I. And you're damn right I feel responsible." He paused, leaning his forehead against his clenched fist. "I *am* responsible."

"Your bullet didn't kill him, Chase."

"I know. That doesn't change things."

Elliot let out a long sigh and plunged his fingers through his hair. No one knew better than he the hell Chase had gone through recovering from the war. He himself had repaired the botched job some quack of a

102

sawbones had done on Chase's leg in a field hospital, and he'd sat through countless nights when persistent fevers and nightmares had held Chase captive. Those nightmares remained with him even now.

The scars Chase bore from the war were not unfamiliar ones. Elliot had seen them in scores of men who'd returned from the horror of battle. Frustration tightened Elliot's throat. He'd learned to heal men's bodies, but he had no idea how to heal the festering wounds that preyed on their minds.

"Have you really thought about this, Chase? I mean, I don't suppose I have to point out that she's a grieving widow—"

"—with a young son and a failing ranch," Chase finished, silencing him. "Her men are quitting on her, and her place is falling down around her ears. What am I supposed to do? Walk away?"

"When are you going to tell her?"

Something tightened in Chase's chest as he thought of that eventuality. "When it's time for me to go."

Elliot let out a long breath and worded his next question carefully. "Do you think you're being fair to her by keeping it from her?"

"Fair?" Chase exploded bitterly. "Hell no. But what about this whole goddamned thing has been fair? I didn't ask the damned Reb to die in my arms any more than his wife asked to be left alone with a struggling ranch. I didn't exactly invite that hunk of metal into my leg either," he added without a trace of self-pity, "but it's pretty damn hard to ignore now that it's there." He shook his head. "A dead man's memory won't help her now. I can. I'm staying. And when I've finished, I'll tell her about her husband and walk away."

Elliot regarded Chase for a long moment. The

haunted look in his eyes was still there, but so was something else Elliot hadn't seen in a long, long time. Not since Chase had returned from the war. Purpose.

Right or wrong, Elizabeth Honeycutt and her ranch had given Chase something to hang on to in the quagmire of a private hell he seemed lost in. If that was true, Elliot decided he could hardly argue with it. "Okay," he answered simply.

Chase turned to Elliot, surprised. "Okay? That's it? No more of the infamous Bradford riposte?"

Elliot's expression was clear of humor as he shrugged. "We've known each other a long time, my friend."

Chase nodded. "Since we were old enough for my father to put us both up on the back of one of *your* father's Thoroughbreds."

"So long," Elliot amended, "that I thought of you as my brother long before your mother married my father."

Chase agreed silently and swallowed back the sudden knot of emotion that rose in his throat. It was as close as either one of them had ever come to expressing that sentiment in words.

"If you say you have to stay, then I believe you. Hell, if I were in your shoes, I'd probably do the same thing. I just want you to tread lightly."

Chase clapped a hand on his shoulder. "Don't worry about me, okay?"

"Worry? Me?" Elliot joked. "Listen, I'm hungry. Are you hungry?"

Chase allowed himself a smile. "I can always count on your stomach to keep things in perspective."

Elliot grinned back, then winced at the pain in his lip. "Ow. It was always a talent of mine. It just so happens I missed dinner last night."

"*You?*"

"A judicious decision, I think, since my teeth were still wobbling around in my mouth at the time."

Elliot crossed to the washstand, poured some water from the pitcher into the porcelain bowl and carefully splashed some on his face, removing the cotton from his nose. "Aw, Jesus," he grumbled when he looked in the small, decorated tin-framed mirror that hung above the washstand. He glanced at Chase. "Pretty bad, huh?"

Chase answered him with a sympathetic smile.

"Damn. You say this Bodine character works for her?"

"Afraid so." Chase stuffed the last of his things into the saddlebags he'd brought up to the room. "I had a run-in of my own with him this morning. Unfortunately, all we exchanged were words."

Elliot let out a whooping laugh. "That must have been a novelty for him. His fists probably outweigh his brain." He slipped out of his bloody shirt and into a clean one. "So," he continued offhandedly, "when do we start?"

Chase stopped in midmotion and glanced disbelievingly at Elliot. "What do you mean, *we?*"

"If you're staying, so am I."

"And do *what?* Doctor her sick horses?"

"Nobody has to know I'm a doctor, Chase. I can 'cowboy' as well as the next man. I came out here to get a taste of the West. I want to experience it, firsthand."

"I think you've already done that," Chase said mildly, indicating Elliot's face.

"No, I mean really experience it. You said her men were quitting on her. She must need extra hands—"

"El, you were born to be a doctor, not a ranch hand. You have a gift. That's where we're different.

105

You'd no more know how to lay a rope around a horse's neck than I would how to . . . how to do what you did for my leg. You wouldn't last a day out there."

Elliot shot him a challenging look. "Oh yeah? Is that a bet?"

Chase recognized that red-flag look. *"No, that's not a—"*

"I say it is. I say if I can learn medicine, I can learn this. I mean,"—he gestured vaguely with his hand—"inexperience doesn't necessarily preclude erudition."

Chase blew out an exasperated breath. "Damn it, El, don't start using those ten-dollar words on me. Speak English for God's sake!"

With a victorious shrug he replied, "How hard can it be to learn to throw a rope?"

Chase's eyes beseeched the ceiling.

Elliot ignored him and ran a hand down his blond mustache, plotting. "A day you say?"

"You are," Chase replied, drawing out his words, "without a doubt, the most bullheaded, addlebrained—"

"Okay," Elliot decided. "Make it a week. No, a month. That's fair. We'll see who makes it and who doesn't."

"What makes you think she's going to hire you in the first place?" Chase said, slinging his saddlebags over his shoulder and heading out the door.

"Desperation." Elliot's unqualified reply came as he followed Chase out into the hall. "If she can hire an idiot like Bodine, she'll surely hire me."

Chase shot him a meaningful look and laughed. "You know, El, you may just have a point there."

*   *   *

106

"Are you sure about this?" Elliot asked, tugging at the creased cuff of the new shirt Chase had forced him to buy at Gold's Mercantile. He glanced down at the new stiff denims and shiny boots with a frown, then tucked his parcel of Eastern clothes under his arm.

Chase eyed him as a portrait painter would his subject. "It's still not right. You're too . . . clean. If you want to fit in, you've got to look more broken in."

Elliot raised an eyebrow. "Broken in? You mean my face doesn't lend that air to this getup?"

"It helps." Chase grinned as he headed into the street and Elliot followed. Sidestepping a burro dozing in the middle of the road, Chase pulled the front of his damp shirt away from his skin. Despite the rising heat of the day, the constant stream of traffic didn't seem to lessen.

Freight wagons stood loaded with goods and supplies. They had come in by way of the Santa Fe Trail. It seemed the merchants took no notice of the Lord's Day, for business went on even as the huge adobe *iglesia* released its faithful onto the streets of the city. Libby invaded Chase's thoughts as he watched women, dressed in their Sunday best, stroll arm-in-arm with their husbands through the plaza. How often, he wondered, had she denied herself the pleasures of a social life for the sake of her ranch? Jonas Harper had been right about one thing: Libby worked too hard. How long had it been since she'd allowed herself the pleasures a woman like her deserved? How long—the thought came unbidden—was it since a man had held her in his arms and made her feel safe?

Several loud pops, like the retorts of pistols, jerked the crowd's attention to the far end of the street. Two trail-dirty teamsters whooped and hollered as they

107

careened their teams of mules into the plaza, full-tilt, each trying to outdo the other with the snapping brand-new "poppers" fastened onto the ends of their whips. People and animals alike scattered to get clear of the two wagons. Chase backed out of the way, ending up beneath the safety of a *tienda* overhang, but Elliot's attention was focused across the street.

"Dear God," Elliot murmured, watching a dark-haired young woman in lavender silk picking her way across the muddy street. She had her nose buried in a book and was apparently oblivious to the teams heading directly for her. "They're going to run her down!"

"Who?" Chase's eyes scanned the street. "El get back!"

There wasn't time to think, only to react. Elliot launched himself into the path of the oncoming wagons and headed for the dark-haired woman.

Chapter Seven

The galloping teams of horses bore down on Elliot as he raced toward the girl. He didn't waste his breath crying out to her. It was too late for that.

She saw him at the last instant. Her sable-colored eyes widened like a frightened kitten's, and a small mewling gasp escaped her before he felt the air rush back out of her as his body collided with hers. They tumbled, as one, out of the path of the oncoming teams. Her book went flying and the small, crocheted reticule dangling from her wrist flew up and tangled around Elliot's neck.

The wagons rushed by them as he and the girl hit the wet ground. He twisted to avoid landing with all of his weight on her. She clung helplessly to him. Over and over they rolled, before coming to an ignominious stop at the foot of a water trough at the far side of the street.

Elliot braced his forehead against her shoulder for a moment, catching his breath, afraid to move. His bruised rib throbbed. The grimy wetness of the street mud seeped through his new shirt to the skin. With his arms still wrapped intimately around the young woman, he felt as if he were holding a wisp in his hands. She was small and delicate as a sparrow, and her slender body provoked his in ways he had no business considering.

As her breath came in choking rasps he had the sudden, sickening feeling he'd broken her, as easily as a china doll, in his attempt to save her. He completely ignored the crowd they were drawing, and carefully untangled himself from her and eased away so he could get a better look at her.

She had a face that another man might have called plain, but Elliot did not find her so. Her doelike brown eyes were stunning. Fringed by thick dark lashes, the sable-colored irises were flecked with gold, the exact color of the raw ore the miners out West had pulled from the earth.

She blinked at him, her expression something akin to terror. Her heart-shaped face was offset by a single dimple in her right cheek which deepened, even as she frowned at him. Coughing, she pushed at his shoulder with one hand.

"Please . . ."

"Don't move," he ordered, rolling off her completely and running tutored fingers down the length of her arm. "Lie still."

"Oh! W-what do you think you're—?"

"Don't move." His gaze took in the mud-smudged porcelain skin on her delicate face and the shock in her eyes. "I might have hurt you."

"Might have h-hurt me?" she sputtered indignantly. "I'm . . . I'm lying in a puddle of mud, for heaven's sake, with a s-strange man—running his hands down my arms. Will you"—she pushed at his firmly muscled chest—"be so kind as to unhand me, sir?"

"When I'm finished," Elliot replied, continuing his meticulous inspection of her. He quickly ran his fingers down the length of her ribs, then aimed for her leg.

110

"Oh! Stop that!" Sitting up abruptly, she grabbed his wrist with one muddy, lace-gloved hand and shot a mortified glance at the crowd of faces gathering above her. "What on God's green earth do you think you're doing?"

Elliot stubbornly freed himself and drew her leg back toward him, running his fingers up her shin bone. Her dress fell away, exposing a black silk-stockinged ankle. "I'm checking for broken bones," he answered matter-of-factly.

She swatted at his hand again. "Nothing's broken, I assure you," she replied hotly, pulling the muddy hem of her gown back into place.

Mesmerized, Elliot watched the woman make a futile stab at trying to repin the lilac silk and netting hat that dangled beside her left ear.

"Here, let me. . . ."

She flinched as if he were going to molest her again. "No! No, it's . . . it's beyond fixing."

They both ignored the murmurs of the gathering crowd. But her eyes widened suddenly when she took in his battered face. "Good heavens! Am I responsible for that?"

"What, this?" Elliot sat back on his heels and touched the swelling around his eye. "No," he assured her gallantly. "That happened last night."

She met him with a blank look as the traffic rambled by on the street behind them.

"In the *cantina*." The ground seemed to shift under him as he dug himself in deeper with the explanation. *What a time to look like I just stepped out of a bare-knuckled boxing match—the loser.*

A look of comprehension dawned on her face. She sniffed, swiping the back of one hand across her dirty cheek. "I see."

"I can imagine how this must look to you, Miss . . . ?"

111

"Somehow I doubt it," she replied, ignoring his feeble attempt at introduction. She struggled to get her feet under her gracefully.

"I mean," he amended, slipping his mud-covered hand into hers automatically, "I don't usually . . . that is, I'm not in the habit of participating in that sort of thing. Brawling, I mean. The truth is, well, I'm a doctor." Elliot raked his muddy hair out of his eyes.

One slender, ebony eyebrow arched up, and she looked heavenward. "And *I'm* Queen Victoria. Really, Mr.—"

"Bradford. Elliot Bradford."

"Well, Mr. Bradford," she went on, plucking at the mud-soaked skirt of her dress, "if you hadn't just saved my life—for which I am, by the way, everlastingly grateful—and if you didn't look like you'd already had a painful taste of your own medicine, I'd have had to slap you for handling me so rudely. But under the circumstances, I think we can both avoid any further embarrassment if you'll just help me up and let me be on my way."

"Of course. But . . . really," he protested, pulling her to her feet, "I *am* a doctor." As if on cue, a pair of brownish gray burros brayed loudly nearby, and Elliot sent them a killing look.

Chase pushed his way through the perimeter of the crowd standing around the pair. "El, are you all ri—? Good God! Miss Harper. Is that you?"

The mud-covered woman in the lilac dress looked up at him, shaking off Elliot's hand. "I'm afraid so, Mr. Whitlaw," she replied, reaching up to pull the daggerlike pins from her hat.

Thunderstruck, Elliot stared back at Chase. "You *know* each other?"

"We, uh, met earlier today," Chase answered,

handing Elliot his hat, which had fallen into the street. "Miss Nora Harper, meet Elliot Bradford. My friend."

"Yes." Nora forced a polite smile as she glanced up at Elliot. "We've already met."

It took several seconds for Elliot to snap his mouth shut and respond. "The pleasure is mine, Miss Harper. I mean, it wasn't exactly a pleasure for you, was it? But it was for me. No, no. What I mean to say . . . that is . . ."

Nora watched his discomfiture with growing amusement, and she pressed her lips together to keep from smiling.

"El always makes a good first impression," Chase interjected, making no attempt to hide his amusement.

"Nora!" the booming voice came from the midst of the onlookers. The appealing smile slipped from her face, and she rolled her eyes. Jonas Harper pushed his way through the crowd.

"Nora! Are you all right? For God's sake, where's your head, girl? Strolling out into the street like that without looking. Thunderation! That's just like you. Frank MacDonald was over at the mercantile and said you were nearly run down."

"I didn't see the wagons coming, Jonas," Nora hastened to say. "It all happened so fast. I . . . I don't know what I was thinking about." Her eyes furtively scanned the muddy street for her fallen book. "I guess I just wasn't thinking. If it hadn't been for Mr. Bradford here—"

"You were to wait for me at the mercantile, Nora. What's gotten into you these days, wandering about with your head in the clouds? Now look at you." Harper clucked through his teeth and, for the first time, glanced at Elliot, who was equally covered with

113

mud. "Bradford, you say?"

"Yes, I—" Elliot began, reaching out a hand to Harper.

"I'm grateful to you, Bradford, for your quick thinking," Harper said, cutting him off and giving his hand a quick shake. He drew a wad of bills from his vest pocket. "You saved my sister's life. I'd like to pay you for your trouble."

Elliot's face flattened with affront. "It was no trouble. Especially rescuing someone as lovely as your sister."

Beneath the layer of mud, Nora's cheeks flushed the color of a wild rose. Her gaze flicked up to meet Elliot's for a moment before she quickly averted her eyes.

Harper peeled off a few bills. "At least let me pay for the clothes you ruined."

"I *said*," Elliot repeated evenly, "it was no trouble, and I meant it." He turned his attention back at Nora. "It *was* a pleasure, Miss Harper. I only wish we could have met under kinder circumstances. Perhaps another time."

Nora lifted her chin and nodded at him. "Mr. Bradford. I . . ." She hesitated, saying more with her expressive eyes than Elliot sensed she would otherwise reveal. A small smile curved her mouth. "Thank you."

He nodded, swallowed hard, and turned quickly before he lost his nerve. He'd never wanted to walk away from a woman less than he did this one. The turmoil in his chest was unfamiliar and, worse, disconcerting.

Harper's eyes narrowed as he watched Elliot go. He turned to Chase. "Whitlaw. I suppose I'll be seein' you out at Elizabeth's place when I come to call on her."

114

Chase didn't miss his implied meaning. "I imagine you will."

"Did you say you were from around here?" Harper asked pointedly.

"I didn't say." Chase replied with a cold look. "Is that required information around these parts?"

"No. I'm just looking out for Elizabeth's welfare, that's all. Woman all alone like she is . . . you can't be too careful."

"No. You can't, can you?" Chase tipped his hat to Nora. "Miss Harper." Without another word, he turned and headed off after Elliot.

Catching up with him at the other side of the street, Chase touched his arm. "You okay?"

Elliot glanced at him as they walked, putting distance between them and the Harpers. "I suppose that would require a qualified answer," he replied testily. "Pompous peacock. Imagine, trying to pay me for helping her."

Chase kept his expression purposefully casual. "Not that it would be of any interest to you, but Nora Harper comes out to Libby's place at least once a week"—Elliot stopped dead and stared at Chase—"and tutors the boy in his schoolwork."

As the possibilities flickered across Elliot's battered face, Chase handed him Nora's muddy book. He'd picked it up from the street and forgotten to return it. "'Course, her brother probably watches her like a hawk."

Elliot's expression faded slightly. "Probably." He grinned back at Chase. "Once a week you say?"

"At least."

Elliot fingered his bruised face with a mud-caked hand. "God, what an impression I must have made. She didn't believe me when I told her I was a doctor."

Chase laughed. "Would you have believed it?"

115

Elliot smiled, flipped the book into the air and caught it. "Nope."

"Well, one good thing came of it at any rate."

"What's that?"

Chase looked pointedly at Elliot's filthy clothes and grinned. "You look good and broken in."

The scent of damp, freshly turned earth drifted up to Libby. Pushing the hair out of her eyes for the hundredth time, she put her weight into the smooth, hardwood handle of the hoe. She plunged the metal blade between the rows of sprouting corn and pole beans, working out the inevitable weeds. Tad had worked behind her, yanking the unwanted plants, until minutes ago, when she'd sent him off, ostensibly to fetch some water to quench their thirst.

Libby shaded her eyes with her hand and smiled when she spotted him. He was splashing in the shallow creek that ran beneath the tall stand of cottonwood. A boy needs time, she reasoned. Time to do boy-things, like splashing in the creek when he should be digging weeds, or daydreaming for a few minutes in a patch of clover when there are a thousand-and-one chores to do.

She felt her heart tighten with love for her son and knew a pang of regret that his father would never see him this way. Lee would never swing Tad into his arms as he once had, or teach him the fine art of baiting a hook. Theirs was a lonely life for a boy. Sometimes, she wondered if she was doing the right thing in staying on the place, so far from others.

Of late, she had felt the lack of balance in their lives. That missing piece Lee had once filled. He had loved Tad in a way, Libby knew, he had never been able to love her—unconditionally. Still, she missed the friendship, the companionship, they'd once shared. But she didn't allow herself to dwell on it.

The midday sun beat down meltingly on her as she turned back to her task. She'd spent the morning working in the breaking pen with several of the mares they'd captured, gentling them to halters. After that, there had been the noon meal to prepare and then the miserable task of hauling water for the stock.

A trickle of perspiration coursed down between her breasts. She pulled a lace handkerchief from her trouser pocket and pressed it to the moisture on her face. Breaking the sandy, New Mexican soil was sweaty and often thankless work. There was good reason farmers hadn't settled here, she mused, as the metal tip of the hoe bit once again into the rain-softened ground.

This land didn't give up its fruits without a fight. More than one of her vegetable crops had withered and died under the intense summer sun. Gardening requires patience, fortitude, and most of all, she thought wryly, hunger. The rain they'd had last night had helped.

If she played her cards right, this year's crop would see them through the winter if she had the time to put up enough of it. That, she decided, was the problem. Time. There never seemed to be enough of it.

"It's too hot out to be doing that now." The deep voice came from behind her.

Startled, Libby jerked her head up to see Chase Whitlaw atop his horse, not five feet away. A corona of midafternoon sun haloed behind him. Her heartbeat skipped in her chest like a flat stone skimming water. The brim of his hat shadowed his face. His posture in the saddle told of his training as a soldier, and she couldn't help but admire the powerful figure

117

he cut. Her giddy smile of relief was instantaneous, unplanned.

"Mr. Whitlaw! I didn't hear you ride up." She brushed her damp, dirty hands against her trouser-covered thighs and, for the first time, noticed the other man who sat astride a sorrel gelding beside Chase.

"You always work out in the midday sun like this?" Chase asked.

"I'm used to it," she replied, wiping the beads of perspiration from her brow. "I'm glad to see you decided to come back."

Surprised, Chase leaned a forearm across the horn of his saddle. "Did you think I wouldn't? I told you I'd be back."

Libby remembered another man, another soldier, who'd spoken those same words to her. But the war had claimed him just as surely as the need to move on would claim this man. "Frankly, Mr. Whitlaw, I've found that it doesn't pay to count on anyone but yourself out here."

"A reasonable philosophy," he admitted. "But if we're going to work together, I'd appreciate it if you'd stop calling me Mr. Whitlaw. My name's Chase. Just Chase."

Dismounting, he met her gaze with an intensity she'd come to expect from him, though it made her insides feel like they were made of gelatin. A warm gust of sage-scented desert wind ruffled her hair, and she swayed against the handle of the hoe. Whether it was the heated wind or Chase Whitlaw that had her suddenly feeling light-headed and dizzy, she couldn't be sure. She watched his eyes roam over her sun-streaked hair before he spoke.

"This is a friend of mine, Elliot Bradford."

Libby glanced over at the stranger, who was sliding down off his horse as well. He was as dirty a cowhand as she'd ever laid eyes on, with dried streaks of mud from chin to boot tips. Beneath the equally dirty brown hat he wore, she caught sight of several nasty bruises on his face. As if he had had a run-in with a brick wall. Or something equally determined. Just what she needed on the Double Bar H, another hot-headed wrangler.

Elliot tipped his hat politely to her. "Mrs. Honeycutt. Chase said you were short of manpower, and I'm looking for work." He brushed at the dried flakes of mud on his sleeve. "I'm afraid I'm not much on making first impressions today . . . but I hear you're looking for hands."

His educated manner of speech surprised her. Looking as he did, it was utterly incongruous, but she kept that observation to herself. She sized him up with an experienced eye and decided he had possibilities. "Are you any good with horses, Mr. Bradford?" she asked.

"Horses?" His sky blue eyes brightened a bit. "Why, yes. As a matter of fact, I was raised around them."

"Did Mr.—did Chase tell you about the wages here?"

"They're fine, ma'am. Whatever you think is fair."

"Fair and manageable are generally two different things, Mr. Bradford," she replied bluntly. "I'm afraid you'll have to settle for something in the middle. You can put your things in the bunkhouse over there." She pointed toward the low, adobe building near the corral. "That is, unless you have the same aversion to bunkhouses your friend has."

"No, ma'am. The bunkhouse will be just fine." Elliot sent Chase a covert, victorious wink.

Two riders kicked up a spray of sandy mud as they headed into the yard—Early and Trammel Bodine. As they pulled up beside them Chase noticed that

119

their horses were lathered from the long ride. Bodine angled a sideways glance at Elliot, but his expression hardened when he saw Chase.

"What you doin' back here, bluebelly? Lose yer way to town again?"

Libby watched Chase's fists tighten ominously at his sides. Elliot Bradford glared at Bodine.

"I've hired both him and Mr. Bradford to work for me," Libby answered before either could respond to Bodine's challenge.

"Whoo-ee!" Bodine hooted like an out-of-place hog caller. He aimed a triumphant grin at Elliot. "Hey, I got it now! Couldn't place ya right off on account'a yer duds is different. But hell if'n you ain't the same greener I laid my fist to last night!"

Elliot narrowed his eyes and pushed the brim of his hat back on his brow. "Hell if I'm not," he agreed humorlessly, brushing at the caked mud on his chaps.

"You two have met then, I take it?" Libby inquired, looking back and forth between the two men.

"In a manner of speaking," Elliot confirmed dryly.

Bodine whistled through his teeth. "You're shore a fancy talker, greener. You smooth-talk them clothes off some cowpoke takin' a nap in a mudhole back in Santa Fe, did ya?" Bodine let out a sarcastic snort of laughter.

"Nah," Elliot retorted, straight-faced. "I just looked up your tailor, Bodine. He fixed me right up."

Early let out a loud guffaw while the smile slipped from Bodine's face.

"Did you find the mare?" Libby asked Early, pointedly changing the subject.

The older man doffed his hat and wiped a sleeve across his sweaty forehead. A sudden grimness ate at

120

his expression. "Yes, ma'am. We found 'er. What's left of 'er that is."

"Coyotes?"

"They might'a picked at her bones, but they ain't what done kilt 'er."

Gooseflesh crawled on Libby's arms. She knew before he said it what he was going to tell her.

"It was Goliath, sure as I'm a-standin' here. Found his three-toed track near the carcass."

"No!" Libby flung the hoe to the ground with a thud. "Not again." Anger and stomach-wrenching fear battled for control within her, but she swallowed both emotions back. She'd learned long ago that giving in to either was a waste of time. She needed to be clearheaded about this. "Don't you go worryin' about ol' Goliath," Early said. "We'll git him."

Frowning, Elliot took a step toward them. "If you don't mind my asking, who—or what—is Goliath?"

"Griz," Bodine answered laconically. He uncinched the drawstring on his bag of Bull Durham with his teeth and poured some onto a thin brown rolling paper.

"Griz?" Elliot repeated, slightly wide-eyed. "As in . . . grizzly *bear*?"

"Griz as in *devil*," Early answered, running an anxious hand over the graying stubble on his face. "Meanest sonofabi—" He glanced up at Libby guiltily and cut off his words. "Meaner'n a norther blowin' down a summer day. Ain't been see'd in nigh on two years, but once is more'n enough fer me, an ever'body else in these parts."

"Last time, he kilt two men who was trackin' him. Doubled back on 'em and got the jump 'fore they know'd what was up. That bahr is sly as ol' Satan hisself."

"And he killed five of our mares, and three colts," Libby added. "That's a loss we can't afford again."

"Grizzlies usually come down this low?" Chase asked, glancing up at the jutting peaks of the nearby Sangre de Cristos.

"Goliath ain't no usual bahr," Early answered. "He don't follow no rules. He's a bad'n. His right front paw looks like it was half-blowed off by some fool's shotgun. You kin tell by his track he favors it."

"You found fresh sign?" Chase asked.

Early nodded. "We found fresh skat and some tracks leading up past Piñon Flat, two miles from the box canyon where we keep most of our stock. Sign's no more'n a few hours old. We left Miguel alone up yonder with the horses, but I'm thinkin' we need to double that lookout. Goliath gets in with them horses we got penned there," Early warned, "and what he don't kill, will be scattered from here to the Cimarron."

Libby let out a harsh breath. "Early, you and Bodine best get yourselves some fresh mounts. I'll pack some food and be ready within the hour." Tromping through the freshly turned ground of the garden, she headed for the house.

"Whoa, there!" Early said, grabbing her arm. "Where you think yer goin'?"

"I'm going with you to find him."

"You can't be serious," Chase replied incredulously.

"Oh, yes she is," Bodine put in with a grin.

"Do you have a problem with that, Mr. Whitlaw?" she asked.

"As a matter of fact—" he began, but Early cut him off.

"Gol' dang it! *I* got a problem. I promised old Malachi when he was a-dyin' I'd look out fer ya. Tanglin' with Goliath ain't what he had in mind when he left this place to you."

"This is *my* place now, Early," she argued. "My

122

land. My mare that devil killed. And God knows how many more will die before he's through. I can't sit back and let what happened two years ago happen again. We're *all* fighting against the same things here, Early. Don't ask me to stay tucked away at home like some pressed flower when things go down hard. I won't do it."

Early shook his head and ran a hand through his gray-streaked hair. "Tarnation, Libby. Sometimes you're the dadblamedest . . . orneriest female this side of the Canadian River. Ya know that?"

She grinned grudgingly in reply.

"I reckon Straw kin watch things here fer a day or so," Early concluded. "What about the boy?"

"Tad will leap at the chance to share the bunkhouse with Straw and help him with the chores," Libby answered. "He probably won't even notice I'm gone."

In the distance, she saw Tad and Straw—the aging white-haired wrangler who'd worked for the Honey-cutts for the better part of his life—walking side by side, near the shallow part of the creek. Straw was pointing out the fine art of minnow-watching to the boy. Straw had taken Malachi's place and, to a smaller degree, Lee's in Tad's life. Though Straw had his faults, she was grateful for the time he spent with Tad. She knew her son would be in good hands while she was gone.

Libby glanced back at Chase, and caught his bewildered expression before he rolled his low-crowned hat back on his head. Clearly, he didn't approve of her going, but that didn't matter, she decided.

No doubt women where he came from were femi-nine and frilly, and batted their eyelashes to get men to do what they wanted. It was a skill she'd never acquired, growing up out here where the land demanded a different sort of behavior from a woman.

Yet she felt a fleeting prick of envy for those pampered Eastern women who'd probably caught Chase Whitlaw's admiring eye. She fingered her plain golden braid self-consciously and turned away from him. She could only be who she was. No use wishing it was any different. Not for any man.

"How 'bout you two?" Early asked Chase and El. "I don't reckon you two done planned on a-fightin' griz when ya hired on, but we shore could use a couple extra pairs of eyes in the trackin'."

"I wouldn't miss it," Chase answered, tossing an unreadable look at Libby.

"I'm in," El answered, scratching the back of his hand where mud had caked and dried.

Libby allowed the tension in her shoulders to relax a fraction. She'd seen Chase Whitlaw handle a gun and was glad he'd be with them. But her reasons went beyond that. A ripple of excitement passed through her like an ill-blown wind at the thought of being near him for the next day or so.

Her curiosity was pricked by Chase the way Pandora's was by that little box in the myth. There would be nothing but trouble in it for her, she knew. But that didn't stop her from wanting to know what secrets he kept locked behind those troubled green eyes.

Libby looked toward the breaking pen to where Miguel's son, fifteen-year-old Esteban worked halter-breaking a stallion. "Tell Esteban to pack his gear. He'll be riding with us as far as the box canyon to meet Miguel," she said. "I'm going to go talk to Straw and Tad. I'll expect everyone to be ready to leave within the hour," Libby then strode off toward the house, not daring to look back.

Chapter Eight

Tongues of flame licked the underside of the blackened graniteware coffee pot that hung on the hook over the fire. Libby fed the blaze a few cropped branches of fallen pine and listened to the sap sputter and pop as the heat met it. The fragrant smoke drifted up in a lazy spiral toward the star-crowded night sky. Beyond the circle of fire, all the men but Early, who had drawn the first watch, had spread their bedrolls out and long ago settled down to sleep.

They'd spent the day climbing higher over the volcanic black rock at the base of the Sangre de Christos. After finding the bear tracks Early had located with Bodine, they had turned up nothing more than a wallowed-out blue elderberry patch and a scuffed bear track that dead-ended at the foot of a rocky copse. The search had been as frustrating as it was fruitless. With the onset of evening, they'd made camp here, beneath a canopy of quaking aspen and pine, in a field of long grama grass. The heat of the day had given way to the inevitable high desert chill of the evening.

Libby heaved a sigh and dug the fine boar-bristle brush Lee had given her before the war out of her saddlebags. After gently loosening the tangle of hair from her braid, she pulled the brush through her tresses, and listened to the chorus of night crickets *chirring* in the darkness.

Shivering, she shrugged the woolen blanket around her shoulders and pulled it across her chest. She was weary, but not sleepy. Over the past few years, she'd discovered the very different meaning of those two words.

It wasn't a physical weariness that assaulted her now. She was used to the long days of riding on the back of a horse and working on the land. In truth, she admitted, it was out-and-out loneliness that invaded her soul now. It was an emotion she didn't allow herself often. But tonight, under the broad expanse of glittering sky, she felt it acutely.

The enormity of the task she'd taken on seemed overwhelming. There were times when she feared she'd made the wrong decision, but out of stubbornness she had refused to give up. Perhaps even Lee would have called her foolish for what she was trying to do. That thought cut the deepest, for it was his legacy she sought to save for their son.

A coyote howled mournfully in the distance as if he'd been privy to her innermost thoughts, and another answered from a long way off. The tops of the nearby aspen and blue spruce rocked to and fro with the sibilant breeze that whispered against them.

Libby wished that, only for a few minutes, someone would take the burden from her; hold her tight and tell her that everything would be all right.

Her gaze roamed, as if of its own accord, to where Chase lay on his bedroll. Silhouetted by the fireglow, he lay with his hands propped beneath his head and his booted feet crossed at the ankle. An unbidden rush of heat sparked deep within her as she stared at him. What would it be like to be held, caressed by a man like Chase? she wondered. What would his lips feel like on—?

Libby cut the thought off abruptly. Appalled by the direction her thoughts had taken, she stood and turned her back on the men. She couldn't allow herself to get carried away, wishing for things that should never be.

Pulling the blanket about her, she rose, gathered up her rifle, and headed into the thicket of aspen to see to her private needs. The pine needles crunched beneath her boot heel, and branches brushed across her face. The stark, three-quarter moon, partially hidden by the trees, dappled the land with eerie blue shadows. She had always been blessed with a good sense of direction, and had no fear of getting turned around in the dark as she made her way to a sheltered spot out of sight of the encampment.

When she'd finished, Libby headed back the way she'd come. From a branch far above her, a great horned owl hooted in the darkness. With her eyes trained on the uneven ground, she picked her way carefully around fallen branches, squirrel holes, and rocks.

Without warning, she ran smack up against the solid, unyielding wall of a man's chest. She let out a small, gasping cry and heaved her weight instinctively in the opposite direction. His steely hand on her arm held her fast.

"Libby," the man whispered, "it's me. Chase."

Relief clamped her throat shut for a second, and she stopped struggling against him. Her whole body shook. He hadn't made a sound to warn her. How had he gotten so close without her knowing?

"Good Lord!" she whispered back when she found her voice. "You scared me to death! What are you *doing* out here? I thought you were asleep."

"Insomnia is my excuse. What's yours?" His voice, low and gravelly, sent shivers through her.

"I . . . well . . . I needed some privacy." She was grateful for the dark now, so he couldn't see the color flooding to her cheeks.

He released her arm, but made no move to let her pass. "Have you forgotten why we're up here? One wrong step and you could have blundered into some animal's nighttime digs."

"I wasn't far from camp."

He glanced at the rifle in her hand. "Far enough. At least you thought to bring a gun with you."

"Well, of course I did. You talk as if I'm some tenderfoot who's never been off the farm," she said, taking the small gun from his hands. "I know this country. Every nook and cranny of it. I've lived here for the better part of my life."

"Then you should know it's unpredictable as hell."

"You don't have to tell me that. I thought we'd settled this little argument."

"We haven't settled anything if you're foolish enough to wander off in the dark without anyone knowing where you are."

Libby had only heard one word in all that. *"Foolish?* What gives you the right to—"

"Libby, I'm only trying to protect you."

"Spare me your good intentions, Mr. Whitlaw," she retorted sarcastically. Her steamy breath battled with his.

"Next time, you tell me before you go off alone. I'll stay close enough to give you protection and far enough to give you privacy."

She practically laughed. "Don't be ridiculous."

"Libby"—Chase took her by the shoulders, his

128

powerful hands nearly enveloping her—"you're a stubborn woman." His voice was gruff, and he held her a little too tightly.

"Yes, I am." The fervor in her voice matched his. "I have to be. Otherwise, I would have given up on this ranch long ago." She braced her hands warningly against the ridged muscles of his chest. Whether she did it to keep the span of distance between them or to close it, she wasn't sure. She felt his body go still at her touch, his heart thud heavily against her fingertips.

"Don't get me wrong," he said, "I admire that quality in a woman." He searched her face in the moonlight. "I admire it in you. You're a survivor. We have that in common, for whatever that's worth."

For whatever that's worth. What did he mean by that? The haunted expression she'd seen before in his eyes, now lurked in his voice, but his words had borne no trace of self-pity, only brutal honesty.

His thumbs, she realized suddenly, were tracing slow, possessive arcs across her shoulders, catching in the locks of hair that had fallen over his hand. The gesture was unmistakably sensuous. Unsettling. The shock of it traveled like sheet lightning down her limbs and curled low and unexpectedly in the pit of her stomach.

Instinct told her to pull away. Something else— perhaps an unaccountable craving for the human touch—held her there. His breath fanned across her face, warm, with a hint of the coffee he'd drunk earlier. When he spoke again, he softened the imperative roughness in his voice.

"Please, Libby," he went on. "Don't be stubborn about this. I don't want anything to happen to you."

"I'm a grown woman, Chase."

"That's obvious."

"I don't need watching over like some hatchling."

"Even grown women have needs."

Shocked into silence by his implication, Libby started to pull away, but he held her firm.

"You're only one woman. And you can't make the ranch work single-handedly. You'll dig yourself an early grave. I'm here to help you. All I'm asking you to do, is let me."

His hands slipped from her shoulders as abruptly as they had settled on them, yet his long, lean body stayed a whisper away from hers.

Belatedly, Libby let her own hands slip from his chest, where they'd found temporary haven. Disappointment warred with relief as she realized she'd been hoping he'd pull her closer rather than let her go. What was wrong with her, letting this man affect her so?

"All right," she relented grudgingly. "If it will ease your mind, I'll tell you from now on before I go off on my own."

"Thanks." He picked up his Henry from its place against the tree. "We'd better get back. I don't suppose you got much sleep the other night, not with that foal."

"No less than you, I suppose."

Chase glanced back at her and frowned, wondering how she could know that.

"I saw the lantern burning in the barn until late in the night," she ventured in explanation. "Did you find the haymow uncomfortable?"

"No." Chase shifted the rifle to his other hand and fitted his right hand into the crook of her arm as he moved toward camp. He avoided looking at her. "It was fine. I just don't sleep much."

Libby stopped and looked him in the eye. "You were serious about suffering from insomnia, then?"

Oddly, Chase had never thought of insomnia as something to suffer. Insomnia kept him sane. No, sleep was the enemy he fought on a nightly basis. Night sweats. Dreams of battle-ravaged bodies, the explosion going off in his—

Chase moistened his dry lips and tightened his grip on her arm. It was some kind of mental weakness that had come along with the physical one, when his leg had been damaged. Nostalgia. That's what that young contract surgeon who had treated him in the army hospital had called it. Said he'd seen it often enough in men who'd seen too much battle, too much death. It seemed a simplistic diagnosis, made by one who'd not been there in the thick of the grisly horror of battle.

Nostalgia. Personally, Chase reflected grimly, he called it hell.

"I'm sorry, I shouldn't have pried," Libby offered when his silence lengthened.

"It's all right. It's just something that's been with me since the war. I don't talk about it." They had reached the campsite and Chase stopped at Libby's unfurled bedroll. "You'd better get some sleep now. We'll have a long day tomorrow."

Before she could respond, he turned and headed into the darkness beyond the fire, toward his own bedroll. The hitch in his step was back, and she saw him rub his lean thigh absently as he walked. Was it pain that kept him from sleep at night, she wondered, or did it have more to do with the haunted look she'd seen more than once in his eyes?

Libby settled on the soogan that padded the hard ground beneath her bedroll. She rebraided her hair and pulled her blankets around her. The quiet sounds of the night did nothing to soothe the stir of emotions roiling inside her. She ran the palms of her

131

hands slowly up her arms and squeezed her eyes shut tight. Damn him, she thought, for making me want more than I had learned to settle for. Damn him for resurrecting emotions I'd given up for dead so long ago.

A fine morning mist shrouded the mountains like a ghostly vapor, sending chilly fingers of dampness into Libby's bedroll. She cracked one eye open, trying to guess the time. The palest of pink tinged the midnight sky overhead through the fringe of pine boughs. Though the sun had not yet touched this side of the mountain, she guessed it was past six.

She shivered, wanting only to retreat into her blankets and sleep. Early was squatting near the fire, already pouring himself a fresh cup of coffee. Perhaps it was later than she thought. There was no sign of Chase or Bodine, but she could see by the top of Elliot's blond head, which poked through his blankets, that he was still asleep.

"Mornin'" said Early, sipping the steaming brew in his cup.

"Morning. Where is everyone?"

"Chase took the watch last night. I reckon he's still out there somewhere. Bodine . . ."

Before he could finish, Bodine staggered from an oak brush break, snapping his suspenders back into place over his shoulders. The jingle bobs on the rowels of his spurs jangled like bells in the thin morning air as he walked. Seeing Libby watching him, Bodine grinned as he rubbed his hands up and down the sleeves of his long johns.

"Cold as a witch's tit this mornin'," he muttered, squatting down beside Early. A small cloud formed as he blew into his hands. He poured himself some coffee and wrapped his hands around the steaming cup. "Ain't it, Miz Libby?"

Libby flicked the leather thong from the tip of her braid and began running her fingers through the knots. "I don't have any personal experience with witches' tits, Trammel," she replied causing Early to spray a mouthful of coffee into the fire as he tried to contain his laughter. "But I'm certain, if we had the slightest interest—which we *don't*—in witches' tits, you could enlighten us all."

Bodine's wily smile faded for a moment before it returned. Clearly he'd expected to ruffle her again, and it gave Libby some small measure of satisfaction that he hadn't succeeded. He took a long, deliberate pull off his cup of coffee and redirected his attention toward Elliot's sleeping form. "Sleepin' Beauty still ain't come up fer air, I see." Bodine gestured with his cup at Elliot's form.

Libby pointedly ignored him, and began redoing her braid.

"Leave 'im be, Trammel," Early said with a grin. "You was a tenderfoot once yerself."

Trammel snorted disdainfully. "Can't remember ever bein' that tender. Hell, you could bait a hook with that one. I'm a-thinkin', all he needs is a good reason to get up." He set down his cup of coffee and crept over to where Elliot lay, his spurs jingling quietly. He grinned like a recalcitrant child as he bent over Elliot and got good and close to his ear.

"*Rooooaaaarrr!*" he growled, sounding like an enraged bear, flinging the covers over El's head, before he stepped back to watch.

El's screamed expletive was an instantaneous response. Arms and legs flailed helplessly within his bedroll as he struggled against the tangle of blankets and tarpaulin. Finally he broke out of it, his face pale

133

with fright. He staggered to his feet, dressed solely in his red long johns. In his hand was his Colt revolver, poised and ready to be fired at the "beast" attacking him.

"Haw, haw, haw!" Bodine guffawed, slapping his knee with genuine glee. "I thought that'd get ya up, greener!"

"Sonofabitch!" Elliot yelled, kicking a puff of dust and pine needles into the air. "What the hell did you do that for?"

Bodine dropped to the ground, rolling in a fit of laughter. Chase chose that moment to wander back into camp, his rifle slung over his shoulder. With a look, he took in the situation and nonchalantly headed toward the fire.

Elliot clenched his jaw, realizing he'd been the brunt of Bodine's twisted idea of a joke. "Wh-what the hell is that?" he demanded. "Some kind of warped cowboy initiation rite? I could have shot you for God's sake!"

Bodine gasped for air and looked up long enough to say, "Inishi . . . What? Hoo-hoo-haa!"

Elliot stood with feet spraddled, wishing he could wring Bodine's scrawny neck.

"Any tinhorn"—Bodine fought his laughter long enough to talk—"sleepin' sound as you's bound to . . . bound to git his nose bit clean off by some wild animal. Mebbe even . . . ol' Goliath. Ain't that right, Early?"

Early was too busy laughing to answer.

"Well, take my word fer it, pard"—Bodine chuckled—"I was just a-helpin' you out."

Elliot nodded impotently, wordless with anger. His scowl took in Libby's attempt to keep a straight face as she pulled the brush through her hair and Early's shaking shoulders as he hunkered down

134

further by the fire. Only Chase seemed to find little humor in Bradford's trick.

"My name," El said at last, turning to Bodine, "is not Greener, nor is it Tinhorn, and by no stretch of the imagination am I your *pard*, Bodine. I'm Bradford, to you. And if you *ever* do that to me again, you're gonna lose more than just your nose. Believe me when I say, my intimate knowledge of the human anatomy could make my revenge an extremely unpleasant experience."

"I can vouch for that." Chase winked at El.

Bodine's eyes narrowed as if he hadn't quite caught all those five-dollar words, but he snapped back. "Gratifyin' to know yer good fer somethin', Buford But if'n my human anatomy ever needs rearrangin', you'll be the last one I'd call. Haw, haw, haw! It's yer turn to unhobble the stock and bring 'em in. Best get to it, before they graze over the mountain."

Chase could almost hear Elliot's brain clicking as he stalked to his bedroll and pulled on his clothes, trying to think up some dastardly scheme to get back at Bodine for having gotten him twice. Chase almost felt sorry for Bodine. For knowing Elliot, if the opportunity arose, revenge would be not only sweet but thorough.

135

Chapter Nine

"We're gettin' nowhere faster'n a junebug paddlin' upstream in a spring flood," Early announced two hours later, when their joint search had flushed out nothing more than a pair of jack rabbits and a disgruntled badger. "I say we split up and try our luck that way."

Libby took a firmer grip on the reins of her mare, Lady, who pawed at the needle-covered earth that edged the small stream they stood beside, then glanced down at Chase's broad back. He was hunched over the swift-flowing stream, sluicing cool water over his face and down the back of his neck. When he stood, he turned and found her watching him. Droplets clung to his sooty lashes and his eyes held a look that should certainly have turned the water to steamy white vapor. He ran a hand slowly down his face, never taking his eyes from her.

Her stomach somersaulted like the current tumbling over the smooth creek-bed rocks. She pulled her gaze from his. It was downright irritating that he could unsettle her by merely standing there in the morning sun with the water sparkling in his dark hair. Her attraction, she decided, was purely physi-

136

cal. She should certainly be able to control her physical reactions to him. After last night, putting distance between them seemed the best answer.

"I'll take the south fork of this stream toward Harper's range," Bodine said, pouring some cigarette makings into a thin brown paper. "Maybe they've had some run-ins with old Goliath, too."

Early nodded. "Libby, you an' Whitlaw head north an' see what you kin scratch up." As Libby opened her mouth to protest, he added. "I'll take Bradford since neither him nor Chase know this country. We don't want them two gettin' lost or we'll end up havin' to hunt them instead of that bahr."

Early was right, Libby knew, and to argue his decision would only bring attention to her uneasiness about being with Chase. But she saw her plans to keep away from him going up in smoke.

"Goliath's a-goin' to hafta git close to the water sooner or later," Early said, turning his horse sharply to the right. "When he does, we'll find him."

The late afternoon sun slanted shadows across the stand of ponderosa pine where Chase spread his fingers across a set of three foot-long slashes in the furrowed bark of one massive trunk. The shredded gouges began two feet higher than his arm could reach, even mounted. He knew without a doubt what had made them.

"Bear tree," Libby noted as she pulled up beside Chase. "Probably passed through within the last day or so."

"How do you know that?"

She pointed to the gashes in the orange-colored bark. "See here? The sap's still oozing from the tree." A scent, oddly like vanilla, permeated the air.

137

"He's . . . bigger than I imagined."

Libby nodded with a wry smile. "You seem surprised."

Chase stared in awe at the evidence etched in the bark.

"Usually a sign like this," she said, "or some cache of carcass he left behind is all you'll ever see of a grizzly. But I caught sight of this one once from a long way off. On all fours, he was nearly the size of a Texas horse. On his back legs, near twice as tall."

"I'd heard stories, but . . ." His voice trailed off. He'd seen bears before. Plenty of them in the hills of Virginia. Black bears, brown bears. But this . . . A healthy ripple of fear passed through him as he gauged the enormity of the animal; fear for the woman beside him, fear for himself.

Chase dismounted, his gaze scouring the ground near the tree. The hind footprints he found there were huge—twelve inches long and as wide as the spread of his hand. The fierce-looking claw marks were another matter altogether. "Good God." He turned to face Libby who was still sitting taciturnly atop Lady. He shook his head in wonder. "You know, yet you came out here after him. Aren't you afraid of anything, Libby Honeycutt?"

She looked at him straight, without the pretext he often saw in the eyes of women he'd known before. "I'm only afraid of being afraid," she replied.

"A little fear is a healthy thing, sometimes."

"I didn't say I was a fool," she replied, the corners of her mouth softening. She threw her denim-clad leg over Lady's back and dismounted. "Everyone thinks because I'm a woman, I shouldn't do things that scare me. But you're a man and you're afraid, aren't you?"

His silence answered her question.

"Yet here you are, believing you should be chasing that devil down and I *shouldn't*."

"Well, I'm not the one who couldn't snag a coyote pelt to save her life the other night."

She arched an eyebrow indignantly. "Are you saying I can't shoot a gun?"

"I don't know. I only have Early's word on it. Can you?"

Libby grinned and fairly swaggered to the rifle boot in her saddle. She pulled the Smith Carbine from its place. "See those two pine cones hanging low on the branch of that ponderosa over there?"

Chase pointed to a towering pine forty feet away. "That one?"

"No," she scoffed, redirecting his gaze. "That one, yonder."

One hundred and twenty yards up the trail stood a massive ponderosa whose branches spread like great sheltering wings over the mountainside. The huge cones in question were, at this distance, the size of withered prunes.

Chase allowed himself a moment of smugness. He could shoot that pine cone down with his eyes closed. Marksmanship was the one talent the army had left him with. It was a dubious distinction when it came to killing men, he mused grimly, but firing at pine cones was a different story.

"Are you telling me you think you can hit those from here?" he asked.

"Are you saying you can't?" she countered with a laugh.

He pulled his Henry Repeater from its boot. "That sounds like a challenge."

Libby shrugged, her gray eyes sparkling provocatively. "Shall we make a friendly wager on it?"

"Let's hear your terms."

"If I hit the cone, you'll stop treating me as if I'm a helpless female and trying to talk me out of running my ranch. If I miss, I cook you a plum duff. All yours, no sharing necessary."

"Done. And if I hit my mark? What do I get?"

A line furrowed her brow as she considered that. "Well, uh, you . . . you get . . ."

Chase watched her brow furrow in thought. His gaze traveled to her heart-shaped mouth as she moistened her lips with her tongue. "A kiss."

"*What?*" Libby's startled eyes widened.

"One kiss, if I hit the cone." Since long before he'd met her, he'd wondered what it would be like to kiss her, just once. It would be, he told himself, just an innocent gesture. Having his curiosity satisfied would put an end to his wondering.

"No."

"You said a friendly wager," he argued. "It would just be a friendly kiss."

"D-do you find me a . . . a woman of loose morals, Mr. Whitlaw?"

"If you were a woman of loose morals, Mrs. Honeycutt, I'd be taking that kiss, instead of asking for it."

Eyes, startlingly the color of the pine needles around him, met Libby's. "Just . . . just a friendly kiss?" she repeated, intrigued and wary at once.

He nodded.

She'd already seen him shoot. There was little doubt in her mind he'd make it. Why, to say yes would practically be admitting she wanted him to kiss her. Yet . . . it had been a long time since she'd kissed a man, friendly or otherwise. Even Jonas Harper had only dared kiss her on the cheek.

She glanced at Chase and her heart pounded a little faster. Hadn't she wondered what his lips would feel like on hers? She felt the heat of that admission warm her insides. "All right. But you have to hit the cone."

"Right," he agreed. "And if I miss, I cook *you* the plum duff." At her surprised look he grinned and added, "Ladies first."

"Right." Libby licked her thumb and touched it to the end of her rifle for good luck. Cook her a plum duff, indeed! That would be the day she'd found a man who knew his way around a kitchen without setting the place on fire! His kiss would likely be the safest bet they'd made.

Pressing the stock against her shoulder, she cocked the hammer and took a careful bead on the cone. She braced herself for the kick and squeezed off the shot.

The pine cone on the left exploded, leaving the heavy branch swaying to and fro. Libby lowered her gun, rubbed her shoulder, and gave Chase a cocky smile.

"Well, well," he murmured, still staring at the void where the cone had been. "I'm impressed."

"And to set the record straight—in spite of the rain being in my eyes, I did hit a coyote or two the other night before you got there. I just wasn't prepared for an all-day siege." She reached into her ammunition belt for another cartridge to reload. "It's your turn."

Chase cocked and shouldered the Henry, squinting at the cone. Though he'd gambled often enough on his ability with a gun during the war, never before had the stakes been so sweet, nor his wish to win so strong. Her playfulness had come as an appealing surprise and only added to her mystique. Beside him, she tapped the toe of her boot in the soil. Waiting.

He looked down the sight of the rifle and squeezed the shot off. The pine cone obligingly exploded on cue. With a quick second shot, he picked off one of the fat quail that rushed into the air from a hedge of

141

brush close by. Turning to her, he said with a twinkle in his eye, "Dinner."

She glanced at him sideways. "Good shot."

"Looks like we both made our shots."

"Um-hmm." She took a step forward. "I'll, ah, go fetch that quail. We wouldn't want to lose din—"

He stepped in front of her, blocking her way. "Wait. What about our bet?" He took the rifle from her hands and leaned it, with his, up against the tree.

Libby's eyes were now level with the half-open placket on his white cotton shirt and the fine mat of dark hair exposed there. It was easier if she didn't look at his face, so she concentrated on the third button from the top of his collarless shirt. Clearly, there was no graceful way out of this.

"All right," she replied. "No one's ever accused me of welshing on a bet." Half in anticipation, half in dread, she closed her eyes, coiled her hands tightly behind her back, presented him with her puckered lips, and waited.

Nothing.

She opened her eyes to see him standing, arms folded across his chest, staring at her. The humor in his eyes lit the short fuse on her temper. He was laughing at her!

Arms akimbo, she glared at him. "Well, what are you staring at? I thought you were going to kiss me."

"I am. As soon as you unkink enough to let me."

"Unkink!"

"Loosen up, Libby," he said, shaking loose the tension in her shoulders. "I'm not gonna bite you. I'm only gonna kiss you."

"I'm not afraid, if that's what you think."

"Aren't you?" His fingers circled her wrists and he drew her balled fists away from her hips and pulled them to his chest. The rest of her body followed, until

142

she was as flush against him as moss on a tree.

"Holding me this c-close wasn't part of the bargain."

"I don't remember discussing any ground rules on holding," he retorted in a low voice.

She was close enough to see the beginnings of stubble on his cheeks, inhale his scent—woodsmoke and saddle leather and the particular masculine fragrance that was his alone. *Lord, Libby, now you've thrown kerosene on the fire.* "This was a bad idea. . . ."

He moistened his lips with the tip of his tongue. His eyes told her he thought she was wrong. They captured the afternoon light and sparkled like the finest jade when they met hers. His hands slid slowly up her arms to her shoulders, setting off waves of heat in their wakes. Deliberately, he lowered his gaze to her mouth.

"It's been a long time since a man's kissed you proper, hasn't it, Libby?"

Libby swallowed hard. *Proper? Was there anything proper about what they were doing?* "I told you, my . . . my husband, died two years ago in the—"

His arms tightened around her. "I know. Shhhh," Chase's whisper implored, while his thumb lightly traced her lips. "No ghosts allowed in this kiss. This one's just between you"—his knuckle trailed a path of heat down her cheek—"and me."

His voice was low and smooth as fine whiskey and went straight to her head. Thoughts of Lee, guilty, useless thoughts, spun away with Chase's caress of her cheek. She kept her hands curled tightly against his chest, as if she could keep him from doing to her heart what he was doing to her body. Oh, why had she agreed to this foolish bet?

143

Because Chase is right, a quiet voice answered. It had been a long time. Too dangerously long. And his tender touch was reminding her of how many years she'd done without that. And if she refused to marry Jonas Harper, of how many more she'd be alone.

Cupping her face with his hand, Chase dipped his head down toward her. Like the whisper of a breeze that surrounded them, his lips brushed hers—once, twice—before claiming them fully. A sinking feeling of pleasure curled through her. His mouth on hers was firm, yet achingly gentle; at once, demanding and entreating.

Beneath her fingertips she could feel the quickening beat of his heart, whose tempo seemed to match her own. Her hands explored the taut, well-defined wall of muscle on his chest. She knew in that instant how capable he was of both tenderness and great violence. But it didn't make her afraid. It made her want him more.

Somewhere in the dim recesses of her mind, while her body turned to molten liquid, she knew this wasn't the friendly kiss they'd agreed on. But as his tongue urged her lips apart, and he explored the dark, long-untouched recesses of her, she ceased to care.

A sound, a moan, came from deep in his chest while he pressed her closer still. She silenced the answering sound that sprang from within her, but couldn't silence the heavy thudding of her heart. Heat raced through her veins and settled in her belly in an aching throb. Her traitorous knees ceased to support her, and she leaned against the strong arm that circled her back. Like a skein of wool, too tightly spun, Libby felt herself unraveling as his kiss deepened and changed.

Chase hadn't meant to kiss her like this, but as he'd

felt her body give in to his, the flame that had sprung to life inside him had trebled. She was sweet, so sweet, just as he'd known she would be. She smelled of fresh mountain air, piñon smoke and . . . wild lilacs?

While his mind pondered the puzzle of that scent, his fingers skimmed the flaxen tresses she wore pulled back in the braid. He itched to let her glorious hair loose and plunge his fingers into it, just as he'd longed to last night. His hand skimmed the graceful arch of her neck, the small of her back, the sweet firm curve of her bottom; pulling her closer against his hardness. "You're so beautiful, Lib," he murmured against her lips, and dipped his head down for another taste of her honey.

He forgot, for a moment, to think; to remember who he was, or to wish she wasn't the wife of that reb soldier. For the moment, she belonged to him. Every fiber, every inch of her. He felt it in her surrender, in the way her hands let loose of the folds of his shirt and spread across his chest like fingers of fire. He felt it in the slow mindless dance her tongue was doing with his and in the way his blood pounded in his veins, washing away all thought and caution—and every shred of his common sense.

Only the ominous rumble of the ground beneath their feet brought him to his senses, though at first he was sure it was the echo of his own heartbeat. Like growing thunder, the rumble grew louder, and he grasped Libby by the shoulders and set her slightly away from him. "Listen."

Her startled gaze met his. His kiss was still evident in her gray eyes as it was on her reddened lips, but clearly she heard the sound, too.

"What is that?" he asked, scanning the horizon in search of the source. The sound grew like the warning roar of white water on a dangerous river.

Libby spotted them before he did, and dragged him backward toward the copse of rock behind them. "Mustangs!" she screamed. "Get back!"

Grabbing the horses' reins, Chase yanked them behind the outcrop of rock. The horses jerked the reins in fright and stomped their hooves into the pine straw-covered ground. Chase placed himself between the oncoming herd and Libby, sheltering her against the rock with his body.

They came over the forested rise to the north like foam on a cresting wave—a herd of wild mustangs so large Chase had to blink to believe what he was seeing. In color and pattern, he'd never seen horses to rival these. The mares and younger horses moved as one, crashing heedlessly through the brush breaks and in between the stands of ponderosa and white pine. The air churned with dust and the pungent smell of sweaty horseflesh. Where only moments ago there had been silence, there was now the deafening din of pounding hooves and high-pitched squeals.

Though the *manada* of mares and younger horses seemed endless, Libby and Chase were left staring after them in a matter of seconds.

"Incredible!" Chase murmured in awe when the last of them disappeared into a thicket of trees to the south. He eased his body away from Libby's. "I've never seen anything like that."

"Wild horses run simply for the love of it most times," Libby answered with a frown, running a disconcerted hand over her unruly hair. "But these were spooked. Panicked. You could see it in their eyes."

"Panicked . . . by the bear?" he asked, glancing in the direction they'd come. An uneasy feeling crept up his neck.

"Any number of things could have done it. But the thing that has me worried is the stallion."

"What stallion?"

146

"Exactly," she replied, gathering up Lady's reins. "Where was he? He wasn't with the herd. Stallions follow the flank of the herd, not only to keep it together, but to guard it from any danger. Nothing but death or defeat by a challenger separates a stallion from his *manada*."

"How do you know you didn't miss seeing him in all that?"

Libby mounted, slipped a new cartridge into the breech of her rifle, and slid it back into its boot. "There's only one stallion in these parts with a *manada* as big as that one. It's Diablo. Believe me, if you'd seen him, you'd never forget him." She nudged Lady forward, heading back in the direction the mares had come.

Chase yanked at Blue's reins, throwing them over the horse's head. "Where are you going now? Hey! Do you realize how many head of horses just passed us back there?" he called, mentally calculating the size of the herd and what its capture could mean for Libby's Army contract. He swung up on Blue's back. "Why aren't we following them?"

"We will . . . after we get what we came for," she called over her shoulder. Urging Lady into a lope, she followed the churned earth and headed toward a wide canyon that veered off to the east.

Chase frowned and rode to the spot where the quail had dropped. After fastening it to his saddle with his whang strings, he tightened his knees around Blue and urged him on, cocking his Henry one-handed as he went.

It wasn't until he and Libby reached the mouth of the ravine that he heard a sound that sent his neck hair rising—the furious scream of a horse, and the answering bestial roar which echoed hollowly across the walls of rock.

Chase grabbed for Libby's reins and pulled his

147

own mount up short. Years of military training had made him wary of riding blind into a potentially dangerous situation. He'd learned to approach a problem like this tactically. Clinically.

The narrow arroyo was surrounded on two sides by steep, nearly vertical walls of loose shale rock, while the center of the canyon spilled open to a panoramic view of the valley below. The arroyo floor was clogged with ferns, brittle stands of brushwood, and the remnants of ancient rock slides.

Fifty yards away, a giant of a grizzly and an ebony black stallion were squared off in battle. The bear, up on his hind legs, let out a bawling roar and made a sweep with his powerful paw at the stallion. His four-inch claws glittered in the sun like bloody daggers, and Chase noted the torn flesh on the horse's neck. This time, however, the bear misjudged his swipe and the stallion reared up and connected with the grizzly's head with a vicious sharp-hoofed kick.

They were downwind of the bear, and both Lady and Blue balked and tossed their heads in near-panic at the scent of him. Chase and Libby fought to keep them under control. "Not here," Chase told her, yanking Blue's head around. "Up there." He pointed to the narrow trail that led to the rim overlooking the narrow gorge.

"He'll get away before we can get up there," Libby protested.

"Better that, than cornering us in that arroyo the way he has the stallion. Going in on his level would be suicidal. It puts all the advantage in his corner. From above, the advantage will be ours. And from the looks of him, we'll need all the help we can get. Let's go." He kicked Blue and started up the steep trail that skirted the gorge.

It took them less than a minute to reach the top.

They tied their nervous horses to the branches of a chokecherry bush and flattened themselves to the ground. Below, the screams of the stallion had grown frantic. His neck and forelegs were bloody, his coat flecked white with foamy sweat, but incredibly he was holding his own against the grizzly.

Chase cocked his Henry and shouldered the gun, taking careful aim.

"Don't hit the stallion," Libby warned, shouldering her own rifle.

"He's a dead horse, either way," Chase predicted grimly. Diablo's magnificent black mane and tail tossed like gleaming raven's wings and his eyes boiled with fury. Chase's heart pumped harder at the sight of him.

Thoroughbred blood ran in that horse's veins, pure as that of any stallion his father had bred for the Bradford stable. In truth, Chase had no wish to kill him. But the stallion was wounded. There was no question about that. How badly, it was hard to tell. "It would probably be doing him a favor to put him out of his misery."

"No," she cried, grabbing his arm. "Just try. For my sake?"

The stricken look in her eyes took him aback. Wondering briefly what stake she had in the horse, he nodded. "I'll do my best." Taking aim again at the bear who was charging the horse with a series of daring feints, Chase squeezed back the trigger. Just then, the stallion reared and dove at the bear's upper body. The bullet drove harmlessly into the wall of rock behind Goliath.

"Damn," he cursed through clenched teeth. *Hold still, you bastard.*

Taking aim again, he pulled off another shot. A spurt of blood erupted in the haunch of the moving bear, drawing an enraged howl from the beast. Goliath bounded around, eyes red with fury, seeking the source of his pain. He tossed his head violently. Saliva dangled from his teeth.

Frozen in panic, the stallion hesitated to take the freedom Chase had offered him. Forelegs planted unevenly before him, Diablo let his frenzied black eyes meet Chase's gaze for a long moment. They were proud, fierce, wild eyes that reflected a spirit so indomitable even the bear could not break it.

"Get out of there, horse," Chase urged under his breath. As if his words had broken through Diablo's terror, the horse bolted from the circle of rocks he'd been trapped in. Goliath reared on his hind legs, and roared in fury as the stallion made good his escape, careening in a flash of gleaming ebony past the mouth of the canyon.

Chase aimed his gun once more. He had Goliath's heart centered in the sight of his gun. From here, he knew he couldn't miss. Carefully, he squeezed the trigger, only to hear the dull pop of a misfired cartridge. Nothing but smoke emerged from the tip of his rifle, but the sound drew the bear's furious gaze upward. With a snarling shake of his tawny head, Goliath bounded up the slippery wall of shale directly toward them.

"Uh-oh . . ." Chase muttered, slapping the side of his rifle.

"He's coming," Libby warned taking aim.

"My gun's jammed," he told her, still trying to shake it loose.

"Don't tell me that," she cried, squeezing off a shot at the oncoming bear. Her bullet pierced Goliath's shoulder. He stumbled and slid on the shale before getting his feet under him again. She cursed under her breath.

"Reload!" He tossed his rifle aside and dragged the revolver from his holster. Pain shot up his leg from the uncomfortable position he was in, but he ignored it.

Libby fumbled to reload. Her hands were shaking, making it all the more difficult. She fired again, hitting the grizzly in the upper chest, but the bullets seemed to have little effect on him. "Chase—he's not stopping!"

"I know. I know." He aimed the revolver, a determined grimace on his face. "Die, you—" His Colt exploded, drowning his words and a bright red splotch appeared on Goliath's right shoulder. The slippery shale carried the bear five feet down the incline. But it didn't stop him. He came on again, like some indestructible killing machine.

"Get the horses," Chase ordered. "Give me your gun and ammunition. I'll hold him off until you're on Lady."

"No! You come, too!"

"Libby! Do it!" He fired another round into the bear. "We've got to get out of here. We don't have the firepower to stop him now. Hurry."

She knew he was right. Unfastening the cartridge belt from her waist, she placed her rifle beside him. She rose on her hands and feet to go, but felt the shale rock suddenly give beneath her left heel. An ominous splintering sound accompanied her sudden plunging slide.

She heard Chase call her name, but the sound was swallowed by her own wretched scream as she slid downward, toward Goliath.

Chapter Ten

"*Cha-aase . . .*"

Libby clawed at the shale rock at the top of the rim,
trying desperately to stop her downward momen-
tum. Its sharp edges bit into her fingertips and
scraped her arms, leaving bloody gashes, and the rock
slid from her grasp like shifting sand.

Chase made a desperate grab for her, but she slid
just out of his reach. "Libby! The branch—get hold
of the branch."

Three feet below the rim of the ledge, she slid past a
lone, stubborn shadscale bush poking out of the
rocky soil. Her fingers found the slender woody stalk
and closed around it. The bush jerked from the shock
of her weight, but held fast. Below her, a mere twenty
feet away, Goliath roared defiantly and pounded up
the incline. For every step he took he slid back two.

Libby's heart felt like it had risen and lodged in her
throat. Tears sprang to her eyes. Above her, she could
see the helplessness in Chase's expression as he
strained to reach her. Dangling against the side of the
hill, Libby tried to get her feet under her.

"Hang on," Chase called. Stripping off his jacket,
he waved it over his head to get the bear's attention.
Once he succeeded, he took aim and tossed the

garment into the air. It sailed down and landed squarely across the beast's face. Goliath tore at the jacket as if it were a live thing, biting it and shredding it, all but forgetting—for the moment—about the real prey above him.

Chase flattened himself to the ground again and extended the butt of the rifle to Libby. "Grab it, Lib."

She did, clamping one hand around the slender stock.

"Both hands!" Chase ordered.

A metallic taste filled her mouth. Blood seeped from where she'd bitten her lip. She glanced again at the dizzying drop below her. The land seemed to be moving, shifting. "I . . . I can't!"

"C'mon, Libby, don't look down. Just grab the gun with both hands. I'll pull you up."

"What if I—?"

"Libby, don't think, just *do* it!"

Taking a steadying breath, she dove for the rifle and felt herself swing against the sharp black rocks. But Chase held her.

He released a breath. "Good girl. Look at me, Lib. Right here. Now hang on. Help me with your feet if you can."

She focused first on his strong brown hands just above hers, then on his arms. His muscles bulged and strained against the blue chambray fabric of his shirt. Her gaze leaped to his face. She could almost hear his teeth grind together as he lifted her, but his green eyes didn't leave hers. Not for a second. She clung to them like a drowning swimmer to a floating piece of driftwood.

Slowly, she felt herself being lifted. The toes of her boots fought for footing in the shale. Below, she heard the rocks slide again with Goliath's weight. "Chase! He's—"

"Don't look down, honey," he told her through

gritted teeth. "Just look at me. You're almost there."

The crack of a gunshot rent the air. Chase heard the ping of shale rocks splintering and Goliath's answering roar. *What the—?*

Two more shots followed in quick succession, each digging into the grizzly's thick coat with a dull thwack. The bear bellowed in fury and tumbled down the slope. Enraged, he headed at his new tormentor at a limping gallop, but a final, killing shot between the eyes sent Goliath crashing to the earth like a fallen ponderosa giant.

Chase didn't have time to wonder who had done the shooting. He wrapped a fist around Libby's belt when she came up even with the ledge and hauled her toward him.

She landed on top of him and together, they sprawled backward in the dirt. Panting for breath, they lay there, too exhausted to speak.

Libby closed her eyes and the shaking started. The tremors began at her fingertips and knifed through the rest of her. She clamped her teeth together to keep them from chattering. Chase pulled her up against him and tightened his arms around her. She could feel him shaking, too.

"It's all right now. Shhh, you're safe," he whispered. His lips brushed the top of her head. She gave in gratefully to his comfort, because she needed it right then. Needed to feel someone's arms around her.

"Hey, up there!" called a voice from below. "Are you two all right?"

Chase eased up, one arm still around Libby. He shook his head at the man on horseback at the bottom of the arroyo. "As always, Bradford, your timing is impeccable. You couldn't have cut that any closer, could you?"

154

A half-smile curved El's mouth, and he rested the stock of his Winchester against his thigh. "As Father always said, timing is everything. Good God, is that what you call a bear in these parts?" he asked, looking at the grizzly. "I've never seen anything quite so . . . huge."

"He looks a hell of a lot bigger when he's getting ready to make a meal out of you," Chase replied humorlessly.

"Thank God we weren't too far off when we heard your shots," Elliot went on, running a hand through his tousled blond hair. "Early and I found no sign of the bear along the south fork of the stream, so we were headed back this way, looking for you. But we ran into the prettiest herd of mustangs you ever did see just south of here. Galloping like blazes. Early was running down a few head when we heard the shooting start. I split off from him to come and find you."

"Lucky for us." Chase pulled a still-shaky hand down his face.

Elliot gestured to Libby. "Is she hurt?"

Chase glanced down at the scrapes on Libby's arms.

"I'm fine," she declared, trying to quell the tremor in her voice. "Really."

"Give us a minute, El. We'll be right down."

"Sure," he answered, glancing uneasily at the carcass of the bear. "I'll just . . . uh, stay here and . . . keep an eye on him. Make sure he doesn't . . . move or . . . anything."

Chase glanced at Libby, realizing how close he'd come to losing her. She was still shaking like a leaf and was white as chalk. "You're not going to faint on me are you, Lib?"

She managed an indignant look and pushed a

strand of straw-colored hair from her eyes. "I don't faint."

"Is that a hard and fast rule or do you make exceptions after being chased by renegade grizzlies?"

The amused sparkle in his eyes wrenched a reluctant smile from her. "I've never fainted in my life and I'm n-not going to start now. I'm just . . . sh-shaking a little. That's all."

His arm tightened around her, and he rubbed his hand briskly up and down her arm. "You're shaking a lot. I'd offer you my coat," he said, casting a forlorn look at the tattered remnants of the garment strewn on the slope, "but I'm afraid it wouldn't do you much good."

Libby leaned into the comfort of his embrace, needing it as much as she'd ever needed a caress. "I'm sorry about your coat. I . . . I'm indebted to you again, Chase. Truly, I'm usually not this much trouble."

"No?" he asked with a grin. "How much trouble are you usually?"

A shiver rattled through her as she brushed the dirt from her scraped arms. "That d-depends on who you ask." She let out a nervous little laugh. "Thank you."

"For what?" he asked, his brows rising questioningly.

"For saving my life, for not saying I told you so."

Chase smiled. "If you're referring to our little encounter with Goliath, you've got nothing to be ashamed of. Most women in your position would have had the vapors at the first sight of that bear. You did well, Libby. Better than well. Besides, what happened was more my fault than yours."

Libby looked at him as if he'd lost his mind. "What do you mean?"

He let go of her and picked up his jammed gun. "I mean it's El you should be thanking for saving you." He picked up his rifle. "I got us into more trouble with this gun than we counted on."

"You couldn't have known it was going to jam that way," she argued. "Guns are unpredictable. It could have happened to anyone."

But it happened to me. "Yeah, just another piece of bad luck, I guess," Chase muttered with a hint of sarcasm.

Libby jerked her head toward him. "What's that supposed to mean?"

"You've been having more than your share of it around here, from what I hear."

"Where did you hear that?"

"C'mon, Lib. It's no secret. Even your pal Jonas Harper mentioned it. I think this might be a good time to fill me in."

Her shivering stopped abruptly and she stared at him. "You say that as though you think your gun's jamming was no accident."

"I'm not saying anything until I have a good look at my rifle. I just like to cover my flank," he admitted. "Why don't you tell me what's been going on?"

Libby looked down at her hands. "It was nothing at first. Just little things after Malachi died. Gates left open, horses getting out, a brush fire on some of my best graze acreage. It took us nearly a day to put that out. Then, the men started having accidents. One of my hands, Will Barlow, was thrown from his own horse when his cinch broke in the middle of chasing down a string of horses. Shattered his leg and ended his career as a buster. He was the first to leave.

"The rumors started around that time that the ranch was jinxed. That blew it all out of proportion. I mean, those things happen on a ranch. But, it didn't

157

help that a woman was running things. There are those who resent me for it. Nate and Wilson, the two who left the night you came, were next."

"And you believe these things were all accidents?"

"Not one of my men is careless, Chase. I don't know how else to explain it. Do you?"

He looked at her for a moment, unsure of how to answer her. His gun hadn't simply jammed. It had been tampered with. He ran a hand down the brass-plated stock. The last bullet he'd fired had been light on powder and had traveled mere inches down the barrel. Had he fired off one more round, the bullet would have collided with the half-spent one in the barrel, blowing both him and the gun to kingdom come. Possibly Libby, too. Neat, and nearly impossible to prove—after the fact.

He'd seen dozens of men die in the heat of battle that same way during the war. It had made him meticulously careful when loading his gun. A light cartridge and a full one felt decidedly different. He would have known, unless the cartridge had been tampered with after he'd loaded it.

His jaw tightened. He had his suspicions, but wasn't ready to voice them yet. She had enough to worry about. But if someone had tampered with his gun, he vowed silently to make damn sure he found out who it was.

He eased himself up off the ground, gritting his teeth against the old ache that shot down his leg, then offered her a hand up. "Let's get those cuts cleaned up and get you home. Time enough to think about the rest later."

She took his hand and felt his strength travel down her arm like a shockwave. Yes, she'd think about all that later, she decided shakily. Right now she wanted to concentrate on keeping her knees from knocking together, so Chase wouldn't know how really frightened she'd been. Nor how much she wished he'd just keep holding her like he had. It had been a long time since she'd felt a man's arms around her, giving her comfort.

Too long.

The men crowded around the long wooden table in Libby's common room passing plates of corn-bread, greens, and the fat mint-wrapped trout Straw and Tad had caught earlier in the day. Elliot was animatedly regaling Tad with an exaggerated ver-sion of the grizzly adventure while Bodine, Early, and Chase savored Libby's cooking.

"But was Goliath tall as the roof, Elliot?" Tad asked, wide-eyed.

El shook his head conspiratorially.

"Bigger?" Tad gasped.

"Biggest darn bear I've ever seen," El replied with somber-faced seriousness. "Why he'd eat the bears back East in one bite. Gobble 'em right up."

"Naw . . ." Tad stared at him suspiciously.

El threw his hands up and looked to Chase for corroboration. "Am I lying, Chase?"

Chase, lost in thoughts of his own, didn't answer. "Chase?"

He looked up and stared at El blankly. "Huh?"

"See," El replied with magnanimous sarcasm. "Even Chase was so stunned by the size of that bear he can *hardly* put the words together."

Chase smiled and shook his head at El. "Oh yeah. Goliath kind of defies description. We're all lucky El came along when he did, Tad. That's a tale you'll want to tell your grandchildren." Chase's eyes met Libby's over the table, and the smile slid slowly from his expression.

She wasn't sure if the room had grown hotter or the

heat of his look had suddenly made her overly warm. Looking away, she pushed her chair back and went to the stove to refill the bowl of greens. She took her time, listening to the animated conversation going on behind her. When she sat back down with them, he was still watching her.

"More greens, anyone?" she offered.

"Thanks," Chase said, reaching for the bowl. Their fingers brushed as he took it from her, and she nearly dropped the bowl right into his lap. Deftly, Chase caught it before anyone noticed the bobble. He smiled a thank you and turned his eyes to the food.

"Well, if'n you ask me," Bodine put in after stuffing his mouth full of food, "we would have been better off if'n Goliath had killed that black devil stallion today."

"What've you got against that stallion, Bodine?" Early asked.

Bodine shrugged, clutching his fork in one hand. "He's an outlaw. A widow-maker. Ever'body knows it. Just as soon kill ya as look at ya."

Libby's expression tightened. "That's not true. I've known man-killers in my time. Diablo doesn't deserve that reputation. Rankin was tormenting him. He gave Diablo no choice."

Bodine snorted and stuffed another forkful of food in his mouth. "Stomped Rankin's brains to mush and would'a done the same to the fellers he was with. He'll try it again on any man who comes close enough to them hooves of his. Steals mares from every herd within fifty miles, too."

Libby started to reply, but Chase cut her off.

"Diablo's a thoroughbred," he put in. "Pure-blooded too, if I don't miss my guess. He doesn't belong out there with those rangy Spanish horses. Where did he come from?" He watched Libby's gaze

160

flick up uneasily to Early and then back down to her plate. He glanced at Early questioningly.

Early cleared his throat. "Fact is, he belongs to the Double Bar H. He's a Honeycutt horse."

Chase stared at Libby in surprise. "You own the stallion?"

Libby shook her head. "No one can really own a horse like Diablo."

"What she ain't tellin' you," Straw explained, in a raspy tobacco-roughened voice, "is that years ago, Malachi Honeycutt—Lee's pa—bought Diablo from a Thoroughbred breeder name of Williamson in California. Diablo was the get of a sire named Belmont, fastest stallion this side of the Mississip'. Malachi paid a fortune for Diablo. Had him shipped here special when he were a three-year-old."

"For breeding purposes?" El asked, intrigued.

"Eh?" Straw cupped a hand at his fleshy ear with a horrified look. "For *circuses*, you say?"

"No, for breeding purposes," El shouted, containing his smile.

Straw shook his head and took a bite of fish. "Oh, that, too. Mostly though, he had in mind racin' him."

"Racing?" El echoed in surprise.

Straw's shaggy eyebrows went up, and he laughed heartily. "Well, it ain't the kind of racin' you Eastern fellers do on them little postage stamps you call saddles. But it suits us fine. Anyways," he continued, "Malachi was sittin' at his peak just then, 'cause the ranch was thrivin'. But a few deals gone sour had made him nervous about the future. Many folks thought Malachi was puttin' good money after bad buyin' that horse. They was proved right, too. Ee-yup."

"Did Malachi race him?" Chase prodded.

161

"Never got the chance," Early replied.

Libby continued the story. "Malachi was so confident, he had wagers set on the stallion even before Diablo's arrival. When Diablo got here, Malachi threw a big party. The other ranchers were green with envy. Malachi pampered that horse like it was a child. Broke him gentle like, and started training him to race. But running was in his blood."

Chase's eyes were on her now, caught up in the story. "What happened?"

Tad leaned forward in anticipation of the part of the story he'd liked best. "Yeah, Ma. Tell him how he got away."

Libby smiled patiently at him. "No one knows exactly how it happened, but one night, only months after his arrival, Diablo jumped the corral fence during a terrible thunderstorm and got away."

"He joined up with a herd to the north and managed to avoid every attempt Malachi and Lee made to recapture him. Seemed he preferred the freedom of the hills to a racetrack. Soon, Diablo had his own *manada* of mares and, to add insult to injury, started stealing mares from our own herd. The horse Malachi had worshiped became his enemy. He put a price on the stallion's head."

"To recover him?" El asked.

She shook her head. "To kill him. Rankin, the man Trammel referred to, was a bounty hunter. He was the only one ever to catch Diablo. He was a cruel man, and since Malachi had put a price on the horse's head, Rankin wasn't obliged to bring the stallion back alive." Libby's voice lowered. "But he underestimated Diablo's will to live. That cost him his life."

"After that happened," she continued, "the stallion was too quick to catch, too cunning to get in

162

range of any man's gun. And things seemed to go sour for Malachi. The war not only hurt his business, it took his son from him." Libby swallowed, darting a quick look at Tad. "When Malachi died earlier this year, he was a broken man, with broken dreams. He blamed it all on that horse."

"You don't seem to share his bitterness," Chase remarked, holding her gaze.

"No," she answered. "Malachi had enough bitterness for the two of us. What he was too shortsighted to realize was that Diablo has mixed his bloodlines with half the foals born on our range. Every year, the quality of the stock improves because of him. The colts we're breaking this year have Diablo's strength and endurance. And no matter what happens to us, whether or not we make a go of this ranch, a piece of it will stay alive for generations through Diablo."

"Yer shoutin' down rainbarrels, Miz Libby," Bodine muttered, wiping his mouth on his sleeve. "Diablo ain't never gonna be more than an outlaw. If he ever comes fer me, he's gonna have a bullet betwixt his eyes fer an answer. A sidewinder's a sidewinder, no matter what name you give it."

Chase shot a look at Bodine and smiled without humor. "Snakes come in all different sizes, isn't that right, Bodine?"

Trammel's expression tightened, and he glared at Chase. "You got a big mouth, Whitlaw."

"No bigger than yours."

Trammel stood up at the table. "You got a bone to pick with me, say it out straight. Maybe you an' me ought to settle things outside."

"I've got nothing to prove," Chase answered. "Do you?"

The younger man's fists worked at his sides, and he glanced around the table to gauge the others' reac-

163

tions. "We'll see, Whitlaw. We'll just see." He gathered his hat, with its leering rattlesnake band, and stalked out the kitchen door, slamming it behind him.

Libby met Chase's eyes across the table and, for the first time, realized what a dangerous opponent he could make. She was suddenly very glad he was on her side.

But her smile was met with a scowl, and Chase gathered his hat up too, excusing himself with his meal still half-finished. Libby watched him go, wondering what she'd done wrong.

The full moon hung low in the sky as Libby tucked the covers around Tad, slipping them between the rope webbing and the straw-filled mattress.

"Wash your face and hands?" she queried, smoothing the clean cotton sheet with her hand.

He nodded.

"Behind your ears?"

"Aw, nobody looks behind my ears," he argued, pushing the back of his head down into his pillow.

"I do," she said, her quick kiss just a peck on the nose. A low croaking sound came from under the covers. Libby frowned, listening. "What was that?"

Tad's eyes widened innocently. "What?"

"That sound?"

"Prob'ly just my stomach, Ma," he lied straight-faced, tightening his arms over the covers to keep them in place. "I'm hungry."

"Since when does your stomach croak?" she asked with a sly smile, pulling back the covers.

On the sheet sat a fat brown toad that seemed clearly relieved to be out in the open. She grimaced, holding the squirming toad by two fingers. "Is he . . . new?"

"Yep," Tad answered proudly. "Found him just today. Can't I keep him, Ma?"

"As long as you don't sleep with him. I'll tie some cheesecloth over the top of a bucket and he can spend the night in there. Tomorrow, you can make a proper box for him. Deal?" Libby slipped the toad into a pillow case.

"Deal." Tad nestled noisily down under the covers and smiled up at her.

"Ma?"

"Mm-hm?" Libby stroked his blond hair back from his eyes.

"Is Diablo really an outlaw like Trammel said?"

"In a way, but he's not hurting anyone. He simply wants to live his own way."

"I wished I could'a seen him fightin' ol' Goliath. Must have been some sight." Tad's young eyes grew wide, imagining.

"It was, darlin'." She'd carefully edited out of the tale her close brush with death. What was left must have seemed like a grand adventure for an eight-year-old boy.

Libby leaned down and pressed her lips to his soft cheek. It reminded her of how close she'd come to never having this sweet experience again, how close she'd come to leaving Tad alone in the world. Guilt sliced into her like a sharp-edged knife.

"Kin I come next time?" he pleaded.

"I hope there won't be a next time, son." She patted the covers and reached to turn down the wick of his kerosene lamp. Moonlight spilled into the room and the sweet fragrance of roses drifted in on a current of night air.

Tad's face drew into a thoughtful pout. "If there is . . . I bet Chase could teach me how to shoot a gun. An' then I could be ready." He pointed an imaginary gun in the air. "Pow, pow! I'd get the next griz'

165

before he could hurt that stallion again or eat any of our mares." His expression lit with a new thought. "Maybe tomorrow I kin help Chase with them new mares Early brung home today."

"Brought," she corrected. "And you know Miss Nora is coming with your lessons day after tomorrow. You need to do your studying." At his disappointed expression, she added, "But, we'll see."

Moonlight spilled into the room from the barred window above Tad's bed. In the dark, he looked so much like Lee it made her heart ache. "Go to sleep now, Tad. Sweet dreams."

"Ma?"

"I . . ." Tad chewed on his lower lip.

"What darlin'?"

"You like Chase?"

His question made her heartbeat falter. "Why do you ask?"

"I think he likes you." A secretive smile lit Tad's small features.

Libby blinked in surprise and let out a nervous laugh. "What makes you think so?"

"I saw him watchin' ya tonight when you was servin' up supper. He was lookin' at ya fine."

Libby flinched at his words, knowing the truth in them. It had simply never occurred to her that Tad knew anything about the way a man looks at a woman. The memory of the way Chase had kissed her up on the mountain returned unbidden, sending a rush of warmth through her.

"He was probably just hungry," she replied and nearly groaned as she said it. Hungry would certainly describe the kiss they'd shared. She smoothed down Tad's blankets.

"But if he did like ya," Tad persisted, "you think you could like him a little?"

"I like him fine, Tad. But he's only here for a little while," she reminded him. "He'll be moving on after the herd's together. Don't go getting attached to him. It'll only cause you hurt when he leaves."

Tad pondered that for a moment. "Like Pa's goin' hurt, you mean?"

Libby stiffened at the analogy. "That was different. He was your pa and we . . . we loved him. He went to fight for a cause he believed in." *Even if it meant leaving us behind—alone.* "Chase is . . . just a hired hand, and he'll be moving on just like all the rest."

Tad frowned, obviously failing to see the distinction she was trying to make. "I think I'll like him whilst he's here and save my *not* likin' fer when he's gone."

Libby sighed, knowing his logic was faultless, if blessedly naive. She couldn't shelter him from the pain of life any more than she could protect herself from it. She brushed away the thought and bent down to kiss him again. "Go to sleep now, darlin'. Sweet dreams."

"'Night, Ma."

The clock on her bedside table had just struck one when Libby pummeled a feather-ticked pillow and then sprawled disconsolately across her broad, cold bed. Several wisps of down exploded into the air and hung on the colorless beams of light filtering through her window before drifting back down to her. She scowled at the one that landed mockingly on the tip of her nose.

She swiped at it and made another pass at sleep. Squeezing her eyes shut, she forced herself to breath deeply. Relax. Empty her mind of thought.

167

It was, she decided after another minute, clearly hopeless. Her eyes popped open again as if by a will of their own. She flung herself onto her back and tugged the covers up under her chin. Her thoughts had run in circles for hours, like hovering scavengers, keeping sleep and peace of mind at bay. Tad's words, Jonas Harper's proposal of marriage, and Chase Whitlaw's kiss were all jumbled with the day's events. By far the kiss was the most confusing.

Chase's fault in what had happened was no greater than her own. She'd not shrunk away from him. In fact, to her everlasting regret, he'd weakened her knees, knocked her off kilter, left her wanting more.

Libby ran two fingers over her lips remembering the feel of his mouth covering hers, his tongue plumbing the depths of her. She realized with a guilty start that Lee's kisses had never come close to inciting the riot of feelings Chase had let loose. How was it possible for a kiss from a stranger to be more intimate than a kiss from one's own husband?

I saw him watchin' ya tonight. . . . He was lookin' at ya fine. Yes, she'd seen Chase watching her, his eyes stalking her every movement the way a cat stalks a doomed bird. It had made her heart flutter like wing-beats. She'd done her best to keep her gaze from meeting his through the meal, but once or twice their looks had collided over the supper table.

You're beautiful, Lib. Chase's voice echoed in her thoughts.

Beautiful? How could he think her beautiful in the raggedy man-clothes and cowhide boys' boots she wore? He'd known many more sophisticated women in the East, she reasoned. Women who wore beautiful gowns like those in the drawings in her dog-eared copy of *Godey's Lady's Book.* Women who knew how to use a fan and talk about silly things like

168

stitchery and the weather. Even if she'd needed to learn those things, which she hadn't, she suspected they would be very boring after a time.

Except, perhaps, to a man like Chase Whitlaw.

No, it was more likely pity he felt for her. Perhaps he used those same words on all the lonely widows he kissed as he drifted through the Territory on his way to God-knew-where. The thought sent a shaft of hurt through her.

Libby tossed her covers aside, realizing the non-sensical turn her thoughts had taken. Nothing had happened between them that couldn't be forgotten.

She pulled a match from the punched-tin holder beside the bed and lit the lamp again. Pale golden light filled the room, softening its starkness. Yes, she thought, tossing her night wrapper on and yanking the sash tight around her waist. She'd put his kiss completely out of her mind. Forget it ever happened. Forget about Chase Whitlaw and the things he made her feel. It was the only way.

Chase leaned heavily against the corral post, tipped his head back and took one more pull off the silver flask of whiskey in his hand. He raised the nearly empty vessel in salute to the inky star-splashed dome above him. The liquor burned a fiery path down his throat. Heat seeped languidly into his limbs, but seemed to deliberately avoid his brain. He tugged on the buttons at the throat placket of his red union jacks, then shoved the flask into the back pocket of his denims.

Numbness, he decided disgustedly, was becoming increasingly illusive. Despite his best attempts to reach that pinnacle of oblivion, his senses seemed clearer than ever and his thoughts focused with vigilant tenacity on the cause of his discomfort.

Libby.

He'd already cursed himself, called himself every kind of fool for kissing her, letting his guard down with her. He'd wanted to satisfy his curiosity about her, but instead he'd stirred up a longing in himself. A woman like Libby could rope a man's heart and cinch it tight before he knew what hit him.

She was ripe for the picking, but the plain fact was, he wasn't in the market. And if he was, he wouldn't even be in the running. A man like Jonas Harper could offer her more than he ever could. Security, a good home with no leaking roof, even an education for Tad. Things he could never give her.

If that was all Libby wanted, she'd have accepted Harper's proposal long ago.

Chase frowned at that thought. So what *did* she want? Several words came to mind: companionship, loyalty, love.

Love? He let out a harsh breath of laughter. Can't squeeze blood from a stone, he thought grimly. The thought twisted at him like the sharp edge of a knife, and he tipped the flask upside-down again and took another swig.

"Here's to you, Lee Honeycutt, you lucky bastard," he grumbled with annoying sobriety. "You didn't know what you had 'til it was too late. Now, it's too damn late for both of us." He clamped his eyes shut, steadying himself against the split rail.

Maybe he was drunker than he thought.

The cool night breeze sang through the aspen leaves above him. The air was pure and clear as a mountain brook. It tingled as it washed over his sweaty face. He tipped his head back and leaned against the fence, allowing the earthy, familiar smell of horses to relax him.

170

"Do you always sleep standing up?"

Libby's voice knocked him off balance, and he nearly fell before catching himself on the rail. He blinked at her, scowling. It was frightening how he'd conjured her up with his thoughts. *Bloody hell! Isn't any place around here sacred?*

Chapter Eleven

Eyebrows arched, arms akimbo at the waist of her night wrapper, Libby awaited his answer.

"You shouldn't sneak up on a man like that," he told her, reaching up irritably to rebutton his shirt. He watched those steely gray eyes of hers fall to the dark snatch of hair peeking out, then jerk back up to his face.

"I wasn't sneaking," she protested. "I didn't even see you until I was almost out here, in fact. I couldn't sleep, and I just came out to get some air."

"Yeah? So'd I."

A line formed between Libby's eyes as she sniffed delicately in his direction.

"S'matter?" he asked, wondering as he said it why his words were so slurred. That red-eye really packed a wallop.

Her nostrils flared again. This time her expression sank into shock. "Why . . . you . . . you've been drinking!"

His gaze skimmed down the length of her flannel wrapper and slowly ran back up again. He swayed against the fence. "Iz there a law against having a drink or two on your own time?"

She narrowed her eyes. "You, Mr. Whitlaw, are drunk as a skunk."

"How indelicate of you t'say so. Been compared to a lot of animals in my time, but never a . . . skunk." He grinned lazily at her. He was tempted to reach out and touch her face. The way the moonlight kissed it made it look like smooth, carved ivory. But she seemed to be weaving just out of reach. Chase folded his arms across his chest and swayed against the post. She was right. He *was* drunk.

But not nearly drunk enough.

She was studying him as if he were an obscure puzzle piece that didn't quite fit into the whole.

"Is . . . is it your leg?" she asked hopefully.

His good humor bled away. "What?"

"Your leg. It seems to bother you from time to time. Is that why you're drinking, to dull the pain?"

He stared at the question in her eyes and considered—for one wild moment—telling her the truth. Considered getting the locket out of his saddlebags and handing it to her. Just like that. It would, after all, make everything easier, cleaner. She'd tell him to pack his things, and he wouldn't be tempted to do what he wanted to do right now.

But just as quickly, he discarded the idea. She needed him. Oh, not in the way it seemed right now. She needed his help. If the rifle incident this morning was any indication, she needed him more than she knew.

"Yeah," he answered at last. "It's my leg."

She nodded sympathetically, her gray eyes meeting his. "Did it happen during the War?"

"Yeah." He turned away, hoping to close the subject, but she persisted.

"How long ago?"

He kept his eyes trained on the mares resting in the paddock. "Two years."

"Two years," she repeated quietly. "My husband, Lee, died two years ago in the Wilderness outside of Chancellorsville. . . ."

A muscle in Chase's cheek jumped, and he pulled his flask from his pocket, taking another long pull. Perhaps he meant to shock her into silence. Mostly, he wanted her to leave him alone. He wiped the whiskey from his lips with the back of one hand and glared down at her.

"Two years is a long time," she murmured, unperturbed by his menacing look. "A long time to be in pain."

Chase wondered suddenly if she was referring to herself or to him. She'd been alone as long as he had. The whiskey was making his head throb, and he squeezed the bridge of his nose between his thumb and forefinger. "Libby—"

"I have some liniment in the barn. Perhaps it would help to rub some on—"

He grabbed her by the shoulders. "Libby, you were right. I *am* drunk. Go back in the house."

Libby didn't move. She felt his fingers digging into her shoulders. She should have turned and run at his words, but something in his expression held her there. Her racing pulse thudded in her ears. "I . . . I can't sleep."

"What is it you want from me?" he demanded, giving her a little shake.

"I—I . . . nothing. I don't want anything. I just wanted to get some air."

He dropped his hands disgustedly and started for the barn.

"No, that's not true," she blurted out, stopping him but failing to turn him around. "I want to know

174

why you kissed me that way today." She wished she could call back her question, but it was too late.

He turned around now. "What way?"

"Like . . . like you meant it."

A grin tipped one side of his mouth, but didn't reach his eyes. "I always mean it when I kiss a woman."

"I see." She gathered her arms across her chest. His answer stung, as she supposed he meant it to.

He started to turn away from her, but his bad leg buckled beneath him and he made a grab for the fencepost. Without thinking, Libby jumped to help him, grasping his arm and hauling him back up.

He mumbled a curse. "I can make it on my own."

"Sure you can, if you want to sleep in the paddock. Come on. I'll help you to bed." She wrapped his arm around her shoulder and aimed for the barn. His limp was pronounced now, and he wasn't bothering to try to hide it from her.

Draping his arm around her neck, he dipped his nose into her hair and filled his lungs. "You smell good, Lib—"

"And you smell like whiskey." Libby frowned.

"—like lilacs. . . . How come you smell like lilacs?"

"Lilac soap," she told him, keeping her focus on the barn door. "I make it out of the wild lilacs that bloom in the spring, higher up."

"He was a fool. . . ." Chase muttered under his breath.

Libby looked up at him. He wasn't talking to her, but to the star-speckled night sky. She kept walking. "Who?"

"Thought he was a goddamned hero. . . ."

It was the whiskey talking, Libby decided. She pulled open the door to the darkened barn. The

175

only light came from the moonlight spilling through the doorway. The milch cow and several horses shifted restively.

Libby looked up at the loft and realized she'd never get him up there. She scanned the stalls and found an empty one. "Over here."

"A hundred thousand heroes, only . . . there weren't any heroes," he slurred. "Only fools."

The straw was fresh in the stall, and she intended to dump him unceremoniously into it. But to her dismay, when she started to disengage his arm, he took her hand and pulled her down with him. In a tangle of arms and legs, they fell together, landing in the cushion of straw.

The weight of his leg across hers pinned her where she was. Her first panicked thought was that he'd passed out on top of her. His body lay sprawled over hers with all the intimacy of a spent lover's. The thought sent fear spiraling through her. She pushed a hand against his shoulder. "Chase . . ."

"Hmmm?"

His voice was startling close, his breath warm against her ear and cheek.

"Let me up."

He didn't answer her with words. Instead, his hand slid up her rib cage to cover one breast and knead it sensuously. She inhaled sharply. Her traitorous nipple beaded into a hard nub beneath the flannel of her wrapper, betraying her, and her pulse throbbed.

"Chase—don't! Let me up," she appealed, pushing his hand away. The straw rustled beneath them as he slid down lower. "You're drunk!"

"Not drunk enough," he answered ruefully against the ivory column of her throat. "Not nearly drunk enough . . ." Then, his mouth slashed diagonally over hers, exploring the moist, dark cavern of her

176

mouth with languid skill. His tongue flicked boldly in and out, teasing and tempting her. Traversing the smooth outline of her teeth, he dared her tongue to join his.

Dizzy and confused, Libby tasted the whiskey he'd drunk. But it was passion, not whiskey, that drugged his kisses now, and she found herself unable to deny the heat rising within her own body. His heartbeat thudded in crazy unison with her own.

His fingers went to the braid that fell across her shoulder and dangled over one breast. "Let your hair down, Libby," he said, pulling out the ribbon. He ran his fingers down the plaiting, loosing thick, golden tresses.

Libby bit the inside of her lip as his gentle fingers massaged her scalp, and she leaned into his touch like a cat being stroked, shamelessly wanting more. A soft moan escaped her. It had been years since a man had run his fingers through her hair or touched her the way Chase was touching her now. It felt wonderful yet dangerous. Heat traveled, like wildfire, through her limbs. She rocked her head back and forth against the straw in useless denial of the pleasure he was giving her.

"It's n-not . . ." She stuttered, unable to complete a coherent thought. "We shouldn't be—"

"You're right," he told her, dipping his head to the hollow at the base of her throat once more and pressing his lips to her thudding pulse. "So, tell me to stop, Lib." His beard rasped her skin erotically, while his lips burned a trail of kisses down her throat. Showers of sparks traveled down her limbs setting fire to her skin.

"S-stop . . ." she whispered, but the word caught in her throat like a lie.

He shook his head slowly, brushing the curve of

her breast with his lips. "Say it like you mean it, Lib."

Libby let out an incoherent sound as her own help-lessness came back to haunt her. She could no more stop him from doing what he was doing to her than she could stop her heart from pounding in her chest.

Dipping lower, like a bee to the nectar of a flower, he pushed aside the fabric of her nightdress and eased his hand inside to cup a bare breast. His thumb traced a maddeningly slow circle around the beaded crest.

"You're so damn pretty," he whispered against her skin. Now he teased her nipple with his open palm. "So soft."

His mouth continued its torturous exploration of her throat and began to move lower. He worked his way down the curve of her chest with long, wet kisses.

Then his mouth closed over the dusky crest of her nipple. Sucking and tugging at the puckered nub, he drove her to the brink where pleasure became pain before transferring his attention to her other breast. His tongue took deliberate pleasure in laving and teasing her there. Libby moaned, giving voice to the unbearable pressure that gathered at the back of her throat. Arching her back instinctively, she gave him freer access to the swollen mound.

Never had Lee's touch made her quake with need as Chase's did. Never had she felt so helpless to stop herself from wanting. Her heart slammed in her chest and her breath came in short raspy gasps.

Chase groaned in response and shifted his weight across her leg until the evidence of his passion pressed fully against her hip. His body was taut and hot. His heated skin scorched hers where his hands roamed over the rest of her body, exploring, discovering.

"Ah, Libby . . ." The word was a breathy hiss. His

palm closed over the mound of her femininity, full of heat even through the flannel wrapper, and her eyes slid shut. Rotating that hand in slow, sensuous circles, he inched up the fabric of her gown with the other, and the night air whispered across her naked legs.

She wasn't so naive she did not realize where this was leading. What they were doing was wrong. So wrong! She wanted him to stop, but just as desperately, she wanted him to finish what he'd begun. The longing that had started as a flutter in her belly had spread and deepened to an inexorable ache between her thighs. What he was doing to her was torture: sweet, erotic, and bordering on pain. Her fingers twined into Chase's thick hair, while her other hand clutched his broad shoulder. "Please, Chase, please."

Chase heard her through the pounding of his blood. He groaned out loud. God, he wanted her. Wanted her the way he'd never wanted a woman in his life. But his need for her had sobered him up like a strong shot of coffee. What they were about to do was a mistake, and he knew she'd hate him for it later.

Yet, the desperation in her voice just now told him they'd gone too far to stop. He couldn't keep himself from satisfying her now, any more than he could have held back the kiss that started it all.

His weight crushed her against the straw as he dragged his hand up her bare inner thigh, up toward the soft triangle between her legs. Libby gasped as he dipped his fingers into the damp slickness there. She clamped her legs tightly together at the shock of his touch. "No!"

"Open up to me, Libby." His fingers found her again, relentlessly. "Let me do this for you."

"No," she said. Shock tightened her throat. "Lee never . . ."

179

Chase's expression hardened and his hand stilled. "Never what? Never touched you this way?"

Her head rocked back and forth against the straw. "We just . . . just . . ." She halted. Embarrassment kept her from saying more.

Chase cursed silently. Lee Honeycutt was more of a fool than he'd thought. "Open up to me, Libby." Once more he dropped his mouth to her beautiful breasts and laved an erect nipple with his tongue. "You'll like it. I promise."

Libby moaned and allowed her legs to relax slightly as his hand once more touched the heated ache between her legs. In and out his fingers slid, wet from the moisture within her, until she thought she could bear it no more. The motion of his fingers caused her hips to undulate against his palm in an ancient primal rhythm she had no control over.

Her body went taut with urgency; a thirst rose in her, one that could be quenched only by his touch. He went on touching her there while his mouth teased and tugged at her breast. She was on fire. A searing heat and tension curled low, first in her belly, then gathered strength and took her like a hot, gusting wind eddy, spinning her out of control.

Libby plunged her fingers into his hair and pulled him closer as release shattered her into fragmented pieces of light in the darkness. A cry wrenched from her, but he muffled the sound with his kiss. His breathing, she discovered was as ragged as her own, and she could feel his strong body tremble under the palms of her hands.

His mouth left hers abruptly, and he dipped his forehead to her bare shoulder, trying to get his breathing under control. "Ah, Libby . . . Libby."

Confused, Libby blinked in the darkness. Was he going to stop now and not make love to her? She

180

swallowed and smoothed back the hair from his sweaty forehead. "Chase, don't stop . . . I want you to—"

"No," he told her harshly, shaking his head against her chest.

Stunned that he would deny himself after what they'd just done, she took his face between her hands and forced him to look at her. "Why not?"

His eyes met hers in the darkness. "I can't. Don't you see? You'd hate me for it later." He rolled off her and threw an arm over his eyes.

"You're wrong. I wouldn't hate you for doing something we both wanted."

"Yes, you would," he repeated with the conviction of a man who knew the truth. "What happened was my fault, and I'm sorry. I'm sorry I started this. I was drunk. I'm not drunk anymore."

She stiffened beside him. "I thought . . . Does that mean what happened here didn't mean anything to you? Was it just the whiskey?" A tremble in her voice betrayed her pain at the thought.

He let out a harsh breath. God, how he wished it were that easy. But nothing about his life had been simple since he'd met her. "No," he answered, "it wasn't just the whiskey." His body was still hard and hot for her. If she touched him again he wasn't sure he'd be able to stop himself the next time. "Libby, get out of here before I change my mind."

She reached out and touched his arm, and he jumped as if she'd burned him. He pushed her hand away and sat up abruptly. "Libby . . ." he warned.

She sat up beside him in the dark, pulling the sides of her wrapper together. Her eyes burned and her chest ached. She suddenly felt foolish and exposed and angry. But more than any of those things, she felt hurt. Hurt that he could turn her away like this. "All

181

right. If that's what you want, I'll go. I suppose I've made enough of a fool of myself for one night." She started to get to her feet, but he grabbed her wrist, stopping her.

"It's not you, Libby. Don't ever think that. It's me. If I thought . . ." He couldn't finish. He dropped her wrist. "Trust me when I tell you I can only hurt you. You don't belong with a man like me. I can't be what you want, Lib. I'm sorry. Hell, I've already made a mess of things."

Libby turned toward him, and her heart caught in her chest. Even the darkness couldn't hide the agony she saw written on his face. She had no idea what *things* he was talking about, but she sensed there was something he wasn't telling her. He was a man full of secrets. A man with a past she'd probably never know. But she was too proud to beg him for answers he wasn't likely to give, or for the kinds of things a woman wanted from a man. The kinds of things she needed from him.

She rose slowly with her back to him. "I think it's best if we put this behind us and pretend it never happened," she said quietly.

His silence answered her. She took it for consent. Stiffly, with her head held high, she walked out of the barn toward the house, trying hard not to break into a run.

Chase watched her go, uncorking the top on his flask of whiskey. He upended it, letting the liquor burn a path of fire down his throat. Maybe if he got drunk enough, he could forget the things she'd made him feel and the burning ache that had settled in his loins. Maybe he could even forget the hurt he'd heard in her voice.

He tipped his head back and took another swig, hoping the liquor would accomplish what reason couldn't. Someday she'd be grateful for what he hadn't done. He knew damn well he would never be.

Smoke . . . choking and thick . . . the roaring noise of cannonade and men screaming. He was running, but not moving. His gaze fell to the red water at his feet. Nausea roiled at his gut. They were coming . . . and he was sinking into the crimson quagmire. His skin crawled with the knowledge. Panic tightened his chest—his breath came hard and fast, burning his throat.

Futilely, he searched for the gun he already knew was gone. On the blazing shore, the Rebel soldier reached out to him from amidst the fire. Chase looked away, helpless. The man's scream of agony was higher pitched than usual. Looking again, he saw that it was Libby's face that watched him from the flames. A silent scream tore from his body. . . .

Chase jerked awake from the nightmare, drenched in sweat and panting in fear. The dream was a brutally familiar one, except for the ending.

That, he realized grimly, was new.

He blinked in the half-light of dawn, turning his cheek against the scratchy straw, and repressed a groan. A herd of horses was stampeding through his brain. Where the hell am I? he wondered.

Blinking in the half-light, he struggled to reorient himself. Surprisingly he found he was not in the loft but in a stall, and fully dressed, boots and all. How the hell had he gotten there?

Then, with unfortunate clarity, he remembered all of it—the whiskey, Libby, what he'd done to her.

A noise stilled the curse he was about to utter aloud.

Chase opened his eyes to the shadowy light of

dawn with sudden, pulse-pounding alertness. He had the distinct and unsettling feeling he was not alone. His fingers tightened over two fists full of straw. He was listening.

The sound came again.

This time, he recognized the stealthy scrape of boot leather on wood, the sifting fall of straw to the barn floor, the footfalls of a man who did not mean to be heard.

Chase sat bolt upright just as the man evaporated into the hazy morning light through the double barn doors. Instantly, he regretted the haste of the movement and clamped a hand to his forehead. Nevertheless, he lurched out of the stall, aiming for the barn door. The man, if indeed it had been a man, was gone.

Chase considered the possibility that all this had been a figment of his cobweb-cluttered mind. Perhaps no one had been in there. After all, the sneak had disappeared, seemingly into thin air.

On the other hand, if someone had been in the barn or, more to the point, in *his* loft, what the hell was he doing there? Chase's gear was up there. Saddlebags, bedroll . . . *gun*.

Chase narrowed his eyes and made his way up the ladder to the loft. Picking up the rifle that lay beside his things, Chase unloaded it, checked his ammunition carefully, and reloaded. There were no signs that the gun had been tampered with. A frown pulled at the corners of his mouth.

Then his eyes fell to something lying on top of the hay near his bedroll. Chase reached over and picked up a small packet of brown cigarette papers. He recognized them instantly. They belonged to Bodine. It didn't surprise him that he'd been right about the

184

little bastard. But he was disappointed at not catching him in the act.

What had he been doing? Setting some kind of trap? And more importantly, why? If Bodine *was* the one trying to sabotage Libby, where did Chase fit in? Why would Bodine be trying to kill him? And more to the point, why would a two-bit wrangler be trying to undermine Libby's operation? None of it made any sense.

He stuffed the cigarette papers in his pocket, gathered up his gear, and climbed back down the ladder. He had a few questions to ask Early and the other men. He planned to keep close watch on Bodine until he could prove his suspicions.

Behind him the barn door's heavy hinges creaked. Blanking his mind of all thought, Chase dropped his gear and swung his gun around, leveling it at the figure silhouetted by the morning sun.

Chapter Twelve

Chase's heart kicked back into rhythm. It was Tad.

"Holy Moses, Chase! It's just me," the boy exclaimed.

Bloody hell! He could have blown Tad's head off. He lowered the gun, easing down the hammer. "Hell, boy. You and your ma have a bad habit of sneaking up on a man."

"Were you gonna shoot me?" Tad asked incredulously, coming nearer. His blond hair was rumpled from sleep and his shirttails hung out of his suspenders.

"No." Chase answered shaking his head. "I'm sorry I scared you."

"That's okay." Tad reached deep into the pocket of his britches. "I brung ya somethin' to see."

Chase rested his rifle against the wooden beam that supported the loft and hunkered down on the balls of his feet to see the plump creature Tad was holding. A smile curved his mouth. "Well now, that's a fine horny toad, Tad. Where'd you find him?"

"Down by the creek. His name's Charlie. Ma says I gotta make a proper box fer him today or I can't keep him. But he likes my pocket best of all." Tad stuffed the squirming toad back into his britches.

"You're probably right," Chase agreed, ruffling Tad's hair, "but mothers can be downright touchy about toads in the house."

"Yeah." Tad screwed up his mouth in thought. "I was thinkin' . . . maybe . . . um . . . you could help me build him a box." Tad glanced furtively at Chase through a fringe of blond lashes. "I got me some flat tree bark and . . . um . . . string."

Chase knew there were a hundred more important things to be doing. None, however, that meant a fig to Tad. He felt a strange tightening in his chest. This was the kind of question the boy should have been asking his pa. "You got any nails?"

The boy's face brightened. "Nails? Sure! You think we'll need nails? I got 'em. Lots of 'em! And a hammer an' saw, too. You just wait right here," he said, flying toward the tool room. "I'll be back quicker'n you kin say horny toad."

"I'll be right here," Chase answered with a laugh, and he leaned back against a stall partition. His questions could wait a few minutes more. Sometimes, he decided, horned toads and eight-year-old boys took priority.

Chase looked up to see Elliot walking into the barn.

"Morning, big brother," El said with a broad smile. On closer inspection, he added, "Or is it? God, you look like hell, Chase."

"Thanks."

"Don't mention it." El lifted his saddle off the saddletree and slipped a bridle from the tack wall.

"Where are you headed?" Chase asked.

"Box canyon. I drew watch for the day. Early's going to show me the way. We're rotating a few head back up to the canyon, and he wants you along to

187

help him bring another bunch back for breaking."

"Where is Early?"

"Back in the bunkhouse. He was just rolling out of bed when I left."

"What about Bodine?"

El frowned. "I don't know. He was up before me. The less I see of that bastard, the better. Why do you care?"

Chase ignored the question. "Then you haven't seen him this morning?"

"No." El stared at Chase for a long moment. "Why do I get the feeling there's some significance to these questions?"

"Because someone was in here this morning while I was asleep in a stall, and I'm fairly certain it was Bodine. He was up in the loft going through my things."

El's expression turned serious, and his gaze went to the Henry. "Your gun—?"

"Wasn't touched. I checked it. He wouldn't be stupid enough to try the same thing twice." Chase had shared his suspicions with Elliot last night after supper. The same thought seemed to have occurred to both of them.

"Damn," Elliot cursed. "What the hell's going on here? You sure it was Bodine?"

Chase nodded slowly, holding up the cigarette papers. "He left a calling card."

"But why?"

"That's what I intend to find out." Chase stood up stretching his long legs. "Tell Early I'll be ready when he is. I have a few questions to ask him."

Tad came clanking out of the tool room, arms full of saws, hammers, and tree bark slabs. He dumped them at Chase's feet. "First," Chase added with a grin, "I've got a toad box to build."

"A *toad* box?" El repeated with a laugh.

188

Tad pulled the wriggling creature from his pocket. "For Charlie."

"Ah, I see." El gave the brown, lumpy animal an appraising look, then rubbed one finger between the toad's beady black eyes. "That's a toad worthy of a toad box if ever I did see one." Straightening, he added, "Good luck, men. Chase, I'll meet you outside in a few minutes."

"El," Chase called, stopping him and meeting his gaze. "Watch your back."

El nodded. "My thoughts exactly."

A thin line of perspiration beaded Libby's upper lip. The smell of homemade lye soap wafted up to her as she leaned over the oversized kettle of bubbling water and lifted steaming lace-trimmed under-drawers and camisoles out with a flat wooden paddle. After dunking them in another kettle of cool water, Libby wrung the moisture from the garments and carefully hooked them on the line to dry, anchoring them with wooden clothespins.

The heated afternoon breeze flapped through the line of clothes already hanging there. Alongside her personal things, sheets, socks, and some of Tad's britches were bleaching dry under the blazing New Mexican sun. Out of modesty, Libby did the laundry behind the house, out of sight of the corrals and bunkhouse.

She placed her hands at the small of her back and arched backward. Fatigue crept up her spine and made her muscles ache. She'd spent the morning scything fresh grass—hay in the north pasture with Tad and Straw. It was for the horses they kept corralled at the ranch. Replenishing the supply of feed was a job that had to be done several times a week. She thanked God the pasture in the narrow-

189

ended box canyon, where they kept the rest of their herd, had plenty of graze.

Like the horses Chase and Early had taken this morning, the ones still penned here would be rotated back to the canyon after being gelded, broken, and hair-branded with the Honeycutt mark.

Libby's mind kept pace with her hands as she worked, wringing out the wet clothes and hanging them up to dry. Tad had prattled on endlessly about how Chase had helped him build the bark box for his latest pet, and the box never left Tad's side that whole morning. It had served as a constant reminder to Libby of Chase's small kindnesses.

She'd been glad for the physical labor and had thrown herself into the task, as she had done with the washing. But no amount of work could push away the memories of what she and Chase had done last night.

Libby felt an unwanted tightening of her nipples at the memory of his hands on her bare flesh. The ache he'd stirred in her was with her still. She'd spent a sleepless night thinking about what he'd said to her. *You don't belong with a man like me. Trust me, I can only hurt you.* She'd accepted it then. She'd tossed and turned and cried into her pillow.

And finally, she'd decided he was wrong.

Wrong to deny the chance they might have together. Wrong to think he could only hurt her. He was a man filled with heartache. The utter loneliness and vulnerability of his kiss last night had proven that to her. Why couldn't he let himself love her?

What makes a man close himself off so? she wondered. The war? She'd only heard stories of the ugliness of it. And though she'd lost her husband to it, she couldn't begin to know what they must have gone through. She knew enough to know it changed men. Perhaps he only needed the kind of softness a

190

woman like her could give him. She had that softness in her, and only last night realized how much she'd missed sharing it with a man.

Drifter or no, Chase Whitlaw was the best thing to happen to her in a long, long time. But it wasn't as simple as that.

She had fallen in love with him.

It had come to her—just like that—as morning filtered through her bedroom window. She loved him. It didn't matter that she'd only known him a short time. It didn't even matter that he wasn't the type of man she'd envisioned herself with. He was so unlike Lee or even Jonas Harper. Chase Whitlaw was a hard man, self-contained—with troubles she could only guess at. But there was another side to him he'd allowed her to glimpse last night. A part that told her he was kind and gentle and, yes, even vulnerable.

There'd been something between them since the moment he'd met her out in that storm. Something as strong and inevitable as the sun rising in the morning or the steady thudding of her heart. And she knew, despite what he'd said, he felt it, too.

He'd ridden off that morning before she'd even seen him. Her mind was made up. When he got back from the box canyon, she'd—

"Well, ain't them purty little things a-hangin' there?"

Trammel Bodine's low, husky voice, next to her ear, made her jump. She dropped her freshly washed camisole into the dirt. Whirling around, she found him standing close behind her, a smile on his face. Her hand went to her throat and she backed up three steps, eying him warily.

The sleeves of his blue chambray shirt were rolled up past his elbows, revealing darkly tanned, muscular arms. His trousers rode low on his narrow hips, held there by a silver-buckled belt. Over them, he wore a pair of worn-looking leather chaps held up by a single rawhide thong that traversed his lower belly.

He bent down to pick up the dainty, then pushed his hat brim up with a finger. "Aw, now that's a darn shame. Now yer gonna have to wash it all over again." Spreading the delicate garment between his two hands, he gave her a slow smile. "Lace'n all."

She snatched it from his fingers, her cheeks flooded with color. "What do you want, Trammel? I thought you were over in the breaking corrals, gelding the horses with Straw."

"Oh, I was," he said, taking a step toward her, at which she took an equal one back. His heavy-lidded brown eyes raked suggestively down the length of her. "We're done pluckin' prairie oysters. Straw an' the boy decided to hunt up some more trout for dinner."

Libby scanned the distant paddocks. He'd spoken the truth. She was alone with him. A wave of apprehension swept over her. Bodine had always been arrogant and teasing, but he'd never before been so bold. She ducked under the laundry, walked to where the black kettle hung over the fire, and flung the camisole back into the hot water. "Have you halterbroken those stallions Early brought in yesterday?"

"Not yet."

At the jangle of Bodine's spurs, her gaze darted back to the clothesline. He parted two pairs of her cotton underdrawers that were hanging out to dry, and let them slide through his hands. He shrugged as he drew up beside her, hooking his thumbs into his belt. "I just had a hankerin' fer some of that buttermilk you keep inside—if you still have any."

"You want buttermilk?"

"If it ain't too much trouble. Gelding them horses

4 BESTSELLING HISTORICAL ROMANCES BY YOUR FAVORITE AUTHORS CAN BE YOURS, FREE!

Kensington Choice, our newest book club now brings you historical romances by your favorite bestselling authors including Janelle Taylor, Shannon Drake, Rosanne Bittner, Jo Beverley, and Georgina Gentry, just to name a few! Each book is filled with passion, adventure and the excitement of bygone times!

To introduce you to this great new club which is part of Zebra Home Subscription Service, we'd like to send you your first 4 bestselling historical romances, absolutely free! And once you get these 4 free books to savor at home, we'll rush you the next 4 brand-new books at the lowest prices available, as soon as they are published.

The way the club works is that after your initial FREE shipment, you will get our 4 newest bestselling historical romances delivered to your doorstep each month at the preferred subscriber's rate of only $4.20 per book, a savings of up to $7.16 per month (since these titles sell in bookstores for $4.99-$5.99)! All books are sent on a 10-day free examination basis and there is no minimum number of books to buy. (And no charge for shipping.) Plus as a regular subscriber, you'll receive our FREE monthly newsletter, *Zebra/Pinnacle Romance News*, which features author profiles, contests, subscriber benefits, book previews and more!

 So start today by returning the FREE BOOK CERTIFICATE provided. We'll send you 4 FREE BOOKS with no further obligation: A FREE gift offering you hours of reading pleasure with no obligation...how can you lose?

We have 4 FREE BOOKS for you
as your introduction to
KENSINGTON CHOICE!
To get your FREE BOOKS, worth
up to $23.96, mail the card below.

FREE BOOK CERTIFICATE

Yes! Please send me 4 Kensington Choice (the best of Zebra and Pinnacle Books) Historical Romances without cost or obligation (worth up to $23.96). As a Kensington Choice subscriber, I will then receive 4 brand-new romances to preview each month for 10 days FREE. I can return any books I decide not to keep and owe nothing. The publisher's prices for Kensington Choice romances range from $4.99-$5.99, but as a preferred subscriber I will get these books for only $4.20 per book or $16.80 for all four titles. There is no minimum number of books to buy and I may cancel my subscription at any time, plus there is no additional charge for postage and handling. No matter what I decide to do, my first 4 books are mine to keep, absolutely FREE!

Name _____

Address _____ Apt. _____

City _____ State _____ Zip _____

Telephone ( ) _____

Signature _____

(If under 18, parent or guardian must sign)

Subscription subject to acceptance. Terms and prices subject to change.   DF02K7

4 FREE
Historical Romances
are waiting
for you to
claim them!

(worth up to
$23.96)

See details
inside....

KENSINGTON CHOICE
Zebra Home Subscription Service, Inc.
120 Brighton Road
P.O.Box 5214
Clifton, NJ 07015-5214

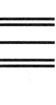

AFFIX
STAMP
HERE

works up a man's thirst." He slowly ran his tongue over his lips while his eyes held hers.

Libby's gaze went from his mouth to the blood spattered on the front of his shirt and the tips of his boots from the gelding. Her stomach roiled. If buttermilk would get rid of him, then she'd get some. "It's no trouble at all. I'll . . . uh, I'll be right back with it."

The house was dark and cool as she went in through the back door. She walked straight to the kitchen, braced the palms of her hands on the wooden table, and took a deep steadying breath. She didn't know why Bodine scared her so, but something about the way he looked at her sent chills up her spine.

She poured a cupful of cool buttermilk from the pitcher she kept in the adobe niche. When she turned around, she almost ran smack dab into his chest. A gasp of surprise escaped her.

He caught her by the upper arms, and his mouth crooked into a smile. "Scare ya?"

"Yes," she said pulling away. "You did. I didn't even hear you come in. Why didn't you wait outside for me?"

"It's hot out there," he said, relieving her of the cup. "Thought I'd save you the trouble of bringing it all the way out to me." He gestured toward the pitcher. "Have some with me?"

"I'm not thirsty." Libby backed up a step and watched while he downed the buttermilk in one long gulp. He wiped his mouth off on the shoulder of his shirt, then handed the tin cup back to her.

"Much obliged, ma'am."

"You're welcome," she said, turning to put the cup on the counter near the dry sink. "Now if that's all—"

Trammel trapped her there against the counter by bracing an arm on either side of her. "Not necessarily . . ."

Shocked, Libby let out a harsh breath and bent backward against the sink. Their bodies didn't touch, but Libby could feel the heat radiating from his skin. He smelled of sweat and horses and, dully, of tobacco. The look in his eye was a frank invitation. "Don't—" she began.

"Don't what? Don't look at you like you was a woman? Is that why you wear them britches all the time?"

"You're making a mistake." The warning in her voice was clear.

He didn't move closer, nor did he back away. "You're a fine-lookin' woman, Miz Libby. You know, seein' them frilly things out there and"—he filled his lungs with her scent—"smellin' you just now made me think how lonely it must get fer a woman like you out here without a man."

"Trammel . . ." She closed her eyes and swallowed hard. Fear twisted, like a fine thread, around her throat. No one would hear her now if she screamed.

"Then again"—he shifted his hips, but still didn't lay a hand on her—"maybe you ain't so lonely. Maybe you already found somebody to scratch that itch."

Like flashing images, pictures of her and Chase together darted through Libby's mind. Could Trammel possibly have seen them together? The mere thought of it made her sick to her stomach. "You don't know what you're talking about," she declared and pushed against his arms to free herself, but she might as well have been trying to escape the steel jaws of a trap. "If you don't let me go right his minute, I'll—"

"Step away from her, Bodine, before I blow your head off."

Libby whirled to see Chase standing in the doorway of the house, his rifle primed and aimed straight at Bodine's back. His voice was hard and cold as a winter freeze.

"Well, if it ain't the bluebelly," Bodine taunted, easing his hands away from the counter, freeing Libby.

Libby had never been so grateful to see anyone in her life, but she found herself frozen to the spot by the deadly violence she read in his blazing green eyes. "Chase—"

"You gonna shoot me for talkin' to the lady, Whitlaw? I ain't armed," Bodine told him with a smile, lifting his arms away from his hips. "I didn't touch her. Ask her yourself." Chase's hard gaze slid inquiringly to Libby.

Libby was furious with Bodine for scaring her, but she couldn't let Chase kill him over it. "He didn't touch me, Chase. He's telling the truth."

Chase sneered. "You don't have to touch a woman to get her dirty, Bodine. Move away from her. Outside."

The smugness had fled from Bodine's expression. Raw anger had replaced it. He backed up, keeping his eye on the weapon poised inches from him. "You got no call to keep that thing pointed at me. I told you I'm unarmed."

The heat outside hit them like a wall, fueling the tension between them. "Funny you should mention this gun," Chase said without a trace of humor in his voice. "It's been a little unreliable lately. In fact, it nearly blew up in my face the other day. You wouldn't happen to know anything about that, would you?"

Bodine paled. "How would I know about yer gun?"

"Because I think you're the one who rigged it, that's how."

"Chase . . ." Libby gasped. "What are you saying?"

Bodine's Adam's apple bobbed in his throat. "You accusin' me, Yankee?"

"Are you denying it?"

"Hell, yes, I'm denyin' it. What would I want to cripple yer gun for?"

"I've been asking myself the same question. You had the opportunity that morning when you were saddling the horses. It would only have taken a few seconds to empty a cartridge of powder and replace it in the breech."

Bodine let out a snort of laughter and looked to Libby. "You ain't gonna listen to this, are ya? He loads a bad cartridge into his gun and he's accusin' me of tryin' to kill him. I think this Yankee's playin' with a few cards shy of a full deck."

Chase pulled a cartridge from his vest pocket and threw it at Bodine who fumbled to catch it. "Those pry marks look familiar, Bodine? That bullet was tampered with. I say you did it."

Bodine's dark eyes narrowed into slits. Sweat beaded on his forehead. "He's crazy. That's what. You hired yerself a goddamn lunatic, Miz Libby."

Libby's shocked gaze went from Bodine to Chase.

"Oh, yeah?" Chase pressed, taking a furious step toward him with the gun. "What about all the other accidents happening around here, Libby? Doesn't it strike you as a coincidence they all started about the time Bodine came to work for you? The fire, losing stock, Will Barlow's accident? All of it aimed at chipping away at the underpinnings of the Double

196

Bar H. All aimed to make you fail. And every time, Bodine was there—with the opportunity.''

"And so was every other man on this place!" Bodine growled. "You can't pin any of that on me. You ain't got one lick of proof.''

Early stepped around the corner of the house and took in the situation with one look. His mouth was drawn in a thin, hard line, and he clenched and unclenched the fists he held at his sides.

"Tell him, Early,'' Bodine pleaded. "Tell him it ain't so. You was there all them times, just like I was.''

"Miguel remembered seein' you with a knife in yer hand comin' away from Will Barlow's horse.''

"A knife!" Bodine let out a desperate croak of laughter. "I was . . . uh, I was pickin' stones out of the horse's shoes! That's all. That cinch weren't cut with no knife. It wore clean through!''

"A man can cut a string girth to make it look worn out.''

"You ain't sidin' with *him*, are ya, Early?'' Bodine demanded of the older man who stared dispassionately at him. "I don't believe this. Yer gonna take that damn Yankee's word over mine?''

Early stared at him with silent accusation.

Libby pressed her fingertips against her eyes. "Wait a minute. Chase, these are serious accusations. Have you got any proof of all this?''

"He was up in my loft this morning, going through my things.''

The color left Bodine's flushed face, and his mouth dropped open. "He ain't got no proof. He was asleep. He didn't even see—'' Bodine's mouth snapped shut as he realized what he'd said.

Chase lowered his gun and smiled grimly. He held up the cigarette wrappings, sealing his case. "You

197

dropped these." He threw them at Bodine's feet.

A hot breeze whipped at Bodine's stony face, buffeting his hair. A muscle clenched in his jaw.

"Why, Trammel?" Libby asked, shaking her head with disbelief. "Why would you do those things to me? To the ranch?"

"Shee-it. You got *nothin'* on me. *Nothin'*," Bodine replied hotly, digging the blood-spattered toe of his boot into the sandy soil. "I didn't do none of them things Whitlaw said. And last I heard, bein' up in a hay loft weren't no crime."

Chase's green eyes had gone dark with fury. He took a menacing step toward Bodine. "You almost killed me, you sonofabitch—"

Early grabbed his arm, stopping him. "Messin' with another feller's personal things is crime enough to get yore sorry ass thrown off'n this place, Bodine," Early told him. "Get your gear together and drift."

Incredulous, Bodine looked to Libby in a last-ditch effort to save his job. "You're buyin' all this? You're gonna take the word of that no-account Yankee over mine? You need me, lady." He jabbed an angry finger in her direction. "You know it and I know it. Without me, who's gonna break them horses for you? Huh? How you gonna get that contract in on time?"

Libby turned her head away, unable to bear looking at him. "We'll get by. You heard Early. You're fired. Get your gear together. Early will draw up your pay."

Bodine blew out a harsh laugh and sent a snarling smile Libby's way. "You're just bent out of shape because I looked at you like you're a woman today, instead of the man you're always tryin' to be—"

Chase's fist smashed into Bodine's face before he could get the whole insult out. Bodine was nearly air-

198

borne with the force of the punch, and he landed hard in the dirt several feet away. Chase reached down and grabbed the dazed man by the front of his shirt. "That was for Libby," he snarled into his face. "Personally, I'd like to break your worthless neck." Instead, he shoved Bodine back down into the dirt and started to walk away.

Bodine sat up, grabbed his aching jaw, and dabbed at the blood trickling down the side of his mouth. "You got more guts than brains, Whitlaw."

Slowly he got to his feet and picked up his dusty hat. His smile was slow and he looked as dangerous as a coiling snake when he turned back to Libby. "I'll go," he said, backing up a step or two, "but while yer pointin' fingers, why don't you ask this lily-white drifter what he's doin' with that little trinket of yours in his saddlebags? The one with yer picture inside."

Chapter Thirteen

The color left Chase's face in a rush as he wheeled on the wrangler. "Goddamn you, Bodine!" Chase launched himself at him again, driving him back against the rounded adobe *horno*. Bodine's head cracked against the rock-hard outdoor oven, but he brought a fist up and snapped Chase's head back. Chase staggered back a step, but, then in a mindless rage, dove at Bodine, sending them both crashing to the ground. Over and over they rolled, pummeling each other with their fists. Dust billowed up in a cloud around them. Vaguely, Chase heard Early shouting at Libby to stay back.

He wanted to kill Bodine, string him up by his heels and make him suffer long and hard for telling her this way. His hands closed around Bodine's throat and his fingers tightened, cutting off the other man's airway.

Only Libby's plaintive cry kept him from snapping Bodine's windpipe in two.

"Stop it! Please, Chase! Let him go!" she cried, dragging at his arm. "Don't kill him."

For the first time Chase could see Bodine's face, see his eyes bulging from lack of oxygen, and he realized

200

how close he'd come to killing the man. He slackened his grip on Bodine's throat and rolled off him.

Trammel groaned and flung his head back, gasping for air. "Sonofa—" he rasped, unable to complete the word for the ache in his throat.

Chase got up slowly. His chest heaved with the effort to control the sickness welling up inside him. He swiped at his bloody mouth with the back of his hand, and the fight left him as soon as he looked into Libby's stricken eyes.

"Get up, Bodine," Early ordered. "Get yer gear and get out." Bodine slowly rolled to his feet, massaging his reddened neck.

"No." Libby put a hand on Early's arm. "Not until he tells me what this is all about. What were you saying, Bodine? What did you mean about the trinket?" she demanded.

"Go on," Bodine taunted in a hoarse voice. "Why don't ya ask him? Ask him how he come by that little silver locket of yours. Maybe he's been stealin' right out from under your trusting little nose."

Libby's gaze went from the taunting mockery in Bodine's eyes to the misery in Chase's. Confusion muted her senses, and she stared at him blankly. "Silver locket? What's he talking about? I don't have a—" The words died in her throat and a cold knot formed in her stomach as she met the grim, confirming look Chase was giving her. She'd had a locket like that . . . once.

Stunned, she watched Chase turn and walk to his horse as if he were a condemned man headed to the gallows. He reached inside his saddlebags and pulled something out. Libby's heartbeat pounded in her ears. Silently, she prayed it was all a mistake. A horrible mistake.

Chase reached for her clenched fist and opened it

201

with his fingers. Gently, he pressed the warm metal into her hand and closed her fingers around it.

"I didn't steal it, I swear to you. But I never meant for you to find out this way."

Numbly, Libby opened her hand and stared at the silvery object he'd placed in it. The filigree locket winked in the sunlight as she touched it with trembling fingers. It had been years since she'd seen it, since she'd given it to Lee when he'd left for the war. But it had been her mother's before that and was as familiar as her own hand. These past two years, she'd assumed it was buried with her husband in Virginia soil.

Bewildered and cold with shock, she looked up at Chase. "This belonged to my husband. H-how did you get it?"

Chase stared at her, unsure of what to say now that the moment he'd dreaded for so long had arrived. He'd meant to plan his words carefully. Choose his time.

Bodine smiled victoriously. "There's yer thief. He ain't so all-fired noble now, Libby, is he?"

Libby turned angrily to Bodine. "Get out," she gritted through clenched teeth. "Get out now, and don't let me see your face on my ranch again."

Bodine's mouth narrowed into a straight line. "You're still takin' that thief's word over mine?"

"I've had enough of you to last me a lifetime, Trammel. I'm happy to have the excuse to be rid of you, if you want to know the truth."

"Fine. I'll go," he replied. "You just make sure you have my pay ready. I got *five* days comin'."

"I'll have it ready," Early replied, shoving Bodine toward the bunkhouse. "Not that you deserve it. Get movin'." Bodine stalked away, slapping his hat against his thigh to rid it of dust. Early turned back to

Libby and gave Chase an up-and-down look. "You need me here, Miz Libby?"

"No." The word was strangled and abrupt. "Leave us alone, will you, Early?" The older man nodded curtly and walked off after Bodine. Libby clutched the locket to her breast and glared at Chase. "Well?"

"I think you should sit down first," Chase said, touching her elbow and guiding her toward the house.

She shrugged off his arm and planted her feet where she stood. Dread seeped into her bones like a draft of cold air. "Don't touch me. Say what you have to say."

Chase sighed. "Libby, I'm sorry you had to find out this way. I meant to tell you before—"

"Tell me what?" she asked in a broken whisper. "How did you come by this locket? Lee would never have parted with it willingly. I know that as well as I know myself."

Chase raked a hand through his hair. "He gave it to me as he was dying."

"You s-saw him die?" She shook her head, still not understanding. "But why would he give it to you? You . . . you're a Yankee. He was . . . how could he have . . . ?"

"We fought for the same piece of ground in the Wilderness campaign in Virginia." Chase's jaw tightened. He wished he could lie, but he knew varnishing the truth would only make things worse. "I shot him."

Libby sucked in a lungful of air and felt the blood rush from her face. She swayed on her feet and braced herself against the sun-warmed adobe wall behind her. She could barely hear for the roaring in her ears. "No . . ."

He extended a steadying hand toward her, but she

203

shoved it away. "You k-killed my husband? You killed Lee?" After several long heartbeats, he answered her.

"Libby . . . let me explai—"

Her open hand connected with his face in a ringing slap that sent Chase staggering back a step. As if he'd expected it, there was no surprise written on his face, only four red welts where her fingers had stung him.

She pressed her own stinging hand against her lips. *"Damn you."*

Chase's jaw tightened and he looked away from her. "It was war, Libby. I didn't know him. I didn't know *you.* I only knew what I was there to do. What we were *both* there to do. Your husband and I fell together in an explosion that ripped the ground from under us."

Numbed into silence, Libby could only shake her head.

Chase turned away from her, his voice growing clipped and unsteady. "Both of us were lying there in the middle of that . . . that piece of hell. He was dying. He wouldn't have given that locket to me if he'd had a choice. But there was no one else. He asked me, begged me to get it to you . . . to tell you . . ." Chase faltered, feeling sick right down to his soul.

"What? Tell me what?"

". . . that he loved you. He wanted you to know that he loved you."

"Ohhh, God," she moaned, staggering away from him toward the house. "Lee . . ."

"Lib—"

She whirled on him, her eyes filled with such hatred he rocked back as if she'd struck him again. "Don't call me that. You have no right to call me that. How could you come here and . . . how could you let me think—?"

204

"Please, listen to me—"

"Why?" she demanded, tears glimmering in her silvery eyes, threatening to spill down her cheeks. "Why didn't you tell me?"

"God, I—I wanted to. So help me, I was going to. I should have." From her expression, he knew she was remembering all the times he could have told her and didn't, and he cursed himself again.

Dragging his hands over his face, he shook his head. "But I thought you needed my help then, more than you needed the locket. That's what I told myself anyway. I planned to give it to you when I was . . . done."

"Oh, did you?" Libby let out a laugh that bordered on a sob. "Well, you can go to hell, Chase Whitlaw. What gives you the right to go around playing God, meddling in other people's lives? How dare you make a decision like that for me? You were holding onto *my* locket, *my* memories as if they were some kind of ransom."

The words poured out of her like venom. She saw him wince, and was glad of it, as the sharp edges of her words penetrated. "Did you think you could ease your conscience by helping out the poor woman you made a widow? Did you think it would make it easier to look me in the eye and tell me this if you made me . . . care for you?" Her throat momentarily closed as she held back tears. "Or was it your plan to c-completely humiliate me before you were done?"

"No." His back was ramrod straight and his fists were held tightly at his sides. But his eyes were squeezed shut with misery. "I'm sorry about your husband. Sorry that I made a mess of things here. I never meant for things to . . . I never meant to hurt you, Libby."

Libby clutched the silver locket against her as if it would protect her from the feelings she'd harbored

205

for him only minutes ago. Her emotions were too raw for her to feel anything but hatred for him now. "Why did you come here? Why didn't you just send me a letter like the army did two years ago?"

Ah, that was the question. Why had he come? His reasons seemed unjustifiable now. Indefensible. "I gave him my word," Chase replied slowly. "I felt . . . I owed you more than a cold letter in the post."

"You were wrong. You don't owe me anything. I think you had better go." The words hung in the sweltering air between them for several long heartbeats.

Chase bowed his head, ringing the brim of his hat in both hands, his emotions draining into that yawning black pit that had grown in him since the war. "Is that what you want?"

Libby's voice, when she spoke, was harsh and unforgiving. "Do you think I could ever look at you after today without seeing the man who took my son's father from him? Do you think I could ever forgive you for this?"

She saw that his eyes had gone flat and lifeless as blades of sun-faded grass. He stared out past the broad sweep of land dotted with chamisa and sagebrush, at the still-white peaks of the Sangre de Cristos, and she felt the smallest pang of remorse. But not enough to take her words back.

"No," he answered at last. "I figured it this way." He sounded defeated, beaten. He ran a hand through his long dark hair and slowly settled his hat back on his head. "I'll get the last of my gear together and get out of here. Should I . . . say good-bye to Tad?"

"I'd rather you didn't. He liked you. It will only make it harder for him."

He nodded and swallowed hard. "All right. Good luck to you. I hope . . ." Words failed him, and he looked up at her one last time to see tears cutting a path down the dust on her cheeks. "Good-bye, Libby."

"Just go. Please. Just go."

Libby held back her sobs until she'd crossed the darkened threshold of the adobe, and she didn't look back until she heard Chase riding off the Honeycutt ranch and out of her life. Forever.

"It's all *your* fault," Tad accused, his young eyes filling with tears.

A string of fish Libby wouldn't have the heart or stomach to cook that night, dangled from his small fist, water dripping onto the *jerga*-covered common-room floor.

"He was gonna teach me to whistle, an' we was gonna catch fireflies tonight for Charlie. *Why* did you send him away?"

"I'm sorry, Tad." Libby battled her own tears and ran a hand comfortingly over Tad's arm. She saw no point in telling him the truth. It would only shatter whatever memories he had of Chase. "He had to go."

Tad pulled away angrily. "No, he didn't. He liked it here. He liked me, even. You had a fight and you made him go, didn't you? Just like Pa."

"*What?*"

"Just like Pa, you made him go away."

His words cut her like a knife. "I didn't make your pa go away. He wanted to go."

"You was cryin' then, just like now. I heard you arguing about it with Pa when you thought I was asleep. And then he went away. And he never came back." Tad flung the fish into the dry sink and stood with his back to her. The setting sun was framed in the open back door.

"Tad, that was a long time ago."

"I remember," he retorted defiantly.

"Your pa went because he wanted to go. I didn't want him to leave, Tad. I was begging him not to go. That's what you heard us arguing about."

"You didn't like Chase. That's why you sent him away."

"That's not true. I did . . . like him. But it was time for him to go."

"He didn't even say good-bye to me," Tad said in a small voice.

"He was sorry about that, Tad. He said so."

"Is he gonna come back?"

She slowly shook her head. Tad sent her one last accusatory look and disappeared at a run out the back door.

Libby sat staring after him, feeling suddenly as fragile as an autumn leaf in the wind. Tad's words about his father had hurt. She'd had no idea he'd blamed her for his father's going.

Perhaps she should have told him the truth about Chase. He had a right to know what happened to his father, after all. But no. As painful as it was for her to know—at last—the circumstances of Lee's death, it would be twice as hard on Tad. Someday she'd tell him all of it and give him the locket—his father's last legacy.

Tell her I loved her. How she'd longed to hear those words from Lee when he was alive. Now they were all she had left of him. Those and the locket.

Her fingers tightened around the keepsake in her hand. Slowly she sprung the lock and opened it. Inside was her photograph, the one Lee had made her have taken in Santa Fe one month before the war had stolen him away. How young she had looked then. How naive she'd been before life had taught her such hard lessons.

She took a deep breath, holding back the latest round of tears that threatened. Guilt lay heavily upon her, for the tears she'd shed that day weren't so much for Lee. She'd done her grieving for him years ago. This time they were for Chase, the one man who'd made her believe she could love again—the man who'd done nothing, but lie to her from the start. She'd cried until her chest hurt; then she'd cried some more.

But her tears had changed nothing.

The foolish notion of love had died in her this very day. She had to be practical now. Wasn't that the word Jonas Harper had used? When he'd said it a few days ago, it had sounded so cold and hard. Now she knew he'd been right. She couldn't make this ranch work with three men and a boy. With Bodine, Chase and most likely Elliot gone now, there was no way she could meet her deadline for the Army contract. Without that contract, her ranch would be taken over by the bank that held the mortgage.

She had no choice, really. No choice at all. Tomorrow morning she'd do what she should have done a long time ago. She would lay to rest all of her romantic notions and be practical for a change.

The setting sun bloodied the snow-covered slopes of the Sangre de Cristos with crimson light. Dark clouds scudded along behind the craggy peaks, shadowed by approaching night. To Chase's right, thick stands of aspen and arrow-straight spruce marked the subtle rise in altitude. At nearly seven thousand feet, the air temperature dropped perceptibly as the sun began to sink behind the mountains. Chase indifferently shrugged on his leather-caped duster and stared straight ahead at the sage-dotted high desert without really seeing it.

Neither the eerie beauty of the mountains nor the darkening sky captured Chase's interest. He'd headed Blue, for lack of a better destination, toward the box canyon at the edge of Libby's ranch, where El was standing watch. But he felt no particular need to hurry. For the first time in years, he had nowhere to go and nothing to occupy his thoughts but regrets. He paid little notice when Blue stopped now and then along the way to crop at the tufts of blue-green grama grass or to trim the delicate yellow flowers from the tips of sage.

His thoughts weren't on the cold or the raw sacred beauty of the land around him, but on the woman he'd left behind. Guilt ate at him. A hollow ache, the kind he'd never expected to feel again, twisted his insides. How had everything ended up so wrong? He'd meant to help her and had ended up hurting her.

What did you expect? That she would forgive you for lying to her?

No.

That she would welcome you back into her arms after she learned you killed her husband?

No, damn it. She has every right to hate me. I got exactly what I expected and certainly what I deserved.

Except you didn't expect to fall in love with her, did you, Whitlaw?

With gut-wrenching, head-over-heels intensity, the realization hit him. Chase reined in his horse with a jerk and took a few deep breaths. Blue stamped impatiently, snorted, and gave a shake to his bridle.

It was true, by God. He *was* in love with Libby. He'd thought himself incapable of ever feeling such a tender emotion again. The death and destruction he'd seen during the war had hardened him against ever again taking such a foolish risk. But Libby hated him now and would always hate him for his part in Lee's death. There wasn't a damn thing he could do about it.

A whisky-jack's shrill cry came from the branches of a nearby stand of aspen, and the jay swooped in a flash of gray out of the trees. Blue's ears pricked up at the sound, and Chase leaned over to lay a soothing hand on the horse's neck.

He heard the distinctive click of a gun's hammer and saw a flicker of movement in the trees, just as he was struck across the right temple with a fiery blow. Lights exploded in his head, and he fumbled frantically for the gun strapped to his hip. His hand closed around it, but before he could lift it up, two more bullets tore wickedly into his side and shoulder.

Chase groaned and doubled over the saddle as he fought the hot, branding agony. Bloody hell! He hadn't even seen it coming. Fury rose like bile in his throat.

Bodine.

Gritting out a curse, he made a grab for the saddle horn and hung on as Blue lurched into a jarring run. Darkness closed in on him in an ever-tightening spiral. He sensed that his hands were losing their grip as he slipped inevitably into that nebulous black void. He felt himself falling, falling.

As the hard earth rose up to meet him, his last conscious thought was of Libby. He should have told her he loved her. This time there'd be no one to tell her that when he was gone.

Chapter Fourteen

Jonas Harper felt every one of his forty-two years as he led the spirited sorrel gelding into the fragrant barn and lit the kerosene lamp that hung from the rafter. Yellow light spilled across the straw-strewn floor, illuminating the large well-equipped stable. He rubbed a hand tiredly across the back of his neck.

It had been a long day, spent branding and ear-marking the late spring calves. His foreman, Cal Stembridge, and most of his men were gone from the ranch, driving the herd south to Fort Sumner and the Bosque Rodondo for sale to the Navaho and Apache reservations. So Jonas had worked hard alongside his small crew of ropers and dallymen. But his muscles were complaining from the work. He wasn't as young as he used to be. He worried about that as he slid the heavy saddle off his gelding and led it into the freshly strewn stall.

The order and cleanliness of the barn suited him. He'd worked hard for this, had built his ranch with his own sweat out of nothing more than dirt. Now it boasted one of the finest *haciendas* in the territory and stock barns to make the wealthiest Eastern landowner jealous. Through sheer determination and know-how—and an economy hungry for cash—he'd acquired almost as much land as Manuel Delgado or Fernando Ortiz, two of the largest of the old Spanish land-grant owners in the territory.

Only two things were still missing from his life: a woman to share his bed and an heir to take it all over when he died. Elda, his wife of eight years, had died three years ago, giving birth to their fourth still-born child. She'd been a fragile city-bred woman, like his sister, Nora. Not at all suited to the hardships of territory life.

When he set his sights on finding a new wife, his first requirement was that she be young enough for childbearing, white-skinned—he'd be damned if he'd leave all this to some half-breed greaser brat—and accustomed to the rigors of New Mexican life. That the flaxen-haired Elizabeth Honeycutt fit perfectly into all those requirements and had extraordinary beauty as well, only made Jonas want her more.

He had fantasized for months about her lying beneath him on his bed, her golden hair wrapped around him as he plunged himself into her ripe softness and got her belly hard and swollen with his seed.

Jonas felt himself grow hard just thinking about her. He decided to seek out Maria tonight, the Mexican whore who worked in his kitchen. She was a lusty one, more than happy to take care of his needs. But every hand on the ranch dipped into her honey pot from time to time and that dulled the pleasure he took from her. It wasn't like having a regular woman in his bed, one he could call his own. He wanted Elizabeth there, and he meant to have her. She'd be so grateful to get out of that shack she and her boy lived in she'd . . .

The scent of burning tobacco cut off the thought, and a shuffle of straw behind him sent Jonas spinning around. In the shadowy light, Trammel Bodine leaned casually against the stall door. The tip of his cigarette glowed red in the dark. It took a minute for Harper's heart to settle back into place. Bodine's long, aquiline features were accentuated by the pall of shadows cast by the lantern light and by a two-day growth of beard.

"Bodine, what the hell are you doing here?"

"Evenin', Harper." He grinned broadly, blowing a smoke ring that drifted lazily toward the other man.

Harper yanked the cigarette from Bodine's mouth and put it out in the water bucket in the corner of the stall. "Are you trying to burn my barn down? Nobody smokes in my barn."

Bodine threw his hands up in front of him. "Okay, okay. Don't get yer dander up. Hell, yer about as touchy as a rim-fired mustang."

Harper pulled the headstall off his horse, clapped it on the backside and sent it toward the manger already filled with hay. "What are you doing here? You're supposed to be at Elizabeth's."

"Yeah, well, there's been a change in plans."

Jonas's gaze narrowed. "What the hell does that mean?"

"It means she cut me loose today."

"She *fired* you?" Harper exploded. "Hell and damnation! For what?"

"It ain't my fault," Bodine argued, setting his jaw so the lean muscles there bulged. "It was that bastard Whitlaw. Somehow, he had it all figured out how I been fixin' things to go wrong on her ranch. Flat out accused me of it in front of everybody."

"And she believed him?"

"I told you she has eyes fer him. Hell," Bodine grumbled, "if she was a chicken she'd a bought a bag of feathers from him. She swallowed the story lock, stock, and barrel. Only thing Whitlaw could prove

214

was that I'd been up in the loft goin' through his things."

Harper raked his fingers through his graying hair. "Damn it!" He paced back and forth for a few seconds before turning back to Bodine. "Did you at least find out who he was—what he wanted—like I told you to?"

"Yeah, but that ain't important no more."

Harper narrowed his eyes. "What are you talking about? You just got through telling me—"

"I mean Whitlaw ain't gonna stand in the way of your courtin' the Honeycutt woman from now on, that's what."

Harper stared at Bodine for a long moment. "You mean he . . . left Elizabeth's?"

Bodine smiled coldly. "You might put it that way. I like to think that I discouraged him like you told me to. Permanent like."

A cold sensation crept up Harper's spine and settled in the pit of his stomach. "You . . . killed him?"

"He had it comin'," Bodine said, rubbing his sore neck. "He tried to kill me first."

Harper leaned a flattened palm against the fragrant barn siding. "God Almighty, I never told you"—he swallowed hard—"to *kill* him."

"See, I don't remember it that way. I remember you wanted him dealt with. I dealt with him. My way."

"I said to stay within conscionable limits, you fool!"

"Ah, see, there's the basic difference between you an' me." Bodine's mouth twisted into an ugly smile. "Good Lord didn't saddle me with a conscience. But I figure that's why you hired me for this job. 'Cause you didn't have the stomach for it yerself. Ain't that right?"

Jonas stared at him disbelievingly. He suddenly

215

felt himself sinking into the mire of his own well-laid plan. "I paid you to convince Elizabeth to marry me by making it impossible for her to manage that place on her own—to see she didn't meet that contract she needs so badly. But I didn't pay you to kill anyone. Now, by God, you've botched that job and implicated me in a murder."

"I done my job, just like you asked. The way I see it, with Whitlaw and me gone, her choices just narrowed down to one. You. Ain't that what you wanted, Harper?"

"Hellfire and damnation!" Harper paced restlessly, but he grudgingly admitted the hardhead might be right. "Are you sure he's dead?"

Bodine pulled Chase's engraved Colt pistol from his belt. "The coyotes used what was left of him fer bait by now. You think he would'a parted with this willin'ly?"

"Put that thing away! Did anyone see you?"

He snorted. "Nobody saw me but Whitlaw. But it's a fact, we didn't part on the friendliest of terms. There's a fair chance the law might try to match me with the doin' of it. But nobody's likely to find his body 'til I'm long gone, and there ain't nobody to connect me with you. Unless, of course, you don't see this thing my way."

Harper's black eyes leapt to Bodine's. "Your way?"

"It's gonna be my neck ridin' under a cottonwood limb if I get caught. The money we agreed on at the start of this job ain't gonna be enough. I figure I need some more to get out of the Territory for a while 'til things cool down."

Sweat trickled down past Harper's ear. "How much more?"

"Five thousand should just about cover it."

Harper let out a snort of disbelief. "You're insane."

Trammel's smile faded and he took a step toward the older man. "Maybe I am. Maybe I'm just crazy enough to tell yer little blond-haired widow what you been doin' to win her over."

"Are you threatening me?"

"If I don't get what I came for, it ain't a threat—it's a promise."

Jonas curled his hands into tight fists. "You little bastard. I paid you well for this deal. You've got no right to blackmail me for your mistakes."

"When you play dirty, you get dirty, Harper. Just ain't no way around it. You keep the money in your house?"

"I don't keep that kind of money around," Harper denied, straight-faced.

"Bullshit," Bodine barked. Cocking Chase's gun, he aimed it at Harper. "Everybody know's you don't hold no cotton with banks. I ain't playin' *games* here Harper."

Harper stared at the gun and thought briefly of the one still strapped to his thigh. He had no chance of getting the drop on this bastard now. "All right. There's no need for that. I'll get it for you. You wait here."

Bodine grabbed his arm and pressed the barrel against Harper's throat, a wild look lighting his eyes. "Do I look *stupid* to you?" He slipped Harper's gun from its holster and stuffed it into the back of his belt. "I ain't waitin' anywhere's fer you. We're a-goin' together."

Heat lightning lit the eastern sky, illuminating the way back to the house. They passed beneath the expansive adobe archway that led to the outer courtyard of the fine rectangular-shaped *hacienda*. The mica-specked sand that made up the adobe's smooth outer layer glittered and winked in the moonlight.

The prospect of imminent death heightened

217

Harper's senses and cleared his mind. It had been a mistake to get involved with Bodine in the first place. *When you play dirty, you get dirty*. That was right. He felt irreconcilably dirty now, his good intentions turned into something else altogether. It was he who'd been stupid to trust Bodine with Elizabeth. He'd kill him for this. Someday, he'd kill him.

Nora was walking into the parlor with a cup of tea when Jonas came out of his study with the stranger and led him to the ornately carved front door. The two were exchanging quiet words she couldn't quite hear. Suddenly, the stranger turned toward her and caught her watching them. Though a hat shaded most of his face, she saw his mouth curve into a slow smile. The man's insolent gaze traveled the length of her before he slipped out the door into the darkness.

Nora frowned. The stranger had looked familiar somehow, and though she couldn't place him, she knew she'd seen him before. His look had sent a chill right down to her toes. She clamped a hand on the throat of her thin cotton wrapper and watched her older brother shut the door. He turned back to her slowly, his expression clouded with anger and something else that kept him from meeting her eyes.

"Jonas?"

He brushed past her. "Did you save some supper for me?" he asked abruptly.

"Of course," she answered, following him toward the kitchen. They passed through the well-appointed dining room with the lace-covered mahogany dining table and sideboard they'd had sent West from New York. Beneath their feet, a colorful rug imported from Persia cushioned the cold earthen tiles.

"I saved you a plate," Nora said, reaching for the plate she had warming on the black iron stove that heated the corner of the kitchen. "You were very late. I didn't even hear you come in."

"We had a lot more mavericks than we expected this season. We're still not finished with the branding." He settled himself at the small wooden kitchen table with his food.

Nora sat tentatively beside him. "Jonas, who was that man?"

"Nobody." Harper stared at his plate of food.

"He couldn't very well be nobody," she persisted. "I saw him with my own eyes. Who was he?"

Harper's fork hesitated on its way to his mouth. "Just a cowboy lookin' for work."

"At *this* time of night?"

"He was just passing through."

"Did you hire him?"

"No." His fork twisted in his beefy hand. His agitation was growing.

"I'm glad. I didn't like the looks of him."

"You *forget* about that man," Jonas nearly shouted. "Forget you ever saw him. You *hear* me?"

Nora stared at Jonas, shocked by his harsh words. Then she tipped her chin up in anger. "Don't make the mistake of thinking you can speak to me the way you did Elda, Jonas. I'm here at your invitation, and I can go back to Richmond the same way I came. I won't be talked to as if I haven't a brain in my head. If you're hiding something from me, I have a right to know what it is."

Jonas pounded his fist on the table, making the silver rattle. "Damnation, woman! It's no wonder you're still a spinster. No man would put up with that mouth of yours!"

Nora colored deeply and drew her lips into a thin straight line. "Fine. If that's how you feel, I'll be packed and gone by—"

"Nora . . ." Jonas's chair scraped against the tiled

219

kitchen floor and he stopped her with one hand.

She flashed a furious, wounded look at him.

"I didn't mean that," he told her with a sigh. "Forgive me. It's been a trying day, and I'm afraid I took it out on you. You know how much I appreciate your coming here. I don't know what I would have done this past year without you." His black eyes appealed to her. "I don't want you to go. I'm sorry."

Silent, Nora stared at the floor. She'd never heard Jonas apologize to anyone before, and the gesture softened her anger. "You're right, you know. I'm twenty-four years old. I am a spinster. And sometimes my mouth goes on ahead of my brain."

Jonas shook his head. "You've got more between those ears than any other woman I know. Elda, God rest her soul, had half your brains and none of your looks. Any man would be lucky to have you."

She forced a smile. "I have the children I teach. That's enough. I'll be going out to see Tad and Libby tomorrow, by the way."

Jonas stiffened at the mention of the Honeycutts. He turned away and sat down to his food again. "Give Elizabeth my best."

"I will." This time Nora let his curious unease pass, determined not to stir the waters again. Jonas hadn't yet explained who the stranger was, nor why he'd gotten so angry about him. It was probably just as Jonas had said; he was overworked. Still, that man's presence had made her uncomfortable. She decided to keep her eyes open to be sure he didn't come back.

Only death could account for the cold that penetrated him like fingers of ice, Chase decided foggily, as his eyes opened to utter darkness. He must be dead.

Why else would he be sucking in dirt with every breath?

A low moan issued involuntarily from somewhere deep in his chest when he lifted his head and turned his cheek slightly to one side. He pressed his lips shut and tried to swallow. His mouth felt like a dried-out tumbleweed and his throat flat-out refused to cooperate. But he was much relieved to find himself on top of the soil, instead of underneath it. He suddenly craved a long, slow pull of forty-rod whiskey. . . .

A puff of warm, moist air *whuffed* oddly against the fingers of his outstretched right hand. That strange sensation was accompanied by a demonic kind of snort close to his ear. Unnerved by the sound, Chase cautiously turned his head and chanced a look up. He could see nothing of the beast save a pair of Satanic-looking wide-spread eyes glinting in the darkness. But he could tell the creature was large . . . huge . . . the color of night.

Pain seared into his shoulder and side like a hot poker, repaying him for his sudden movement. Chase let his eyes shut again, allowing the blackness to obliterate the horrific vision.

Damn. He'd died and gone to hell.

The wheels on her buckboard spun over the rocky soil in a whooshing, rhythmic tempo as Libby urged the team down the two-mile rain-rutted lane to Three Peaks, concentrating on their *clackety-clack* sounds that broke the stillness. It was early. The morning sky still boasted the dusky rose blush of sunrise. In the endless pastures surrounding Harper's *hacienda*, cattle still lazed in the long tufts of grass and blue-green chamisa where they'd spent the night.

Libby had no worry about the decorum of the hour. She knew Jonas would be up, tending to business by the time she arrived. And once he learned her purpose in coming, she doubted he'd be offended by her visit.

She flicked the reins over the mare's back and swept a hand over the fine clair de lune-colored muslin gown, tugging at the lace-trimmed neckline. It felt strange to be corsetted and flounced. Uncomfortable, in fact. The last time she'd worn a dress, it had been her black widow's weeds for Malachi's funeral. But widow's weeds seemed somehow inappropriate today, considering her intent.

Tiny mother-of-pearl buttons marched up the front of her bodice and along the outsides of her sleeves from elbow to wrist. They seemed to be choking her. It was more likely resolve that was caught in her throat, she decided, but she'd made up her mind and there was no changing it now.

She was nearly to the house when she saw Nora standing in the lane, waving to her. Libby took a deep, fortifying breath and returned the gesture.

"What a wonderful surprise! Jonas didn't tell me you were coming to call this morning." Nora ran up to greet her.

Libby pulled the mare to a stop, wrapped the reins around the brake handle, and climbed out of the buckboard, holding her skirts out of the way with one hand. "Jonas didn't know I was coming by. In fact, I didn't even know it until last night. I hope it's not an inconvenient time."

"Oh, heavens! We're up with the chickens around here," Nora said, waving off Libby's worries. "But I was going to come to your place today myself, for Tad's lessons. Just yesterday, I received that new McGuffey Reader I told Tad about. I was getting

222

ready to come when I saw your buggy burning a path down the lane. Look at you," she said, eyeing Libby's dress. "You look just wonderful, Libby. I can't remember the last time I saw you in such a pretty gown."

In any gown, Libby thought, tugging at the neckline again. She knew that, coming from Nora, the comment wasn't meant as a criticism, so she didn't take it that way. Pressing her cheek to Nora's, she gave her a warm hug and an extra squeeze for courage.

Nora pulled back and looked squarely at Libby. Her clear brown eyes reflected her concern. "Is anything wrong, dear? You're not ill, are you? You look a bit pale."

Nora's concern made it difficult for Libby to keep tears from forming in her eyes, but she blinked them back ruthlessly and managed a wan smile. "I'm perfectly fine. Nothing's wrong, Nora. I've just come to my senses, that's all."

Nora's eyebrows took a dip. "Come to your senses? Are you sure you're well? I have a pot of sage tea brewing. Won't you come in and have a cup with me?"

Tea sounded wonderful, and Libby was tempted to accept the opportunity to delay. But she couldn't. "I . . . I'd love to Nora. But I really came to talk to Jonas. Is he . . . home?"

"He's still inside, finishing his morning coffee. He's just about to head out to the range to finish the branding with the men. He's been so out of sorts lately. I'm sure your coming will cheer him up. C'mon, I'll take you to him." Nora gestured to a sun-browned cowhand who was on his way to the barn. "Missouri, see that Mrs. Honeycutt's horses get watered."

223

The bowlegged man nodded and shifted the wad of tobacco around in his mouth. "You want me to unhitch 'em, too?"

"No," Libby answered, too quickly. "I won't be here that long."

The inside of Harper's home was as grand as the outside. Thick adobe walls—whitewashed and pristine—kept the *hacienda* cool. Colorful calico strips protected them from floor to shoulder height. Jonas Harper's success was reflected in his dwelling, from the rich carpeting that covered the floor, to the fine furniture, imported from the East, that filled its rooms. A grand piano took up one side of the common room. Libby's fingers' brushed the fine, ebony wood as she followed Nora through the house.

Harper's coffee cup rattled in it's saucer when he looked up from his copy of the *New Mexican Weekly Gazette* and saw her standing in the dining-room doorway. He shot to his feet. "Elizabeth."

She managed a tremulous smile. "Good morning, Jonas."

"What . . . what a surprise." Pleasure and shock registered in his dark eyes. And something else was there, too. It made her distinctly uncomfortable, though she couldn't put her finger on it. His gaze quickly traveled down the length of her, taking in the blue-gray gown she wore. "Come in. Come in. You look lovely, my dear. A dress? To what do I owe this honor?"

Libby cleared her throat and glanced at Nora.

"Won't you join me for a cup of coffee or tea?" he asked. "Have you eaten yet? I can have Soo Ling bring in something for you."

"Thank you, but no. I'm not hungry." The truth was, she'd been unable to stomach the thought of food before coming here. Now, she just wanted to get this over with. She gazed at Jonas unsure how to begin. He frightened her just a little, though she couldn't say why. Perhaps it was the determined light in his dark brown eyes, or the self-confidence he exuded.

For a middle-aged man, he was in remarkably good shape; no paunch softened his middle, though his barrel chest made him appear larger. Only a hint of gray streaked his hair and beard, and he was strong. A self-made man. She didn't now feel any attraction toward him in spite of his earnest pursuit. In time, perhaps that would change.

"I . . . I have something I need to discuss with you, Jonas." She glanced again at Nora, hoping she'd be able to talk with him in private. As close as she felt to Jonas's sister, she had no desire for her to know the cold details of the conversation they were about to have.

Nora smiled and touched Libby's arm, taking the hint. "I'll leave you two to talk. I'll see you when you're finished, Libby."

Jonas motioned Libby to a chair, and she perched upon the edge of it, nervously fidgeting with the fabric of her skirt.

"What can I do for you, Elizabeth?" he asked. Leaning back in the leather-backed chair, he sipped his steaming coffee.

"I've come"—Libby cleared the resistance from her throat—"to accept your proposal of marriage."

225

Chapter Fifteen

Harper bobbled his cup, causing the hot coffee to spill over onto his fingers and the front of his shirt. He let out an involuntary curse and shook the hot liquid from his hand, then sent Libby an astonished look.

She took up a linen napkin and handed it to him. "Are you all right?"

Harper dried his hand and dabbed at the coffee on his shirt. "Yes, yes, of course. It was nothing. Did you say you've decided to *marry* me?"

Libby didn't know what to do with her hands, so she folded them tightly in her lap. "If the offer is still open."

"Open?" he nearly choked. "God Almight—" He caught the curse before he could finish it. "Elizabeth, do you know how long I've waited to hear you say that?" He pulled one of her hands free and sandwiched it between his. A smile creased his sun-bronzed face. "Are you sure about this?"

"Yes, very sure," she answered. "There are, however . . . a few things I'll need in return." Discreetly, she withdrew her hand from his and twisted her fingers together.

Harper made a small inquisitive gesture with his hands. "Anything. What is it?"

She took a deep breath. "First, I'll need a signed agreement from you stating that Honeycutt land will remain in my name after our marriage. You, of course, will have water and grazing rights to it until the time my son, Tad, turns eighteen, when the deed shall revert to him. If he should want to start a ranch of his own, I want him to have that as an inheritance from his father and me."

Jonas studied her thoughtfully before answering. "I am not in great need of more land. Although I'm not averse to using the water on your land for my expanding herds, I have no desire to take that from you and your son. I will have my lawyers prepare an agreement to that effect, if it's what you want."

"I have my own lawyer in mind, if it's all right with you." Libby's palms grew damp with perspiration.

Harper frowned slightly, but gave a brief nod of concession.

"Second," she continued, "as you know, I have a contract with the Army for sixty saddle-broke mustangs due the first of August at Fort Union. It appears now . . . that I won't be able to make that deadline." Her fingers twisted deeper into the fabric of her gown. "I lost two of my men yesterday."

"I'm sorry to hear that. Did they quit on you?" Harper asked, brows raised.

She answered in a whisper. "I'd . . . I'd rather not discuss it."

His face was implacable. "As you wish. I'm sorry all the same."

"That's not why I'm telling you this, Jonas. I'm not looking for sympathy."

Harper leaned back and propped the knuckles of

227

one hand against his lips. He watched her silently, waiting. "Why are you telling me, then?"

"I am . . . loath to renege on the promise to the Army," she went on. "Malachi made it in good faith, and I feel obliged to fulfill it. I would consider it a great favor if you would lend me a few men to finish out that contract so I can leave the Honeycutt reputation intact. Of course, I'll pay you for their time after the herd is delivered."

"My men are cowmen, for the most part. Not horse wranglers."

"I know that. I also know you have a few bronc-peelers working on Three Peaks with your own *remuda*."

Harper smiled slowly. "That's true. I do. I suppose I can spare two men if you're determined. Between my men and yours, I'm sure they can meet your deadline. Just leave all that to me, Elizabeth."

Libby straightened her shoulders. "I intend to see this contract through personally for the Double Bar H, Jonas," she told him firmly.

"Don't be ridiculous, my dear. There's no need for you to—"

"Until I do," she interrupted, "I won't feel free to leave the ranch or the past behind me. Please understand, bringing the herd together is something I feel I must do. It's still my ranch. I'm responsible. It's important to me. We can marry after the herd is delivered."

His long silence told her he wasn't pleased with her decision. Finally, he said, "You're a strong-minded woman, Elizabeth Honeycutt. I suppose you've thought this all through."

"I have," she admitted.

"We could be married this week. You and Tad could be out from under that albatross of yours and living here, under my roof. No more hard work day in and day out. No leaking roof falling down around your ears. Why, you could wear a gown like this every day. Even better gowns. I'll take you to that Jew seamstress in town, Sarah Levinson. I'll have her make you a dozen of them. As many as you like. Think again, Elizabeth."

"I'm not interested in gowns, Jonas. Don't you understand?"

He shook his head. "I'm afraid I don't . . . But what man ever understands a woman? I suppose I have no choice in this, then. You must know I'm anxious to marry you." He placed his hand over hers.

She could feel the dampness of his palm and how his hand trembled. Guiltily, she couldn't help but compare him to Chase and the feelings he'd evoked from her with a mere touch. There was no such experience when Jonas touched her. But then, she'd never expected there would be. For once, she was doing the practical, sensible thing. Such feelings had no place in an arrangement like this.

Libby swallowed hard, enduring his touch. "It won't be long. Only six weeks. After that, I'll be free to be a wife to you."

He smiled a little wistfully, and the fine lines around his eyes crinkled. "Six weeks can seem like a lifetime when you're alone."

Libby was taken aback by the loneliness she heard in his voice. She'd never considered that he might be as lonely as she. Perhaps there was some common ground between them after all.

A smile trembled over her lips. She knew she was pushing her luck. "There is one more thing. When you proposed to me months ago, you asked me to think of the advantages my son would have living here at Three Peaks. Well, I have given that a lot of thought. And you're right. I'll never be able to give him the things he deserves on my own. The one thing I've always wanted for Tad is a formal education. Nora is wonderful, and she will take Tad as far as she's able. But I need your word that in a few years you will allow him to go East to finish his schooling."

"You won't have to worry in that regard, of course. Tad will be taken care of as if he were my own son. Is there . . . anything else?"

If Jonas was a bit peeved over her requests, he concealed it well. She was grateful to him for that. She glanced up shyly, wondering what it would be like to stare over the breakfast table for the next twenty years or so at him.

She felt nothing. Not the slightest pounding of her pulse, not the vaguest lift to her heart. Disappointment scuttled through her, but she managed a smile despite it.

"No," she answered at last. "There's nothing else. Thank you for being so understanding, Jonas. I'm very grateful to you."

Harper rose and took her by the shoulders, bringing her to her feet. He drew her closer to him and unexpectedly kissed her, full on the mouth. She went rigid with surprise, and her mouth remained firmly shut against his eager kiss. His lips were wet, hot, and demanding, and they tasted of coffee and tobacco.

Her stomach roiled. Not simply because of the unpleasantness of his kiss, but because the gesture sealed the bargain she'd made to sell her soul—and so cheaply.

He pulled back and searched her eyes intently. "Elizabeth, is it only gratitude you feel for me?"

She swallowed and checked the urge to wipe his kiss from her mouth. "I won't lie to you, Jonas. I . . .

230

respect you, but I'm not in love with you. Perhaps," she suggested, "it's too soon to expect such feelings."

"It is my hope that one day you'll feel for me what I already do for you. It makes me tremble to simply hold you in my arms," he said, sliding his palms up her arms and drawing her close. "You won't regret marrying me."

She pulled away, unable to look him in the eye. "I . . . I will try to be a good wife to you and to make you happy, Jonas."

He tipped her chin up toward him with his finger. His brown eyes darkened. "While we're laying our cards on the table, I think you should know this, Elizabeth. I want children. And soon. I want an heir. My first wife was never able to give me one."

Libby nodded. She remembered Elda, the fragile, mousey woman who'd been his wife. In all the years Libby had known her, Elda had never carried a child to term, though it had seemed the woman had been almost constantly pregnant. Was this to be her own fate as well? she wondered. Tad's birth hadn't been an easy one, but the midwife had told her the first ones are always the hardest.

Sharing Jonas's bed was part and parcel of the bargain she'd struck. It was something she'd have to endure. Maybe a child would help to bring them closer.

"Good," he replied with a smile. "Nora was coming by today with an invitation to the Independence Day celebration we're having here in two weeks. I think that would be a good time to announce our wedding plans, don't you?"

"Whatever you think is best," she answered without enthusiasm.

"Elizabeth, you've made me very happy today."

Libby smiled tremulously and turned to go. "I'm

231

happy too," she lied. "I . . . uh, I must be getting back. There's a lot to do between now and then."

He led her outside into the morning air that already held the promise of heat, then helped her up into the buckboard, where she pulled on her gloves.

"Can I expect your men soon?" she asked.

"I'll send them over within a day or two."

"Thank you, Jonas. I'm very . . . grateful."

"It is I who should be grateful. I've waited a long time for this." He gave her gloved hand a squeeze.

Nora came out of the barn, leading a sidesaddled mare and wearing a riding habit of black silk. White lace frothed at her throat, hem, and cuffs. A jaunty black velvet hat was perched atop her coiffed hair. The contrast with her pale ivory skin, Libby decided, was striking.

"Want some company?" Nora asked as she drew near. "I might as well ride over with you since I was coming later anyway. That way we'll have a chance to visit."

"Of course, that will be wonderful," Libby told her and tried to sound convincing. She doubted she'd be very good company for anyone this morning.

Nora tied the reins of her mare off at the back of the buckboard, drew her rifle out of her saddle sheath, and placed it on the floor of the wagon beside Libby's.

"You two wait right here," Jonas told them, helping Nora up to the hard wooden seat beside Libby. "It's not safe for you to go gallivanting around the countryside on your own. Your mind is always up in the clouds somewhere, Nora, instead of where it belongs. God know's what kind of trouble you can run into on your own. I'm going to have a man follow you over to the Double Bar H."

"And have one of your hands waste a whole day of

work?'' Nora protested. ''Don't be foolish, Jonas. It's only eight miles and we're both armed.''

''Is it foolish to want to protect my sister and the woman who will soon be my wife?''

Nora's gaze flew to Libby. ''Wife? Libby, does that mean . . . ?''

''Elizabeth's agreed to marry me,'' Harper supplied proudly as he headed off to find one of his men. ''Don't go anywhere until I get back.''

Libby tried to look happy, but her smile was strained. She wished she'd been the one to tell Nora.

''Oh, Libby, I'm so . . . happy for you.'' Nora took Libby's hand.

''I would have told you, but—''

''Don't be silly! The groom should be the first to know.'' She looked at Libby intently. ''Are you happy?''

Startled by the question, Libby met her gaze. ''Happy? Of course.'' She brushed back the tears that refused to stay safely hidden. ''I'm just emotional, that's all.''

A warm smile spread across Nora's face and she patted Libby's hand, but Libby could see the doubt her reticence had planted in Nora's eyes. ''You'll be happy here, Libby. You'll see.''

Within a few minutes, Harper introduced a young, bandy-legged cowhand named Will Tuerney to them. Tuerney was to join them as their guard. After saying farewell to Jonas, they were off, heading back down the lane that led away from Three Peaks.

Libby glanced back at the *hacienda* disappearing in the cloud of dust behind them, knowing that soon she would call that place home. A sadness that felt like defeat swept through her, but she merely straightened her back, gave the traces a jangle, and hurried the team toward the place she loved. The

233

land where her heart would always be.

She and Nora talked of many things on the trip back home; Tad's schooling, her ranch, the Fourth of July celebration Jonas had planned, and his secret surprise. All topics, Libby noted gratefully, which carefully avoided discussing her impending marriage to Jonas.

They were nearly halfway back when Will Tuerney turned back to them and signaled them to pull up.

"What's wrong?" Nora shouted to him as he galloped his buckskin gelding back toward them.

He pointed toward a dapple-gray horse cropping the long grass in the far distance. "That horse is carryin' an empty saddle," he said flatly. "Any notion who owns it, Mrs. Honeycutt?"

Libby shaded her eyes with her hand, and scanned the horizon until she spotted the horse. Then her stomach took a sickening plunge. *It can't be.* "Oh, my God," she breathed out. "It's Blue."

"Blue?" Nora repeated.

Libby gripped the side of the wagon seat tightly. "It's Chase's horse. Chase Whitlaw. But he rode away yesterday. . . ." Her mind whirled with a dozen different possibilities—all of them bad. She remembered that Chase could call the horse with a whistle. If he were able to, wouldn't he have done it? The thought that he could be lying out there somewhere, hurt, tore at her insides. She flicked the traces and steered the wagon overland toward the grazing horse without a single thought as to the inadvisability of such a move.

Will Tuerney was right behind her. Blue lifted his head and nickered at the sight of them. He trotted over to the wagon as they pulled up. Libby scanned the hilly landscape. There was no sign of Chase anywhere.

Will rubbed a finger across the dark smudges on Chase's saddle and looked grimly at the two women. "Blood."

"Oh, no . . ." Libby whispered.

Will twisted in his saddle to get a better look at the surrounding area. A mile or so away, they could all see the ominous circling of turkey vultures high overhead in the cerulean blue sky. Libby's heartbeat faltered at the sight.

Will tied Blue off to the back of their wagon. "You ladies stay right here and keep yer guns out and ready. I'm goin' to go see what them scavengers is a-waitin' for."

"I'm coming with you," Libby told him, jumping down from the buckboard before he could stop her.

"Ma'am"—Will cleared his throat uncomfortably—"Mister Harper told me to watch out fer you two. I think it's best if you stay with the wagon."

Ignoring him, Libby mounted Nora's sidesaddled horse. "Nora, you follow us as best you can. We'll need that wagonbed if we find him."

Will anxiously lifted his hat off, then settled it back on his head. "Aw, heck . . . all right, c'mon then."

With a touch of her heels, Libby nudged the mare into a lope toward the stand of aspen and pine, a mile distant.

Will was the first to spot the black stallion, Diablo, standing like a sentinel in the distance. The animal reared, slashed his front hooves at the cloudless sky, but strangely, made no move to escape them as they neared.

Even from far away, Libby could see the white scars from the grizzly's claw marks on the stallion's neck. Diablo trotted in agitated circles as if he were waiting for them. Thirty feet away, sprawled in his bloody duster, lay Chase, as still as death.

"Damnation," Will muttered. "That black devil's

killed him." He drew his rifle from its scabbard and pulled off a shot at the horse. His bullet tore into the ground at Diablo's feet, sending the horse to galloping. His black mane and tail flew behind him. Will pumped off two more shots, but the stallion escaped, vanishing into the thick copse of trees a half-mile away.

Libby was off her horse and running before the dust had settled. She dropped to her knees beside Chase. Blood and dirt caked his cheek and forehead, and stiffened the beige fabric of his duster at shoulder and side. Merciful God, he'd been shot!

"Oh, Chase . . ." Libby cried. Her hands trembled above him for a moment. She was afraid to touch him, afraid to know. *Please, God, don't let him be dead.* He was so pale and still. She placed trembling fingers at his throat and felt a pulse—weak, but steady. Relief poured through her. Despite the awful things that had happened between them, she never wanted something like this to happen to him. Tears gathered behind her eyes.

At her touch, he moaned low and stirred. "Get up . . ." he murmured in a gravelly voice. "Gotta get up. I'm gonna kill that bastard." He rolled over onto his side and tried to push himself to his feet.

"Chase, please, don't move," Libby warned, holding him down with her hands. "You're hurt."

"Libby?" Chase swallowed and turned his head toward her, blinking away his double vision. A sharp pain ricocheted through his head. He was hallucinating again. Only this time his vision was of an angel, not a demon. She was wearing a dress. *His* Libby never wore dresses. He winced at the pain in his upper back.

"Chase," she whispered, unwittingly smoothing back the shock of dark hair that fell over his eyes.

236

"You're going to be all right, Chase. We're going to take care of you."

He squeezed his eyes shut. "Lost my horse . . . tried to walk back. . . . I didn't get very far. . . . The stallion—"

"Shhh. Don't talk now. I'm here. Just rest. Nora's bringing a wagon."

"Couldn't make it back to the road. How'd you find me?"

"We found Blue first, a mile or so away. Then we saw Diablo. He was practically standing beside you. We thought he was the one who hurt you."

His head rolled against the dirt. "It was Bodine."

She sucked in a breath. It shouldn't have surprised her that Bodine was capable of something as ruthless as back-shooting, but it did.

She bit the edge of her lip as she pushed the duster aside to get a better look at Chase's wounds. She couldn't tell much without ripping his shirt open, but he felt too cold to do that now. The bleeding had mostly stopped. The least serious of his injuries seemed to be the bloody gash at his temple, though she knew only a fraction of an inch had saved him from instant death. Will grimaced as he joined her at Chase's side. "God Almighty!"

She nodded. "It wasn't Diablo. He's been shot—bushwhacked. He said it was Trammel Bodine."

Will shook his head and let out a silent curse.

"We've got to get him back," Libby said. "He needs a doctor."

"Ain't no doctor closer than Santa Fe," Will reminded her. "That's three hours back and forth on a fast horse." He didn't say the obvious: neither of them was sure Chase could hold on that long.

"Get Elliot," Chase told her in a raspy whisper.

"Elliot? All right," she replied, remembering they were friends. "I'll have one of the men send for him. He'll want to know—"

"No," Chase told her. "He's a doctor . . . he'll know what to do."

Dear God. Elliot Bradford, a doctor?

Nora pulled up in the wagon behind them and jumped down. "Good heavens!" she cried. "Has he been shot?"

"One of my ex-ranch hands . . ." Libby explained briefly.

Without a thought to Will's presence, Nora lifted her skirt and tore a length of cotton ruffle from her petticoat. "We'd best wrap those wounds before we move him or he'll be bleeding all over again."

After they'd bound him, Will helped lift Chase into the wagon, then turned to Libby. "You say this Elliot fella's in the box canyon up near Piñon Flats?"

Libby nodded. "Tell him to hurry, Will."

"You watch yerselves," he ordered. "That feller Bodine could still be around here. Keep yer rifle primed." Will pulled himself up on his horse and took off for the canyon at a gallop.

"Libby . . ."

She turned back to Chase. His bloody fingers brushed hers and then closed desperately around her wrist. The intensity in his green eyes was startling, combustible, belying the weakness of his body. His voice, when he spoke, was barely a whisper, audible only to her.

"I'm sorry. So sorry about this, about everything. You have to know that, don't you?"

Libby bit the inside of her cheek to keep from crying. He was looking for absolution, and she wasn't sure she could give it. She was sorry, too, that he hadn't ridden cleanly out of her life as he'd

238

promised, that he'd been hurt this way. But most of all, she was sorry, so sorry, she still cared enough for him to feel as if her heart were being torn out.

"I know, Chase," she told him at last. "I know. I'll get you home."

Home. He sighed, and his eyes slid shut as he gave himself over to the pain. He'd just hang on until she got him home. Home with Libby.

Chapter Sixteen

"Is he alive?" Elliot demanded from the doorway of Libby's room. His expression was stark, wretched. She could see he'd ridden all this way expecting the worst. Carrying a small, black leather bag, he crossed to the bed on which Chase lay facedown and pale as the white sheets he rested on.

"He's alive, but he's lost a lot of blood," Libby answered, swabbing the last of the dried crimson from Chase's upper back with a vinegar and water solution. "He told me you were a doctor. Is that true?"

El nodded, taking a closer look at the small, dark hole in Chase's shoulder. "It's true." He exchanged a look with her that said they'd talk about that small deception later.

"Thank God. There isn't another doctor for miles. I . . . I'm afraid for him, El. Is he going to die?"

"Not if I can help it." El raked his blond hair back with one hand, then pulled a stethoscope from his bag. He slipped the instrument in his ears and listened to Chase's breathing and heartbeat.

When he'd finished, Libby pulled the sheet down

240

past Chase's waist and said, "The other bullet passed straight through his side, but I don't think it hit anything vital."

A muscle worked in El's jaw. "Damn that little bastard Bodine."

"Will told you?"

El nodded grimly. "The bullet in his shoulder's going to have to come out. It missed his lung, I'm fairly sure. No sound of fluid there." El frowned and touched the gash on Chase's forehead. "How long has he been out?"

"On and off since we found him. Will gave him some whiskey before we moved him. He woke up while we were driving back and passed out again when Early and Straw carried him in here."

"Has he had any nausea? Vomiting?"

She shook her head.

"I have ether, but I'd rather not use it on him because of the head wound. Let's get that bullet out while he's still unconscious."

"What will you need?"

"Hot water and strong soap to wash my hands and instruments in."

"All right. Elliot?" Libby dropped her gaze to the man on her bed. "I never meant for this to happen," she whispered in a choked voice. "Despite our differences . . ."

"Libby," El asked gently, "did Chase tell you the real reason he came here?"

She nodded.

"Will told me Chase was leaving the ranch yesterday when this happened. Is that why he was going? Did you send him away?"

She turned silvery eyes up to him, in them something akin to defiance. "You can't expect me to for-

241

give him for what he did? He *killed* my husband."

El stared at her for a long heartbeat. "Is that what he told you?"

"It's not important now, is it?"

El let out a long breath. "I think it's more important than you know, but we'll talk about this later. Right now, I want to save his life. I'll need some more light in here if I'm going to dig out that bullet. And get Will to give you the rest of that whiskey. Chase will need it if he wakes up."

Libby stood, dropping the bloody towel she held. "I'll get a lamp and some whiskey for you," she said and walked stiffly from the room before she embarrassed herself by crying.

Nora passed Libby as she entered the room. She was carrying another bowl of hot water and some clean linen towels. She nodded to Elliot. "Mr. Bradford."

El smiled half-heartedly at her. "Ah, Miss Harper. It seems we're doomed to meet under the most unpleasant of circumstances." He took the bowl of water from her and set it near the bed. From his bag, he pulled a two-pronged tuning fork.

"Apparently so," she agreed, pushing back a strand of dark hair that had fallen against her cheek. "I suppose this means you weren't lying that day when you told me you were a doctor?"

"No. I wasn't." He sent her a faint smile and turned his attention to Chase. After tapping the tuning fork against the side of his hand, he rested the tip of it against Chase's teeth and watched him closely for a reaction. "Good," he murmured when he saw no wince of pain come from him. "At least the bullet didn't crack his skull."

"A tuning fork can tell you all that?" Nora asked, leaning over his shoulder for a closer look.

242

"The vibrations tend to gather at the fracture, if there is one, causing a great deal of pain. Even an unconscious man will react to it." He glanced up at her again. "Are you sure you want to be in here? Most women can't tolerate the sight of blood."

Nora smiled sadly. "I spent two years volunteering in the Confederate hospital back in Richmond. That experience inured me to the sight of blood."

El's eyebrows rose in surprise. "You were a nurse?"

"Not formally. The surgeons considered women unsuited to that kind of work. In the beginning, we just rolled bandages and wrote letters for the men. But, toward the end of the war, they were so desperate for help, they finally let us do the same things as your Mother Bickersdyke's nurses were doing up North."

Elliot regarded her with new respect. "Ever assist in a surgery?"

"Quite often."

"Would you mind assisting me here? I'm going to need some help."

Nora tipped her head to one side. "I'd be honored. I'm certain I owe you that much for doubting you the other day. Not to mention saving my life. I wondered if I'd ever get the chance to repay you."

Chase stirred and moaned softly, but didn't regain full consciousness.

"We'd better hurry," El replied, lifting one of Chase's eyelids to check his pupils. "I don't know how much longer he'll stay out. It'll be much harder if he's awake."

Libby sat in the rocker in the common room, her arms wrapped around Tad. She'd changed out of her bloodstained gown and replaced it with her usual attire: denim pants and an oversized red flannel shirt.

The chair rocked back and forth against the hard-packed dirt floor in a steady, soothing rhythm. At the table, a few feet away, sat Straw, Will, Early, and Esteban, nursing tin cups of cooling coffee, listening for sounds from the other room. Nearly forty-five minutes had passed since El had started the surgery on Chase. Twice Libby had heard Chase cry out in pain. The sounds had torn through her like knives.

Early skittered his chair against the table leg and Libby jumped at the sound.

"Just gettin' me some more coffee," he assured her. "Damn, that boy is takin' his sweet time in there, ain't he?" He set the graniteware coffee pot back on the stove with a clang.

Straw hushed him with a gnarled hand. "Can't hurry doctorin' if'n it's good doctorin'. Anybody can dig out a bullet. But not to kill the man whilst yer doin' it . . . that's the trick."

Esteban nodded and his black eyes flashed. "He won't let Chase die. *Ellos son hermanos.*"

"They're brothers?" Early repeated, staring at the boy.

"*Sí.* He told me this up in the canyon when I teach him to make his *hondo* sing," he replied, referring to the sound the lariat made when spun correctly. "They are not brothers of blood. But Chase's mother is the wife of El's father. Even before that, they were friends for many years. *Son hermanos del corazón.*"

Brothers of the heart. Libby stared at the boy, wondering how many other secrets Chase and Elliot had kept from her. How could she have thought she loved a man she knew not at all?

"Ma?" Tad asked in a small voice. "You ain't mad at Chase anymore, are ya?"

Libby's arms tightened around her son, and she kissed his cheek, avoiding the question.

Just then, the door to Libby's room swung open and Elliot came out, wiping his hands on a towel. His sleeves were rolled up against his tanned arms. He looked exhausted, but relieved. As one, the men and Libby rose expectantly to meet him.

"Well, it's about time," Early grumbled impatiently. "How is he?"

"I got the bullet out," El answered with a tired smile. "He was lucky. His shoulder blade deflected it upward and so it missed his lung. It took some digging to get it out."

Libby let her eyes drift shut in thankful prayer.

"I gave him a few drops of laudanum," El went on, looking pointedly at Libby. "He can't be moved. What we have to watch for now is any sign of infection. Just pray it doesn't happen."

"He can stay where he is," Libby assured him. "I can share Tad's room."

Early rubbed a hand over the suspicious moisture in his eyes, then picked up his hat and clapped El on the shoulder. "A doc . . ." He grinned. "Hell, I should'a guessed by them hands of yours. They ain't never seen the raw side of rawhide before you come here. But it's lucky fer that feller in there they was trained fer somethin' besides catchin' horses."

"Thanks, Early. He's not out of the woods yet, but he's got a chance now."

"Tad?" Straw called. "Why don't you come with me, boy? I bet by now you got some nice fat flies caught for ol' Charlie toad in that fly trap o'yourn."

"Can't I see Chase now?" he asked.

"You kin see Chase later, when he wakes up," Straw promised.

Tad brightened a bit. "Tell me when he wakes up, okay, Ma?"

Libby nodded, and Tad reluctantly followed Straw

and the other men out the door.

El turned to her. "What about you? Do you want to see him now? He asked for you."

Libby avoided his eyes and started stacking the empty coffee cups in the dry sink. *If I see him now, I'll just embarrass myself, and I can't afford to do that anymore, not with Chase Whitlaw.* "No. I have a hundred chores that need tending to . . . I'll go in later."

El frowned and helped himself to a cup of coffee. He sipped it slowly, watching her. "I think we should talk about this. Don't you?"

Libby braced her hands against the counter, her back to Elliot. "There's nothing to say."

"I think there is. Sit down, Libby."

She turned on him, suddenly angry. "Look, I know he's your friend and I . . . I pray he doesn't die. He's welcome to stay in my room until he gets well . . . but don't ask me to care about him again. He lied to me, Elliot. You *both* lied to me."

"Neither of us lied," El corrected. "We simply didn't tell you the whole truth. I still don't think you know it."

"*I* know it. I know he killed my husband."

"No. He didn't."

Libby's eyes darted up to his, and she felt her heartbeats stagger. "*What?*"

"He didn't kill your husband."

Her face went pale. "But . . . he said—"

"He said he shot Lee, right?"

She nodded.

El sighed. "That was true. He shot him—in the arm. A flesh wound, not the fatal wound that ultimately killed Lee."

Confused, Libby shook her head. "Then how . . . ?"

El wrapped his hands tightly around his cup.

246

"Chase, like hundreds of other men, has lived with a lot of guilt since the war. Your husband wasn't just one of the faceless men he was forced to kill in the name of the Union. Lee Honeycutt became something more to him. A symbol, if you will, of everything that was wrong with that bloody travesty of a battle.

"If Chase convinced himself that he was responsible for your husband's death, it's because he had killed dozens, maybe hundreds, of others just like him. After a while, the distinction becomes blurred."

"What is the distinction?" she asked bitterly.

El sighed. "I couldn't begin to describe the hellish conditions they were in when it happened. The men who survived it didn't call it a battle. They referred to what happened there as murder. Federals and Confederates struggling through undergrowth so thick and choking with smoke, they couldn't see three feet ahead of them."

El's eyes took on a faraway look, and Libby sank down on the chair opposite him.

"Chase fired at the enemy—a Reb soldier—and, like your husband, he was trying to survive. Most likely, they would have killed each other then and there, but an artillery shell from God knows which side exploded nearby, throwing them both into the same ditch. Your husband took a mortal wound to the stomach, and Chase took a bad hit to the leg."

Libby's throat tightened as she imagined Lee's suffering and remembered the limp that stiffened Chase's walk.

"Your husband was dying," El went on. "He knew it. He begged Chase to return the locket to you, knowing there was no one else to ask." He looked directly at Libby. "Chase could have refused. A lot of men would have in his position. But he didn't. He

247

made a promise to him. And he kept it."

Libby locked her hands together on her lap; then she stood and gripped the back of her chair. "He should have sent it. He shouldn't have come here."

"Maybe not," El agreed with an irritated shrug. "Maybe he shouldn't have comforted the enemy who lay dying either. Maybe doing the honorable thing doesn't have a place in such situations." He gestured toward Libby's room. "Look where it's gotten him."

She studiously avoided glancing that way. "You call lying to me honorable?"

"I know he wanted to help you."

"How? By making me fall in love with him? By letting me think he cared about me?"

Elliot paused. "Are you in love with him?"

Libby fell silent, staring at the cup of coffee in El's hands.

"I don't know what happened between you two," El said, "but I do know he felt he owed you for saving his life."

"Owed me for . . . ? What are you talking about?"

"I haven't told you everything."

Suddenly Libby was afraid to know what El meant to tell her. "Well, I don't think I want to hear anymore," she said pushing away from the table.

El jumped up and grabbed her arm, jerking her toward him. For the first time, she saw anger in his eyes. Anger toward her, anger toward the injustice of the whole awful situation.

"Well you're going to hear me out," he snapped. "He's suffered enough on account of this whole business. I'm going to tell you what Chase never will. *Then* you can decide whether or not to forgive him for doing what he did. Now sit down."

Libby sat down hard in the carved pine chair.

Elliot ran two hands through his hair and composed himself for a moment before beginning. "Chase never meant to hurt you. You must know that. Why, the man's been half in love with you since he first saw your picture in that locket two years ago."

Libby's lips parted in shock, but she could only stare at him.

"After he was wounded, he was brought to a field hospital. He was lucky to keep his leg, but he took a fever and nearly died. A nurse found your husband's locket inside Chase's pocket. She assumed, naturally, it was a picture of his wife. She gave it to him so he'd have something to hold on to, something to fight for."

El laughed humorlessly. "Ironic, isn't it? But it was your picture that saw him through the worst of his illness. He had nothing else to keep him going."

"He has no family?" Libby asked. "No woman?"

"There was someone, before the war, but she married another man shortly after Chase joined the Army. His family—me, his mother, and my father— we didn't know until later where he'd been sent. When we did find him at last, I brought him home to Baltimore and did a second surgery on his leg."

"He still has pain from it, doesn't he?"

"Some. He was lucky to live through it at all." El shook his head. "The war changed him, Libby. It hardened him. Closed him off. When he told me he meant to come out here, I tried to talk him out of it." El laughed with genuine affection. "He told me either to go to hell or come along, because he wasn't changing his mind. So here I am.

"To tell you the truth," he went on, "you're the only thing Chase has really cared about since the war. Meeting you, seeing that he could help you, made him feel like he was a part of something again, like he

249

had a reason for being. That's why he couldn't just give you the locket and walk away."

Libby was silent for a long time. She pressed her fingertips against her aching eyes. "What do you want from me?"

El leaned forward in his chair. "I have no right to ask you for anything. I can only imagine how hard this must be for you. But as Chase's friend, I'm asking you to think about what I've said. He's not a saint, Libby. He's human. He needs your help and your forgiveness."

Forgiveness? A shudder ran through her. She wasn't sure she had anything like forgiveness in her anymore. "You ask a lot, Elliot."

"I know. Just think about it, will you?"

Reluctantly, she nodded.

He smiled and dragged a hand across the blond stubble on his cheeks. "I'm a mess. . . . Do I, uh, still have a job here?"

Libby smiled, too. "Of course, if you still want it. I need all the help I can get."

"I don't think Early can spare me right now. You'll have to look out for Chase for the next few days. Can you handle that?"

"I suppose I don't have much choice," she replied with a lift of her eyebrows. "After all, he is in my bed."

El grinned and got up from the table. Libby walked him to the front door. "Make a poultice of two parts linseed oil and three parts milk for him. It'll need to be changed a few times an hour until the threat of infection is past. The gash in his head worries me, as well. He'll want to sleep, but don't let him go too long in one stretch. Wake him periodically."

El touched Libby's shoulder. "Thanks."

"For what?" she asked with an arched brow.

"For hearing me out. For finding him before it was too late. For taking care of him when it's the last thing you want to be doing. You're a special woman, Mrs. Honeycutt. Chase knows it, too."

Libby closed the door silently after El left and then leaned back against it. She stared at her bedroom door and wished she could turn and run. But she couldn't. She'd have to face him sooner or later. Her head was spinning with confusion after everything Elliot had told her. *He's been half in love with you since before he met you . . . he didn't kill your husband . . . he needs your forgiveness. . . .*

She heard Jonas's deep voice as well. *You've made me very happy . . . you won't regret marrying me, Libby . . . is it only gratitude you feel for me?*

She pressed her fingers to her temples. She felt like she was being pulled in a hundred different directions at once. Chase, Elliot, Jonas, Tad—everyone wanted something from her, and she wasn't sure she had anything left to give.

"What about *my* feelings, *my* dreams," she wondered aloud. "What about what *I* want?"

Only silence answered her.

"Oh, Libby," she scolded herself, "when are you going to start thinking with your head instead of your heart?"

Nora looked up when Libby came into the room carrying the pan of milk and linseed oil. Nora had stripped off the jacket of her black riding habit and now wore a simple white batiste blouse rolled up at the sleeves. She was wringing out a cloth she'd just dipped in cool water.

Chase lay on his side, eyes closed, his breathing

251

deep and even. His skin was pale, and sweat matted his hair to his forehead. The sight of him like that gave Libby a queer sensation in the pit of her stomach.

"How is he?" she asked in a whisper, putting the pan down on the bedside table.

"Resting easier," Nora whispered back. She stood and gathered up her jacket, slipping it over her shoulders. "He was in some pain, so I gave him some more whiskey and he fell asleep. Your Dr. Bradford did a good job. He's a fine surgeon. It was fortunate he was here."

"And it was lucky you were here, Nora. I can't thank you enough for your help." Libby watched two spots of color appear on Nora's cheeks.

"I'd better go before we wake him. I hope he'll be all right. He seems like a good man. It just doesn't seem fair, does it?" She shook her head sadly, patted Libby on the shoulder, and slipped quietly from the room.

What about life is fair? Libby wondered, wringing out the cloth she'd dipped in the poultice. Carefully, she peeled off the pad of gauze Elliot had placed over the hole in Chase's side and she laid the warm, moist towel in its place. She did the same for his shoulder wound.

Chase jerked awake and took in a long, hissing breath. He blinked up at her. "Libby?"

"I'm right here."

He reached for her free hand like a man grasping for a lifeline. Hesitantly, she obliged him. His strong fingers wrapped around hers, and she let him squeeze until the pain eased. Even after that, his hand remained clamped on hers as if they were two parts of a whole, forged together by the heat of their touch.

"How bad am I?" he asked in a raspy voice.

"Elliot got the bullet out of your shoulder. Nothing vital was hit. The one in your side passed straight through." She squeezed his hand. "You're going to be all right, Chase," she told him, trying to believe it herself. "What you need now is rest."

"Damn careless of me to get caught that way," he mumbled.

She shook her head. "Trammel didn't give you much choice, shooting you in the back the way he did. Are you sure it was him?"

He nodded and managed a grim smile. "He made a point of making sure I was awake so I could feel the toe of his boot connect with my ribs. He wanted me to know he left me there to die."

"Oh, Chase . . ." She'd seen his bruised ribs, but had assumed he'd gotten them in the fall.

"He took my gun and my horse."

"We found Blue a mile or two from where we found you."

Chase grimaced as he tried to ease some weight off his shoulder. "That stallion . . . stayed with me . . . all night. . . . Don't know why. . . ."

"I saw him. Thank God he was there or the coyotes might have killed you."

"Libby—"

"Shhh, don't try to talk anymore. Go to sleep," she told him.

He had some things that needed saying, but his strength seemed to be dissipating like morning fog.

"Lib?" He swallowed and rolled his eyes shut. "Sit with me a while, will ya? Jus' 'til I fall asleep?"

"I'll be right here."

"Thanks," he murmured.

A smile tipped one corner of her mouth, and she

253

brushed his hair from his eyes. "Go to sleep now, Chase," she said, but she realized he already had.

Outside, El leaned his palms against the wooden water trough and hung his head. He was shaken. Not just by the sight of Chase so gravely wounded, but by Libby's anger. He could have predicted things would end this way between them. But he could never have imagined Bodine shooting Chase in the back.

He splashed water on his face and let it drip off as he stared into the water. If he ever saw the bastard again he'd . . .

Another face joined his reflection in the trough. He straightened.

"Are you all right?" Nora asked, touching his arm tenderly.

El scraped the water from his face with one hand. "I'm . . . Yeah. Just great."

"I'm sorry about Chase. It must have been awful for you to have to doctor him yourself."

"I've done it before."

"You're a wonderful surgeon, Dr. Bradford."

"It's Elliot, and right now I'm feeling pretty damn helpless."

Nora shook her head. "You've done everything you can. He'll pull through. You said so yourself. He's lucky to have a friend like you."

Elliot really looked at Nora for the first time, taking in the empathy in her sable eyes. "We practically grew up together. His mother married my father after they were both widowed, but he's always been a brother to me. These past few years have been hard on him. I've watched him go to hell and back." Anger made El's words harsh. "He didn't deserve this."

"No, he didn't. No one deserves something like this," Nora agreed. "But you can't blame yourself for that."

El sighed and stared out across Honeycutt range. "Bodine's to blame. If I ever see him I'll kill him myself."

Nora's voice was soft as she laid a hand on his arm. "Elliot, your calling is to heal, not to hurt."

Her touch brought his gaze around to her face. He had the craziest urge to draw her into his arms and hold her. Propriety checked it. Instead, he smiled and lifted the back of her hand to his lips. "The best nurses always know how to keep the doctor in line. I was glad to have you in there to help me."

"I am, sir, humbly at your service," she replied with a grin and a curtsy. Together they walked to where Will Tuerney held her horse in readiness for her. El helped her mount and she smiled down at him. "I'll be back in a few days to see how Chase is doing. I pray, for your sake and his, he'll be all right."

Chapter Seventeen

Fever hit Chase on the second day, despite all their precautions. Infection had gotten a toehold in the wound in his side in the hours he'd lain outside after being shot. Libby sat with him for two days straight, with Elliot spelling her every few hours. They sponged him down with witch hazel and packed the infection alternately with woundswart and a mixture of charcoal and yeast. They forced feverfew and sage teas down his throat by the cupful. All to no avail.

On the third day, Chase ranted feverishly, struggling and thrashing against their every effort to help him. He called out to soldiers on the field, as if he were in battle, and twice mentioned her husband's name. More often than not, however, it was Libby he called for. That nearly broke her heart.

At times, he clung to her hand as if it were the only thing keeping him in this world. Despair rimmed Elliot's tired eyes when he ministered to his friend, and Libby steeled herself for the very real possibility of Chase's death.

Tears of exhaustion and frustration coursed down her cheeks that night as she once more changed his poultice. Her movements were stiff with fatigue and weighted down with the knowledge that she might never be able to right things between them. She alternately cursed him and pleaded with him to live, and finally, sometime during the third night, she fell into an exhausted sleep beside him on the bed.

Chase cracked an eye open and stared into the semidarkness of dawn. Pain rolled over his body like the wheels of a heavy cart. There wasn't a place on him that didn't hurt, though some hurt considerably more than others. He blinked, trying to focus his eyes. He was in Libby's bedroom, in her bed, naked beneath the sheet that covered him to the waist. Sweat soaked the bedding and pooled in the curves of his bare torso. He vaguely realized that the blessed coolness he felt was in sharp contrast to the furnace he'd felt inside him a short time ago.

He glanced at the barred window, wondering if it was morning or night. How long had he been out? Hours? The last thing he remembered was asking Libby to sit with him.

Candlelight danced across the smooth adobe wall, creating flickering shadows. It came from a stubby, nearly spent candle beside the bed. The air was scented with the slightly medicinal fragrance of herbs and witch hazel. These mingled pungently with his own sweat. In the corner, he saw El sprawled negligently in a chair, head thrown back in exhaustion, snoring softly. Gradually, he became aware of something else.

Someone was holding his hand.

He turned his head on the damp pillow and found Libby sprawled across the bed in a cloud of tangled blond hair. Her fingers were twined with his as naturally as if they belonged in them.

257

He ran his thumb across her smooth knuckles, tightened his fingers around them and gave her a gentle squeeze. "Libby . . ."

Nothing. He watched the gentle rise and fall of her back.

"Libby."

Her head came up with a jerk. "Huh?" A curtain of hair fell over her face, and she pushed it away with her free hand. She seemed astonished to find him watching her. She looked, in fact, as if she were seeing a ghost.

"*Chase?*"

"Hi." His voice was rough as sandpaper and barely a whisper. "Have we been holding hands like this for long?"

She glanced down at their joined hands and let out something between a laugh and a sob, then covered their clasped hands with her free one. "Oh, my God, Chase. I was afraid—" The word was choked off, and tears gathered in her eyes. She noted the sheets, drenched with his sweat. "Your fever broke."

"How long have I been here?"

The blank look on her face suggested she'd lost track herself. "This is . . . ummm, the fourth day. Elliot and I . . . we thought . . ."

"*Four days?* You were here with me that whole time?" he asked, amazed.

"She *was*, you stubborn cuss." Elliot appeared at Chase's bedside, struggling to hide his own powerful emotions. "And you can thank her for keeping you alive. It's about time you kicked that fever."

Chase grinned at the sight of him. El's hair stuck up at odd angles and his shirttail was half-in and half-out of his trousers. "You look like hell, Elliot."

"That's the thanks I get." El's relief showed clearly through the lines of fatigue on his face. He crossed to

258

the bed and put a hand on Chase's forehead. "For a while there I thought you were going to do some permanent damage to my medical reputation by dying on me, brother."

Chase moistened his parched lips and smiled. He could see from the tethered expression in El's eyes, he'd come mighty close to doing just that. "Next time I nearly die, I'll make sure I have another doctor," he parried weakly.

The rising sun had peeked through Libby's window, washing the room with soft golden light. Turning his gaze back to her, Chase noticed the bruise that darkened her cheekbone. His stomach took a plunge. He reached up to touch it, but she flinched away from his hand. "Did I do that?" he asked, horrified.

Her fingers brushed over the spot. "It's nothing. You were out of your head," she told him dismissing it. "You were thrashing around and—"

"I'm sorry."

Gray eyes collided with green. His apology covered more than just the bruise, and they both knew it.

"How do you feel?" she asked, changing the subject.

One corner of his mouth tipped up in a parody of a smile. "How do I look?"

She realized her question was ridiculous. His drawn face was shadowed by a four-day growth of beard that emphasized the new hollows in his cheeks. Dark blue smudges beneath his eyes were his only claim to color, save the green in his eyes. He'd lost weight in the past few days. Chase Whitlaw's sheer size insured he could never appear frail, but he looked, just now, as close to being so as Libby could imagine.

"You look like . . . well, you look like the rest of us," she said, including El in her gesture. "Only worse. Here, have some water."

She slipped a hand behind his head and helped him sip from the tin cup she held. Her nearness made his heart skitter along his ribs. Her fingers were warm against his skin, and he wanted to haul her into his arms and kiss her for all her gentleness.

Instead, he let out a long sigh and tipped his head back against the pillow. Weariness pressed down on him like a weight. He was having trouble keeping his eyes open, but he couldn't fall asleep. Not yet.

"Libby, I need to talk to you," he said groggily.

"Later. You must sleep right now," she argued.

"Libby's right, Chase," El agreed. "Don't tax yourself now. Get some rest. When you wake up again, we'll ladle some broth down that ornery throat of yours and get you back on the mend."

Chase didn't have the strength to fight them both. He was disgusted by the weakness that assailed him and surprised when his eyes slid shut as if they had a will of their own. Later, he decided as he gave in to the need to rest. I'll tell her later.

When he opened his eyes again, he guessed it was late afternoon. Sunlight slanted into the room from the south-facing window, warming the air. Outside, cicadas buzzed in the cloying heat.

He rolled over onto his back cautiously. There was still pain, but nothing that wasn't manageable. He felt better—considerably better—than he had that morning.

"Ma! He's awake!"

Tad's shrill voice jolted Chase, and he looked over to see the boy sitting up close to the bed on a straight-backed chair, watching him intently.

"Hi, Chase! You're awake," Tad informed him.

"Hi ya, Tadpole."

Tad grinned at the nickname Chase had given him. "You got shot, huh?"

Chase nodded.

"Did it hurt a lot?"

Chase grinned. "I wouldn't recommend it."

"We all thought you was gonna die. Ma stayed up all night with you. I seen her cryin', too. She didn't want me to know. But I did. She told me to come in and watch you. I was real quiet, wasn't I? I didn't even wake you up."

At that moment, Chase caught sight of Libby, standing in the doorway, holding a bowl of steaming soup. A blush tinged her cheeks. She'd clearly overheard her son.

"Tad, Chase is in no shape to be answering all your questions now."

"He's not bothering me," Chase told her.

She smiled at Tad. "You did a good job of watching Chase for me. Why don't you run out to the paddock now and tell Elliot he's awake."

"Okay." Tad tilted his head at Chase. "You're gonna be all right now, ain't you?"

Chase let out a small chuckle. "Yeah. I guess I have your Ma to thank for that."

The soup bowl rattled against the plate as Libby set it down on the bedside table. Libby avoided his eyes but felt them on her.

Tad slipped off the chair. "If you get bored, I've got a checkers game. And Straw and Early taught me how to play five-card draw the other night when I had to sleep in the bunkhouse."

Libby's mouth dropped open. "They *what?*"

Tad grinned sheepishly. "Oops. I wasn't s'posed to tell ya that. I'll go tell Elliot now." He slipped out the door.

Chase smiled when she turned back to him. "Cute kid."

"Too cute for his own good sometimes. I brought you some broth. Can you take some?"

261

"I'm hungry," he admitted.

"That's a good sign."

She eased him up gently and propped him up with an extra pillow. A shock raced through him at how weak he really was. Though his left shoulder was the injured one, his right arm shook so he wasn't able to manage the spoon on his own. She fed the steaming broth to him slowly. Surprisingly, half a bowl was all he could manage. He eased back down on the bed as she gathered up the soup bowl, preparing to go.

"Do you have to go?" he asked. "I'd like to talk to you."

"No, I can stay here for a minute."

He was hungry for the sight of her, hungry for something he couldn't even name. Chase let his gaze drift down her—over her face, her breasts, the shapely denim-clad legs she'd tucked beneath her. At that moment, it didn't have so much to do with his overwhelming desire to enfold her in his arms and show her what she meant to him—though that desire was undeniably compelling. No, it was more a need to affix her in his memory, like postage on a letter about to be mailed. He watched the color heighten in her cheeks as his gaze went back to her face.

"What I said earlier," he began awkwardly, "I meant it. I'm sorry for bringing all this trouble down on you. I wouldn't have blamed you for leaving me out there."

She looked shocked by the suggestion. "Don't be ridiculous. I could never have—"

"No, you couldn't. I know that." His fingers brushed hers with the barest of touches. "I had a lot of time to think, lying out there, Libby. Time to wonder what I'd done with my life. It didn't amount to a hell of a lot. I've been running from the past, myself, and everyone else for so long now, I'd forgotten what it was like to *feel* anything.

262

"You made me feel something again," he continued. "You made me feel alive for the first time in years. I don't want to run from that anymore." He paused, moistening his lips. "I took the easiest route of escape by leaving the other day instead of facing what I'd come here to do."

Libby stopped him. "Chase, Elliot told me."

He frowned. "Told you . . . ?"

"About Lee. About the locket. Everything."

He leaned his head back against the pillow. "Oh."

"I understand some things now I didn't before," she said quietly. "I was wrong not to let you explain, but I was angry and . . . hurt. I'm still not sure what I feel."

"I didn't kill him, Libby. God knows I killed my share of men, but your husband wasn't one of them. The rest of them, I never knew. Having your husband die like that next to me—and nearly dying myself that time—stopped me cold. Froze me up like a rusted hinge. I lost track of who I was. In fact, what I'd been doing with my life seemed to make no sense at all."

"How long did you fight?" she asked.

"Four years in every hellhole on earth, it seemed. Shiloh, Bull Run, Chancellorsville, the march through Atlanta with Sherman, where we burned everything in sight; houses, barns—some with innocent people still inside." His voice caught as he made the admission. "Then . . . The Wilderness. Four years of hell until that shell took me out with your husband." He laughed, a bitter, weary laugh. "I was almost grateful when it happened. I was ready to die and get it over with. Lee gave me something to live for, as strange as that sounds."

Libby's heart tightened at the thought of the pain he'd known. Not only physical but emotional. It answered so many questions she'd not understood

263

about him; the strange reactions he'd had to the fire popping that first night, the deep, bitter emotional wounds that kept him safely hidden from others. She touched his pale fingers, and they curled around hers.

"What happened between Lee and me," he went on, "I don't suppose you can forgive me for it. I never even expected that. But I promised you I'd help you see this contract through. Let me do that when I get back on my feet again, Libby. Just, please, let me do that for you." He paused, taking in the wary look in Libby's smoky, passionate eyes, her mouth, the shadow that pulsed at the base of her throat.

Libby's skin tingled at every point Chase's gaze touched. Despite his weakness, his look was stunningly powerful, seductive. She found she couldn't deny him that after all he'd been through on her account. But she couldn't lie to him either.

"You can stay. But, Chase . . . I think you should know this. After the herd is delivered, I'm going to marry Jonas Harper."

If he hadn't been lying down, her statement would have knocked him flat. *"What?"*

"I was coming from his ranch when I found you. I agreed to marry him in ex—" She stopped abruptly, thinking better of what she was about to say. "He's already sent men over to help with the roundup. I'm going to marry him as soon as the order is delivered."

He felt like he'd been poleaxed. "Do you love him?"

Libby dropped her gaze. "I . . ."

He grabbed her hand. *"Do you love him, damn it?"*

The look she flashed at Chase was hollow, suddenly angry. "What's love got to do with anything? It's not practical, and it certainly won't save my ranch from the bank or give my son the kind of life I want for him. I owe him that much." She looked

264

down at his hand on hers. "I can't give it to him if I remain here. Jonas can. He wants me—us. He'll give us a good home. It's the best thing for everyone."

A muscle jumped in Chase's cheek. "What about you, Libby? Is it what *you* want? Are you willing to sacrifice yourself to a man you don't love?"

"I love my son, Chase. That kind of love I can trust; it's something I can hold on to. The other," she said, avoiding his eyes, "is just a romantic fantasy. You said yourself I was crazy to try to hang on to this place by myself."

"That was before I knew you," he replied quietly. "Before I knew what you were capable of."

She let out a sigh of frustration. "I'm tired of being the one everyone depends on. I've made a promise to Jonas, and I intend to keep it."

"I see." Chase's mouth was drawn into a thin line. The tension between them was a palpable thing. Damn! He'd bloody well pushed her into Harper's arms by leaving. She'd done the only sensible thing. After all, what could he offer her? Certainly not what Jonas Harper could. He loved her, but love wasn't what she needed, wasn't enough to hold her to him. "You're probably right, then," he said at last. "It's for the best."

"It is."

Chase absently ran a hand over his sore shoulder. "I'd still like to stay, if it's all right with you."

Libby stood and picked up the bowl of soup on the table. "Do you think you'll be up to it?"

"Just give me a few days."

"All right. I'll need all the help I can get." She turned to go, but Chase's voice stopped her.

"Just tell me one thing, Libby."

She looked back at him.

"Was the boy telling the truth? Did you cry when you thought I might die?"

Libby's lips parted briefly in surprise, but her mouth snapped shut quickly. "What kind of a question is that?"

"An honest one. Just answer me. Do you feel anything for me, Lib?"

"I . . . don't know what you mean."

"When I woke up that first time, you were holding my hand. And you did that at other times. I remember now. Why?"

Her cheeks paled. "I would have done the same for any man as badly hurt as . . ." The lie died on her lips, and she stared at him, flustered. "I held your hand because it was the only thing that seemed to calm you, help you. Because the last time you were badly wounded, El said you were alone and I . . . I didn't want you to be alone."

Chase's face remained grim and he closed his eyes, weary beyond words. "That's all I wanted to know."

"Let it be, Chase. Just let it be."

Libby turned on her heel and fled the room, leaving Chase alone to brood over what she'd told him—and everything she hadn't.

Chase frowned. She'd saved his life for a second time. Only this time, she'd been there beside him, holding him, urging him to live. Why? Who was he to judge her for marrying Harper? And what did he know about love and marriage? He was more of a stranger to it than she was. She'd been married once to a man who did love her, and look where it had gotten her. He had no right to mess in her life anymore. That was what his head told him. The twisting in his gut told him something else.

Let it be. That was what she'd said. Let *her* be, was what she'd meant. Undoubtedly, good advice. The problem was, he wasn't sure he'd be able to do that, even if he wanted to—which he didn't. The problem was, he was in love with her.

Chapter Eighteen

"Hold *still,* will you?"

"I'm trying, woman, but you keep coming at me with that thing like you want to slit my throat."

Tempted, Libby lowered the hand that held the straight razor, and she glared at Chase's soap-lathered face. His expression was perfectly serious, so she did her best to hide the grin that crept to her lips. "Believe me, *Mr.* Whitlaw, the last thing I intend to do is incur any more injuries that I'll have to nurse. Now, I'm perfectly capable of doing this."

He grabbed her arm before the lethal-looking razor could touch his face. "Had a lot of experience shaving men's faces, have you?" he jibed.

"As a matter of fact," she said, shaking his hand off, "I have." She didn't expound on the fact that she'd shaved Malachi nearly every day after his first heart attack until he'd passed away. She decided she'd rather let Chase wonder.

"Well," he grumbled, running a hand through his damp, freshly washed hair, "I told you, if you'd just give me a mirror, I could do it myself."

She raised one unbelieving eyebrow and decided to let him leap into that muddy water on his own. Thrusting a small tin-framed mirror into his left hand and the razor into his right, she smiled. "All right, Mr. Sunshine. Go right ahead."

His scowl traveled from the mirror he now held to her. Libby recognized the determined set to his jaw. Less than two days had passed since his fever had broken, but that was long enough for her to realize he was a man who had no patience with being bedridden. He was bored and sore, and his temper was as foul as a wet cat's. He certainly wasn't used to having to rely on someone else to do for him.

Libby went about her business, folding up an extra blanket, and pretended to ignore him. At the foot of the bed, Patch lay where he'd taken up residence, his ears perked expectantly, watching Chase.

Chase dipped the razor into the bowl of warm water in his lap and cautiously approached his bearded face. The mirror rattled in his left hand with the effort it took to hold it up, but he doggedly made an attempt. He cursed the weakness that left him unable to handle the simplest of tasks. The first stroke was punctuated by a crass oath, and a bright red spot of blood appeared on his throat. The second stroke was worse.

"Damnation!" He threw the razor into the pan of water.

Libby pressed her lips together to keep from smiling.

"And don't you laugh at me either, Miss I-can-do-everything. The razor's dull as an old dog's teeth."

"I just stropped it," she told him, dangling the razor strop between two fingers. "It's perfectly sharp. Let me know when you're finished," she told him, mercilessly as she swept out of the room, blanket in hand, "and I'll empty that water for you."

"Libby." The word was nearly shouted.

She stuck her head around the door frame. "Yes?"

"Could you—would you—please shave me? I, uh, can't seem to manage it one-handed after all."

"Please?"

"Ple-ease," he gritted out.

She couldn't resist taunting him. "With sugar on top?"

"Now wait just a minute," he growled.

"Oh, never mind," she replied, joining him at the bed. "Please will do just fine. In fact, it's the nicest thing you've said to me all day. I think you woke up on the wrong side of the bed."

He muttered something about any side being the wrong side, as she took the razor in her hand and tipped his head back. Her fingers pressed against the base of his neck where she found his pulse thudding furiously. From anger or sheer frustration, she couldn't be sure.

He glared at her through narrowed eyes while she stroked him with the razor, tipping his head first one way, then the other. "I guess I *have* been—"

She shushed him as the razor followed the curve above his lip, then went to his chin. He flattened his lower lip against his teeth to give her better access. He had to admit, she did this well. He wondered if she'd practiced on her husband and if she planned on doing this for Harper after they were married. A shaft of jealousy darted through him. He didn't allow himself to think too long on that. He concentrated on the feel of her fingers against his skin.

"You were saying?" she asked, paying close attention to his jawline.

"I was saying, I guess I *have* been a little touchy lately. It's just being in this damn bed for so long." He glanced down his nose at her. "Was that Jonas Harper I heard pull up outside this morning?"

The razor nicked his chin. "Ow!"

"Sorry. Yes, it was."

He grunted and angled his head sideways. "He stayed long enough."

"He brought me a new dress. He wants me to wear it at the party."

"Party?"

"Independence Day."

Chase's eyes narrowed, but Libby pressed on, changing the subject. "He was asking about you. He was quite concerned about what happened."

A sardonic smile curved his lips. "Ha. I suppose he wasn't too thrilled with the idea of me being in your bed, was he?"

She stilled her arm and stared at him. "Why, Chase, what a lowly thought."

His eyes met hers, serious now. "If you were mine, it would have been my *first* thought."

Libby hesitated above the tender skin near Chase's ear. What Jonas had minded most was that Chase would be staying on at the Double Bar H when he got well. But she didn't need to tell Chase that. It would only add fuel to the fire. It was plain he didn't think much of her arrangement with Jonas.

"Well, you're still weak as a kitten," she said at last. "You're hardly in any condition to pose a threat to me."

A wicked look lit his eyes. "You sure about that?"

The blade nicked him again in retribution.

"Ow!" He grabbed her slender wrist and held it away from his face. "Damn it, woman! I think I could have done a better job of it myself."

Their eyes met over the straight razor. The humor in hers faded as his look became hotter and infinitely more dangerous than the teasing one it had been only a moment before. His gaze dropped to her parted lips and hovered there for a moment before returning to search her eyes.

270

"Then again," he murmured, "maybe it's worth losing a little more blood, just to be able to watch your eyes catch the sunlight that way."

His words caught her off guard and spread through her like warm honey, overshadowing the pang of warning she knew she should heed. With his free hand, he picked up the towel and wiped the remaining soap from his face. It was a gesture so blatantly male that it made her breath catch in her throat. Her pulse was spinning in an involuntary reaction to his nearness. She forgot to resist when he pulled her closer still, his warm fingers still around her wrist.

"Did I ever tell you what your eyes do to me, Lib?"

"Chase, please . . ."

"They make me want things from you I know I have no right to want. Crazy things I imagine we'd both regret." His eyes roved over her face, searching for an answer to his unspoken question. "Then again, maybe we wouldn't regret it." His fingers burned into her skin, pressing against her thudding pulse. "Does Jonas Harper do this to you Libby? Does he make your pulse race? Does he make your skin get hot the way it does when I touch you?" Chase pulled her close, so close their breaths mingled.

"I told you," she whispered, "it doesn't mat—"

His lips brushed hers, tasting, tempting, silencing her excuses. "And when he kisses you," he whispered against her mouth, "does he light a fire in those smoky eyes of yours, like I do?"

Libby was horrified by her body's involuntary response to his touch. Yet she couldn't deny the memory of the ecstasy she'd found in his strong arms. No, Jonas's touch was nothing like this. But that was before . . . before everything had changed. How could she still feel such things about a man who'd turned her life upside down and helped to strip her of

271

everything she loved? It was wrong. It had to be.

A voice from the doorway sent them both crashing apart guiltily.

"So, how's the"—El hesitated for only a second, taking in their expressions—"patient?"

Neither of them spoke and both avoided El's questioning stare. "Did I interrupt something?" he asked. "I can come back."

"No. You didn't interrupt a thing," Libby told him, gathering up Chase's shaving things. "I was just trying to make Chase look like a human being again." Her eyes flickered to Chase's momentarily to find him watching her.

El looked from one to the other and shook his head. "And you've managed to do it. Barely. I don't know about his temper though. He's been more like a bear lately than the Chase I know and love."

"Yes, see if you have something in that little black bag for that, will you?" Libby requested before she stalked out of the room, slamming the door with a force that left it rattling in its frame.

El raised an eyebrow as he turned to Chase, who lay abed, scowling. "Wanna tell me what that was all about?"

"Not particularly."

"Okay. Let's try something else. How are you feeling?"

"Great. Just great," Chase fumed.

"Ah-hah."

Chase gritted his teeth as El bent over him and undid the bandages at his shoulder and side, inspecting his wounds. El let out a satisfied grunt and bandaged him back up.

"Get me out of here, El."

"You're not ready to get out of this bed. Trust me. That fever took a lot out of you. Give yourself a few days."

272

"Get me my pants."

El stared at him. "Chase . . ."

"Get them."

Reluctantly, El handed the denims to him, then folded his arms across his chest and stood back to watch.

Dizziness made Chase's head swim as he swung his legs over the side of the bed, but he refused to be daunted. Chase tugged the pants on with an effort, buttoning them halfway up. He steadied himself on the bedstead and on shaky legs stood. Almost immediately, black spots danced in front of his eyes and he swayed toward El, who had moved in to catch him just as his knees buckled.

"Convinced?" El asked, helping him back down onto the bed.

"Damn it."

"Your body's been through a shock. I told you it will take a few days to recover. What's the problem anyway?"

The answer came in an impassioned rush. "I'm feeling pretty goddamn useless, that's the problem. I should be out there working, instead of in here trying to convince Libby not to do what's best for her." He lowered his voice and slung an arm over his eyes. "Damn it, El. What am I going to do?"

"You're in love with her, aren't you?"

It took Chase a few seconds to answer. "Yes."

"Then," El shrugged, "maybe you should marry her."

Chase let out a bark of laughter. "She's already engaged . . . to a man who had nothing to do with the death of her first husband, I might add."

"In that case, I guess you'll have to do what you've always done best with women."

"Which is?"

"Change her mind." El snapped his medical bag

273

shut and handed Chase a letter from his attorney, Maxwell Foulard, postmarked Baltimore. "Father forwarded it to you, and I picked it up in town when I went to wire him about what happened."

Chase frowned at the letter in his hand, then stuffed it into his saddlebags to read later. He wasn't in the mood for any more bad news. "You told my mother about this?" he asked, rubbing his side. "You know what a worrier she is."

"I didn't tell them how bad it really was," El replied. "Just that you were going to be all right. Oh, and Nora Harper was here earlier."

"Is it my imagination, or has she been coming by quite often lately?"

El cleared his throat. "Actually, she's been by every day since you were brought in. She was quite concerned about you."

"Somehow, I doubt it's me she's coming to see."

El glanced up at Chase through a fringe of blond lashes. "She's something, you know?"

"Is she?" Chase asked with a knowing grin.

"Um-hmm. Oh, she, uh, wanted to invite us, *personally*, to the wingding they're having at their place next week for the Fourth of July. If you're feeling up to it that is."

"A *party* at Harper's?" he repeated in a flat voice.

"Libby's going," El pointed out with a shrug. "You could drive her there."

Chase scowled. "I'll think about it."

"Some of Nora's friends, the Winfields, are driving up a few days early from Albuquerque for the party. They have a whole passel of kids, and she and Libby thought it would be a chance for Tad to play with some children his own age. He'll be in heaven." El rubbed his chin thoughtfully. "She asked if I would drive Tad over to her place on Saturday night and, uh . . . stay for dinner."

274

"I see," Chase said, with a slow grin. "So you're interested in her?"

"She's an interesting woman," El allowed with an easy smile. Tipping his hat back on his head, he headed toward the door. "Give yourself another couple of days to get your strength back. I'll see if I can dig up something innocuous to keep you occupied until you're back on your feet. Stay in bed. Hear me?"

Chase watched him, then threw the bedclothes off again and sat up. He would get out of this room as soon as possible—before confinement or Libby Honeycutt drove him crazy.

The next day as Chase sat beneath the portico outside, mending harnesses, the young U.S. Marshal from Santa Fe, John Pratt, rode out to hear firsthand what had happened between Chase and Bodine. Pratt was an easy-going man, whose outward calm, Chase guessed, was deceptive. He seemed surprisingly knowledgeable and capable, and bent on upholding the law. When they'd finished talking, he told Chase that he'd be issuing a wanted poster with Bodine's name on it to all the Territorial Marshals from Texas to Arizona and to the *alcaldes*, or mayors, of surrounding towns.

And before he left, he warned Chase to leave Bodine to him. Chase gave the marshal a grim, silent smile. Only if I don't find him first, he thought, watching the marshal ride off. Otherwise he's a dead man.

Every muscle in her body ached. All Libby could think about, as she forked the last of the hay into the paddock, was sprawling across the bed in Tad's room and sinking into blissful unconsciousness. She had pushed herself hard for the past few days, working

275

side by side with her men in the breaking corrals.

Today, she'd been stepped on, had her arms nearly jerked off by an ornery gelding that took exception to being saddled for the first time, and, despite wearing gloves, had gotten a rope burn on her hand from the thirty-five-foot manila lariat she'd been throwing and dallying around the necks of the stallions who needed halter breaking.

But she wasn't through yet. She had supper to fix, and Tad had to be helped with his schoolwork. Frankly, she wasn't sure she could focus her eyes long enough to do it.

The evening sun hovered over the tips of the mountains to the west by the time she dragged herself into the house, to be met by the smell of corn chowder cooking on the wood-burning stove. Libby blinked in confusion at seeing soup simmering in the pot and smelling the fragrant aroma of fresh biscuits baking.

What in the world . . . ?

The sound of whistling came from her bedroom— sweet soulful whistling that reminded her of a song she'd heard once but couldn't place. The haunting sound stopped and she moved closer to her bedroom door, which was slightly ajar.

"Like this?" It was Tad's small voice she heard.

"That's it," Chase encouraged quietly. "Keep your tongue tight up against your lower teeth . . . like this. Uh-huh. You control the sound with the shape of your mouth and your tongue. Just let the air sail over it, like a breeze whistles through the aspens, like this. . . ."

There it was again. That song. She recognized the tune this time. It was "Lenora," a song popular with both the North and the South during the war. It was one of her favorites, but she hadn't heard it in a long time.

276

He stopped again, and Libby moved closer, peeking through the crack in the door. Tad and his dog, Patch, were sitting companionably on the bed beside Chase, who leaned back against the pillows behind him. In spite of the gauntness from his illness, he was the most handsome man she'd ever seen.

He'd unbuttoned his red cotton shirt, revealing the well-defined muscles of his chest and abdomen. The dark triangle of hair on his chest tapered down to a thin line and disappeared below the waist of the denim trousers that hugged his long, muscular thighs. The fingers of his right hand rested in Patch's fur just behind his ears.

The familiar pang of desire hit her like a wave, and she leaned against the doorway. This was why she'd worked herself ragged for the past few days. This was the reason she couldn't put herself in the same room with him without making a fool of herself. She didn't know what she felt for him anymore or what was right. But watching him filled her with a longing she couldn't deny. And seeing him with her son, she wished, for one bittersweet moment, that they could have met in another time and place.

A noisy wet rush of air escaped Tad's puckered lips, along with a hint of a note.

"Hey! That was the best one yet," Chase praised.

"Wait, wait! I can do it." Tad puckered up and tried again. This time, one fine, pure note escaped his mouth, then disintegrated with his delighted laugh.

Chase grinned broadly and reached over to ruffle Tad's hair. "I told you you could do it."

"I did it! Wait 'til I show Ma!"

Tad nearly collided with Libby on the way out of her room. "Ma! Chase taught me to whistle."

"I heard," she replied, hugging Tad and walking

277

back into her room with him. "And did you cook dinner, too?"

"Chase and me did it together. We made it fer you, Ma," Tad answered proudly.

From the bed, Chase gave her a wink and an easy grin. "Are you all packed up, Tadpole?" Chase asked. "Elliot will be here any minute to take you over to Nora's."

"'Cept my marbles and my toad."

"I think you'd better leave Charlie here, darlin'," Libby told him. "He might get lost in all the excitement over there."

Tad's face fell. "But who'll feed him? He'll starve without me takin' care of him."

"I'll make sure he gets a few crickets while you're gone, Tadpole," Chase promised.

"Tonight? He'll be hungry tonight."

Chase held up his right hand solemnly. "Promise."

"Okay. I'll get the marbles and go see if Elliot's ready to go. Wait 'til I show Nora I know how to whistle. . . ." Tad hurried off happily to do what Chase asked, whistling his one note.

Libby shook her head. "You shouldn't even be out of bed, Chase, and look at you."

"I must admit, I'm a little tired now. But no more than you." His gaze roved over her face. "You look exhausted. You shouldn't be working so hard. You've got some extra men now."

They both knew why she'd chosen to stay away from the house.

"I'm all right." She sat down tiredly on the edge of the bed and traced a finger along the wedding-ring design of the patchwork quilt. "It was nice of you to teach Tad to whistle."

Chase shrugged. "I've been promising him."

"Thanks for cooking dinner, too, because I don't

278

think I could have tonight. It smells wonderful. Where did you learn to cook?"

"I had to teach myself to cook in the Army or go without."

It was then she noticed his saddlebags stacked neatly by the door beside his rifle. She looked back at him. "Are you going somewhere?"

He nodded. "I'm giving you back your room tonight. I'll be fine in the barn."

"But your shoulder—"

"—is healing up just fine, thanks. You need this bed more than I do tonight. I've kept you out of it long enough. Besides, with Tad gone"—he paused— "I think it would be better if I was out of here."

Disappointment tracked through her. She would miss having him here in her house. He was right, of course, about propriety, but knowing that did nothing to ease the lonely ache that started in her at the thought of being completely alone again.

Without him.

His gaze fell to her sore hand, which she cradled in the other one. "What's that?"

"It's nothing. A rope burn."

"That's not something to ignore, Libby." He took her hand in his. "Come here."

"It's nothing really, I—"

"Libby . . ."

Reluctantly, she let him examine her hand. His thumbs smoothed the roughened skin on her palms, carefully avoiding the sore spot.

He frowned. "Don't you wear gloves?"

"I did," she replied. "If I hadn't, they would have been a lot worse. It was just this ornery gelding. My hand nearly got caught in the dally knot."

Chase cursed silently. He'd seen men lose fingers and sometimes hands by getting caught up against the saddle horn in the knot like that. He shook his head and reached for the salve she'd been plying him with all week. Gently, he stroked the fragrant balm onto her palm; then he massaged the rest of her fingers, one at a time.

Libby allowed it, closing her eyes at the wonderful sensation of his caresses. No one had ever done this for her before, and she found she didn't want him to stop. His strong fingers worked their way up to her wrist and arm, stroking, massaging, working out the soreness there.

She opened her eyes to find him watching her intensely. His hand stopped its movement. Libby pulled her hand from his and felt the heat of color rise in her cheeks.

"I . . . I think I smell the biscuits burning," she said without moving, held by his eyes.

He nodded. "Better go check 'em then, Lib."

"I . . . yes." With her heart pounding in her ears, she left him sitting on the bed, watching her go.

Tad and Elliot rode off together toward Three Peaks a short time later. Except for those posted on watch in the canyon, the other men rode off to town for their Saturday night blow out. Libby and Chase shared the supper of corn chowder and biscuits. Though they both ate slowly, and talked of inconsequential, safe things, the meal was over all too soon. Chase helped Libby wash the few dishes they'd dirtied. Then he gathered up his things and came back into the common room.

"I guess I'll head out to the barn," he announced quietly.

"Yes," she answered, not looking at him.

He set his saddlebags on the floor beside him and

took her by the shoulders. He felt an involuntary shiver race through her. "I just want to say . . . thank you for everything. I'm beholden to you, Lib."

Disappointment flashed through her silvery eyes. "Chase . . . you don't owe me anything," she answered, searching his face. This time there was no malice in her words. Only sadness.

"You're wrong about that."

He bent closer, and for a moment she thought, hoped, prayed he was going to kiss her. But his lips only brushed her cheek and then he was gone.

Chase angled the letter he'd received from Max Foulard toward the soft yellow glow of the lantern, read it, and then, with a frown, crumpled it in his hand. Three weeks ago, the letter would have been cause for a celebration. After all, the news that his modest investments had done well in the recent stock-market surge, nearly tripling in value, should have made him happy. It wasn't a huge sum. Twenty thousand didn't make him rich, but it gave him a base to work from. Max had other news as well: an offer by General Grenville Dodge, a Union surveyor he'd met during the war, to come and work for Dr. Thomas Durant's Union Pacific Railroad outside of Omaha.

The job offer gave him pause. It wasn't as if such offers had jumped out of the woodwork. In fact, after this whole business with Libby, he had no plans for the future. But he couldn't bring himself to think about any of that right now. He couldn't imagine a future that didn't include Libby.

The night was full of sounds. A pack of wolves howled in the distance, their plaintive cries hanging on the night air. The hoot owl in the cottonwoods joined in, too. But it was the chirping chorus of crickets that made Chase remember his promise to Tad about Charlie. Tad would never forgive him if the toad was neglected.

Cursing, he climbed carefully back down the loft ladder and hunted up a couple of fat, black crickets. He wrapped them in a rag and started toward the house. He knew where Tad kept his toad box. It was just a matter of . . .

Chase frowned. The lights in the house were still on. Libby had been exhausted. Why was she still up? Maybe, he reasoned, she was having as much trouble as he was getting to sleep.

He knocked on the door, but got no reply. "Libby?" Chase called. Letting himself in, he called again. "Libby?" Her bedroom door was partway open, and the room within was dim with candlelight. She'd probably fallen asleep before she'd even turned the lights down, he reasoned.

After depositing the crickets in Charlie's toad box, he pushed Libby's door open, thinking he'd blow out the candle she'd left burning. A thread of panic seeped into him when he saw that her bed was empty. Her work-soiled clothes were there, cast carelessly on the floor. He picked up her lacy camisole and without thinking pressed it against his mouth and nose, inhaling her scent. He felt his gut tighten.

"Libby?" *Where the hell are you?*

The hinges on the back door complained as he pushed it open and headed toward the privy—the last place he could think of looking. His heartbeat quickened as he strode toward it. What if she was sick and needed help?

But the privy was dark and empty.

Heat lightning split the sky in the distance, in an eerie display of blue light. Chase plunged a hand through his hair and let out a curse, scanning the yard around the house. He cupped his hands around his mouth and was about to cry out for her again, when he was stopped by the glint of moonlight off the water-filled hip bath parked beside the back door, There, with her head tipped back against the copper tub, was Libby, chest-deep in water, sound asleep.

Chapter Nineteen

Chase's stomach sank at the sight, and he walked slowly toward her. His loins tightened with every step. Damn. There was no question of leaving her there. Once the water cooled, she'd catch her death of cold. But how did a man gracefully awaken a naked lady who'd fallen asleep in her tub?

He knelt beside her. She was beautiful. The water appeared black in the moonlight, but he could make out the outline of her breasts just below the surface. Her knees lazed against one side of the tub, partially out of the water. Steam rose off the water in foglike tendrils as it hit the cooler night air, but that didn't account for the heat growing within him.

He pulled his gaze to her face. Her hair was bunched up on top of her head in a knot. Her lips, slightly parted, glistened with moisture. Her lashes moved slightly against her cheeks as if she were dreaming.

"Libby." He ran a finger down her cheek. She sighed and leaned into his caress as a cat might. "Honey, wake up."

She smelled of lilac-scented soap and heat, and he couldn't resist brushing his lips against the softness of her cheek. It was a mistake and he knew it, but he couldn't keep himself from stealing that taste of her. She moaned and, still half-asleep, turned toward him and settled her lips over his in a seeking, answering kiss that shook him to his very soul. He let out a moan and deepened the kiss. Her lips parted, welcoming his tongue and meeting it with her own.

His breath came hard and fast, and he forced himself to pull away from her, cursing himself for being every kind of fool for taking advantage of her this way. Libby's eyes fluttered open only inches away from his. A sharp gasp escaped her as she came fully awake. "Chase!"

"You fell asleep."

"I . . . I did?" She glanced down at the water, glittering in the darkness, and made an attempt to cover herself. But as her gaze went back to him, she let her hands fall away from the breasts she'd tried to hide. He'd expected to see fear, or maybe anger, in her eyes when she woke. But there was nothing close to that in them when her gaze returned to his.

"I thought I was dreaming . . . but I wasn't. You kissed me."

His jaw tightened and he nodded.

Chase froze as she sat up in the water, letting its protection fall away like a drawn-back curtain. Chase's gaze dropped to her breasts—full, round, and perfect—above the cooling water. The chill air puckered their areolas. Her breasts rose and fell with each breath, causing little ripples. Chin up, almost challengingly, she watched him, waiting, daring him to walk away from her.

He started to sweat. Her eyes told him the things she couldn't bring herself to say, and begged him for the very things he wanted to give her. Slowly, her hand came out of the water to touch the scar at his temple with a wet caress.

He felt his good intentions crumple at her touch.

"Ah, damn it all, Libby . . ." His mouth crushed against hers with none of the gentleness he'd shown before, but with a driving reckless hunger that demanded satisfaction.

On a moan of yearning, Libby wrapped her wet arms around his neck and drew him closer until her breasts flattened against his hard chest and soaked the front of his shirt. Without a thought to reason or consequence, her lips moved over his, demanding, feeding the fire already raging inside them both. It was too late to deny the intensity of what was between them. Even if she'd wanted to turn him away, she was utterly incapable of doing it. His kiss had stolen her senses and robbed her of all will, but to be here in his arms.

Without breaking apart from her, he stood, bringing Libby with him. He drew her ever closer, until she was crushed up against the steely, unyielding length of him. She felt an almost violent tremor pass through him. Sliding his hands down the slick length of her, he cupped her buttocks and drew her hips to him. His arousal pressed hard against her belly. He slanted his mouth, and his kiss settled deeper, more provocatively against hers, while their tongues mated.

If it was cold, Libby didn't feel it. Her body was on fire for him. He broke the kiss long enough to reach for the flannel wrapper she'd left draped over the end of the tub and wrapped it around her. One arm slid beneath her knees, and Chase lifted her in his arms, heading for the house.

"Your shoulder—"

His mouth captured hers again, silencing her protest and making it clear he was in no pain from the effort. He yanked the door open and kicked it to make way for the two of them. Like her breath, his came fast and hard, and they shared air as his mouth hovered a whisper above hers.

"We've both wanted this for a long time. You know that, don't you?" he asked.

"Yes" was her breathless reply.

He carried her to her room and set her on her feet in front of her bed. If it hadn't been for the caress in his jade green eyes and the sudden awe in his expression, she would have felt vulnerable, exposed, standing naked before him. He slid the wrapper off her shoulders and wadded it up in his fist. With slow, sensuous strokes, he dried her, dragging the flannel over her still-damp body. Her hands touched his shoulders, feeling his strong muscles bunch and flex beneath her fingers.

The soft fabric rasped over her breasts, her hips, her stomach; and his warm hand trailed behind it, exploring, discovering her. When he was finished, he tossed the wrapper to the floor.

Libby's head dropped back as his palms cupped and lifted her breasts. He dropped his mouth first to one, then the other, taking each nipple into it with reverent passion.

Suddenly, he drew her against him again and buried his face in her hair which had pulled free of the knot and now covered her shoulders in a blond froth. She tightened her arms around him, her hands playing over the ridges of muscle on his back and along his spine. His shirt was wet where she'd touched it, but his skin was hot beneath the fabric.

"Ah, Libby . . . you're so beautiful."

He took her face between his two large hands. His gaze took in every detail and told her there would be no turning back for either of them this time. His look was predatory, utterly male, and sent a shiver of pleasure through her. She didn't want him to stop.

Beyond caring what was right or wrong, she could only proceed where her heart led her—into the quiet storm of his lovemaking.

With his arm behind her neck, he lowered her to the bed, then lay down on top of her. Crushing her into the feather mattress, he again claimed her mouth with his. She met him halfway, shaping her mouth to fit with his. Tongue, teeth, lips ground together in a desperate hungry feast. His body was rock hard, and his hips arched into the cradle of hers.

She reached up to fumble with the buttons of his shirt, needing the feel of his skin against hers, but he didn't have the patience to wait. He ripped his shirt open, buttons popping off and rolling on the floor in little circular spirals. Before he had even shrugged the garment off, her hands were beneath the fabric, touching, exploring his heated skin. They trailed lovingly over the healing scar at his side, the bandage that still covered the wound on his back.

He let out a moan of pleasure and rubbed against her, caressing her breasts with his hair-dusted chest. "Libby . . . ohh-h, Libby . . ."

"Love me, Chase. Just this once. I need to know—"

"You're so soft . . . you taste"—his tongue laved the still-damp skin near her ear—"so sweet." Raining kisses down her throat and chest, he slid downward until his mouth closed over one swollen nipple. He sucked and gently bit the tender place with the edges of his teeth while his rough palms caressed her belly and moved lower, ever lower.

His long fingers found the silky triangle of curls at the vortex of her legs. Her eyes flew open, and she found him watching her with the same fierce expression she'd seen often on his face. It was a look that frightened yet thrilled her.

Chase watched her eyes roll shut and her lips

slacken with pleasure at his touch. Her hips moved against his stroking palm in an ancient rhythm. Chase trailed his tongue across her quivering belly and back again to her breasts. She whimpered. She was hot and ready for him, but he wouldn't take his pleasure too soon. He wanted it to be good for her, because he sensed it never had been before. He wanted to remember every touch, every brush of her lips against his skin, the soft, pillowy weight of her breasts in his hand . . . every sigh his touch evoked. And oh, how he loved to touch her.

Their joining was as inevitable as the fate that had brought him here. He could no more stop himself than he could stop breathing. She was water to his thirst, filling the deep, aching well that had been growing inside him since the war.

He would show her, even if he couldn't tell her, what she meant to him. With every kiss, every stroke, he wanted to make up for all the hurt he'd given her, all the pain she'd suffered. He would love her until she couldn't think, or speak, or remember all the reasons she shouldn't be with him—until all that was left was the fiery dance of their mating.

Libby couldn't believe what he was doing to her. Exquisite shattering feelings rocked her from head to toe, centering deep in her womanhood, curling like a ball of fire and spreading out in tongues of flame. Of all the imaginings she'd had, all the sinful, reckless remembrances she'd harbored, this went beyond them all. He was driving her wild with wanting, and she was desperate to feel him inside her. She moaned his name, but he muffled the sound with his mouth, wresting one long, wet kiss from her.

He pulled away long enough to tug his boots off, then stood to undo the buttons on his trousers and slid them down over his lean hips. Her eyes widened when she saw his arousal. It awed her that she could stir such a need in him and that he could do the same to her.

Then her gaze fell to the terrible scar on his right thigh. Her breath caught in her throat. She'd seen it once, that night when he'd been wild with fever. But then it had seemed paltry compared to the injuries he fought to survive. Now, if indeed it symbolized everything that stood between them, she no longer cared. She wanted to reach out and touch it, heal it—take away the pain he'd gone through.

He stood above her, watching these thoughts play across her face. "It's an ugly scar," Chase said, glancing at his leg.

She shook her head and reached for him. "How could it be ugly if it's part of you?" she asked as he stretched his body out on top of hers. She enfolded him in her arms.

"Ahhh . . . I walked around half-alive before I met you," he murmured, nuzzling her breasts. His lips played against her skin, sending shivers up and down in her. "You make me feel whole again. You're a part of me, Lib, you always will be."

Libby felt her heart lurch painfully at his words, but his stroking hand pushed all thought from her mind. She felt the hard, silken heat of him against her leg. Satin and steel, he was. He wanted her as much as she did him. Chase let out a convulsive shudder as her fingers brushed, then closed around him. He moaned, pressing his face into the curve of her shoulder.

"Libby . . . what you do to me . . ." he murmured. "Can you feel it? Can you feel how much I want you?"

Leaving a fiery, damp trail of open-mouthed kisses in her wake, she answered him, exploring the firm muscles of his chest, teasing his salty nipples with her tongue the way he had hers. With untutored

290

strokes, she discovered the part of him she craved.

"Ahhh . . . yes," he sighed. "Just like . . . ahh . . ."

All the while his hands roved over her breasts, gently squeezing them, rasping the tightened dusky crests with the flattened palms of his hands. Like flint against steel, their hands skimming over each other's body, feeding the growing fire within them until it burned white hot.

With a growl, Chase rolled back on top of her, the limits of his control finally snapped. He wasn't gentle as he pushed her legs apart with one knee, then settled commandingly between her thighs. He dipped his mouth down to pull one nipple fully into it, teasing the bud with his teeth. She gasped his name before he captured her mouth with his own. Then he taught her tongue to explore his mouth as she had the rest of him.

A long shuddering sigh escaped him as he slid inside her, savoring the feeling of the tight, slick sheath welcoming him. With slow steady movements, he rocked against her, easing himself deeper into her velvety warmth until she'd taken all of him.

Libby moaned, her hips straining against his in a steady building rhythm. Heat fused them together. Long, wet strokes, agonizingly slow, quickened the current he felt within her. Her body arched and writhed, trying to get him closer, ever deeper inside her. He drew his hand between them once more and found her. The sounds of pleasure that came from her drove him to the edge of control.

The netting of ropes beneath the mattress creaked with their movement. The heat lightning from outside flashed against the stark adobe walls of her room in a brilliant clash of light and darkness as his thrusts became stronger and more demanding. He drew back to see her face. She was dazed, as fevered as he, her lower lip caught between her teeth.

If he lived a hundred years he would never forget the way she was looking at him right then—head thrown back in passion, her heated breath mingling with his in the space between them. Her eyes told him what he needed to know.

Arms trembling, hands frantic and clinging, hot, slick, flesh against flesh, he lost the last ounce of control he had. His movements inside her became frenzied and his breathing roughened as he approached his own release.

Libby cried out and dug her fingers into his back, "Chase . . . Chase—"

"Don't hold back . . . Come with me, honey, let it happen," he told her, burying his face against her slender neck. His restraint was gone. With his hands on her hips, he brought her up to meet him fully as he drove into her.

She could no more have held back the spiraling, mind-stealing pleasure that eddied inside her than she could have held back a brilliant sunrise. The fever and tension inside her mounted unbearably until, like a thread, it snapped.

Together, in the spiraling eddy that had captured them both, they found their release. The miraculous sensation crested and ebbed within her like a wave crashing on the shore. She cried out and, at the same moment, heard his groan of completion as his body shuddered over hers.

Spent and shaking, they lay together, both stunned by the violent beauty of their mating. Neither of them spoke, as if they were afraid of spoiling the moment they'd just shared. Instead, they clung together for a long time while their breathing returned to normal and their heartbeats slowed.

Chase's breath rasped against her cheek as his lips brushed it. He tasted the salt of her tears and raised up to look at her.

"Libby . . . ?"

She looked up at him, and ran her fingers through his hair, brushing it back from his face. "I'm all right."

"You're crying. Did I hurt you?" He would rather die than think that he had hurt her again.

"No, you didn't hurt me. I've never . . . it was . . . I never felt that way before."

They shared a smile, and he rolled off her, taking her with him in his arms. "You're not alone there, you know." No woman had ever fit him so perfectly or made him lose control so wonderfully before. "You are so . . . beautiful." His hands ran sensuously down her spine. "Libby, I never meant for that to happen, but I don't regret it. Tell me you don't either."

She dropped her cheek to his shoulder with a sigh. "I'd be lying if I said I did." She looked up at him, her shining gray eyes meeting his. "I should have stopped it, too, but I couldn't. I didn't want to. But that doesn't make what we did right."

"Who's to say what's right or wrong?" he asked, pressing his lips to the top of her head.

"Oh, this was wrong." She sighed. "But more than that, it was dishonorable."

He turned her face up with his hands. "Why? Because we finally admitted what we were feeling for each other?"

She shook her head and slid off his sweat-slick body. "Because of *who* we are. Because there's no future for us and I'm promised to another man now."

"You don't owe Jonas Harper anything, Libby. You can tell him you've changed your mind—"

"I haven't."

Her words stopped him cold. "You're going to go through with it?"

"I made a promise to him. This has changed

nothing." *Except me, forever and always.*

He blinked disbelievingly, hurt pouring through him like a bitter infusion. "How can you say that?"

Libby buried her face against her arms. "I'm not saying that what we did meant nothing to me. It meant . . . everything to me. But marrying Jonas isn't about you or me or even my happiness, Chase, don't you see that? It's about Tad and his future. I can't let Tad grow up without some kind of security. Jonas can give him that. I can't. I know that now."

Chase rolled up on one elbow and faced her. "And what about your life? Your happiness? It doesn't count?"

She frowned. "I'll be happy. Jonas Harper is a good, respectable man. He'll take care of us and see that Tad gets all the things he needs."

Chase grabbed her suddenly and pulled her under him again. Her hands went up to brace against his chest.

"What about *your* needs, Lib?" he demanded, fondling her breast, which instantly beaded into a tight bud. "Can Harper do this to you? Can he make you feel what we just felt together?"

She looked away and shook her head. "It doesn't matter."

"Tell me, Lib. Can you live the rest of your life without this?"

She was startled to feel him grow hard against her belly again. "Chase, don't . . ." she pleaded, trying to push him off her.

"Don't what?" he asked, flexing his hips toward hers. "Remind you of what you'll be missing?"

She grew quiet and looked away. "Yes."

After a moment, Chase rolled off her and sat with his back to her. He draped one forearm over his knees. "This is still about Lee, isn't it? You can't forgive me for that, can you?"

A long pause followed. "I've forgiven you," she said at last. "It's myself I can't forgive."

He turned his head to look at her questioningly. "What do you mean?"

"Never mind." Libby threw back the covers and started to get up. Chase's hand lashed out and stopped her.

"Wait a minute. You've got nothing to feel guilty about, Libby. Lee's dead. You're a healthy young woman. He wouldn't have expected you to live alone for the rest of your life, mourning him. You have a right to live again . . . even love—"

"The man who shot him?" she asked before she could stop herself. Libby saw the blow had hit its mark, and she felt herself wither inside. "I'm sorry. I shouldn't have said it that way."

He shrugged and let out a long sigh. "It's true, though, isn't it? But you know, I've often asked myself why it was me that ended up with that locket of yours—why some other poor sap wasn't caught lying in that ditch beside an enemy soldier who only wanted to see his wife one last time. And why, of all things, I was driven to bring the locket to you myself. You know what I decided, Libby?"

She shook her head.

"That I came here because I had no other choice, just as neither one of us had a choice tonight. We're two of a kind, you and me. We're both lost as hell and scared of something that could make us happy."

"I'm a realist, Chase. Even if you and I could overcome the problems we'd face, what about Tad? Do you think I could keep your part in his father's death from him forever? Sooner or later he would find out and end up hating you."

"And what about you? Would you end up hating me, too?"

She pulled the sheet up around her neck. "Forgiving you and letting myself . . . love you are two different things. I can't think about the other."

"Can't or won't?" He pinned her with his eyes while he stood and pulled on his denims. "Watch out, Libby. You just might let yourself be happy for once." He shrugged on his shirt. "You know, sometimes children can surprise you. Sometimes their instincts are a hell of a lot better than ours. Maybe it's because they're so . . . uncluttered by guilt and all those other nasty things we worry about. They live for today, not for the past or the future."

She was about to reply when he swooped down and stole one last stinging kiss from her. Shaken, she stared up at him, while his kiss vibrated through her.

"I love you, Libby, but I'm not the type of man who'll beg," he said gruffly. "It's your decision. Harper or me. I'll be waiting. Good night, Lib." Then he turned and walked out the door.

She lay awake brooding about what he'd said for most of the night, and she kept running up against the same wall. It couldn't be right to love the man who'd played such a part in her husband's death. Could it? Yet, despite what she'd told him about not allowing herself to love him, she knew it was too late for that. She loved him already.

How could loving Chase seem so right and Jonas so wrong?

I won't beg you, Libby. It's your decision.

Her heart ached at what she'd seen in his eyes. Making love to him had been a selfish mistake, and she wished she could take back all the hurt she'd put in his eyes.

Lord in heaven, how could she turn him away? she wondered desperately. But more important, how could she allow him into her heart?

296

Chapter Twenty

The sound of guitars, strolling mandolins and lively chatter filled the air at Three Peaks as Chase pulled the buckboard to a stop next to the large corral where a host of buggies were parked. The corrals were festively decorated with red, white, and blue banners. Pole-hung lanterns were ready to light the place at nightfall.

Smoke billowed fragrantly from the two barbecues at the side of the *hacienda* where beef sides turned, sizzling with dripping grease over the fire. Another fire sported a huge black kettle of beans. Beneath the shade of the willowy aspens, long plank tables had been set up atop barrels and covered with white sheets and patchwork quilts. The yard was already crowded with people. Some of the oldest families of Santa Fe were there: the Delgados; the Ortizes, who had seven children; Jose Sena and his wife, Isabel, who, wearing a black lace *mantilla,* looking every bit the prosperous rancher's wife. Libby tried to imagine herself taking her place among them in society, but the idea held little appeal.

The diminutive scout and Indian fighter, Kit Carson, who'd ridden down from Taos, was there, too. As usual, he was surrounded by admirers and trailed constantly by young Billy Bonney, a boy of Tad's age, who had several times drawn Tad into games of tops in the streets of Santa Fe when Libby had taken her son to town. Libby nodded to Billy's mother, Mrs. Antrim, who ran a neat boardinghouse in town.

There, too, was the marshal, John Pratt. He and his wife, Cynthia, were talking with Nora, who was laughingly fending off a sneak attack by four of the Winfield children. Libby watched Chase's gaze take it all in: the rambling buff-colored hacienda, the rich barns and corrals, the expense Jonas had gone to for this party.

Chase's jaw tightened as he wrapped the reins around the brake handle and jumped down to the ground. Except for Straw's constant banter from the back of the buckboard, their ride here would have been—like the day that preceded it—silent. Chase had only come here at El's insistence that he needed to get off the Double Bar H and have some fun. From his grim expression, Libby guessed that fun was the last thing he expected to have. Libby tore her attention from him and searched the crowds for Tad.

El pulled up beside them on his horse and adjusted the string tie at his neck. "Looking for anyone in particular?" he asked, teasing Libby.

She grinned guiltily. "I can't help it. Tad's never been away from me this long before."

"He was with Nora, who adores him, and about a dozen of those Winfield children," El reassured her. "Believe me, he was in good hands."

"He probably didn't even miss me," she admitted with a smile.

"Oh, I wouldn't be too sure about that," El chuckled. "Look."

298

Tad came racing toward the buckboard, just as Chase was handing Libby down from it. Jonas wasn't far behind.

"Ma!"

Libby scooped him up in her arms and gave him a spinning hug. "Ohhh, you! I missed you so much!" she cried.

"Me, too. Hi, Chase!" he called over his shoulder. "Guess what, Ma? Jarrod Winfield taught me how to pitch horseshoes and Jackson traded me a cat's-eye marble for a rock I found that had plain old *mica* in it and Miss Nora's old white, barn cat had kittens! *Four* of them, and she said I could have one if I wanted. . . ." His voice trailed on, telling Libby all the excitement he'd had in the two days he'd been gone.

A pang of desire hit Chase as his gaze fell to Libby. She looked beautiful with her flaxen hair pulled back neatly into a chignon and her cheeks rosy with excitement. The elegant magenta silk gown she wore had drop shoulders, a tightly fitted basque, and a full skirt. It suited her hourglass figure perfectly. The fact that it was a gift from Harper, however, made Chase wish she were wearing nondescript trousers and boy's shirts again. And as Harper approached, his pleased, possessive look sweeping over Libby, Chase wished it even more.

"Hello, Elizabeth." Jonas's deep voice rumbled from his barrel chest. A catlike grin lit his face as he kissed her cheek. "You look . . . radiant, my dear. Lovely. If I do say so myself, the choice of magenta for your gown was the right one."

"Thank you, Jonas. Your place looks wonderful."

"Nora's doing, I'm afraid. She's had Tad and all those Winfields hopping to all week."

"Are we the last ones here?"

"Not at all," he answered, "but I'll admit, I've been anxious to see you."

Tad pulled on his mother's arm, desperate to show her the barn kittens. "C'mon, Ma. There's a little black one that's—"

"Tad!" Jonas snapped. He frowned and laid an ominous hand on Tad's shoulder. "You forget yourself, boy. Your mother will be along in good time, and it won't do to be yanking her by the arm as if she were a yearling calf." He pointed off in the direction of the barn where a swarm of boys were hitting a metal hoop with a stick. "You run along now and play with your friends."

Tad blushed furiously and looked up at Libby, confused.

Speechless at Harper's disciplining of her son, she bent down and gave Tad a peck on his cheek. "You go on. I'll be along directly. We'll pick out the prettiest of those kittens for you to take home. Okay?"

Tad managed a smile, but his joy had dimmed with Harper's taking-down. He turned and ran off toward the other children.

Libby couldn't bring herself to look Jonas in the eye. Instead she glanced at Chase, who was visibly seething over Jonas's dismissal of her son.

Jonas took her hand and patted it, clearly misunderstanding her anger for embarrassment. "Don't worry, my dear. His lack of manners is perfectly understandable considering he's been fatherless so long. A boy like Tad needs a firm male hand. I'll see he gets it."

Libby's teeth ground together. Tad's enthusiasm had been perfectly understandable, considering he hadn't seen her in days. She would have to set Jonas straight about how she intended Tad to be raised. But this wasn't the time.

Jonas nodded to Elliot then glanced at Chase who was unhitching Blue from the back of the wagon. "Mr. Whitlaw, I'm glad to see you're on the mend."

"I'm doing fine, thanks to Libby," he replied.

Jonas didn't flinch. "Yes, she's quite a woman, my Elizabeth," he answered, offering her his elbow.

Libby hesitated. "Oh, I brought some apple pandowdy," she said, reaching for the cloth-covered pan at the back of her wagon.

Jonas took it from her hands and passed it to Chase. "I have some people to introduce you to, my dear. I'm sure Mr. Whitlaw won't mind carrying it in for you, will you, Whitlaw?"

Chase sent him a scowl and took the pan. "Not at all." He touched the brim of his hat to Libby and smiled meaningfully. "Ma'am."

Libby returned his smile nervously then allowed Jonas to lead her off to the party.

"I don't like that bastard," Chase grumbled to El, who'd come to stand beside him.

"That makes two of us. When I came to Nora's for dinner with Tad, he spent half the time grilling me about you."

Surprised, Chase turned to El. "What did you tell him?"

El laughed. "Nothing, of course. But I think you make the man nervous."

A bitter smile curled Chase's lips. "I wonder why? He's got what he wants."

"Could be the way the object of his desire looks at you. . . ."

Chase glanced sideways at him. "Do me a favor and tie Blue up over by the barn, near the water trough, will you? I'm gonna get rid of this pan and see if there's anything to drink stronger than lemonade over there."

301

"The day's young, Chase," El warned, taking Blue's reins.

"Don't remind me," he tossed back over his shoulder as he walked away.

Nora had planned a full day of events aimed at keeping the children entertained. Sack races, foot races, even a greased pig-catching contest. To no one's surprise, men and women joined in the fun, participating in their own three-legged races and tobacco-spitting contests. Nora and Elliot entered the three-legged contest together, much to the delight of the children. They ended up in a tangle on the ground halfway to the finish line, laughing hysterically. Tad and Jarrod Winfield reigned victorious, defeating all the eminently clumsier adults.

Jonas served as judge in the dessert contest and, amid jesting cries of partiality, picked Libby's apple pandowdy over all the others.

It was, however, the target-shooting contest that peaked Chase's interest. Over the rim of a strong cup of Switchel, a drink made with rum and molasses, Chase watched the men line up for the contest. Among them was Jonas Harper. The prize: a fifty-dollar purse of entry-fee money. Intrigued, not by the prize, but the opportunity to go up against his nemesis, Chase quietly retrieved his Henry rifle from his saddle and joined the others.

"That's a fine-looking rifle," Jonas commented, eyeing the etched brass breech. "But can it shoot as good as it looks?"

"All depends on the man who's shooting it, I suppose," Chase answered, dropping his two-dollar gold piece on the entry table.

Jonas licked his thumb and swiped at the sight on the barrel of his Spencer Repeater. "That's a fact," he agreed with a chuckle. "The proof, as they say, is in the pudding. Let's see what kind of a cook you are, Whitlaw."

"It'll be my pleasure, Harper."

The targets were empty bottles, set up in long rows across a fallen cottonwood trunk. Each man had three shots in the first round, eliminating any who missed by more than one shot. Both Chase and Jonas easily hit their marks, as did Early and several of Jonas's men and the slender blond-haired marshal, John Pratt. In all, fifteen went on to the second round which was moved back ten paces from the firing line to increase the difficulty. This round drew more of an audience, including the women who'd hung around on the outskirts of the cooking.

Libby was one of them. A smile crept to her lips. She'd seen Chase shoot, and if it had been ladylike to lay odd's on his winning, she would have done so. Her heart beat faster as she watched him shoulder his Henry and pick off three bottles in quick succession. Juan Ortega, a Santa Fe gun merchant, John Pratt, and Jonas each picked off their bottles, too.

The third round was moved back another ten paces, with only the four men left. Gunpowder smoke hung in the air. A murmur of excitement passed through the crowd as the men reloaded their guns. Jonas cast a glance at Libby and winked at her. Chase glanced at her, too, but there was no mischief in his eyes, only a confident grin that said, "This is for you." She looked away quickly, afraid someone would notice the heat passing between them.

Ten more paces put the prize out of reach for Jonas who missed his last bottle. He swore and lowered his gun slowly, not a little disgusted with himself. He gave Chase a grudging tip of his head as he walked away from the firing line to stand beside Libby. Ortega, too, missed one, eliminating him from the competition. That left John and Chase.

"Let's make this interestin'," called James Johnson, a bushy-faced merchant from Santa Fe. "Both of these fellers is crack shots. I say to choose the best shot between 'em, we let 'em have a go at a movin' target."

A roar of approval went up and Johnson was chosen to do the honors. The onlookers became divided into cheering factions, each supporting one of the two contestants. Six bottles were thrown for each and twelve were hit. On the signal, Johnson threw two more into the air. John hit one and missed one. Chase exploded both of his.

A roar went up from all sides, and John walked back to shake Chase's hand. "That's some kind of shooting, Whitlaw. Where'd you learn that?"

He shrugged. "Army." Chase fended off the claps of congratulations that came dangerously close to his healing shoulder. "You're not half bad yourself, Marshal."

John smiled wryly. "Good to know the Army wasn't a complete waste of our time, isn't it? You ever need a job, you come look me up, Whitlaw. I could use a gun like you."

Chase shook his head. "I'm not looking to be a hired gun. The only man I aim to see justice for is Trammel Bodine."

John rubbed his square jaw as they walked toward the shade of the aspen grove near the corral. "Matter of fact, I heard some news about your 'friend' just yesterday. Seems he's running with a feller name of Clay Allison. Bad feller, too, that one. Had me a couple of run-ins with him in my jail. He was working at a spread over on the Rio Grande. Apparently, Bodine worked there at one time, too.

"Allison killed two men over there. Couldn't prove it wasn't self-defense, but I know it wasn't. Anyways,

304

seems Allison and a feller fitting Bodine's description was seen rustling some cattle down near San Miguel and killed a ranch hand in doing it. So your friend just progressed from attempted murder to murder and cattle stealing."

"San Miguel you say?"

Pratt nodded. "He's probably long gone from there by now, but the *alcalde* there did tell me before they done it, this feller calling himself Travis Barlow"—he carefully enunciated the initials T. B.— "wearing that rattlesnake hatband like the one you described, was spending money like he had it to throw away."

Chase scowled. "Where would Bodine get that kind of money?"

Jonas interrupted them before Pratt could answer. "Congratulations, Whitlaw," he said curtly, handing Chase the jingling bag full of prize money. "Have to admit, you're a damn good shot."

"Thank you," Chase replied, his eyes flashing to Libby's.

"I reckon fifty dollars will come in handy with your job at Elizabeth's dryin' up soon, won't it?" he asked pointedly.

"I imagine fifty dollars would always come in handy, unless I was too rich or too drunk to notice."

Jonas let out a sharp laugh. "You have plans to move on after the herd's in, do you?"

Chase smiled with deceptive ease. "I don't hold much store with plans. I like to take things one day at a time. Sometimes," he continued, brazenly sliding his gaze to Libby, "fate can step in and change what we mere mortals have in mind."

Libby blushed furiously in response, dipping her head so no one would notice. Her temper flared like a sulfur-tipped match. She knew what he was trying to

305

do, blast him! She hardly needed a reminder of what happened between them less than thirty-six hours ago. Yes, and she'd counted every one, hell that they had been. Indeed, destiny may have put Chase Whitlaw in her path to stumble over, but she'd be damned if she'd make a fool of herself over him again.

"My, but it's hot," she commented, sending Chase a scathing look and fanning herself with her hand. "Jonas, could I bother you for a cup of Haymaker's Punch? I saw a bowl on the refreshment stand earlier."

He hesitated only a moment, giving Chase an appraising look. "It would be my pleasure, my dear," he replied, heading off to fetch it for her. A pair of strolling musicians passed him, strumming guitars.

The raven-haired wife of the marshal, Cynthia Pratt, sneaked up behind her husband and gave his arm a playful tug. "If you men are through talking business, maybe you can drag yourself away to pour me a cup, too."

Pratt grinned and shrugged. "Women. They always want something from you," he said, allowing his wife to lead him away.

"And what is it you want from me, Libby?" Chase asked coolly when he and Libby were alone.

"Nothing," she snapped, "except that you don't try to make a fool of me here in front of all these people."

"I have no desire to make a fool of you."

She flashed a pleasant smile at a couple who passed by, but it abruptly disappeared when she turned back to Chase. "Are you deliberately trying to embarrass me, then?"

"Why would I try to do that?" His expression was unreadable.

306

"I'll thank you to stop making comments about fate—"

"I've always been of the conviction that fate spoke for itself," he replied.

"—and to stop looking at me the way you do."

A sudden grin curved the straight line of his mouth. "And which way is that?"

"Like . . . like you want to . . ."

He folded his arms across his chest, and one dark eyebrow arched inquiringly. His gaze dropped to her lips. "Like I want to what?"

It was there in a flash, flickering in his eyes. All the heat of their joining, the pain of their parting. But the look was gone as soon as it came, replaced by the solid blank wall he'd again erected around his heart over the past two days. He was a proud man, and she loved him for that.

I won't beg you Libby. No, she didn't want him to beg her. Frankly, she didn't know what she wanted, but the silence between them had grown unbearable.

Flustered, she tore her gaze from his and stared at the ground. "I don't want to fight with you. Not after everything that's happened between us. Can't we be friends?"

Chase's eyes glittered like cold jade, and he shook his head. "If it's a friend you're looking for, better shop someplace else. I'll have all of you or none of you. That's the kind of man I am, Lib. If you can't handle that, you'd better stick to something safer." He gestured, with a hitch of his chin, behind her. "And here he comes now."

Before Jonas could reach her, Chase had turned on his heel and disappeared into the crowds of guests.

Jonas handed Libby the cup of cider vinegar and molasses punch. "What did he want?"

"Nothing," she lied, staring after Chase.

307

"I don't like him."

"You don't even know him."

Jonas narrowed a look at her. "It's a gut feeling. I don't trust him. I don't want him getting friendly with you."

Libby smiled sadly and looked at Jonas. "No worry about that. I saw Nora getting the dinner ready. I think I'll go give her a hand."

Chase stalked to the barn, where he'd seen Tad and some of the other boys go. He'd promised the boy to look at his kitten. Maybe it would help to cool him down.

Slim chance of that.

"You should have left it alone, Whitlaw," he muttered to himself, "given her the locket and let her get on with her life—gotten on with your own!"

He slammed his palm against a corral post. The first time! The first damned time he'd allowed himself to feel anything for anyone since the war, and she'd slapped him in the face with it. It didn't matter that he'd opened his heart and soul to her the other night. It didn't matter that she'd seen a part of him no one had since the war had stolen tender feelings away from him. She was going to marry Harper, and there wasn't a thing he could do about it.

Damn it to hell! A man had his pride! He could only take so much. He'd been right the first time. It was safer to feel nothing than to live with this kind of agony. His chest ached with it, and it gathered like a fist in his throat. Why had he let El talk him into coming? To see Libby reject him publicly? Maybe he'd hoped to change her mind. But it was clear she'd made her decision. *And it wasn't him.*

From inside the barn, he heard voices whispering in frantic hushed tones.

"Step on it, Jarrod! Holy cripe, it's smokin'!"

"I am! It won't go out. Oh, Lord! Ma's gonna kill me."

Chase heard Tad's voice, too, as he headed into the darkened barn.

"I told ya not to, Billy! Hit it with yer coat, Jarrod!"

Chase heard Jarrod wrestling with his coat and didn't wait to hear more. The pungent smell of smoke reached his nostrils.

Chase made a grab for the saddle blanket hanging over a saddletree and sprinted to the stall where the boys were stomping on a small, burning patch of straw. He lunged at the fire while the twelve-year-old Jarrod Winfield, Billy Bonney, and Tad stared wide-eyed at him. Chase beat the small pile of flames into submission with the thick, woven blanket, and the fire sputtered and went out. A small charred circle of straw was all that remained.

"Go get a bucket of water, boy," Chase told Billy.

"I didn't do it," Billy said defiantly. The other two flashed him a disbelieving look, but kept silent.

"That wasn't an accusation," Chase told him. "It was an order. Go get some water before this straw starts up again."

Billy escaped out of the stall and disappeared out the double doors of the barn. Chase turned to Jarrod and Tad, who stood trembling and wide-eyed before him.

"What are you boys thinking of, smoking in a barn full of hay? Don't you know what could have happened?"

Both nodded miserably.

Silent, they stared at the charred hay, unwelcome tears welling behind their eyes. Yes, Chase imagined they did know what they'd almost done. That kind of a scare can stay with a boy for life. He remembered

309

the time he and El had done much the same thing in the silo one summer afternoon, starting a minor fire that sent smoke billowing up the tube like a chimney. El's father had made sitting pretty damned uncomfortable for both of them for quite a while after that.

But it wasn't the whipping he remembered. It was the realization of what the fire could have done— what their carelessness could have cost everyone— that stuck with him. By their expressions, he suspected this wasn't an incident they'd soon forget either.

Chase ran a hand through his hair. "Jarrod, I'm not your pa. Lucky for you no real harm was done here. But I'm going to trust you'll do the right thing and tell your father what's happened here. You're almost a man. You can use your own judgment about when to tell him."

"Yes, sir."

"Now git."

Jarrod hesitated for only a moment. "I'm sorry, sir. I . . ." He faltered and sprinted from the barn.

Tad hung his head and scuffed his toe in the ashes at his feet. "I'm sorry, too, Chase. Are you gonna tell Mr. Harper on me?"

Chase had seen a taste of Harper's justice. He had no wish to submit Tad to it, considering the little damage that had been done. "Do you think I should?"

Tad stiffened his jaw and shrugged.

"It's not my place to tell him," Chase said finally. "I'm not *your* pa, either."

"I wish you was," Tad mumbled.

Chase's heart jumped in his chest and a feeling of tenderness swept over him. Lord, he'd miss Tad when he left.

"I wish I was too, Tad," he said, wrapping an arm

around the boy's narrow shoulders. "Sometimes things just don't go the way we want them to."

"Do you want to marry my ma?" he asked hopefully.

Chase ruffled Tad's blond cap of hair with his hand. "I guess that's something between your ma and me, son."

Tad wiped his mouth on his sleeve. "I don't remember my pa much. I was little when he left. But sometimes . . . I think he must'a been like you." Tad grew silent as Chase reined in the emotions that made him look away. "Are you gonna tell Ma about . . . ?"

"I'll leave that up to you, Tad. Now start to clean up this mess while I get a bucket of water," he said, handing him the rake that stood in the corner. "Looks like Billy's not coming back."

"Thanks, Chase." Tad threw his arms around Chase's waist.

Chase hugged him back and allowed himself to wonder for one brief moment what it would be like to have a child of his own. He put the thought away. He could imagine no one but Libby mothering his children. And that, he knew, wasn't to be.

The dancing circle was set up after the sun dipped below the horizon and the mountains of food had been almost consumed. Yellow lantern light spilled across the yard. Guitars, fiddles, mandolins, and mouth-harps appeared, and couples paired off for the dancing on the smooth, raked-dirt dancing area. Elliot pulled Nora onto it with a flourish, and she laughed aloud as they whirled to the tune of "Sweet Betsy."

"Dr. Bradford!" Nora scolded teasingly. "My reputation—"

"—Is spotless," El finished. "School teachers are

311

allowed to have fun, aren't they?"

"I suppose. It's just been so long since I have!"

"Well then, now's the time to start." Nora allowed him to pull her closer than was strictly proper as they moved amongst the other couples.

"A surgeon and a dancer, too," she said with a grin. "How many other hidden talents have you, Dr. Bradford?"

"Ah, you've only scratched the surface, Miss Harper," he murmured in her ear, sending a shiver through her. "And may I say, you dance splendidly for a schoolteacher."

She pinned her gaze on the silken string tie at his throat. "You've danced with many schoolteachers, have you?"

"A few. But none as lovely as you."

Color crept to her cheeks, and she laughed. "I'll bet you were a terror in the classroom with that fatal charm of yours."

"Possibly," he admitted mischievously, "but I learned a long time ago that a woman could always tell a lie from the truth." His fingers tightened around hers. "I enjoy being with you, Nora."

She searched his sky blue eyes, then smiled. "I feel the same way."

"It's funny isn't it?" he mused aloud. "We're both from the East, but we each had to travel hundreds of miles to meet each other in the Woolly West."

The song ended and another picked up immediately. This time it was the haunting melody "Shenandoah," that drifted from the musicians' podium.

"Do you miss it?" he asked, weaving Nora through the crowded dancing area.

"What?"

"The East . . . the hustle and bustle of civilization."

"Sometimes. But I'm quite content here," she answered, then glanced up at him. "Do you?"

El drew her closer. "You know, I thought I would miss it more. Before I joined the Army, I'd never traveled farther from home than the city of Boston— to attend Harvard. Then I found myself being sent all over the countryside: Shiloh, Louisville, Philadelphia, Washington. As horrible as the war was, the traveling got into my blood. When it was over, my family expected me to settle down to a practice and start a family. But I was . . . restless. I wanted to see the frontier before it was settled. Tagging along with Chase seemed the perfect opportunity to do just that.

"The West *is* extraordinary," he went on. "And it has its own"—he glanced down at her—"special sort of beauty. Suddenly, I find I can't think of another place I'd rather be right now." His fingers twined with hers. "Have you ever given thought to returning to nursing?"

"I suppose teaching has its share of nursing," she answered. "Wiping bloody noses, cleaning scraped knees."

"No, I meant, working with . . . say, a doctor perhaps."

"There is only one doctor within miles of here, in Santa Fe, and he's old and feeble and not long for the profession, I'm afraid."

"I meant, perhaps, with a doctor like . . . me."

She stiffened slightly in his arms. "Be careful what you say, Dr. Bradford. A spinster like me might get the wrong idea."

He chuckled and brushed a strand of hair from her face. "If you're unmarried, its only because you haven't let any of us catch you yet. You're a woman with a mind of her own. And a good mind at that. I admire that. I've never met anyone quite like you, Nora." He gazed down at her, stroking her face with

313

his eyes. "You haven't answered my question."

Her mouth curved up in a shy smile, and she chose her words carefully. "I suppose it would depend on how much that particular doctor needed me. But, yes, I'd . . . consider nursing again."

Elliot pulled her tighter against him and kissed her cheek tenderly. "That's good to know, Miss Harper. That's very good to know, indeed."

Dancing lightened Libby's mood as she was spun on the arms of three other men and Jonas in the Forward, Backward Eight, a square dance done with four couples. No one called the dance. Everyone knew the steps. The musicians played everything from "Turkey in the Straw" to "Camptown Races," until Libby finally pleaded fatigue and asked Jonas to get her some punch.

Then several cowhands who had already heard Cynthia Pratt's voice, begged her to get up and sing for them. Blushing, she took the platform next to the musicians' and whispered a request to the guitar player.

Libby searched the crowd for a glimpse of Chase. He'd studiously avoided her all day. Once she had seen him walking with Tad and his new kitten, later with several Mexican women who obviously appreciated his good looks. Tonight, she'd seen him dance with nearly every woman at the party but her. She had no right to feel jealous, but she did. Just once, she'd like to dance in Chase's arms, to know what that felt like.

Cynthia started to sing, her sweet resonant voice doing justice to the bittersweet song she had chosen.

"Green grows the laurel, all sparkling with dew,
I'm lonely my darling, since parting with you.

But by the next meeting I hope to prove true,
And change the green laurel for the red, white,
and blue.''

"Hi." The voice came from behind Libby. Even before she turned, she knew who it was. It was eerie, almost as if Chase had read her thoughts.

"Hi, yourself," she replied with a shy smile.

"Care to take a turn with me?"

"I . . . I was wondering if you'd ever ask me."

Chase's right hand closed around hers and his left went to her waist. Her crinolines rustled as they moved together. He spun her slowly across the dance floor in time to the song. He was a wonderful dancer and made the steps seem effortless, in contrast to some of the clumsy attempts of the cowboys on the floor.

"I once had a sweetheart, but now I have none,
Since she's gone and left me, I care not for none.
Since she's gone and left me, contented I'll be,
For she loves another one better than me.''

"Pretty song," Chase murmured against her hair.

"Mm-hm." Libby pulled back slightly, trying to make light conversation. "Did you know it was that song that gave us all the name *gringos?*"

He looked to see if she was serious.

"During the war with Mexico," she explained, "the Irish-American soldiers sang it constantly. All the Mexicans could make out were the words 'green grows.'" She smiled and shrugged. "Gringos."

"You're a wealth of information tonight, Mrs. Honeycutt."

She chuckled. "Are you enjoying yourself?"

He drew her fractionally closer, tightening his hand at her waist. "At this very moment? Yes.

You look beautiful by moonlight, Libby. Did I ever tell you that?"

"I believe you did, one drunken night," she recalled with a bittersweet smile.

"Ah, yes . . ." He smiled, too. "But you have outdone even that memory for me tonight, Libby." His eyes blazed down into hers, and his thumb caressed her waist.

"You're just not used to seeing me in a dress."

"You'd outshine the other women here no matter what you wore. You know that, don't you?"

She looked away, realizing how often since she'd met him he'd made her *feel* beautiful. She felt it right now, with his arms around her. Whether it was heaven or hell to be here, she couldn't decide.

"I saw you talking with Colonel Carson earlier. Were you discussing the herd?" he asked.

Libby nodded. "He's made arrangements to have an army detail meet the herd in Las Vegas on the first of August to escort it to Fort Union."

"Good. That will save us a day or two of driving them."

"Where will you be going after the herd is delivered?" *How will I bear it when you're gone?*

He shrugged. "Omaha. I've had a job offer from Grenville Dodge to work for the Union Pacific Railroad. I suppose I'll go there." *Tell me not to go, Libby. Just tell me.*

"Oh."

"Have you and Jonas set the date yet?"

"I . . . no, not exactly. Right after the herd is delivered."

"Oh."

The music stopped, but he didn't let her go. Instead they stood looking into each other's eyes. He couldn't very well kiss her right here in front of all

316

these people, but he wanted to. Damn it all, he wanted to.

"Elizabeth?"

Jonas's tight voice separated them as surely as if he'd parted them with his hand.

Libby flushed with embarrassment. "I . . . we were just dancing," she said guiltily.

"The music's over," he replied, sending a hard look to Chase. "Come with me, my dear. I think it's time for my little surprise. Mr. Whitlaw . . . stick around. This might interest you, too."

Harper took Libby's hand and led her to the musician's stand. Unable to watch, Chase made his way to the refreshment table and slugged down two cups of strong punch, wishing for something more potent.

It was only out of some kind of morbid curiosity that he stayed. He was a glutton for punishment. And tonight would end it for them. He knew that.

The liquor in the punch left a numb trail blazing down to his gut, and he fought the sudden twinge of nausea that resulted. If he got drunk, so be it. Drunk or not, he'd never be rid of this ache growing inside him.

A silver spoon clinking on crystal brought Chase's attention to the stage on which the musicians stood. He saw Harper and Libby facing the crowd of guests. Assuming a magnanimous air, Harper started to speak.

"Most of you know Elizabeth Honeycutt. Some of you know I've been after her to be my wife for some time now." An expectant murmur rose from the crowd, and Jonas gazed at Libby, who managed a forced smile. "Well, by God, she's finally agreed to change her name to Harper."

Applause and cheers rippled through the crowd as Jonas bent to kiss Libby chastely on the lips. She

317

flushed right down to her toes and wished she could be anywhere but where she was.

"I have a little present for you, Elizabeth," Harper then said, opening the small black velvet box he'd kept in his pocket. From it, he withdrew a stunning diamond ring surrounded by perfectly cut sapphires. To the oohs and ahhs of the crowd, he slipped it on the fourth finger of her left hand.

"It's . . . it's beautiful, Jonas. Thank you," she said, knowing the extravagant gift required some kind of response. The audience approved, with shouts and catcalls.

Jonas turned and smiled expansively at his guests. "I think this calls for some kind of celebration, don't you?" He motioned dramatically to his Chinese cook, Soo Ling, to ignite the charge on the string of fireworks set up in the corral farthest from the house.

The charges exploded one at a time, pitching flares of color into the sky to the delight of the audience, young and old alike. As colors blossomed—red, white, and blue—over their heads, Libby's gaze collided with Chase's. A thousand regrets passed between them in that one look; for each of the days, years, lifetimes they wouldn't share.

Chase tossed back the last of his cup of punch and lifted the empty cup in a silent, mocking salute to her. Then, his stride stiff with anger, he walked to his horse and spurred Blue off into the darkness in the direction of her ranch.

And with him, he took a piece of Libby's heart.

Chapter Twenty-One

Summer burned its way across the valley, scouring the land with heated, moisture-sucking winds and dust storms. The chamisa dried, as did the grama grass, forcing Libby and her men to search the higher altitudes for the foraging herds of wild horses. Will Tuerney and Ladder Hopkins, so named for his tall, lanky body, were sent from Three Peaks to help in the roundup. Together with her men, Libby went out in search of the stock needed to complete their string of horses for the Army. They stole young stallions from every wild herd within forty miles of her ranch, but strangely never ran across Diablo's *manada*.

Days were long and sweltering. Nights cold and, for Libby, endlessly long. Chase avoided her at every turn, speaking directly to her only if she asked him a question. Given the choice, he'd have stayed behind to work with Straw, shoeing the horses, or he'd have ridden ahead with the others if she'd stayed at the ranch. He'd accompanied her reluctantly on a trip to Santa Fe, so she could keep her appointment with an attorney and he could buy a new pistol to replace the one Bodine had stolen from him. But their trip was anything but comfortable. Silence rode along with them like a third companion.

She didn't want things to be left the way they were, but she could find no help for it. The men were set to leave for Las Vegas with the herd the next morning.

It had taken two and a half weeks to round up the last of the mustangs. As she, Miguel, and Ladder drove the last four stallions into the holding enclosure, she noticed the dust cloud issuing from the high-railed breaking pen. But it wasn't until she got closer that she noticed *who* was doing the breaking. A frown crossed her face.

"Of all the hair-brained, idiotic—!"

"Yee-haw!" Straw crowed from his place on the six-foot corral fence. "Hang on to that jigger-brained knothead, Chase!"

"Hoo-hoo! Don't let him make ya meet yer shadow, boy!" Early shouted, cupping his hands around his mouth. "I got money ridin' on ya!"

"Yeah, Chase!" Tad chimed in, "show 'im who's boss!"

The moon-eyed roan gelding in the breaking pen swung madly about, trying to fishtail its rider off, but Chase hung on with a tenacity born of sheer determination and skill. Libby watched from atop her dun-colored mare. She didn't know who she was more furious with: Chase for wanting to ride that fractious beast or Early for letting him do it.

She'd seen perfectly healthy men bleed from the nose or ears after riding a bronc, just from the jolting. Blast him! It had been less than a month since he'd nearly been killed! Whether he was doing this to prove something to himself or to her wasn't important. She kicked her horse nearer the breaking pen.

"What in God's name is Chase doing riding that bronc?" Libby demanded of Early, who was balanced on the top rail of the breaking pen. "How could you let him get near that devil?"

"He ain't a child, Libby," Early admonished her.

320

"He's healed up good, an' he's got a mind of his own. Once he makes it up, you know there ain't no stoppin' him. 'Sides, it appears he's got that sidewinder right where he wants him."

"He's going to kill himself, is what he's going to do," she muttered. "The idiot."

"Maybe," Early agreed, "but he'll have a helluva time a-doin' it."

She couldn't help, however, grudgingly admiring Chase's considerable skill. The man rode like he was born on a horse.

The air was thick with dust churned up by the bucking roan, and the wilting heat made the fine silt cling to every exposed part of the body. Chase's spurs jabbed the horse's flank every time the animal bucked. The roan was wild eyed and furious, but Chase was firmly settled against the bucking roll and showed no inclination to be parted from his saddle. A dark V of sweat made his shirt cling to his muscled chest. Moisture glistened on his face.

"Ride 'im, boy! Hell, that feller kin set that devil!" Will exclaimed, punctuating his praise with a wet stream of tobacco juice.

"Hey, Ma!" Tad called, seeing her. "Lookit Chase! Ain't he somethin'?"

"I see him." She raised the volume of her voice a notch so he'd be sure to hear. "But a fool and his saddle are soon parted!"

Chase made the mistake of breaking his concentration at her taunt. In the moment it took for his eyes to meet hers, the mustang wrangled the upper hand. The animal careened, bucking into the split fence sideways, trying to knock Chase off. He saved himself a smashed femur by pulling his leg up at the instant before the gelding crashed into the wood. It cost him, however, his balance. "Whoa!" he cried, as he was launched off the horse with the next buck. He tucked his head and hit the ground rolling until he ground to a stop, halfway across the paddock. For some moments, he didn't move at all.

Libby's instinct was to rush to him to see if he was all right, but she held back, wanting neither to embarrass herself nor him. Will vaulted over the fence and chased the loose bronc down, tying him deftly to the railing.

To her great relief, Chase slowly got to his feet, apparently unhurt. He was spitting out dirt, scowling at her. Covered as he was from head to toe with dust, only his leafy eyes and the squint lines around them were untouched.

"You still in one piece, Chase?" El called with a grin.

"Yeah . . ." He looked like he'd just taken a roll in a cattle wallow. Retrieving his hat, he slapped it against his chap-covered thigh, sending up a cloud of New Mexican earth. The gelding perked his ears and gave Chase a condescending look from its place at the fence, snorting disdainfully and tossing its head. Chase narrowed his eyes.

Early let out a hoot of laughter. "I think ya just come down a notch in his estimation, boy."

"Yeah, Chase, don't feel bad," Will Tuerney chortled good-naturedly, "He weren't the puniest one of the bunch. Only the second puniest!" Will crumpled into a fit of laughter along with most of the others.

Libby knew only too well the men saved the worst of the lot for last, and they'd nicknamed this particular gelding Lucifer, for good reason. Looking at Chase, she pressed her lips together as laughter bubbled up inside her, too. It was awful of her, but she couldn't seem to help it. It served him right for being so obstinate.

Chase cast a glare at her. "*"Et tu Brute?"*" he

growled, actually speaking to her for the first time in days.

Libby rocked in her saddle, gripping her sides as laughter escaped. It felt good to laugh, to release some of the tension of the last few days. "Brutus, am I?"

"Watch out when he starts quoting Shakespeare," El warned between hoots of laughter.

Chase determinedly shoved his sleeves up past his elbows. "Oh, yeah? You think I can't ride this demon from hell?" he asked, stalking to the wary beast once more. The gelding rolled its eyes and backed into the fence.

The smirk fell from Libby's lips. "Chase! Oh, for heaven's sake! How stubborn can you . . . ? You're not going to—"

"The hell I'm not. I never met a horse that could throw me and get away with it."

"Whoa! Stand back," ribbed Will Tuerney, covering the horse's eyes with his neckerchief. "Whitlaw's gonna give 'er another go. Ho-ho! Five more says he won't get airborne a second time, Early!"

"Yer on!"

"Ya-hoo!" Tad shouted.

Chase mounted the mustang whose feet were splayed nervously out to both sides. This time, Chase decided, nothing would distract him from his job. Including the beautiful blonde glaring at him across the fence.

As soon as Will removed the wipes from the gelding's eyes, the roan was off like a caged grasshopper. It bucked and twisted, fishtailed and spun, employing every means at its disposal to dump its rider back on the ground, to no avail.

Chase stayed in the saddle as if he were glued to it, relying on his instincts to tell him which direction the animal would go in next. Using spurs and quirt to save himself a repeat performance, he wore the animal down methodically, refusing to be cowed or intimidated. Finally, the roan settled into an exhausted trot, allowing Chase to guide him around the ring masterfully. The men let out whoops and hollers of appreciation.

With a light tug on the reins, Chase brought the roan to a stop in front of Libby. A rare, triumphant smile brightened his dust-coated face, and he arched an insolent eyebrow at her. "He who laughs last," he said cockily, "laughs best."

Libby shook her head and raised her own brow. "Ah, but we'll see who's laughing later when you come to me for the liniment." She tossed her golden braid over her shoulder and turned her horse toward the barn.

Chase frowned, watching her go, and absently rubbed his already aching shoulder. He cursed silently but imaginatively, and told Early to saddle up another horse.

"Glad to see you haven't lost your touch, brother," El said, coming up behind him. "I was worried about you for a minute."

Chase stared after Libby. "Horses, I could always handle. Women? That's another story."

"Your mind's made up, then, about leaving tomorrow?"

Chase nodded.

El took a deep breath of the arid, sage-scented air. "I'm sorry, Chase."

"Yeah . . . well . . ." Chase stared at the tips of his boots, unable to find words to express his own regret. He wasn't the kind of man who shared his feelings, even with El. "What about you? I'm sure I can scare up a surveying job for you on Grenville's team." Even before he'd asked, he'd known what El's answer would be. El had spoken of little but Nora since the Independence Day celebration.

"After we deliver the herd, I'll be coming back here for Nora. She said yes to me. I'm gonna marry her, Chase."

"I'm happy for you, El," he said, clapping him on the shoulder. "She's a terrific lady."

"I'm crazy about her." El laughed as if he couldn't quite believe it himself. "We're going to be married in Baltimore. I . . . was hoping you'd come back and be my best man."

After a moment of thought, Chase shook his head. "I'm honored that you'd ask me. But I'm not ready to go back yet, El. There's nothing for me there."

"Except your family. Your ma misses you, and I know Father does, too. They're both worried about you."

Early led a bay gelding into the pen for Chase and motioned him over. Chase looked back at El. "I'll leave it to you to convince them to stop worrying. Tell 'em I'm fine."

"Are you?" El asked doubtfully.

Chase pushed away from the rail, his arms spread wide. "Right as rain." He turned to run a soothing hand down the neck of the nervous bay horse.

El shook his head as he watched Chase work. He could see the old armor returning in the unfathomable depths of his old friend's eyes. *You can convince the world of that, Chase, but who's going to convince you?*

A knock on the door brought Libby's attention up from the meat she was putting in individual packets for the trail ride on the morrow. It was past day, but not quite night. The summer sun stayed out late, and the evening crickets sang outside her open windows. "Yes?"

The door cracked open and Chase stuck his head in. "Hi."

A smirk touched her lips. "It's on the counter."

His eyebrows fell. *"It?"*

"The liniment."

Opening the door fully, he eased into the room. His limp was more pronounced tonight, and for once he wasn't trying to hide it. "Oh, yeah." He chuckled. "Liniment. Your last revenge."

"Hardly. Did you ever hear the phrase, 'The better part of valor is discretion'?"

"Henry IV?"

"You're not the only one who can quote Shakespeare. I'm sure old Henry would have agreed with me today. That was a foolish risk you took."

"Maybe so. But risk is part of life, isn't it?"

"Yes." It wasn't the mustang he was talking about and they both knew it. Libby tied a string around the sack of food and stacked it beside the others. At Chase's curious glance, she explained, "For the trail tomorrow."

He nodded, running a long finger along the pine table. He tried to keep the disappointment out of his voice. "Early tells me you're not coming along for the delivery."

She looked away. "No."

"You trust him to come back with your money?"

"Yes," she replied without hesitation. "Wouldn't you?"

"I suppose I would. He's a great old guy."

Libby smiled. "So . . . did you come for the liniment?"

Chase touched his shoulder without thinking. He was sore and stiff, but that wasn't why he'd come. His gaze traveled down to the locket—"his locket"—she wore around her neck. "Where's Tad?"

She swallowed, thrown off by his change of direction. "He's off catching crickets for Charlie."

"Good. Because I didn't come for the liniment. Unless, of course, you're offering to administer it yourself. . . ."

A look that spoke of all the things they'd once done passed between them, and they shared another smile. The heat between them was still a tangible thing. She felt it in the way his eyes devoured her; he, in the way her skin flushed and her knuckles whitened on the old sack of flour she was holding.

"I came to say goodbye, Libby."

She lifted the flour sack and turned away, clutching it to her. "Oh." She'd prepared herself for this. Yet now a pain centered in her chest and cut off her breath. She pressed a hand there, surprised by the power those simple words had over her.

"Where will you go, then?" she asked, her back still to him. "Omaha? The Union Pacific?" She heard him step closer.

"I suppose. I haven't had any better offers. And you? When's your wedding set for?"

"Four days. The second of August." Lamely, she added, "You're welcome to come."

He laughed humorlessly. "I think I'd as soon jump into a pit full of rattlers. Thanks just the same."

She turned and gave him a weak smile. "Nora told me Elliot asked her to marry him. They plan to be married in Baltimore, with your family. You won't go?"

Chase shook his head. "He'll manage just fine without me. He and Nora are good together. Anyway, it was never my intention to go back there. I suppose it was always his, though. He kept trying to fix the unfixable. He's a good friend."

"You'll miss him." It wasn't a question. Simply a statement of fact.

Chase nodded silently. His fingers reached for the silver locket at her throat. "It looks good on you."

She drank in the sight of his eyes, his clear green eyes, caressing her face. Oh, how she would miss him! "Thank you for bringing it to me, Chase. I was wrong to say you shouldn't have come and I'm . . . I'm sorry for all the trouble it caused you."

"It brought me more good than bad." His gaze stole to her mouth. He wanted to kiss her, but knew it would be a mistake. He remembered with a sudden jolting ache why he'd kept his distance these last few weeks. "When do you plan on telling Tad about me?"

"I'm not sure. He's very fond of you. How do you tell a boy that his hero was really a Yankee who shot his father in the war? How do you tell him that without destroying him?"

From the doorway came a gasp and both turned to find Tad staring at them, horrified. The glass jar in his hands crashed to the floor, and the crickets sprang free.

Libby's heart sank as she saw him. "Tad—oh, my God."

The boy blinked disbelievingly. "You k-killed my pa? You *killed* him?"

"Tad . . ." Chase appealed, his eyes stricken.

Tears sprang to Tad's eyes and his lower lip quivered. He shook his head and backed out the door. "You even knew! How could you, Ma?"

"Tad, wait." Chase started toward him.

"No!" he cried. "Liars! Leave me alone. I never want to see you again, you damn Yankee. I hate you. I hate you both!" He tore out into the dusk, letting the back door slam behind him.

Libby started after him, the color drained from her face. "Oh . . . oh, my God."

Chase stopped her. "Let me go. Please."

"Oh, Chase, he said . . ." She dropped her face into her hands. "I have to go to him."

"This should come from me." He took her by both arms and gave her a reassuring squeeze. "It'll be all right. You'll see. He's just upset and confused. I think I know where to find him."

Libby nodded numbly. She didn't know what she'd say to Tad anyway. How could she explain to an eight-year-old boy what she didn't even understand herself?

"Don't worry," Chase told her, and he disappeared out the door.

Libby watched him go and wondered if her life would ever be the same once he was gone. It was pointless to speculate; for she knew he had changed it unalterably.

The sun was a vermilion ball of fire in the western sky, casting a scarlet wash over the craggy mountains to the east. Chase ran up the stream behind Libby's barn, now little more than a creek in the dry summer heat. His pounding heart kept time with his thoughts. He cursed the timing of this whole mess. Selfishly, he'd wanted to leave Tad with good memories of him. Now, gauging the boy's reaction, there seemed little chance of that.

He stopped at a squatty, young cottonwood whose low fork made it an ideal climbing tree. Patch sat patiently beneath it, thumping his black- and white-tipped tail at Chase's approach. Taking a deep breath, Chase tipped his head back and peered up between the branches. "Tad?"

Silence.

"Tad? I know you're up there. Can we talk for a minute?"

Silence again.

"I know you're upset. But I just want to—"

"Go away!" Tad hollered. "This is *my* tree."

"I know. I just want to talk to you, son."

"I ain't your son. I'm my pa's son. And you . . . you k-killed him."

Chase hung his head for a moment, considering how to approach this. "I'm coming up if you won't come down."

"No!"

Chase fit his foot in the fork of the tree and pulled himself up. "We're friends. At least, we were. That's why you told me about this place, remember? Just trust me for another minute and let me explain what you heard."

A marble, one of Tad's precious marbles, rocketed down between the branches and caught Chase squarely on the top of his head. "Ow!"

"I don't want to talk." Tad launched another missile, this one missing by inches.

"Well, you're going to, even if you empty your marble bag in the process. Look," Chase said, spreading his hands in a gesture of uncertainty, "I know you're angry, but you hurt your ma, Tad. Hurt her bad with what you said. She doesn't deserve that."

"She lied to me."

"*I* lied to you. Not your ma. She didn't find out until a little while ago. But she wanted to pick the time to tell you—"

"That you was a low-down murderin' . . ." *Thwack!* Another marble crashed into Chase's shoulder.

"Now, cut that out! I didn't kill your pa!"

330

"You did, too! Ma said—"

"She said I shot him and that was true. You don't know how I regret hurting you, Tad. I never wanted you to hear about it this way." He eased himself up a few more branches until he was only a few feet below the boy. "Just . . . just listen to me for a minute, okay? Give me a chance to explain this to you."

When Tad remained silent, Chase told him the story of how he'd met his father in Virginia's Wilderness. About how they'd fallen together, about the locket and even how he'd held his father at the end. He'd never shared that part of the story with anyone but El. Why he did now, he wasn't sure. But he suddenly knew it would serve no purpose to omit it.

Confusion darkened Tad's fair features. "But . . . you wuz enemies."

Chase shook his head. "We were just two men fighting for different ideas, Tad. Those ideas put us at opposite ends of two rifles, yes, but that didn't make us hate each other. We never even knew which side fired the shell that killed your pa. It was a mixed-up battle, and there weren't any sides by the end. Only men trying to survive it any way they could.

"I know this is hard for you to take in," he went on, "but I never came here to hurt you or your ma. I just wanted to settle up with a piece of my past, and I was hoping I could make things a little easier for you and Libby."

Tad was silent, mulling it over.

"I know you loved your pa. And you can hate me if it makes you feel better. But you're all your ma's got, and she loves you something fierce. I expect you to apologize to her for the things you said."

A mourning dove cooed in a nearby aspen, punctuating Tad's silence. A fat tear splashed on Chase's knee.

331

"Tad—"

"She's a traitor to my pa for likin' you!" he blurted out, turning away from Chase.

"You liked me . . . once," he pointed out gently.

"N-not anymore." The words were choked out in a mixture of grief and anger.

Chase hadn't expected this to hurt so much. But it did. He kept his voice even and steeled his heart. "Okay. If that's the way you want it. But I'm not going to let you off the hook with your ma. If she did anything wrong, it was to try to protect you from being hurt. You go tell her you love her, 'cause I know you do. It means everything to her."

Tad shifted on the branch, his feet dangling below him.

"I'm leaving tomorrow morning with the others," Chase told him. "So, I . . . I guess this is goodbye."

With his mouth set in a firm, unyielding line, Tad refused to look at Chase.

"I'll miss you, Tadpole. You take good care of your ma for me, you hear?" Without another word, Chase climbed down out of the tree. A last, telling marble hit the ground beside him.

On the way back to Libby, he tightened his jaw with resolve and resigned himself to the truth. She met him outside the door, a dishtowel twisted between her hands. "Did you find him?"

"He's not far. Patch is with him. He's thinking things over, but he'll come around to you."

Libby searched his eyes. "And . . . what about you?"

Chase was careful to keep the emotion from his face, but he couldn't keep a note of bitterness from his voice. "You were right about that part, too, sweetheart. He's mad and hurt. He has a right to be. I can't say I blame him. Disillusionment is a hard pill to swallow for an eight-year-old."

She'd had second and third thoughts about how right she was about any of this. But she could see in his eyes that he had, too. "I'm sorry." That was all she could say.

He raked his fingers through his hair. "Yeah. Listen, I'm going to go before he comes back and sees me with you again." He let his eyes roam over her one last time, memorizing her every nuance. "Goodbye, Libby."

"Chase . . . I won't forget you."

If she hadn't touched him, if he'd kept his distance, he would have made a clean escape. It was no more than a light brush of her fingertips against his, but it cost him his last ounce of control. He took her hand roughly and pulled her up against him. He heard her small gasp of surprise and ignored it. "Ah, hell. Wisdom be damned."

His mouth descended on hers with a fierceness that was so like him. Libby's lips opened to his, and her head tipped back to meet him fully. He kissed her with utter completeness, washing her mouth with his taste, filling her with the memory of him. The kiss was as brief as it was consuming, over before she was ready for it to be.

He set her away from him almost harshly and, without a word, walked out the door.

Chapter Twenty-Two

It took two days of riding to get to Las Vegas. They chose the old Santa Fe Trail route over the more direct, but riskier, mountain pass. Early, Elliot, Chase, and Will drove the remuda hard, stopping only for darkness the first night. New Mexico Territory was a haven for criminals and outlaw on the run. A string of fine horses the likes of these would be easy prey for any rustler and would bring a hefty price. So, even with guards posted, they slept with one eye open and a finger on the trigger of a gun.

Las Vegas was a dusty, ramshackle little pueblo on the banks of the Gallinas River, with more *cantinas* per square foot than most self-respecting Western towns cared to boast of. There was no law outside of the *alcalde,* and few honest men were within its limits. It was said that when a man couldn't go anyplace else, he went to Las Vegas. Dangerous-looking *hombres* prowled the streets, armed to the teeth. Despite the early hour, the noisy *cantinas* were in full swing, brawls occasionally spilling out onto the dusty streets.

Though rumor had it the town was being considered as a possible railhead for a branch of the

Central Pacific Railroad, the prospect had done little to tame this small Gomorrah in the desert. This town was no place for a woman. Libby's decision to stay behind had been the right one, Chase decided.

The army detail met them, as promised, at the small plaza in the center of town. A young lieutenant named Gallagher relieved them of the horses in exchange for a bank draft for fifteen hundred dollars, twenty-five dollars a head—the army's price for ridable horseflesh. With the transactions out of the way, Early and Will Tuerney were anxious to be safely on their way back to The Double Bar H while there was still daylight to travel by.

Early was giving Libby away at her wedding. Though Chase knew he wasn't happy about it, he'd agreed to do it for Libby's sake. Elliot's reasons for returning were different, though equally compelling. The three cut their thirsts at a local establishment, then headed out onto the street again.

"Go with Early and Will," Chase advised when Elliot seemed reluctant to leave with the others. "Safety in numbers."

"Yeah, I know," El answered. "I hate to just leave you here like this, though. I pictured us going through this together, like we have everything else."

"I'm happy for you, El. Nora's a fine woman. She'll be good for you. But I think you can manage this one without me."

El ran a finger and thumb over his neatly trimmed mustache, then offered Chase his hand. "I'll miss you, you crazy bastard."

Chase chuckled over the lump in his throat, took El's hand, and pulled him into an embrace. Then, slapping his back, Chase stepped away from him. "When you see Ma, give her a kiss for me. Tell them . . . tell them I'll be back . . . when I can come."

"I'm sorry things didn't work out with Libby."

Chase shrugged as they walked toward El's horse. "Yeah, well, I guess it wasn't meant to be. I'm headed for that job with Grenville. I'll be out of this dust-hole by tomorrow."

"If you ever need anything . . . anything at all—"

"I know." Chase smiled and watched El mount.

"Keep yer nose clean, an' yer eyes open, *compadre*," Early said with an easy grin, and touched the brim of his hat to Chase.

"'Bye, Early," Chase answered. "It's been a real education knowing you."

"Why thank'ee . . . I think." With a bawdy laugh, Early spurred his horse forward. Will touched the brim of his hat and followed.

"Keep in touch, brother," El called, not wanting to say the words that made their parting seem so permanent.

Chase waved back silently, then watched until the three men disappeared at the edge of town. A swelling feeling of emptiness overtook him and he turned away.

He gave a moment's thought to wallowing in self-pity and disgarded the idea just as quickly. Stopping a young Mexican boy on the street, he gave him two bits for directions to a stable, a hotel, and a meal. And maybe, if he could make the hotel clerk understand him, a hot bath.

"*¡Ay! ¿Guapo . . . tú quieres una mujer esta noche, eh?*"

The sultry, honeyed voice pulled Chase from his reverie and stopped the shot-glass full of tequila half-way to his mouth. The brown-skinned woman gave the ruffles at the bottom of her colorful skirt an enticing shake in time to the music coming from the far corner of the *cantina*. She then ran her slender fingers down his neck. Chase didn't understand her words, but that invitation was clear. Slowly, he set his glass of tequila down on the table and let his gaze trail over her.

She was prettier than most, though not as young as some, with black eyes and a thicket of raven hair that tumbled over her shoulders like a storm cloud. Her low-riding cotton blouse dipped enticingly over her ample breasts, and she thrust these out haughtily to be sure he could see her most compelling attribute. A teasing smile curved her mouth, which was colored bright red with lip stain.

"You speak English?" he asked, wondering what had possessed him to ask.

"Enough," she answered slyly, sliding one finger down his open shirt. "You want to talk, *guapo?* I know better things."

He had enough tequila in him for the offer to seem enticing yet not enough to believe he could truly be interested in her. He slugged down the shot he had in his hand. Gritting his teeth until the burning stopped, he refilled his glass. "Drink?"

"¿Por qué no?" Without further encouragement, she settled herself on his lap and poured the fiery drink down her throat. Tossing her head back, she then breathed deeply, wriggling her bottom intimately against him. *"¡Ay! Qué bueno mescal! ¿No?"*

"It does the job."

She lifted the bottle to inspect it. *"Un gusano,"* she noted, pointing to the whitish worm at the bottom of the bottle. "Is good luck, no?"

Chase hadn't noticed the worm, but somehow wasn't surprised to see it in a place like this. The smoky cantina was full, men stacked along the

337

rickety bar, laughing and swapping stories. Others, seated at the round tables nearby, were playing poker and craps. He had gotten there early, and had this corner table to himself. No one, before this woman, had dared ask him to share it.

"What's your name?" he asked, taking in the cloying musky scent of her.

"You need a name, *gringo?*" She laughed. "You have a favorite? *That* is my name."

"You don't look anything like her," he muttered, tipping the bottle against the glass once more.

"Bueno," she conceded, running her hand through his hair. "Then, it is Argentina."

"Argentina. Pretty name. You should keep it for yourself. When you give a piece of yourself away," he said, feeling the liquor at last, "you can't always get it back."

She watched him thoughtfully. "Most of me is given away, *guapo*. You can have what's left tonight."

"Guapo . . ." He frowned. "What . . . ?"

"How you say . . . ? Handsome," she translated. "You are a handsome *gringo.*" Her hands traced his broad shoulders, and she gave her hair a toss. *"Y fuerte,* strong. I might even let you have me for less." She laughed again, nipping at his ear with her teeth. "Not *too* much less."

That she held not the slightest interest for him, he found surprising. In another time, another place, he would gladly have sought what she had to offer. Tonight and, he decided, for a long time to come, there would only be room for one woman in his heart and in his bed.

He gently pushed Argentina away from his ear. "I'm afraid I wouldn't be good company tonight."

"Dios mío . . ." She breathed out the words, her enticing gaze running over his long, lean body. "I

think you would be good company any night, *guapo.*"

Chase frowned and raised the glass to his lips. Before he could drink he saw something that stopped him cold.

Argentina felt him tense. "*¿Qué pasa?* What is wrong?"

Chase didn't take his eyes from the Colt revolver strapped to the hip of the man seated across the room from him—his Colt. The small hairs on the back of Chase's neck bristled. He would know that gun anywhere by the specially made ivory handle and the etching on the side.

"Do you know that man over there?" he asked. "Sitting at the table by the wall."

Argentina frowned now. "Which one?"

"The one with dark hair and a scraggly beard."

Chase heard her intake of breath. "*Sí, yo conozco.* But you do not want to, *señor.*"

Deliberately, he set his drink back down on the table. "Who is he?"

"All-y-son is his name. *Un mal hombre.* There are many bad men in Las Vegas, *guapo.* He is one of the worst."

"*Clay* Allison?"

"*Sí.*"

Chase's answering smile was cold as a winter snow.

The whore tugged at his shirt. "*Vaya conmigo, gringo.* Come to my room. I will make you forget this other woman who does not look like me."

He glanced up at her and reached into his pocket. "Argentina, how would you like to make more *dinero* tonight than you make in a month?"

Her ebony eyebrows flicked up hopefully. "With you?"

He smiled and shook his head.

The promise of money brought a pacifying curve to her lips. *"¡Pues!"* She shrugged. "If I cannot have you, perhaps money will ease the pain."

Chase sat back and watched Argentina do her job. She was good at it, he realized, as she rubbed against Clay Allison like a cat in season. The outlaw did his best to ignore her at first, intent on finishing his game of poker. But as she became more insistent and intimate with her talented hands, the man's baser needs won out over the poker game.

Argentina wound herself around Allison as they made their way to the back rooms where she plied her trade. Chase felt a tug of regret that a woman as intriguing as she had to make her living that way. He also prayed he hadn't put her in any danger.

After waiting a minute or two, he followed them. There were six cribs at the back of the *cantina*. The hallway was dark and dirty. If he'd had to guess which door was hers, he would have probably guessed wrong. But the button from her gown was on the floor in front of the door, just as she'd promised it would be.

Chase kicked it away, pulled out his gun, and listened for a moment. He heard Argentina's sultry laugh and the sound of heavy boots hitting the floor, one at a time. He checked his gun, unnecessarily. It was loaded and ready, as always.

He let the seconds tick by until he heard Argentina's throaty exclamation. *"¡Ay, hombre! ¡Tan grande!"* He heard the deep murmur of Allison's reply and decided the time had come. With gun cocked and ready, he slammed into the room.

Argentina's surprised shriek came on cue, and Allison's head came up with a jerk as Chase burst through the doorway. His wide eyes went first to Chase's gun, then to his own, out of reach on the chair beside the bed.

"Think you can make it?" Chase asked with a hard-bitten smile, taking in the sight of Allison, naked as a jaybird, atop the whore who'd set him up.

Allison's eyes flicked to Chase again. "Who the hell are you?"

"I'm the man who caught you with your pants down, Allison"—Chase moved closer, his gun still trained on the man's head, and pulled his Colt from Allison's holster—"and the owner of this gun."

Allison paled and his eyes became slits. "You're . . . you're dead."

Chase laughed. "Do I look dead to you?"

Allison swallowed hard. "What do you want, Whitlaw?"

"Where's Bodine?"

"I don't know—"

Chase's finger tightened threateningly on the trigger.

Sweat popped out on the naked man's forehead.

"¡Por Dios! ¡Digale!" Argentina implored convincingly, clutching the sheet to her. "Tell him!"

"¡Basta!" Allison snapped.

"You'd better listen to her," Chase warned. "I've heard you've got a price on your head. No one would think twice if I pulled this trigger. But then this pretty little whore would have your brains spattered all over her sheets."

"Hellfire! Wait a minute," he said, holding his hand up. "I don't owe that little bastard nothin'."

"I thought I could count on your sense of self-preservation. Where is he?"

"He . . . he ain't here. He went back to finish up some business with an old employer."

341

Chase felt his chest tighten. *Libby!* "What the hell are you talking about?"

"Bodine told me you were dead. He sold me that gun when he ran out of money. He went back to get more. Said there was bundles of it where that came from."

"Back *where?*" Chase thundered.

"S-some cattle rancher in the Rio Grande Valley. Harper, I think. Jonas Harper. He bragged how he was workin' for this man Harper, causin' trouble for some woman."

A sickening lurch of realization tore through Chase.

"And he was blackmailin' him over yer murder," Allison continued. "This Harper fella wanted the whole thing shut up. So he paid Bodine to disappear. Only Bodine didn't."

"Go on."

"He was thinkin' he should'a played a bigger hand the first time with this rancher. So, after his money was gone, Bodine headed back for more."

"How long ago?"

Allison hesitated.

"How long!"

"Day before yesterday."

Letting out a low, foul curse, Chase let his gaze fall upon the tools of Argentina's trade stacked neatly in a basket in the corner of her room, among them a quartet of short ropes, undoubtedly used for the very purpose he intended.

"Get up!" he ordered Argentina. "Tie him to the bedstead. Make the ropes tight."

"Ah hell . . ." Allison groaned. "Ya ain't gonna leave me here buck-nekked!"

"I'm leaving you alive," Chase assured him. "Which is probably more than you deserve."

342

Allison muttered another foul curse as Argentina tightened the ropes on his wrists. Chase tore the sheet from the bed and ripped it into strips.

"Gag him."

She did, to the grumbling protests of Allison.

"Now, put something on," he told her. "This was none of your affair, but I'm going to have to tie you, too."

"*¡Bastardo!*" she spat out, but winked at him when her back was to Allison. She slipped a cheap, cotton wrapper over her nakedness and lay back down on the bed beside the gunslinger.

Chase tied her up and gagged her as well. "Someone's bound to miss you by morning," he told them with a cold smile. He slipped his old Colt into his holster and touched the brim of his hat with the barrel of his new gun.

"Sweet dreams."

Jonas Harper closed the study door behind him and walked in the dim light of evening to the cluster of cut-crystal decanters on the small table near the window. Unstoppering a bottle of Napoléon Brandy, he poured two fingers into a snifter, then swirled it and held it up to the light from the window, admiring the fine amber color.

He was pleased. More than that, he was content. Tomorrow Elizabeth would be his. The preparations for the wedding were finished. Guests had begun arriving already, among them men who could make a political future for him in the seat of the territorial government a reality. A smile crossed his face. He was ambitious, yes. He wanted what this land had to offer. All of it. Cattle, power—a place carved out for himself and his offspring. With a woman as attrac-

343

tive as Elizabeth at his side, he could hardly miss.

The flare of a sulfur-tipped match illuminated the room behind him with a heart-stopping suddenness. Jonas turned on his heel, expecting to see that one of his guests had sneaked into the darkened study for some privacy. But when he spotted the figure lounging negligently on his desk chair, he knew he was wrong.

"Damnation! What are *you* doing here?" Harper demanded, slamming his snifter down so hard the thin stem shattered. He glared at the broken glass, then back at the interloper.

Trammel Bodine shook the match out with a flick of his wrist and took a long draw on his cigarette. The red tip glowed ominously in the darkness. "Well now, that ain't a very friendlylike way to talk to an old friend. Ain't you gonna offer me none of that there brandy, Harper? 'Course, I'd like a glass with a bottom still on it."

"How did you get in here?"

"Window—seein's how I didn't get an invite through the door." He took another pull on the cigarette and let the smoke out slowly. "Havin' you a shebang here, ain't you? A weddin' maybe, boss?"

"It's none of your business, but yes. Elizabeth's going to marry me here tomorrow. And don't call me boss. You don't work for me anymore, Bodine. What did you come back for?"

"Not my health, that's for damn certain." He lifted the gun he had concealed on his lap and spun the cylinder.

Jonas hadn't seen it before. He ran a nervous hand over his mustache and chin. "Your health would appear to be a tenuous commodity these days, I would say. In this territory at least."

"I came for money," Trammel said flatly.

344

Jonas laughed and turned his back on Bodine to pour some brandy into another snifter. The lip of the bottle rattled slightly against the glass. He took a long sip, then swung around. "I gave you money. Enough to get you out of the goddamned country."

"It didn't take me that far."

Harper's jaw tightened. "You've gotten all the money you're going to get from me, you little blood-sucker."

"Brave words comin' from a man without a gun."

"I don't need a gun, because you're not going to shoot me."

"Oh, yeah?" Bodine raised the Colt toward Harper. "What makes you so cocksure o' that?"

"Because you're a coward, Bodine. Because you wouldn't get two feet out of this room before one of my men put a bullet in your rangy hide. And I don't think you want to die. Besides, I have no reason to pay you any more money. The man you shot in the back didn't die. Whitlaw's alive."

Bodine's eyes widened. "Yer lyin'! He was good as . . ."

A sneering smile tugged at the corners of Harper's mouth. "Elizabeth happened upon him before the desert could claim him. You're a bungler—even at murder, Bodine. Bad luck for you, but as it turned out, good luck for me. Whitlaw rode off two days ago, out of Elizabeth's life. So you see, Trammel, there's nothing left for us to say."

"That's where yer wrong. You don't want to pay me?" Bodine dropped his cigarette onto the fine wool carpet and crushed it with the toe of his boot. "Fine. I'll just have a little visit with yer precious Elizabeth. We'll see what she has to say about yer part in her ranch failin'."

Harper laughed again. "You *are* a fool. Do you

345

think she would believe you after what you did to her? To Whitlaw? It'll be your word against mine, and everyone will know you're just trying to cover your guilty ass with lies. Show your face anywhere around these parts and they'll string you up so fast you won't need a judge to speak over you. You're a wanted man, Trammel. Not only for the attempted murder of Whitlaw but that little rustling escapade I heard about over near San Miguel, where you killed a man."

Bodine swallowed hard, and a muscle twitched in his cheek. "What do you know about that?"

"I'm surprised you haven't seen the wanted posters, Bodine."

"I seen 'em. I ain't got no use fer readin' is all."

"Pity. If you could read you'd have known that U.S. Marshal John Pratt is after you."

Bodine raised the gun. "Open yer safe, Harper. I come for money and I'm not leavin' without it."

Harper kept his expression even. "I don't think so."

The pistol shook in Bodine's hand and fury darkened his eyes. *"Open the damned—"*

The door to the study burst open and Jonas's foreman, Cal Stembridge, appeared, the shotgun he was holding aimed at Bodine's face. Bodine's shaking gun went from Harper to Stembridge. His expression was wild and desperate.

Cal stepped closer. "If you don't want me to blow your brains out, drop the gun now," the tall ranch hand ordered.

"It's all right, Cal," Harper told him, holding up his hand. "This gentleman was just leaving. Weren't you?"

"Put the gun down! *Now.*" Cal repeated in a low dangerous voice.

346

Bodine's gaze slid back and forth between the two men. Sweat glistened on his upper lip. Trapped, he carefully lowered his pistol to the floor. "I'm doin' it. I'm doin' it!" As Harper bent to pick the gun up, all the words Bodine longed to spit out at him worked at the corners of his mouth.

"This the bastard you been worried about, boss?" Cal asked.

"Yes."

"You want me to send a man for the marshal?"

"That won't be necessary."

Cal frowned. "But—"

"I *said* that won't be necessary." Harper glanced meaningfully at Bodine. "I suggest, however, you get on your horse and ride out of here before I change my mind. Take him out the back way, Cal, with as little fuss as possible. Ride with him to the edge of my property, then give him back his gun."

"Are you sure you want—?"

"That's an order, Cal," Harper snapped.

"Yessir." Cal grabbed Bodine's arm, but Trammel turned back on Jonas with an evil smile.

"Pay now or pay later. It don't matter to me, Harper," Bodine told him. "But you'll pay."

Harper only laughed. "You won't be back. Because if I see your face near my ranch again, I'll have you shot on sight. Is that clear? Now get him out of here."

Bodine stumbled out after Cal, and Jonas shut the door behind them. With a curse, he hurled the snifter of brandy into the adobe fireplace at the far corner of the room and watched it shatter in a splash of amber.

Chapter Twenty-Three

Chase splashed the last of his coffee onto the thirsty ground and kicked dirt over his fire, sending a sputtering plume of smoke into the pink-tinged morning sky. The coffee helped to clear his brain; the crisp mountain air, his spirit. He hefted his saddle up onto Blue's back and cinched it tight.

He'd forgone the longer Santa Fe Trail route they'd taken on the way in and had chosen instead the mountain route back to the valley of the Rio Grande. He hoped to cut off a few precious hours of travel that way. As it was, there was a chance he might not get there in time.

Darkness had forced him to stop for the night on the eastern slopes of the Cristos. But night hadn't brought sleep. Only the gnawing panic that he would reach Libby too late to stop her from making a terrible mistake.

Harper. Chase wanted to kill him slowly for what he had done to her. As he mounted and headed Blue up toward the notched pass in the mountains, he wondered how he could have missed connecting Harper with Bodine. In hindsight, it made perfect sense. Someone had been working long and hard to make Libby fail, but Chase had never been able to figure out why. Libby's stubborn tenacity would have kept her on her ranch despite normal odds, and he imagined she might even have made a success of it. Failure had driven her directly into Harper's arms, just as the bastard had intended.

Chase spurred Blue on. He planned to pay Harper back, not only for betraying Libby but for the small matter of the two bullets that had nearly killed him.

Morning gave way to afternoon as he pushed on through the rocky terrain. A foamy sweat slicked Blue's coat and Chase's shirt clung damply to him under the brilliant afternoon sky. At eight thousand feet, the thin air made the sun seem closer and the effort greater.

There was no warning when it happened. They were moving so fast through the scrub meadow, there wasn't even time for the rattle which would have betrayed the five-foot diamondback that lay sunning on the rock beside the trail. But the strike to the horse's foreleg was deadly.

Blue screamed and reared in fear and pain. Caught off balance, Chase scrambled to free himself from the stirrups just as the gray fell over backward. He hit the ground hard and bounced to a grinding stop, then rolled to his knees, his pistol drawn. The rattler had already struck once more at the horse which was struggling to its feet. This time the snake went for Blue's neck, with deadly accuracy. The frantic horse pawed wildly at the air letting out shrill, squealing cries.

"Noo-o-oo!" The scream tore from Chase's throat even as a round exploded from his Colt, ripping the diamondback in half when it coiled to strike again. He fired again and again into the writhing mass of flesh until the snake moved no more.

His disbelieving gaze went to Blue who struggled to his feet, grunting with pain and taking labored breaths.

"Aw, damn. *Damn!*" He grabbed Blue's loose reins and brought him to a stop. "Whoa, now. Easy, boy." Chase ran his fingers over the bleeding, angry bites in Blue's neck and leg. The horse quivered and snorted in reply.

"Aw, Blue . . . Blue." Chase felt his throat tighten with emotion as he realized what had to be done. Blue tossed his head, then dropped his velvety muzzle against Chase's hand.

"I'm sorry, boy. I'm so sorry."

It had happened so fast, there was nothing he could have done to prevent it. Still, he blamed himself for pushing so hard, letting his guard down, taking the mountain pass when he should have taken the road. Blue was a trusted friend, the last one he'd counted on. Now, even Blue would be gone.

Damn it all to hell.

With a heavy heart, he released the latigo on the saddle, loosening the cinch. The poison was already doing its work on the gelding. As Chase pulled the saddle off, Blue wobbled a few steps, then went down. Chase dropped to his knees beside the stallion, soothing him with his voice and stroking his strong jaw. He unfastened the bridle and slipped it out of Blue's mouth.

"Shh-hh . . . thatta boy. You're gonna be all right now. . . ." Emotion choked his words off. Blue looked up at him with trusting, pain-filled eyes.

Slowly, Chase pulled out his pistol, rested it against Blue's temple and, with a shudder of regret, pulled the trigger. The retort echoed like a shattered promise across the granite cliffs clawing at the stark New Mexican sky.

On a broad outcrop of rock overlooking the sprawling Rio Grande Valley, Chase sat with wrists dangling over bent knees, watching morning steal over the sky. Vermilion edged the wispy clouds high above the flat sweep of land below. Beside Chase were his saddle and tack, which he had lugged seven or eight miles on foot the day before after covering Blue's body with rocks from the meadow. His sense of loss was rivaled only by his sense of impotence.

It was Sunday. Today Libby would marry Jonas Harper and there wasn't a damn thing he could do about it. At least twenty miles separated them. Miles impossible to cover on foot in time. He'd lost and so, he realized, had Libby and Tad.

The shout of frustration welled up inside him like a curled fist until he could do nothing else, but release it.

"Liiib-beee-ee—"

The cry echoed down the mountainside and came back to him like an answer.

Another voice, the one that had kept him alive and fighting all these years, rebelled at giving up so easily. Anger tore through him, a rush of liquid heat.

He could flail a fist at fate, give in to the hopelessness of his cause, or he could fight with everything he had. It might be too late, but he'd try. Damn it, he'd try.

With the decision made to lighten his load, he unwound his canteen from the saddle horn and slid his Henry from its scabbard. It was then he first felt the rumble. The rock beneath him trembled as if from an earth tremor, but in a few seconds he discovered the source of the sound.

The herd of mustangs moved as one across the

351

ripening meadow of high mountain grass below him. It was a large herd—at least fifty head—and if he wasn't mistaken, it was Diablo's. But he couldn't spot the black stallion. There was another dun-colored stallion, younger perhaps, at the rear of the herd, laying claim to his *manada*.

A sharp, squealing whinny brought Chase's head around to the mountainside fifty yards to the north. He shouldn't have been surprised to see Diablo there, but he was. The magnificent stallion reared and pawed at the sky, then stood silent, watching his old herd pass by below him. He still bore the marks of his battle with Goliath.

It occurred to Chase then that the old stallion had lost his claim on the herd because of the wounds he'd suffered in the grizzly's attack. Diablo was an outlaw now. An outsider, just as Chase was.

He waited. Diablo shook his mane and pawed the ground, then caught sight of Chase. Their eyes met as they had twice before. But instead of running, Diablo stood his ground, waiting, too. For what, Chase couldn't know. The horse's ebony coat gleamed in the sunlight. Devil or angel? Chase wondered, acknowledging the irony of their situation.

And a crazy thought crept into his mind. Crazy and desperate. But he was just desperate enough to try anything. Slowly, he reached into his saddlebags and pulled out two lumps of the sugar he'd always kept in supply for Blue. He threaded his bridle over his shoulder, and with slow measured steps—and a silent, offered-up prayer—he made his way toward the skittish stallion.

"Ow! Let go a my ear!" Tad whined, as Early pulled him gingerly toward the *hacienda*. His short

352

wool pants were covered with dust, and one stocking puddled around his ankle.

"Lookit you, boy," Early replied shaking his head. "Got them fancy duds Mr. Harper done bought fer ya all mucked up, like you was a stable hand instead of the ring bearer at your mama's weddin'." He released Tad's ear when they drew near the guests circling a table of punch. He saw Jonas Harper fidgeting with his string tie beneath the stand of quaking aspen, beside him the preacher and several other men. They had wheeled Nora's piano out under the trees, and a woman from church was plinking away at it in preparation for the ceremony.

Early propelled Tad toward the house. "What in the tarnation did you think you was up to, fightin' with that Higgins boy?"

"Nothin'." Tad's expression was uncharacteristically sullen and had been for days. The sudden change baffled Early, but he suspected by the long face Libby had been pulling since Chase left, it was about his going.

Early blew out a sigh and cast a sidelong glance at Tad's blackening left eye. "Didn't look like nothin' to me. 'Pears to me you been itchin' fer a fight ever since we come back from deliverin' them horses. With yer ma, with me . . . heck, even Patch has been stayin' outta yer way lately. You want to talk about it, Taddy?"

"No."

"You missin' Chase?"

"Ha!"

"Ya could'a fooled me, boy."

"I ain't a boy! And he's a traitor," Tad retorted hotly, emotion overriding his reticence.

"Fer leavin'?"

"For shootin' my pa."

353

Early halted his steps. "What are you talkin' about boy?"

"In the war. That's why he came here, to give Ma a locket my Pa give him when he was dyin'. He lied to me and my ma. I hate him."

Early frowned, comprehending at last the missing piece of the puzzle between the stranger who'd ridden in on a storm and Libby Honeycutt. *So that was the way of it.* If he hadn't known Chase so well, he might have bought what Tad had selling for face value. But there was more to it than this. He knew that as sure as he was standing here.

Though his heart went out to the boy, he figured that boulder on Tad's shoulder must be getting a mite heavy and needed shaving down a sliver or two.

"You hate him, huh? You figure a man who fought agin' your pa ain't got no good in him?"

Tad scowled silently and scuffed at the dirt with the toe of his new leather shoes.

"Yep. Well, I reckon as how you're right," Early agreed. "It took a mighty small man at that to come all that way and face your ma head-on instead of throwin' that locket away like any good Yankee might have. And then, well, to stay and help her when he could see she was strugglin' . . . well, I reckon that don't count for much since he never took no money from her fer pay. Told me to give it to yer ma after he left." Early shook his head. "Scalawag."

Tad shot a confused look at him.

"Yeah," Early continued, moving toward the house, the boy in tow. "And then there's all the time he spent with you. Buildin' you a box fer Charlie and teachin' you to whistle. He was a real lowdown buzzard fer that."

"I . . . I know, but he—"

"Weren't who you thought he was, hmmm?" Early

354

finished. "Most folks ain't. But to be a man, you gotta learn to judge a man by who he is today, not on his past. Lovin' and hatin'. They's kissin' cousins, boy. Sometimes, they're so close, you can't even tell 'em apart. You kin let your hate for him eat you up, or you kin let it go and remember all the good he done for you an' yer ma. Either way, I don't aim to let ya spoil yer ma's weddin' day. You buck up boy and wipe that scowl off'n yer face."

They crossed the threshold of the *hacienda* and found Nora making last minute adjustments on Libby's cream-colored batiste gown in the parlor. Libby's face fell when she saw her son.

"Oh, Tad . . ."

Tad shrugged out of Early's grasp and stood before her with his head down. She reached out and tipped his chin upward, grimacing at his bruised face. "What in the world is this all about? How did you get this black eye?"

"I found him fightin' with Bruce Higgins's boy behind the barn. I reckon there's some way to salvage these duds, ma'am, but yer groom is about to jitter outta his britches out there. And the folks is startin' to grumble. The weddin' was supposed to start a half-hour ago."

Libby sighed. "I know. I just had a few last-minute adjustments to make." *And a few misgivings.* "Thanks for finding Tad for me, Early. If you would, tell Mr. Harper I'll be right out."

Early touched the brim of his best hat. "Yes'm. I'll do that."

Nora clucked her tongue and brushed at Tad's clothes with her hand. A cloud of dust billowed up. "Oh, my. We'll have to take a brush to these. Come along, young man."

Libby bent down and kissed the top of Tad's head

before he left. "Tad, you know I love you, don't you?"

He nodded, unable to look her in the eye.

"And I know you love me, even though you haven't felt much like telling me so in the last few days. It's going to be all right, son. You'll see."

Tad shrugged silently and then followed Nora out the door without returning Libby's kiss.

He'd been this way for days now, and she was beginning to wonder if she would ever get him to talk. He hadn't said goodbye that morning Chase had left, but she'd seen him alone in the barn loft, staring off after the men as they rode away. Tad had barely spoken a civil word to her or anyone else since that day.

He was angry, and she thought she understood why. She was angry, too. Chase Whitlaw had succeeded in turning their lives upside down and inside out. But he'd also given them a gift more precious than anything he'd taken: his love.

Not a day went by that she didn't think of him, regret all the angry words between them and her own stubborn pride. But it was too late for regrets. She'd let him ride out of her life. He was gone, and with him, the one chance she might have had for happiness. Now she would have to make the best of what was left.

"They're ready, Libby," Early told her from the door. "Miss Hattie is playin' the weddin' march." He offered her his arm and she took it, trying to quell her trembling. Early reached over and patted her arm with his rough hand. "You sure this is what you want, ma'am?" he asked. "We kin walk away right now and fold this hand if yer a-gettin' cold feet."

"Thank you, no, Early. I suppose cold feet are normal in a situation like this, aren't they?"

"Yes, ma'am. I reckon they are."

Together, they walked out the door toward the stand of aspen where Jonas waited with the preacher. Her stomach churned, and she was suddenly afraid she would be sick. Forty-five guests stood in their Sunday best, waiting expectantly for her. She couldn't turn back now.

Libby's dress billowed in the gusting breeze as Jonas watched her come toward him. He smiled at her, while his eyes raked down the length of her. A shudder raced down her back.

Hattie, whose piano playing was halting but usually accurate, faltered in earnest at the sound of approaching hoofbeats. Jonas turned to look and saw a solitary rider bearing down on the crowd at breakneck speed. The horse was a black demon that flew across Three Peaks land, barely touching the earth. The rancher's expression darkened noticeably when he recognized the man atop the beast.

Chase hauled back on Diablo's reins and brought the stallion to a prancing stop at the edge of the shocked crowd. White foam around the stallion's chest and mouth testified to the strenuous ride he'd just made.

"Don't do it, Libby," Chase shouted, sliding from the horse's back. "You can't marry him."

Libby halted in shock, still grasping Early's arm. Her pulse leapt at the sight of Chase. She checked the urge to run to his arms, for his harrowed, exhausted look verged on being murderous as well. "Chase, wh-what—?"

"It was Harper," Chase answered, pointing to the man he'd named with an accusing finger. "It was him all along."

"Chase . . ." Libby breathed out, horrified and confused.

357

"What the hell are you talking about, Whitlaw?" Harper demanded. "Who do you think you are coming in here, interrupting our—"

"Go on," Chase taunted, his breath coming hard and fast. "Tell her how you fixed it for her ranch to fail, Harper. Tell her how you hired Trammel Bodine to work for you and undermine her until she'd have no choice but to come to you."

Libby's wide-eyed gaze went from Chase to her intended, and her stomach lurched.

"You're out of your mind!" Harper shouted. "Get out of here before I—"

"Have me shot?" Chase finished. "You already tried that once. You couldn't kill me then and you won't now. Especially not in front of all these witnesses. That's not your style, is it?" With the measured steps of a man who knew he was right, he moved toward Harper.

Harper's face mottled with rage, and he backed up a step. "I had nothing to do with that. Or with Trammel Bodine. You can't prove a thing. He's lying, Elizabeth. Can't you see that?"

"Am I?" Chase countered. "Think about it, Libby. When did all your troubles start? After Malachi died? After Jonas proposed to you and saw you had no intention of selling out or giving in? And what did Bodine stand to gain by your failure? Nothing. It was a job for him, pure and simple. Only he wasn't working for you. He was working for your *fiancé*."

Nora, who had been behind Libby, reached out and took her hand, gasping in disbelief. "Dear Lord, Chase . . ."

A murmur of outrage rose from the crowd. Marshal Pratt, who was one of the guests, stepped forward and faced Chase. "These are serious accusations you're making. Do you have anything to back them up, Whitlaw?"

The hard planes of Chase's face sharpened further. "Maybe not enough for a court of law, but while I was in Las Vegas, I had a friendly chat with our friend, Clay Allison, who just happened to be carrying my gun—the one Trammel Bodine stole after he shot me. He said Bodine had sold it to him after his blackmail money had run out—blackmail money Jonas Harper had paid to shut him up about my 'murder.'"

Libby's face had gone pale with shock, and she leaned on Early. "No . . ."

"Hearsay!" Harper claimed. "Nothing but lies, I tell you." Turning to the marshal, he pleaded, "John, you're not going to take the word of some criminal and some no-account drifter over *mine?* It's slander. I tell you I had nothing to do with this. Whitlaw is just jealous because I'm the one who wound up with Elizabeth, that's all. He's wanted her right from the start."

"You're right about that," Chase admitted, without a hint of regret. "I wanted her. I *still* want her. And I'll be damned if you'll have her after everything you've done."

"Well, you can go to hell, Whitlaw. She's promised to me!"

"Not anymore, she's not. Consider the promise broken."

The humiliation of it all rose in Libby's throat like bitter bile. "Stop it!" she cried, loosing herself from Early's protection. "Both of you!"

Ignoring her, Harper swung furiously at Chase, who ducked the punch and landed a savage one of his own on Harper's jaw. Harper's head snapped back and he grunted in pain. But he launched himself at Chase, knocking him to the ground.

"No!" Libby screamed. "Chase stop, for God's sake. . . ."

But it was too late. Over and over, the pair rolled in the dirt, pummeling each other. Blood smeared Harper's mouth and spattered his crisp white wedding shirt and silk waistcoat. A cut above Chase's eye bled freely, but he seemed not to notice it. His arm reared back and connected with Harper's jaw. Colliding with the slender white trunk of an aspen, Harper slid down it, momentarily stunned, but he got to his feet again, lunging for Chase's knees. Both men went down again in a cloud of dust.

The crowd scattered and one woman crumpled in a dead faint at the spectacle. Several men moved to stop the fight, but John Pratt held them off with one arm.

"Let 'em go at it," he growled. "Maybe we'll get to the bottom of this."

Gathering Harper up by the shirt front, Chase plowed a fist into his jaw, but the rancher managed to dislodge his grip with a well-placed blow. Chase landed hard, then staggered to his feet. Harper, too, was on his feet, his fists balled in front of him—dirty, bloodied, and ready for more.

By now the crowd was taking sides. The men shouted encouragement at one or the other of them and circled the pair as if they were spectators at a cock fight.

Libby couldn't watch. She couldn't bear to see Chase being hurt again, fighting over her. Nor could she bear the horrified, pitying stares of the other women. Tears gathered at the back of her throat as she backed away from the crowd, leaving Early and Nora to stare in shock at the battle.

Libby turned and fled to the house. She closed the door behind her and leaned against it, her eyes closed, her palms flattened against the solid, pine slab. Her pulse thudded in her ears so, it sounded like a rushing river. Her confused thoughts seemed caught in the eddy.

Jonas . . . to blame for all the accidents? Hiring Bodine to sabotage me? How could I not have seen, not known it? Worse, how could I have trusted a man like him? Is my judgment so lacking, I could have been fooled so easily?

And Chase—the man who owns my heart, the man who nearly died because of me, is fighting for me still. Have I been wrong about him too? Wrong to deny the love we had for each other? Hasn't he proven himself to me over and over?

Unbidden came the memory of all the things he'd said to her that night they'd made love. *What about you, Libby? What about your needs? Your dreams? Can you live without this for the rest of your life?*

It wasn't, she realized now, the physical act of love-making he was talking about, but the powerful love that bound them together in spite of everything that had sought to tear them apart. To deny that would be to deny herself.

A shuffling noise behind her sent her spinning around. A scream rose in her throat, but Trammel Bodine choked it off by placing one hand over her mouth and the other at her throat. He smelled of horse and stale cigarettes and days on the trail. The dirt from his hand ground into her lips.

"Well, well." Trammel sneered. "Ain't this a piece of luck?"

He dragged her toward him, circling his arm tightly around her neck, choking off her breath as he drew his gun. Her fingers clawed at his arm until she heard his pistol hammer click near her ear.

"One scream, just one, and I'll blow yer pretty little head off."

Chapter Twenty-Four

"I . . . won't . . . scream," Libby rasped, scrambling backward as he dragged her away from the door. His harsh grip on her sent fear shooting down her limbs. "Please, d-don't . . . hurt me."

A self-satisfied chuckle rumbled in his chest. "Ain't so high an' mighty now, are ya, Libby?" Bodine edged toward the window to look out. In the distance, the circled crowd concealed the two fighting men.

Libby's heart sank. No one had even noticed she'd slipped away. Why hadn't she stayed out there with the others?

"What's goin' on out there?" Bodine demanded. "I thought you was gettin' hitched."

"Chase . . . and Jonas . . ."

Bodine gave her neck a mean little jerk. "Whitlaw and Harper, fightin' over you are they? That ought to work out just fine fer you an' me."

"Wh-what do you want from me?"

He hauled her backward toward the next room. "Only what I'm due. And maybe a little more."

Bending her awkwardly in front of him, he reached for the flour sack he'd left on the sideboard before sneaking up on her in the parlor. The bag thudded against her. It was money. Harper's money. The loose coin clattered musically, but paper bank notes also filled the sack.

"Feel that?" he gloated. "That there's poetic justice a-janglin' against yer hip, lady. My future. Harper made it easy for me with all these fine folks he invited here. I just waltzed in, pretty as you please, an' nobody was the wiser." Bodine pulled her through the house toward the back door in the kitchen, his arm still tightly around her neck. Keep him talking, she thought desperately. "You came to *rob* him?"

"I come here to pay him back. See he made the mistake of underestimatin' me. I don't take that"— he shoved the pistol closer to her temple—"from anybody."

There was no mercy in his grip on her. No half-measure in his voice.

He was going to kill her.

The realization struck like a sharp blow to the solar plexus. It made her dizzy and angry at the same time. She tasted the coppery tang of blood on her lip where his hand had crushed her mouth against her teeth, and tried to get a grip on her breathing, to slow it down. If she let him rattle her, she had no chance of fighting him. And she wouldn't go down without a fight.

"I never underestimated you, Bodine. I always knew you had enough nerve for ten men." She felt him pause fractionally. "You have quite a reputation in these parts already."

"That's right. They're gonna be writin' about me someday in them little dime novels."

"I'm sure they will. I wonder what they'll say about you, though, when they learn you hid behind

363

a woman to make your escape?"

"I ain't hidin' behind you," he argued. "I'm takin' you with me. Like a . . . a hostage." He laughed then, as if he'd made a joke. She stumbled over the carpet when he dragged her toward the kitchen at the back of the house.

Heat, from the huge cooking fireplace on the other side of the *cocina*, hit them like a wall. The contents of a large kettle simmered fragrantly over the unattended fire. Several cloth-covered tables full of prepared foods and desserts crowded the kitchen in readiness for wedding feast.

"You don't need me," she pleaded, in the calmest voice she could muster. "No one will see you go. Everyone's out front—"

"You don't get it, do you?" Bodine's grin was icy. "Takin' you is the perfect revenge. I'll have me his money *and* his woman."

"You're wrong, Trammel. I'm not his woman. I know he betrayed me. That's what Chase came to tell me. He found out you were working for Jonas all along—"

Bodine's arm tightened around her neck. "How?"

"C-Clay Allison told him."

"That son of a—"

He edged over to the small wood-barred window and looked out. Cal Stembridge was about thirty feet from the door, watching the fight from a distance. Bodine let out a foul curse.

"Don't you see?" she pressed. "If you take me . . . it will . . . be for nothing."

"Shut up!"

"You'll ruin him when you take his money. Just take it and go."

"*Shut up*, I said! I need to—"

The back door swung open suddenly. Maria,

Jonas's young Mexican cook, froze in the opening when she saw them and went slack-jawed with surprise. Her huge brown eyes widened with fear. *"Madre de Dios—"*

"Maria! Look out!" Libby cried in warning.

Trammel instinctively swung his gun in her direction and fired. But the bullet merely furrowed into the wooden door Maria had slammed shut at the last second as she'd ducked out of the way. "Damn it!" Bodine bellowed, momentarily loosening his hold on Libby.

Seizing the moment, she sent her elbow crashing into his side. With a groan, he doubled over, releasing her and dropping the bag full of money. "Bitch," Bodine moaned, gasping for air.

Libby twisted free of his grip, but only got two feet from him before she felt his hands on her gown. She heard a scream and realized it had come from her. The delicate batiste shredded in his grasp. Hope—thriving in her only a second ago—withered like a spent blossom. Her strength was far outmatched by his. He hauled her toward him. She fought him with her fists until he captured one in his steely hand.

Though she saw it coming, she was helpless to stop it. Lights exploded in her head as the side of his pistol slammed viciously into her temple. The blow sent her flying backward against a table of food, knocking it and its contents to the floor against the door. She crumpled into the debris.

With horrifying awareness, she watched the unlit coal-oil lamp that had sat on the table with the food shatter on the hard tile floor. Its liquid fuel splashed about and bled in a swift, resolute runnel toward the blaze in the fireplace.

Gunshots roused her from her stupor. She blinked up at Bodine. He was pressed up against the thick

365

adobe wall to avoid the bullets whizzing through the small barred window. *Maria!* She must have told someone.

Desperately, Libby fought the blackness that threatened to engulf her. The ringing pain in her head blurred her vision. I can't pass out, she told herself. I have to get out of here! The room seemed to be spinning slowly, and something warm and wet trickled past her ear. With dull, awkward movements, she rolled to her hands and knees just as the stream of coal oil met a tongue of flame. A sheet of fire roared to unholy life, racing toward her, engulfing the table cloth and lapping at the edges of the upturned pine table beside her.

A scream caught in Libby's throat, and she fell backward, scuttling along on her bottom to get away from the heat of the blaze. The door was barricaded by debris that was afire. Her only hope of escape was to go back the way they'd come.

"Holy hell!" Bodine yelped, ducking underneath the window. He shielded his face from the intense heat with one hand. "Get back here, you little she-wolf," he yelled, reaching for her ankle. "You ain't goin' nowhere!" For a moment, he had her, and she kicked at him with the heel of a white kid boot.

"Let . . . me . . . go!" she screamed. "We're both going to die in here, can't you see that?"

"Oh, no we ain't. Not when I got all this money to—" Too late, he saw the sack catch fire. He let out a foul curse and made a grab for it anyway, stomping on the flames with his booted foot.

Libby edged away, choking on the thick black smoke pouring from the fire. Flames licked the ceiling, where pine rafters supported thinner wood planks. They raced hungrily along the dry wood, devouring everything in their path.

Fighting dizziness and the mind-numbing pain in her head, Libby got to her feet and scrambled into the dining room. Just let me make it to the door, she prayed. But smoke was already pouring into that room too, eating up the light and making it nearly impossible to see. Her eyes smarted and teared, and her lungs burned with each breath.

In the smoky light, she collided with a table and fell to the floor. Fire clawed at the doorway to the dining room now, and it was racing up the crisp, calico cloth that hung on the walls. Libby gathered up the hem of her gown and pressed it against her mouth. She crawled a few more feet before she realized she'd lost all sense of direction in the fall. Her vision blurred, and the blackness seemed to spiral around her.

Pulling her knees to her chest, she curled up into a ball and turned her face to the floor in a vain search for air. A thousand regrets flashed through her mind in those last seconds of consciousness: she wished she'd kissed Tad goodbye and given him his father's locket, she wished she'd told Chase how much she loved him, she wished . . .

The darkness closed over her like a sheltering raven's wing, obliterating the dreams she would never fulfill, spinning her into its cocoon of oblivion.

Chase's fist dented Harper at the waist, doubling the rancher over in pain. Both men were bloody and spent, heaving like draft horses yet staggering at each other again. Lips bleeding, knuckles split, neither was willing to concede to the other.

"I should kill you, you sorry excuse for a man." Chase spat out a mouthful of blood.

Harper staggered, unwilling to give in. "Go to hell, Whitlaw." He swung ineffectually at Chase, missing him completely and no longer caring, before stumbling forward and landing on hands and knees just beyond Chase.

Chase dropped to his knees beside him and shoved him over onto his back. In his fists, he gathered Harper's bloodied shirt and pulled him up against the tree trunk behind him. "Tell them," he snarled. "Tell them how you tried to have me killed, and maybe I won't kill you myself."

"Jonas! For God's sake, tell him," Nora cried, unable to hold it in any longer. "Can't you stop this?" she pleaded with the marshal. "He's going to *kill* him."

Elliot came up beside her, taking her arm. "That's enough, Chase. You've proved your point."

"Like hell I—"

Marshal Pratt laid a hand on Chase's shoulder. "Bradford's right, both of you. Nothing's going to be resolved this way. What do you know about this, Miss Nora?"

Regretfully, she shook her head. "I'd forgotten it until just now . . . but that was him that night, wasn't it, Jonas? The night Chase was shot, Trammel Bodine was in our house, talking with you in your study. I didn't recognize him then because it was dark and he was dirty and unshaven." She looked up at the marshal. "He said Bodine was looking for work. But he wasn't"—her accusing gaze fell on her brother—"was he?"

Chase turned to regard Harper. "Tell them. If you have any decency left in you Harper, tell the truth."

Exhausted, Harper shook his head. "I didn't have anything to do with trying to kill you . . . I swear. I never wanted that," he declared, panting for breath.

368

"Bodine hated you . . . for his own reasons. I just wanted you off the ranch . . . away from my Elizabeth." His face was a study in guilt as he looked at Chase.

"You expect me to believe that?" Chase retorted disgustedly, and the crowd around them muttered ominously.

"I don't care what you believe," Harper answered, still breathing hard and fingering his bruised ribs. "I'm telling you the truth. Bodine wasn't the man I thought he was when I hired him. He was completely without scruples. Yes, I told him to make trouble for Elizabeth, to push her toward marrying me. But I only wanted what was best for her. She was too stubborn to see she couldn't make it on her own. She would have killed herself trying to make it work and I . . . I wanted her." Harper's eyes reddened, and his face contorted with emotion. "Damn it, was that so wrong? To want to give her a good life when she had . . . *nothing?*"

Chase released him with an angry shove, and Harper lowered his swollen eyes. "Yes, damn it," Chase bellowed. "It wasn't your choice to make."

"I never meant to hurt anyone. Bodine went way beyond what I'd hired him for out of pure . . . maliciousness. He blackmailed me when I tried to get rid of him. That was the night Nora saw him. God help me, I didn't mean for any of this to happen."

It took a moment for those gathered about them to assimilate the sound they heard next, but when it came again, they had no doubts about it. It was gunfire.

John Pratt drew his pistol from his holster and took two steps toward the back of the house. "What in Hades is going on?"

Chase's frantic gaze took in the crowd. Something

inside him turned to ice when he couldn't find the one face he sought. "Where's Libby?"

Early looked around, too. "She was right here when the fight started."

Chase turned back to the house just as Maria came tearing around the corner of it, shouting in rapid-fire Spanish. Tears streaked her face.

"Fuego! Fuego!" she cried. *"Ay, Dios! La Señora Honeycutt está en la cocina con el gringo!"*

The color drained from John Pratt's face as he translated the one word every Anglo learned and dreaded hearing. "Fire!"

Harper staggered to his feet. "No . . . no-o-o!"

Alarm tore through the crowd as smoke billowed from the adobe. "Get buckets from the barn!" Pratt ordered. "Form a brigade, starting at the troughs. Hurry!"

With Nora showing the way, the men scattered to find buckets, and the women ran to form a line at the back of the house.

Chase grabbed Maria, who was still crying hysterically, and shook her by the shoulders. "Speak English!" he shouted. "Where's Mrs. Honeycutt? Where *is* she?"

"In the house! *El hombre* . . . the man, he has . . . a . . . *una pistola*—a gun!"

"What man?"

"I don't know him," she sobbed. "He shot at me. He is holding *la señora* with the gun!"

"Bloody hell!" Chase exclaimed. "It's got to be Bodine! He's got her."

"No, it can't be," Harper murmured in shock. "The damn fool, wouldn't come back here."

Chase didn't waste time arguing. *Dear God! Libby's in there!* He tore off at a run toward the nearest water trough, stripped off his gunbelt, and quickly submerged himself in the water.

El, who had followed him, grabbed a wool lap blanket off a nearby carriage and plunged it into the water, then wrapped it around himself.

"What do you think you're doing?" Chase demanded, picking up his pistol.

"I'm coming with you!"

Already on the run, Chase waved him off. "Stay here!"

"But you might need help."

"Libby may need a doctor," Chase shouted to him. "I don't want to worry about getting two people out."

"Take this, then," El answered, tossing the sodden blanket at Chase. "It may buy you a little more time."

Chase wrapped the blanket around his head and shoulders as he ran. Out of the corner of his eye, he saw Harper lurching toward the *hacienda*, rifle in hand, a look of stunned disbelief on his face. In a matter of minutes, Harper's whole world had collapsed: he'd lost his fiancée, and his reputation, and now his house was going up in smoke. Chase didn't spare the man a moment of pity, but he could see Harper was planning on going in without taking any precautions.

"Harper! Get back!" Chase hollered in warning. The man ignored him. "You won't last two minutes inside."

"I'll kill him!" Harper ranted.

"You'll get yourself killed."

"He's got Elizabeth."

"Harper, wait!"

The warning proved futile, for at that moment the front door crashed open and Trammel Bodine staggered out under the portico, holding his smoke-blackened neckerchief to his mouth with one hand,

371

firing his pistol with the other. Chase dove for the ground, but Harper made a convenient target as he headed directly toward the door. Incredibly, the bullets that tore into his body didn't stop him.

Harper raised the rifle and fired into the smoky cloud surrounding Bodine, who ran for the cover of the trees at the far end of the yard. The first shot merely ripped Bodine's hat from his head, the second hit him in the leg, knocking him off his feet. He coughed and rolled to his knees dragging the pistol back up to point it at Harper.

Chase took aim and fired before Bodine could squeeze off his last shot. A splotch of red blossomed on Bodine's chest, and his eyes opened wide with surprise. As his pistol slipped from his hand, his pain-glazed eyes turned on Chase; then he collapsed face-first into the dirt atop his singed bag of stolen money.

"Jonas! Dear God, no!" Nora screamed and ran toward her brother. Elliot followed closely behind her, dropping to his knees beside the fallen man.

Chase was on his feet already and running toward the house. He yanked the blanket over his head, gulped in three deep breaths of fresh air and ducked into the doorway. His heart hammered against the wall of his chest. The recurrent nightmare flickered through his thoughts, and he was seized by a sudden, unreasonable panic. Shoving it ruthlessly down, he staggered into the room. He couldn't lose her now. Not now.

His eyes watered immediately. The smoke was thick, and it smelled of burning wood and wool and singed leather upholstery. He wrapped the blanket over his nose and mouth and tried to see past his own hand.

"Libby!"

No reply. Only the whooshing sound of igniting wood as the ceiling caught. Fear clawed at him. She'd been in there much longer than he, and already he could scarcely breathe. A racking cough assailed him. *"Libby! Damn it . . . where are you?"*

He ducked low and discovered the smoke was thinner near the floor. He sucked air through the wet wool blanket, but every breath tortured his lungs. With one hand out in front of him, he swept the floor searching for her. He ran into tables and chairs. Nothing else.

"Dear God"—it was a desperate, raspy prayer—"help me."

He was just about to turn in another direction when his hand connected with her hair. "Libby!" He reached out to find her curled, like a limp rag doll, on the floor. *Oh, God, don't be dead. Don't be dead, Libby.*

She moaned as he scooped her into his arms. Hope surged through him. He faltered on the way to his feet. What was left of his strength was fading. He had to get out, but which way should he go? He took another hacking breath and tried to see the door.

"Chase!"

It was El's voice he heard. He followed the sound like a beacon, stumbling toward the door. "Keep talking," he shouted in a raspy voice which dissolved into a fit of coughing. "I can't . . . see . . . the . . . door."

"This way! Come this way," El hollered. "That's it. You're almost here."

El appeared, ghostlike, at the doorway, beckoning Chase toward him. Before Chase was even clear of the doorframe, he felt strong hands pulling him out. From behind him came the sound of splintering wood as part of the ceiling crumbled in the conflag-

373

ration. Chase nearly collapsed before staggering out the door. El relieved him of Libby, and John Pratt caught his other arm, dragging him across the yard, away from the thick, billowing smoke.

Chase dropped to the ground, retching the smoke from his lungs and taking in deep draughts of clean air. He took the cup of water Pratt offered and poured it down his raw, burning throat.

When he had recovered enough to move, he crawled on hands and knees to where Elliot worked over Libby. Her eyes were closed. Except for the labored rise and fall of her chest, she looked frighteningly still. Her pale face was stained with soot and blood.

"El?" Chase croaked.

"She's alive," he answered. "But she took in a lot of smoke. Her breathing's not too good."

"She was on the floor. She's not gonna"—his voice cracked with emotion—"she'll be all right won't she, El?"

El's answering look was grim. He tipped Libby's chin sideways so Chase could see the bruise on the side of her cheek, then dabbed at it with a wad of lint dipped in water. "It looks like she was hit with something. Right now I can't say if it's the blow, or the smoke inhalation that's keeping her unconscious." Gently, he cleaned the nasty bruise forming on her cheek. "This I can treat. Her lungs . . . we'll just have to see." He looked away from Chase and yelled, "Somebody get me some blankets."

Damn Bodine, Damn him to hell! Chase leaned close to Libby's face, pressing his lips against her sooty skin willing her to absorb his strength. "Don't die. Please, don't die. I love you, Libby. Do you hear me?" He pulled the two blankets Early brought up under her chin and tucked them gently around her sides. "I love you."

"Ma!" Tad tore up to them and slid to his knees on the ground beside his mother. "Mama!" He nearly sobbed. "Is she—?"

"She's alive, Tadpole. But she breathed in a lot of smoke."

Tad's face bunched up with emotion and he slammed pitifully into Chase's shoulder, wrapping his arms around Chase's neck. Tears erupted now, and Tad's small chest was racked by sobs. "It's all . . . my fault."

Chase's arms tightened around the boy. "What are you talking about? Don't even think that, Tad. It's not your fault. Your ma—"

"No!" Tad argued, mashing his forehead against Chase's wet shirt. "I was so mean and . . . and hateful after you left. She tried to . . . t-tell me about you." He hiccoughed on a breath. "About why she . . . loved you, but I just g-got . . . mad at her. I'm s-so . . . sorry."

"I know, son," Chase soothed, rubbing the back of Tad's neck. "I'm sorry, too. But none of this had anything to do with you. I didn't blame you for being mad at me and neither did your ma. Your ma loves you so much . . . she's gonna be all right." *She has to be.*

"P-promise?"

Chase nodded silently, dropping his cheek to Tad's shoulder. But he'd never been less sure of a vow in his life.

Behind them, the house was engulfed in flames. From the back of it came the crash of collapsing walls. The crowd of guests stood back and simply watched, having given up trying to fight the inferno

375

any longer. Smoke and ash floated like specters in the air.

Libby's eyes fluttered open to take in the man she loved holding her son. It was a sight she'd never thought to see and one that made her heart clench with joy. She sucked in a lungful of fresh air and coughed. How it burned! Her head ached fiercely and her eyes stung. But she was alive. *Alive.*

Chase and Tad turned to her as one and stared.

"Libby?"

"Ma?"

She coughed again and managed a wan smile for them both. Her fingers curled weakly around Chase's and her eyes were lined with tears. "I didn't think . . . I'd see either one of you again," she told them in a raspy whisper.

"Oh, Mama . . ."

Chase's lips caressed the back of her sooty hand. "Thank God . . . thank God."

The choking fire, the struggle with Trammel—all came back to her in a fearful rush. *"Bodine,"* she rasped, trying to sit up. "Chase, he tried to—"

"He's dead. He can't hurt us anymore, Lib." He glanced toward Harper's inert body only a few feet away. "Jonas is dead, too. Bodine shot him." Chase stroked her palm with his thumb.

She felt a pang of regret about Jonas, but her pity was reserved for Nora who now sat beside her brother's body. Dear Nora. She didn't deserve Jonas's betrayal any more than I did, Libby thought bitterly. But there would be time enough later to mourn Jonas's treachery. Moments had suddenly become too precious. The boy and man beside her were all that mattered.

Chase's hair was a wet tangle, and his skin was dark with grimy smoke. His face showed the ravages of the fight he'd had with Jonas and of his worry about her. She ignored the curious stares of some of the guests who'd gathered nearby. She felt no shame about her love for Chase. Let them think what they would.

She reached up and lovingly ran a finger along his bruised cheek. "You brought me out." It wasn't a question. She knew the answer already in her heart. "Thank you."

"Ah, Libby, I love you . . . don't you know that by now? When I thought you might—" He broke off, clearing the knot of emotion from his voice. "I'm never leaving you again, you hear? You can argue about the right and wrong of it 'til hell freezes over, but I'm staying right here."

She let out a sobbing, happy laugh. "If you didn't, I'd never forgive you." She drew his battered hand to her lips and kissed it. "Inside the house . . . when it was burning around me . . . I kept thinking how wrong I'd been about us. How, if I could only tell you I love you, Chase," she whispered, looking up into his eyes. "I love you so much."

Heedless of the crowd gathering behind them, Chase dipped his head and his mouth briefly settled over hers. Their lips met with all the tenderness brimming in their hearts.

She tasted smoke on his lips.

He tasted promise on hers.

"And as soon as you're on your feet again, you're going to marry me, Lib," he told her, gathering her in his arms.

"Just try to stop me." She hugged him, knowing she'd be holding on to his strength for years to come and cherishing the gentle fierceness in him that had captured her heart.

A high-pitched whinny came from close by. Libby

looked over Chase's shoulder to see the black stallion prancing nervously between the paddocks. *Diablo*. "Chase, what in the world—? Where's Blue?"

His arms tightened around her. "I . . . lost him coming over the mountains." He nodded toward the stallion. "That's our future you're looking at, honey. Diablo's going to sire the finest horses this country's ever seen for the Double Bar H."

She pulled back to look at his face. "But how did you . . . ?"

He shrugged, still not quite believing it himself. "One refugee to another, I guess. We sort of came to a mutual understanding. But it's a long story for another time."

"We'll have plenty of that," she promised, smiling. "Years and years."

"And I intend to spend every one of them proving how much I love you." He kissed her again, then opened his embrace to include Tad, drawing him inside the circle of their love. Whatever they had to face, they'd face it together—as a family.

"Let's go home," he said, lifting her into the cradle of his arms.

Libby wrapped her arms around his neck. "Yes, love," she answered. "Home."

Epilogue

Summer passed into autumn, turning the valley from verdant green to burnished gold. In the distance, the slopes of the Sangre de Cristos were a patchwork of color: golden aspen, the evergreen spruce and juniper, and cottonwoods garbed in vermilion.

The early November air held the crisp hint of winter, the sky, the promise of early snow. Chase rubbed his gloved hands together, walked the perimeter of the grassy rooftop, and inspected his work. He'd finished replacing the old roof with new wood, first stripping and then replacing its covering of sod. The new rye seed was already thick and green from the fall rains, anchoring the soil.

He bent down and worked a circle of holes into the soft soil with the tip of his finger. Then, dipping into his pocket, he pulled out a handful of flower seeds Nora had given him before she and Elliot had left—a surprise for Libby when spring thawed the land. Carefully he planted them in the rich earth and covered them over.

A wave of contentment passed over him as he stood and looked out over the flat sweep of New Mexico

Territory which he and Libby called their own. Never in his wildest imaginings, had he envisioned this kind of happiness for himself. He had a wife who loved him beyond anything he had a right to expect, a son any man could be proud of, and a patch of ground which, for the first time in his life, he could call home. His chest tightened as he mentally gathered up his blessings and held them close to his heart.

"Admiring the view, or your handiwork?"

Chase pivoted to see Libby climbing onto the roof from the wide wooden ladder at the side of the house. She was wearing the knowing grin she always wore when she knew something he did not.

He smiled and drew her into his arms as she came close. It was a gesture he rarely resisted and one she never objected to. "Both," he answered. "Although I must admit, I fixed the roof for purely selfish reasons."

"Oh?" Libby turned playfully in his arms until her back was against his chest, and she looked out toward the horses grazing in their pastures.

"Yes, well," he went on with a smile, "with winter coming, I figured the less attention you had to give to all those water-catching bowls and falling mud pies, the more time you'd have for me."

"You did, did you?"

"Um-hmm." He nuzzled her flaxen hair, taking in her familiar scent. "What brings you up here? I thought you were putting up the last of the pumpkin from the garden."

"I was." She pulled an envelope from her pocket. "I thought you might like to see what Early and Tad brought back from town."

Chase looked at the return address on the letter.

"Dr. and *Mrs.* Elliot Bradford! By God, they did it!" With one arm still anchored firmly around Libby, he tore open the envelope and scanned the contents of the letter, grinning from ear to ear. "He says Mother adores Nora and they've become"—he laughed—"great co-conspirators, directing all the new landscaping for the stables and grounds. And he says Nora has already set up a temporary school for the ex-slaves who've come to work for El's father. It seems she requisitions an unused tack room in the evenings." Chase glanced at Libby. "That sounds like our Nora."

Libby nodded and smiled fondly, remembering her. "I miss her," she admitted. "I miss them both."

"Well, you won't have to for long," he added, continuing his perusal of the letter.

"What do you mean?"

A grin caught the edge of Chase's mouth. "According to this, Nora, El, my mother, and Thomas Bradford are all heading this way come summer. Since they missed our wedding, my parents decided they can't wait until next year to meet you. And El and Nora just plain can't wait to get back here for a visit."

"Your parents . . . here? They're all coming *here?*" Libby pressed her fingers against her mouth in excitement and turned to face him. "Oh, Chase! I'll get to meet your family." Instinctively, she glanced down at herself—the faded denims she still insisted on working in, the pumpkin-stained apron, her worn boots. She'd always felt comfortable being just who she was, but would who she was be enough for Chase's parents? Anxiety creased her brow. "But . . ."

Chase chucked two fingers under her chin and tilted her mouth up to his. He placed a gentle, reassuring kiss on it. "You're perfect," he told her, "just

381

the way you are." Dipping down once more to taste her, his lips reclaimed hers, chasing away all her doubts.

His kiss sang through her veins and kindled the fire that had only grown hotter between them over the months.

With great restraint, Chase pulled back and smiled down at her. "I love you, Lib. And my family will love you just as much as I do. But if you're not careful, I'm gonna have to love you right up here on the roof."

She took hold of the lapels of his sheepskin coat and grinned enticingly up at him. "Would that be so awful?"

His brows rose fractionally, and a look she could only compare to a stalking mountain lion's lit his eyes. "Ah, Mrs. Whitlaw. You are a wild woman. I do like the way your mind works." His lips captured hers again, while his hand found its way beneath her wool coat to the curve of a breast, caressing its fullness.

"Perhaps we should make the best of our time. After all," she murmured, "I won't be able to climb up ladders too much longer."

"No?" he asked distractedly, searing a trail of kisses down her slender neck. "Why's that?"

"I expect I'll be too fat."

"You? Fat?" He resumed his exploration of the tender skin behind her ear. "Never."

"Oh, yes. I will be," she assured him. "Fat and awkward and terribly happy."

Chase's face went utterly blank for a moment as he pulled back to look at her, trying to comprehend her meaning.

"In fact, your family should be here just in time." She smiled then, a woman's smile.

"In time?" he echoed. "Libby—"

"You should have just enough time to build on that extra room we've talked about, off the—"

"Libby!" He took her by the shoulders. "By God! Do you mean what . . . what I think you mean?"

She bit the edge of her lip, suddenly shy, and nodded. "It'll be June, by my calculations."

Chase's gaze flew to her still-flat stomach, then back up to her face. On his face was a look of wonder and joy Libby knew she would never forget.

Words stuck in his throat when he tried to speak. "A baby . . . Libby . . . are . . . are you sure?"

"A woman knows these things."

Reverently, his hand slid down to her belly and rested over the spot where their child grew. Words failing him, he scooped her into his arms and spun her around with a hearty laugh.

Libby laughed, too, and hugged him tightly. "So you're happy?"

"Happy?" A sly grin crossed his face. With infinite care, he lowered her to the grass carpet that covered the roof and captured her beneath him. "Shall I show you just how happy I am, wife?"

She feigned a shocked expression. "But Mr. Whitlaw! What if someone sees us?"

"Up here?"

"It's a big country," she reminded him.

He kissed the tip of her nose. "As a matter of fact, you're right. Besides I have it in mind to have you entirely to myself . . . under a nest of warm blankets, by the light of a crackling fire."

"Ma?" Tad's voice intruded from below.

Libby smiled and closed her eyes. "My point exactly."

"Have you told him yet?" Chase asked.

"I thought we should tell him together." Libby

383

watched a curious smile of gratitude tip the corners of her husband's mouth.

He rolled off her and tenderly lifted her to her feet. Glancing briefly at the dented soil where he'd planted the wildflower seeds, Chase smiled secretively, imagining all the new beginnings the summer would bring.

"C'mon, Mrs. Whitlaw," he said. "Let's go tell our son he's about to become a brother."